The *Dark* Prince

Book 2 of the Dark Light Series

S.L. Jennings

The Dark Prince

Book cover by Stephanie White of Steph's Cover Design
Book interior design by JT Formatting

ISBN-10: 1483901890
ISBN-13: 978-1483901893

For the dreamers, the believers, the supporters, the lovers, and the risk takers.
For every person that took a chance on me and my dream.
This is for you.

xoxo

Love The Way You Lie (piano version) – Rihanna
Night Of The Hunter – 30 Seconds To Mars
Decode – Paramore
Daykeeper – The Foreign Exchange
Use Me – Miguel
Sex on Fire – Kings of Leon
Kings & Queens – 30 Seconds To Mars
What If – Coldplay
S&M – Rihanna
We Are Young – Fun.
We Are The People – Empire of the Sun
Mars vs. Venus – Usher
Stay – Rihanna ft. Mikky Ekko
Jar Of Hearts – Christina Perri
Talking To The Moon – Bruno Mars
Dreaming With A Broken Heart – John Mayer
Numb – Rihanna ft. Eminem
Monster – Kanye West
The Beautiful Ones – Prince
The Kill – 30 Seconds To Mars
All We Ever Do Is Say Goodbye – John Mayer
Rehab – Rihanna
The Lonely – Christina Perri
Take It From Here – Justin Timberlake
Strawberry Swing – Frank Ocean (original by Coldplay)
Sparks – Coldplay
All I Wanted – Paramore
The Fighter – Gym Class Heroes
This Is War – 30 Seconds To Mars

Stronger – Kanye West
Supremacy – Muse
Alibi – 30 Seconds To Mars
It Ends Tonight – The All –American Rejects
My Songs Know What You Did In The Dark – Fall Out Boy
Radioactive – Imagine Dragons
Moonshine – Bruno Mars
Mirrors – Justin Timberlake
A Thousand Years – Christina Perri

One

Numb.

I have never wanted to be an unfeeling sack of flesh and bone more than in this moment. Because I feel everything. Pain. Betrayal. Grief. Sorrow. Every fucking thing I hate about feeling. Everything I've tried so hard to avoid.

I look down at the photograph crumpled in my rigid grip. It suddenly feels like glowing red hot coal in my hand. It burns me, sears the skin of my palm. In my hand I hold everything that I love. My parents, both adopted and biological. And *him*.

Dorian.

I know what this is. I know this is my truth. My past. My present. My future. It is what I knew all along and, like a freaking idiot, ignored because my beautiful illusion was so much better than my tragic reality.

For once, I had embraced happiness. Bliss. In spite of finding out what I was, finding out that I was a half Light, half Dark inbreed, I was *happy*. Even with a damn supernatural assassin out for my blood, I was content. Because of *him*. He made me whole. A new and improved Gabs. A girl that wanted to be good enough. For *him*.

Fuck. Him.

On autopilot, I stuff the photo into my purse. Then I am mindlessly dressing myself. Right arm in sleeve. Left arm in sleeve. Sweatshirt over my head. Legs sliding in jeans. Feet stepping into shoes. I'm almost there. I'm almost numb.

"Gabi?" my mom asks as I breeze by the living room robotically. I stop in my tracks and gaze at her, my face stoic and unreadable. "Dear, where are you going? Are you ok?"

I look at my adopted parents, the wholesome couple that took me in and cared for me as their own when I was nothing remotely like their own. I am not even human. But they gave me a human life. Despite the pure evil festering within me, bubbling just at the surface, they chose to believe I could be like them. They wanted to believe I could be *good*.

Fuck. *Good.*

I fish the photograph out of my purse and thrust it towards them without another glance or word. What would I even say?

Found this picture of you guys and my birth parents. And by the way, I am screwing that guy in it. Plus he hasn't aged a day. In twenty-freakin'-years. No big deal.

"Where did you get this?" Chris asks, though it sounds like more of a demand in his low timbre.

"I don't know," I hear myself say. "I think it was in Natalia's book. I just found it."

"Oh my God, it's us," Donna replies in her breathy soprano. "Us and your parents, Natalia and Alexander . . ."

"And? And him?" I ask jutting out my finger at his maddeningly beautiful face. Dark hair, impossibly blue eyes, and that sexy smirk that makes me forget my own name. *Him.*

"Him? That's, uh," Donna stutters before swallowing. "He was your father's friend. His partner."

I meet her pale blue eyes and nod, needing no further explanation. "Dorian."

Chris and Donna's brows furrow simultaneously, first in confusion then in terrifying understanding.

"He's here," Donna squeaks, barely above a whisper. "Oh God, no. No. No!"

"Dammit!" Chris shouts. "How the hell did this happen? How do you know him?"

Donna crumbles into chest-heaving sobs. "Oh please, no! Please, Gabriella! Don't tell me . . . don't tell me it's *him*! Don't tell me he's the one!"

She knew. For months she read it in my aura. She knew I was

involved with someone and something had changed in me. She knew I had fallen in love. She just never imagined it could have been with the epitome of all that is corrupt and immoral in their world.

With *him*.

I couldn't say anything. There was honestly nothing left to say. Admitting I was in love with Dorian would only throw salt in the wound. Theirs and mine.

"I have to go," I mutter. I start to turn towards the door then hesitate. The photo. I need the photo. "Can I have that back?"

"Where are you going?" Chris asks. Again, it sounds like a demand. An accusation.

"I have to go," I repeat. "To see . . . him. I have to know." I snatch the photo from his grip and stuff it back into my purse.

"You have to *know*? *Know what?* What the hell is there to know?" Chris shouts.

My face heats with anger, tiny beads of sweat forming on my forehead. I reflexively swipe my sleeve across it. "Why he's here. Why he came. Why he . . . I just need to know."

"Absolutely not! You will not leave this house, do you hear me? Dorian is off limits!"

Chris steps towards me with the intent of grasping me by the shoulders. Yet for some reason he recoils, stumbling several steps back, shielding his wife with his broad body. I hadn't even noticed the lights. Every light in the entire house is blinking rapidly, casting ghastly shadows across their horrified faces. It's happening again.

And then I feel it. My hands are hot; scorching. And though it feels as if I have thrust them into a raging fire, it does not burn me. I look down at my palms, enraptured in a dull red haze, glowing hot with fury. They are trembling uncontrollably. My whole body is. I can't stop it; I can't even understand it. Anger and grief have completely overpowered me.

This isn't numbness. This is wrath.

Tiny icicles assault my retinas, pricking my eyelids until they sting. My eyes feel too cold, frozen even, yet my vision is not obscured. I can see . . . *everything.* As if I have been blind for twenty years. The arteries beating in their rigid necks, the tight flex of their jaws, the fear inscribed in their faces. I see it all. I see *them*. Human. Frail. Infantile. I had always considered myself as one of them, but as I gaze upon them now, they appear alien to me. I can't comprehend this sudden revelation but I know it is real. It is the realest thing I have ever felt.

"Gabriella," Donna whispers hoarsely. "*Please.*"

She's pleading. Begging. *Why?* Her petrified tone startles me and my emboldened resolve falters. The tremors cease, the red glow from my hands extinguished. Even my eyesight has dimmed and the alarming chill has dissipated. I tumble back down to Earth. Back to my humanity.

"There's something you need to know. Please let us explain before you go," she pleads from behind Chris.

I nod stiffly, afraid to do or say more to provoke their fear. I can't be certain what would happen if I did. She steps around my dad cautiously and stands to face me. Chris's eyes dance wildly between us, his fists pressed into tight balls of hard steel.

"Dorian was your father's partner. The one who tried to keep Alex and Natalia's secret. He wanted to keep them safe; to keep you safe. But once word traveled back to the Dark, he was taken. His punishment was harsh but he was spared."

I fold my arms in front of my chest, not completely sure where Donna is going with this. I already knew that from Natalia's journal. "Ok. He was punished; I get that. But he suffered a loss too. He lost his best friend. Why do I need to stay away from him?"

"Dorian is . . . special. And that is the only reason why he was not executed along with your father. He made a deal to save his own life. He was petrified–frozen in time, his magic stripped from him. His sentence was 20 years." Donna takes a step towards me, her expression a mix of fright and concern. "The deal Dorian made was that he had to kill you. Once he was released from petrification, he had to hunt you down and slaughter you. And if he fails, he will be put to death."

I struggle to process Donna's words, my already shattered heart desperately urging my brain to reject it. But even in angst my mind can't hold onto the illusion. I know what she is saying is true. Dorian was sent here to kill me. Everything we've shared, every ounce of passion we've exchanged has been a lie. And somewhere amidst all my hang-ups and denial, I knew it all along. What else could he possibly want from me?

I turn towards the front door when I feel a large hand grasp my forearm. "Where are you going?" Chris asks.

My glazed eyes fall to his grip and he instantly pulls it back. "I have to see him. I have to hear him say it."

"What? Why? Did you not just hear your mother? He will kill you, Gabriella! He does not want you! He does not care about you! You are nothing but prey to him!"

Chris's words sink the knife deeper into my hemorrhaging chest. I laboriously swallow down the bile rising in my throat. "I need to hear him say it," I repeat with a shaky voice. "He's not going to get away with being a coward. If he wants me dead, he has to tell me himself."

"No, Gabriella! Don't do it! He will kill you!" Donna shrieks. But I don't meet her horrified eyes. I don't respond to their pleas to stay in the safety of our home, away from the darkness that craves my demise. I am already out the door, guided by my own darkness festering deep inside me.

I don't notice that I am at the Broadmoor until I am already there. I don't even know how I managed to make it here in one piece. But as I gaze upon the double doors of Dorian's suite, I can literally feel my heart beating out of my chest. I know I've been standing here staring at it but I've completely lost all sense of time.

The door suddenly swings open, startling me out of my anguished daze. And I am face to face with *him*. Dorian. Still dressed in his suit and tie, he is so amazingly gorgeous it physically hurts to look at him. His black hair is styled in its usual disheveled perfection. His jaw is shaved and smooth. Even his eyes seem bluer and brighter. I bite down the gasp at his splendor and fight the urge to melt into his arms.

"Gabriella? Are you ok?" he asks after a moment of my gawking. His eyes rest on my face, no doubt housing a mixture of pain and confusion. "What's wrong? Are you hurt?"

I take a deep breath, my head swirling with questions. I don't even know where to start. How do I even formulate all this into words?

"I . . . know. Who you are, *what* you are. I know," a hoarse voice croaks. I can hardly recognize it as my own.

Dorian's expression darkens instantly, his mouth turning up into a menacing snarl. Even his eyes have turned cold and icy, and I swear I can feel my blood freeze over. He takes a step back, holding the door open wider.

"Come in."

Come in? I've just told Dorian that I know he is an evil, sadistic mythical creature and he wants me to *come in*? Hell no!

Dorian sighs, letting his eyes close for just a moment before looking to me. They are full of emotion–sorrow, regret, anger. *Why?*

"It's ok, Gabriella. I won't hurt you. I want you to come in."

And as crazy and stupid as it sounds, I believe him. I have to. The man before me is my heart and soul. Every part of me screams for him, yearns for him. And even if he has lied to me, I can't deny what I feel for him. I just can't turn it off. And I seriously hate myself for that.

I square my shoulders and will my shaky legs to carry me forward into the suite. Even as I pass him, even as our bodies meet with the slightest brush of the shoulders, I am on fire for him. Even as fear flows through me in staggering ripples, all I want to do is bury myself in his arms and let him ease my trepidation. Trepidation I feel for *him*.

How stupid can you get, Gabs?

The reality of Dorian's real reason for being here nudges me and

I am reminded of Chris's terse words. Dorian doesn't care about me. He doesn't want me. He is completely incapable of ever loving me. I need to let those truths fuel what's left of my courage.

I spin around, my survival instincts kicking in. No matter what I feel for him, he can't be trusted. All pathetic signs of adoration are erased from my face, replaced with disdain and anger.

"You can relax. I won't attack you from behind," Dorian mutters, clicking the door closed. He walks past me and heads to the bar to pour himself a drink, downing it in one hefty gulp. He refills then pours one for me as well.

"You won't?" I ask flatly, taking the crystal glass from his outstretched hand. I take a sip, my throat not even registering the burn.

"No," he responds before running his hand through his silken locks. "That's not how I . . . operate."

"But you will. You will hurt me. That is what you were sent here for, correct?" I take another sip, hoping it brings me one step closer to absolute detachment. It hurts too much to feel.

"Yes." Dorian downs his own poison before looking back at me devoid of all emotion.

"Why?" my quivering voice cracks. "So all this was a lie? I'm just an assignment? A target? You really are some murderous piece of shit? What the fuck, Dorian! Why?!"

I wait for an answer yet Dorian simply continues to stare at me blankly. Doesn't he want to explain himself? Doesn't he have *anything* to say? He just continues to stand there, unreadable and unfeeling. His silence infuriates me and I can't contain my agitation. Even my fear can't override my temper.

"Ummm, *hello*? I'd appreciate an answer, asshole," I spew angrily. Still, Dorian remains silently impassive, causing wrath to take over. "So it's true. You really are a cold-hearted prick who preys on defenseless young women. What kind of man are you? That's sick, Dorian. You are one sick, sadistic fuck."

Somehow my harsh words pierce through his stoic guise and

Dorian's mouth twists into a vicious snarl, bearing his gleaming white teeth. His eyes narrow menacingly and have lightened into the palest of blues, too frightening to be beautiful. And his face–a face so unbelievably gorgeous that I lose all sense of coherent thought–shifts into a place of pure evil.

He is no longer *my* Dorian. The man I love is gone.

"You stupid, little girl," he seethes. Even his voice has lost its velvety tone, becoming more of a guttural growl. I flinch in response, too consumed by fear to run or scream. What good would it do anyway?

Dorian's head snaps forward faster than my eyes can see. "You think I wanted this? *Any* of this? You think I wanted to come to this little, miserable town just to hunt some silly girl? Babysit you like a toddler? You are so fucking clueless, it infuriates me! Don't you understand? Don't you get it? *I. Have. To!"*

Dorian's tirade slices through me like a blade, leaving me open and bleeding. I bring the crystal glass to my lips in an attempt to mask my trembling bottom lip. I can barely taste the scorching liquid as it makes its way down. Then without thinking, without even considering what this could mean for my own preservation, I bring my arm back and push it forward with all my might, slinging the glass directly towards Dorian's head.

Without flinching or batting one of long lashes, Dorian's eyes flicker up to its approach, halting the glass in mid-air just as it is centimeters from his face. He holds out a palm and it easily falls into his grasp.

"Don't do that again. I am a patient and understanding man, Gabriella, but I won't tolerate your tantrums," he says with an amused smirk, abandoning his darkness. And just like that, the Dark monster trying to crawl its way to the surface is caged. He is back to being *my* Dorian.

"Or what?" I scoff, stupidly trying to provoke him. "You already want to kill me. What else could you possibly do?"

Dorian shakes his head. "I don't *want* to kill you. At least the rational part of me doesn't."

"And the irrational part?" I hold my breath awaiting his answer.

Dorian's eyes find mine, flashing white hot before settling into crystal blue. They are full of confusion and loathing. Reluctantly, he nods. "That part of me–the pure, incomprehensible evil–wants to slaughter you right here and now and be done with it. I want to drain every ounce of life from your body, strip you bare of the essence deep inside you. Then discard your pitiful carcass like garbage."

He swallows then cringes, as if his mouth tastes of bile. "I'm Dark, Gabriella. It's my nature to feel those things, to want you dead. I can never change that. The very thing that draws me to you is the very thing I hate."

"You don't mean that," I find myself whispering.

"Yes, I do. And you have to accept that. I'll never be anything other than Dark. No matter how much I wish I could be."

"So what, then? What does this mean?" His indecisiveness is maddening. And here I thought *I* wore that crown.

"It means that you have a choice. Align with us; ascend into the Dark. Or I *will* kill you. And I'll like it."

Of all uncontrollable reactions to have at his ominous confession, I laugh. A crazed, delusional laughter that bends me over at my waist, howling as tears stream down my face. I can't explain it; I can't even stop it. And judging from the scowl that creeps onto Dorian's face, he is not pleased with my outburst.

"That's insane, Dorian!" I breathe between guffaws. "All of this is insane! Shit, maybe even I am insane. Because here I am, in your hotel room listening to you describe killing me like it's a fucking sport, and I am seriously trying to make sense of it. Like I can't even accept that you really are a heartless, disgusting animal. Unbelievable!" I howl.

"Calm down, Gabriella," he warns.

"Why? Why calm down? I'm dead anyway. Hell, why not make it even easier for you?" I screech, throwing up my hands. My laughter begins to shift into rage. "Do it, Dorian. Get this shit over with. All those times you had me sprawled out, naked, while you played with my mind–my heart, for Christ's sake–you could have just done it. Why wait? Why continue the charade?"

Dorian sets down the glass in his hand and takes a small step toward me, his expression tortured. "That's not what it was."

"No? Well, what the hell was it?!" I scream. "You know what, never mind. Just do it, Dorian. I'll never side with you Dark fuckers. Ever. So don't waste your time. Besides, you have already killed me a thousand times over with your lies so let's just get this shit over with. Unless you can't; unless you are too pathetic to actually do what you came here for."

"Watch it, Gabriella," he seethes between gritted teeth.

I am taunting the beast inside him, but my slain pride has taken the reins. He has hurt me, and in turn, I want to hurt him. It's the only way I know how to deal with this pain. It's what I've always done when my heart has gone into defense mode.

"You are a coward. My father trusted you. He thought of you as a brother. And this is how you repay him? By fucking his daughter, you sicko?" I stare him down, disgust etched in my face. "I pity you, Dorian. You are a pathetic waste of power. All you had to do was kill a defenseless girl, and you can't even get that right!"

As if I have flipped some imaginary switch, all humanity drains from Dorian's frame, his body transforming into something dreadfully wraithlike. The bones in his body crack and contortion, wisps of grey vapors writhing around him. His face, pale and ashen, resembles something out of a horror movie–deep set, icy eyes, menacing snarl, razor sharp teeth. Even the air around him trembles in response. His skeletal form lurches towards me, stopping inches from my terrified face. I'm too petrified to even fix my lips to scream.

"Is this what you want?!" Dorian seethes. "You want to see me like this? You want me to hurt you? You want me to end you right now?"

I take in the daunting apparition before me, swirls of blackish smoke enveloping him like a toxic cloak. He is beyond my worst nightmares, encompassing all things evil and cruel that exists in this world and beyond. But even I know that this is a different brand of darkness. This is no ordinary nightmare. He truly is the epitome of Dark.

"No, Dorian," I choke out in a whisper. "This is what *you* want. What you need. You killed me the moment I found out the truth. So just do it."

I feel my eyes pool with fresh tears, unable to blink them away. And why would I? This is the end. There's no use in trying to stifle my agony. It's true; I am dead inside. Without Dorian, without the beautiful illusion of love and true happiness, I am but an empty shell. Even the mirage of my life that pacified me for twenty years cannot pull me back from the ledge. I can't go back to that. Meeting Dorian–*loving* Dorian–has altered my entire being. Life without him is death.

At the sight of my crack of emotion, Dorian releases a bit of the anger that feeds the beast within him, though his darkness is still prevalent. He reaches a pale, spiny hand toward me, plumes of charcoal writhing around it. The sharp pads of his fingertips slide down my cheek, leaving a trail of frigid cold prickles. I bite back the urge to cringe at the chilling sensation.

"I don't want that," he mutters hoarsely. "But you've left me no choice. I'm sorry, little girl." With a sigh, he stows his darkness entirely, his body settling back into its original magnificent form. The olive tone of his skin returns and the ominous grey smoke dissipates, the ice blue of his eyes the only sign of a supernatural threat.

I hear his words but the peril still doesn't register. There is no room left in me to feel anything else but immense pain. I can literally feel my heart splinter into several jagged pieces, the ache radiating in my chest and spreading throughout my body like a cancer. I don't even notice the tears streaming down my hot cheeks until Dorian brushes them away. I resist the urge to burrow my face in his hand.

"So this is it? You're going to do it?" I whisper with a weak, wavering voice. My brash and bold nature has completely abandoned me. I was defeated from the start.

"Yes." The look on his face is pure agony and regret. *Why?* This is what he's wanted all along, toying with my heart just to get close to me. Yet this is not the face of a cold-hearted paranormal killer. This is the face of a man tormented by his own demons.

I let my eyes close, before allowing myself one last glimpse of his beautiful face. *Dorian*. My very own angel of death. "Ok. I'm ready."

I feel his fingers brush a trail from my cheek down to my collarbone, resting there to trace small circles with his thumb against my throat. His warm lips touch my forehead and I ease into the touch. *A final kiss goodbye*. I allow myself to savor it.

Dorian quietly mutters a few strangled words against my flushed skin in his secret, unnamed language. A language I'm not supposed to know, yet this time I understand every word. Words that I have craved to hear from his lips. Words that grip my shattered heart, trying to piece the jagged shards back together.

My eyes flutter open just as Dorian takes a step back, looking down at me in anguish. I let my hazels plunge into his glossy pools of azure as I offer those same words to him in my last dying breath.

"I love you, too."

Two

We stand in silence, staring at each other, an array of tortured emotion etched on our faces. Dorian said he loves me. He knows I can understand his language, the sacred tongue of the Dark. And he knows I love him too. We are both jolted with these revelations, unsure of what to do next. I should be dead right now, but instead, I am gazing up at the most beautiful man ever created. At the Dark Warlock that I love so much it's bound to kill me.

Tension swirls around us, the heat of our bodies mingling with the sexual electricity that neither of us can deny. Seconds ago, I was ready for Dorian to end my life in order to save his own. There was nothing I could do to fight him, and a big part of me didn't want to. Knowing that he has deceived me in the worst way possible was like taking a bullet to the chest. I don't think I could ever survive his betrayal.

Dorian's brow furrows, bewilderment flashing in his eyes. He drops his hand from my throat and cocks his head to the side, causing me to stifle a giggle. I've always found the gesture incredibly cute and endearing. Even now, knowing what he is, he still looks like *my* Dorian. And I will always view him as such.

I open my mouth to speak, but realize I don't even know what to say. What words could possibly sum up my confusion in this moment? I lick my dry lips in exchange, noticing how parched my mouth has grown.

"*Fuck,* Gabriella," Dorian hisses.

Before I can even respond, his mouth is on mine, urgently moving against my lips. I gasp at the sudden assault and Dorian easily slides his tongue inside, tasting my impassioned desperation. He pulls me into him, pushing our bodies as close as they could possibly be. Feeling the rigidness of his artfully muscled physique, his hand on my lower back, the other at the nape of my neck, I completely lose myself and just *feel*. Even after kissing him countless times, even after learning his intentions, his touch completely disarms me. I am putty in his skilled hands, his to mold and shape however he sees fit.

Dorian's tongue explores my mouth with perfect precision, tasting refreshingly sweet as always. I drink in his intoxicating flavor, my head swimming with illusions of hope and redemption. I try not to overthink it and just let myself get lost in the passion radiating from his soft lips. He playfully nips my bottom lip before sucking it into mouth. I sigh against his lips, letting my hands grab soft handfuls of his silky black hair.

God, I've missed him. Even though it's only been a mere 24 hours since I kissed his lips, it feels like it's been months. For a moment, I lost him. My Dorian left me, leaving a horrific beast in his wake. But he came back; he uttered those three little words that completely altered my resolve. And now, as I melt into his arms, our mouths joined in a slow yet heated embrace, hands kneading and stroking generously, I know that I have surrendered to him wholeheartedly. In life and in death.

Dorian sucks my tongue into his mouth once more before reluctantly pulling away from me. He runs his hand through his tousled hair, making my desire for him burn even hotter.

"You amaze me, you know that? I am completely enraptured by you in every way. So much so that I am about to commit suicide," he says, eyes twinkling in the dim light of the room.

"What does that mean?" I breathe, my voice hoarse from shouting and struggling to choke back sobs.

Dorian strokes my cheek with the back of his hand reverently then chews his bottom lip. "It means that I can't do it. I can't hurt you; I won't. I'd rather die than harm you, Gabriella."

I nuzzle into his touch and kiss his palm, as he does with me whenever I touch his face. "I can't let you do that, Dorian. I meant what I said. And even if you were to lay down your life–which is ridiculous, by the way–what is stopping the Dark from sending someone else? Someone that doesn't give a damn about me?"

"You're right," he says with a resigned sigh. "But there is no defeating or deceiving them. We can't win."

We? Is there still a *we*?

"Let's back up, Dorian. You lied to me. You purposely deceived me and made me believe that we had something *real*. How can I ever trust you? How do I know you won't change your mind and decide that I'm disposable?"

Dorian's eyes are on my lips as he runs his fingers through my dark waves. "I never lied to you, little girl. I may have deceived you–and for that I am truly sorry–but I never lied. I can't."

"What do you mean, *you can't*?"

He leads me to the plush black and gold filigree couch, easing me down. I crumple into the cushion, suddenly realizing how fatigued I am after missing dinner, not to mention the emotional roller coaster of events this evening.

"Gabriella, I cannot lie. Ever. I was cursed, unable to ever deceive the Dark, or anyone else, again. So when I tell you that I love you, that I could never hurt you, I mean it. I would gladly lay down my life for you, and that is the realest, truest thing I have ever felt."

I'm rendered speechless at his declaration. *He loves me*. Even the words passing his lips leave me utterly breathless. And now more than ever, I know that I cannot live without him. He is willing to give up everything for me. He is willing to *die* for me. If that isn't love, I don't know what is.

"I can't let you do that," I whisper. "I won't let you do that. I . . . need you. That day in the restaurant, you were absolutely right; I am just now living. And that's only because I met you." I take his hands in mine and relish in the contact, letting it motivate me. Touching him always soothes me. "You changed me, Dorian. You awakened something in me that I never knew existed. And now I can't go back to the life I had before. It wasn't a life at all. Not until I met you."

Dorian gazes at me in wonder, completely taken aback at my earnest confession. "You really mean that?" he asks, clearly perplexed.

I nod and give him a reassuring grin. "Yes. I do. I love you, Dorian."

His eyes are on my lips again, as if he is struggling with the urge to kiss me. He smirks, and shakes his head in disbelief. "I've never done this before, Gabriella. I've never . . . loved. We aren't taught to, even as children." Dorian brings his eyes to mine and they are filled with so much intensity, it startles me. "But what I feel for you–this . . . *love*–is real. I never thought it was possible for me to feel this way. But now that I have it, I never want to let it go. I never want to let *you* go. And I will do whatever it takes to keep you alive."

I don't stop myself from brushing my hand against his cheek, feeling tiny prickles of stubble along his jaw. Dorian turns his face into my palm and inhales before exhaling his serenity.

I raise an eyebrow with question. "When you do that . . . ?"

"I breathe you," Dorian answers with a sigh, finishing my thought. "You intoxicate me, Gabriella. I told you that. Breathing you has become somewhat of an addiction for me."

I pull my hand back and frown. "But can't that . . . *kill* me?" I think back to the passage in Natalia's journal, warning me against those that may seek my presence in order to steal my essence. Part of me always knew that Dorian's ritual was no coincidence.

"It can, if I'm not careful. I try to be. My affections for you are the only way I'm able to show an ounce of restraint," he chuckles.

I plaster on a strained grin, slightly daunted by Dorian's buoyancy at my fragility. I hate feeling so helpless, so feeble. But I know what he's saying is true. He could kill me easily, even accidentally.

"I won't let myself do it. I won't lose control," he mutters, reading my discomfort. "Look at me." Dorian's finger lifts my chin to meet his solemn gaze. "You know that, right? That I won't hurt you?"

I nod weakly, trying not only to convince him but myself as well. "I think so. I hope so."

"Remember, I can't lie to you, Gabriella. You are safe with me." He gives me a forced half-smile laced with pain. "For now."

My eyes cast down to his mouth, unable to look him in his eyes. I focus on the curve of each lip, the tiny dots of black stubble just breaking the surface of his skin. Anything to distract my mind from the inevitable.

Eventually, one of us will have to die.

"Why the sudden change of heart, Dorian? Come on, five minutes ago, I was a goner. You were ready to do it. I need to understand why you didn't carry out your plan a long time ago."

Dorian sighs, and leans back into the sofa, pulling me into his arms. The contact is immensely comforting, and I find myself nuzzling into the patch of bare skin above the collar of his shirt. He's still fully dressed in his suit and I'm tempted to loosen his tie and unfasten the buttons of his dress shirt.

"I told you, I felt it too," he begins in a quiet voice. "The shift when we first met. From that moment, I couldn't get you off my mind. It was maddening, and I was literally sick with myself for feeling so . . . drawn to you. I wanted to resist you completely. But there was this intense magnetism between us that made it impossible."

"I know," I nod against his chest. The moment I laid eyes on Dorian, I knew there was something uncanny about him that drew me to him. I, too, knew that I couldn't resist him from that point on.

"I told myself that once I spent some time with you, got it out of my system, the allure would fade. That I could focus on what I needed to do." Dorian brings my hand up to his face and gently brushes the back of it with his lips. "But then I tasted your lips. I couldn't stop myself from doing it. And I knew I couldn't leave you alone."

"That's all it took? A kiss?" I ask doubtfully. "And just like that, you're off the hook?"

I feel Dorian's jaw shift into a smirk. "Not exactly. When I left after that, I went to Greece. To my home. To try to buy you–*us*–more time. I told them that I could possibly persuade you to align with the Dark. And if you did, there would be no reason to kill you."

My eyes grow wide with a mixture fright and understanding. I sit up and turn to Dorian. "The messages . . . It was you?"

"No," he shakes his head. "Not me personally. But I knew."

"Something tells me you knew about everything," I mutter with an accusing tone, my eyes piercing the layers of his obscurity.

Dorian doesn't respond. What could he possibly say to make me feel better about his deception?

"I had to, Gabriella. To save your life," he finally says, answering my unspoken question. "I needed more time to figure things out. I'm sorry if it frightened you."

"Are you the killer, Dorian?" I ask, growing tired of dancing around the question.

"No. Of course, not." Dorian pulls me back into his embrace and I let him, despite my uncertainty. "I have no need to kill innocents, Gabriella."

"Not even for . . . power?" I ask with a wavering voice.

"I don't need power, little girl."

"Then who?"

Dorian strokes my disheveled mane, making me suddenly conscious of the ragged state I arrived here in.

"I don't know. There was no mandated order outside of mine. We have rules, Gabriella. We don't kill for sport, despite what the Light may believe."

An involuntary yawn escapes me and I try to muffle it against Dorian's chest.

"You're tired," he observes.

I shake my head. "No, I'm fine." There's so much more I need to know, so much I want to ask him. About what he is. About what *I* am. "Are there others? Like you?"

"Yes, of course. Everywhere. Hidden in plain sight."

"I think I saw one. Like you. The night after our first date, in the parking lot. I think it was coming after me. Scary as hell, like some type of freaky ghost-like figure. All distorted and demonic looking. It looked like you did. When you . . . changed. But it wasn't you, was it?"

Dorian chuckles, and I sit up to check if he's delusional. *What the hell is so funny?*

"Aurora," he snickers. "She has a flair for the dramatic."

Aurora? *I knew it!* "So she's . . ."

"Dark, yes. She wouldn't have hurt you though. She was just curious, maybe even a bit jealous. But she has been helping us, watching you when I can't be here. Luckily, her involvement with that boy has made that task easier."

Aurora's sudden infiltration into my life has been more than a nuisance. But the realization that her involvement with Jared was orchestrated to get closer to me brings a tiny smile to my face. I know I shouldn't be pleased with the charade but I can't help but find comfort in the fact that their relationship isn't real.

Way to be a bitch.

"So what's the plan? If it's not you, and it's not Aurora, than how can I possibly elude whoever is out there hunting me? Especially when you don't even know who it could be?" I stifle another yawn with the back of my hand.

"Well, for starters, the necklace," Dorian says, tugging it gently from the inside of my sweatshirt. "It's spelled to track you. You mustn't take it off. This necklace . . . is you, Gabriella. The pearl signifies your human life–delicate, effervescent and so precious–protected by dazzling white brilliance. Yet you are also surrounded by the allure and equally radiant darkness. Just a little girl thrust into the very heart of all of us. Both Light and Dark."

I reflexively place my fingers over the pendent of pearl and diamonds cradled in Dorian's hand. He cups both it and my hand and smiles sweetly, taking my breath away. I don't stop myself from tipping my head up and placing my lips on his. They feel so soft and warm, and before long a light moan erupts from my throat which Dorian relishes. My hands tug at his tie, unsuccessfully trying to loosen it. Luckily, Dorian removes it swiftly, giving me access to the buttons of his shirt where I begin to go to work on furiously. I straddle his lap, fumbling with the buttons as Dorian kneads my backside through my jeans.

"Wait," he says suddenly, pulling my lips from his.

"What?" I ask breathless and confused.

"I have to give you something. And I don't know how you'll take it."

"Ok," I enunciate slowly. "What is it?"

Dorian opens his palm, revealing a tiny vial of iridescent liquid. I have no idea where it came from and I know it hasn't been in his hand the entire time.

"What is that?" I ask, picking it up between my thumb and forefinger.

"*Magic*," Dorian answers. "My magic, specifically. At least in part." He takes the vial from my fingers and unscrews the top. "It will connect us. I'll be able to feel your emotions, especially when you are in danger."

I look at the pearlescent liquid skeptically then gaze up at Dorian with a raised brow. He rolls his eyes then sighs, taking the tiny bottle from me. He dabs a bit onto his finger and sticks it into his mouth. Just the sight of him sucking his finger causes my breath to hitch.

"See, perfectly safe. You have to believe me when I say I won't hurt you, Gabriella. Besides, poison isn't my style."

My eyes widen with morbid curiosity. "Well, what *is* your style?"

Dorian scoffs before flashing me a sinister half-grin. "Let's hope you never have to find out. I'm very good at what I do." He brings the vial to my lips. "Now drink up."

With a final deep breath, I let him tip the substance into my mouth. It's sickly sweet and syrupy and I cringe a bit. A cool sensation sweeps through me, like winter in my veins. Yet, the cold evolves into a burn–a crackling fire in the midst of a snowstorm. It soothes and stimulates me all at once, sending my senses into a frenzy.

"Good girl." Dorian shifts my body so that I am cradled in his arms, laying my cheek against his bare chest. "You will need to rest."

"But I'm not tired," I lie with a yawn.

Whatever was in that potion has suddenly intensified the fatigue. My eyelids feel like lead and even my breathing has grown deep and heavy. But I don't want to sleep. I am afraid of waking up and finding that Dorian is gone. And all this–the reconstructed remains of our shattered relationship–really will be over. I need to see him, feel him in my arms, just so I know he is real. That what we have is *real.*

"Just keep talking to me," I murmur lazily.

Dorian kisses the top of my head, his fingers twisting in the coils of my hair. "What do you want me to say, little girl?"

"Anything," I breathe, letting my eyes close. I burrow my face into the smooth hardness of his bare chest and inhale his amazing scent. "*Mmmm.* Tell me a story."

"A story." Dorian squeezes me a bit tighter, holding me with such care. "Ok. You rest. I'll talk." I kiss his chest in response, smiling against his soft skin.

Dorian sighs heavily then begins his nostalgic tale in a distant tone. "A long, long time ago, there was a boy eager to become a man. But he was not the man that his father intended him to be. The boy was very rebellious, very spirited, yet very talented. He did not want to embrace the life that his father had mapped out for him. He wanted no part of the depraved role he was expected to fill. He rejected his destiny. This is virtually unheard of amongst his kind, especially considering his pedigree.

"The son strayed, choosing to pave his own way and make a name for himself through his own merit. And he did. Against all odds, the young man succeeded and was known for being an asset to the elite brotherhood of assassins he belonged to. He enjoyed it–the carnage, the brutality. He felt empowered; unstoppable. But soon, he realized he was becoming more and more like his father. He was embracing everything he sought out to avoid. Everything he fought like hell to reject.

"Soon the man was faced with a life-altering choice: defy his father, his people, and all he was taught to believe, or protect his friends and their unborn child. The young man knew what it meant to deceive his father; he knew he could never win. No one ever did. Yet, he chose the latter. He wanted to believe in something greater than the constant thirst for power and influence. He wanted to believe in something more substantial just as his friend had. He knew what this choice entailed. It meant that he would go up against the most powerful Dark force there was. He would defy his king. And no one defied the king and lived to tell about it. Not even his son, the Dark Prince."

Before my weary mind can even begin to process Dorian's sad, tormented tale, the heaviness of sleep blankets me, and I fall into the dark, warm depths of my subconscious mind.

THREE

I stir awake, enraptured by complete darkness. The feel of slick satin against my bare legs informs me that I am in Dorian's bed. He's shed my rumpled clothing, draping me in what feels to be one of the satin nightgowns he purchased for me at Cashmere. My hands search for him in the space beside me though I know he isn't there. The faint murmur of hushed voices wafts through the cracked bedroom door. One of the voices is a hitch-pitched soprano. Aurora. She's here, and from the sound of it, urgently pleading with Dorian. Her shrill voice is agitated, exasperated. I place my feet on the ground then lift myself up, successfully muffling the creaks and squeaks of the bed.

Virtually silent, I tiptoe to the door. I can hear parts of their hushed conversation from several yards away. Dorian is standing at the French windows, looking out into the blackness of the night. He shakes his head, his stance tense and rigid. Aurora stands just a few feet away from him, facing his back. Her hands are on her hips and I can tell she has a serious attitude. I strain to hear the details of their exchange.

"How could you be so careless, Dorian? Do you know what your father will do to me if he finds out?" Aurora whispers fiercely.

"What else could I have done? She knew. And it's not like I could lie to her." There's a crystal glass of amber liquid in his hand. He brings it up to his lips and takes a swig.

"But to link her to you? Do you know what that means? You are already giving her too much of yourself. She *will* drain you completely. What if she's playing you for a fool? She could very well already be consorting with the Light and is taking advantage of your weakness."

Dorian's head snaps back to look at her sharply. His eyes are alight with a vengeful warning. Aurora physically recoils at the sight of Dorian's deep-seated darkness. He returns his attention back to the bleak night sky. Aurora swallows loudly, taking a moment to formulate her words more carefully. She takes a step forward, leaving less than a foot between her and Dorian's broad back. Her perfectly manicured hand reaches out to rest on his shoulder. When he doesn't react, she takes the opportunity to place her other hand on his back, and begins to lightly knead. I feel my fists ball at my sides, my jaw tight with rising anger.

"You know, you don't have to go through with this. You don't owe her anything. We could just end her. Now. You could regain your place at your father's side; go *home.* And I would be right there with you, every step of the way. We could do this. *Together.* We could go right back in that room and kill-"

"Enough! You will not speak those words! Do you hear me?" Dorian growls viciously. Faster than I can see, he spins around, and meets Aurora's terrified expression with his own icy glare. The air around him sizzles and shimmies, indicating that his wrath is near. His mouth is mere inches from hers when he seethes, "I am your prince. You *will* obey me. And you *will not* harm her. Do you understand?"

"Yes, Dorian. I . . . I . . . apologize. Please forgive me," Aurora stammers.

Dorian's eyes are still burning into hers, his lips tight with contempt. "You can come out, little girl," he says gently, though his voice does not match his cold, menacing stare. He backs away from Aurora as if he is disgusted with her proximity.

I push the door open tentatively, unsure of how he knew I was standing there, though something tells me he knew the moment I began to stir. I walk across the room, painfully aware of Aurora's embarrassed, yet hateful glare. I meet her eyes momentarily then snap back to Dorian's now contented expression. Just being in each other's presence is mollifying. I can't even dwell on Aurora's blatant disrespect for me or her pass at Dorian. All I see is *him*.

I brush past my lover's bitter ex-girlfriend, and fold myself into his waiting embrace. He looks down at me and smiles before gently pressing my cheek to his chest. He makes me feel so precious, so cherished.

"Go, Aurora. I will summon you when I need you," Dorian says dismissively. I can't see her, but I can almost feel the heated tension rolling off of her.

I don't look back up at Dorian until I hear the click of the front door behind the clatter of Aurora's designer high heels.

"Why was she here?" I try to dispel the nagging desperation in my voice but I need to know.

"I summoned her. I had to inform her of your newfound knowledge."

He leads us to the plush couch, continuing to embrace me lovingly. This time is different from when he first put his arm around me on this couch. Then, he was trying to be conscious of his movements, careful not to rouse any suspicion. Now he folds himself around my frame with graceful ease.

"Summoned her?" So what, he waited until I was asleep to call her? My jaw tenses with irritation.

Dorian nods. "Aurora and I can communicate without words. Telepathically. It's common for our kind. Easier for us because we are . . . bonded," he explains.

Bonded? What the . . . Oh. "Because you two have had sex." Though I already knew they had an intimate past, just saying the words causes my chest to tighten and ache. Imagining Dorian with anyone else, especially Aurora, is like a kick to the gut.

"Yes," he breathes, stroking my cheek. "I am not sure how it will hold once you ascend, but you and I are bonded as well. And more than just physically."

Aurora did say something about a link between Dorian and me. Though I'm pretty sure I can't hear his thoughts. "How so?"

"The vial I had you drink. It connects me to every part of you. I live inside you now."

Dorian searches my eyes for reaction. Part of me wants to be angry with him for doing something so intrusive without my knowledge. But hearing him say that he *lives* in me is just damn erotic. And that's exactly what I want–for him to be at home inside of me in every way.

"So how does that work?" I ask after a beat, deciding that I could possibly be okay with his invasiveness.

Dorian exhales with relief. "I can feel you, every one of your emotions. I'll know when you're sad, happy, lonely, afraid, aroused. But not only that, I will experience those emotions as if they are my own. Your pain becomes my pain. Your joy becomes my joy."

"Wow. *That's* not weird at all," I remark sardonically.

"It's necessary. I can also use through you if I need to. If you are in trouble, I can channel my power through you. But only in extreme cases. It takes twice as much energy from me."

Unable to come up with a response, I simply nod. Dorian has thought of everything and I genuinely believe he wants to keep me safe, especially considering what he is up against. But even through all this, even with my acceptance of who and what he is, I still feel confused. Lost. Stuff like this isn't supposed to happen to unsuspecting, underachieving girls like me. I don't fit the profile. I'm not mousey, shy, or bookish. I'm not frail and awkward. I like to drink, curse too much, and have handed out my fair share of ass-whoopings. Not to mention, my virtue, or lack thereof, is about as mythical as Dorian himself.

I sigh and give my muddled thoughts in my brain a resigned shake. "So, your father is the king?" I ask, hoping to reignite our earlier conversation.

"Yes."

"And you're a prince? *The* Dark Prince?"

"Yes."

"Why? Why give all that up to save me? To keep my parents' secret?" I'm trying hard to wrap my head around it but no sane person, immortal or not, would wage war against his own family, who just happens to be the ruling family of the Dark Ones. *No big deal.*

"I told you. I was becoming everything I was seeking to reject. I was becoming my father. Brash, evil, merciless. All magic has its price. I had to constantly kill just to retain my youth and power. It was becoming all-consuming."

Yikes. I can't imagine Dorian killing anyone. "And now? You don't have to kill to replenish yourself?"

Dorian shrugs. "I have no need to use that much power anymore. The night sustains me enough, though it takes time. And I'm ashamed to admit that I breathe so much of you, I have no need to acquire any other source," he says sheepishly. That's comforting, I guess.

"And how do you know if you breathe too much?"

"If I take too much of you, my love, I will kill you. So I am very careful, and I give you *me* in return. But I worry. I'd be lying if I said that I don't and you know that's impossible for me," he chuckles lightly. "I worry about not being able to resist you. Or how it would affect you in the long run."

"What do you mean?"

"You are the Dark Light. Half Light and half Dark equally. But I am afraid of you becoming more Dark. I don't want to eclipse the Light in you. I don't want to change you."

I contemplate Dorian's words. He is right; I've worried about being more Dark than Light even before I knew about him. Could this be the fortune teller's prophecy? She said that the Dark would consume me, yet I would welcome it. Was she killed because of what she saw in me?

"You're hungry," Dorian remarks.

"Huh?" I ask quizzically. There was only a faint rumble in my stomach. Even I didn't really notice. Geez, he must have bionic hearing. Tack that on along with the psycho phantom face and the telepathy.

"Whatever you feel, Gabriella, I feel. So let me feed you," he smiles.

After Dorian calls down to room service, we lounge on the couch, eating late night junk food like a regular couple on a Friday night. Even with our volatile showdown earlier and the unexpected arrival of Aurora, it's nice. It still feels right. I can tell that Dorian has made every effort he possibly could not to scare me, even though I internally cringe every time his gaze turns icy or he moves too swiftly. He's trying though; he's *here*. And I'm alive. At this point, that's all I could really ask for.

"When did you start to understand?" Dorian asks.

"Understand?" Realization hits me before Dorian has a chance to answer. "Oh, the language. I started getting bits and pieces at first. That night in the limo up at Breckenridge. I heard you and Aurora talking. About . . . killing me." I give him my hard, unapologetic glare, refusing to let him slither out of this with a vague answer.

"Gabriella, we weren't discussing killing you. You misunderstood. She was informing me of the Dark's presence at the club the night before I arrived. She ensured you were safe, watched you. Like I said, there is no separate order for your death, not since I negotiated a deal with my father. However, I don't trust anyone, and neither should you."

"But you trust Aurora?" I say with a bit of nastiness, making it sound more like an accusation. I take a sip of wine to wash away the bitter taste of jealousy.

"Yes. To an extent."

I suck my teeth and roll my eyes. "And that's all she said? She didn't mention someone being in my room later that night?" Something tells me Aurora at least knows about it, if not orchestrated it.

Dorian's head unnaturally snaps around to face me, his eyes igniting with molten blue flames. He sneers menacingly, the dim light glinting off his teeth. "What?"

I gulp, instantly regretting telling him about it. But me and thinking things through have never really gone hand in hand. "I mean, I saw someone in the shadows and then they just disappeared. I wasn't hurt."

"And where was she?" he demands.

"Oh, um, she was . . . busy. With Jared."

Dorian grounds his teeth and a low hiss escapes. Crap. Hope Aurora is a fast runner. Or the Dark have an excellent health insurance plan.

Dorian takes the wine glass from my trembling hand and places it on the coffee table before cupping my face in his grasp. "I apologize for that. Please forgive me. Aurora will be dealt with."

I perk up into a reassuring smile before leaning forward to press my lips against his. There's so much more I need to know and I need to restore Dorian's casual disposition to sift those answers from him. In return, Dorian eases into a half-smile, his eyes returning to their glittering hue.

"There's something I need to show you," I say, pulling his hands from my face. I spy my purse crumpled a few feet away and go to grab it. After a few seconds of rummaging, I place the photo in his hands, awaiting his reaction.

Dorian strokes the picture with his thumb, his initially surprised expression growing warm and nostalgic. "Where did you get this?" he asks without looking up.

"I can't be sure. I found it in my room. My mother, Natalia, she left a journal for me. You know, I never knew who I was or where I came from. On my birthday, my parents–um, I mean, Chris and Donna–gave it to me. Twenty years of complete and utter confusion, and then all of a sudden, I'm bombarded with all this shit," I say with a wave of my hand.

Dorian looks up at me with a furrowed brow. "So all this time, you really didn't know what I was? I think I made it pretty obvious."

I take a deep breath and shrug my shoulders. "Part of me always knew. A big part, actually. I just didn't want to believe that the first guy I was really, really into wasn't a guy at all," I chuckle nervously.

"Then there's the whole crazed-killer-out-for-my-blood thing. I figured that if you really were Dark, I'd be dead."

"Right," he responds dryly.

"What do you mean, *you made it obvious*? Isn't that against the rules or something?" I ask, my eyes narrowed with question.

Dorian nods, setting the photo down on the coffee table before grabbing his own glass of wine for a hearty sip. "I thought if you knew–if I showed you what I was–it'd make it easier. I was constantly trying to motivate myself to do it. To kill you. I thought if you knew, I'd have no choice but to follow through."

"Oh yeah? And how's that working out for you?"

"Not so great," he laughs, leaning back beside me. His laughter is infectious and I join him. Given our impending doom, there's not much else we can do.

"So what do we do now? Where do we go from here?" I ask once our chuckles have ceased.

"I try like hell to keep you alive, being the fragile little thing that you are for now. And then once you turn 21, the choice is yours."

Twenty-one. I was simply looking forward to buying booze and getting into nightclubs without flashing my fake ID. Now knowing that my ascension will save my life, and potentially Dorian's, it all has new meaning. I just need to make it to twenty one.

I look to the Greek god sitting next to me, making the conscious decision to do whatever it takes to save both our lives.

"So I take it you're not twenty five."

Dorian shakes his head. "Our physical forms stop aging when our power reaches its full potential. Using ages us but we can replenish in . . . various ways. My body stopped changing after 25 years." His mouth twists with mischief, making him look young and ridiculously adorable.

He turns to me, his eyes flickering with nostalgia. "Gabriella, I have lived for two and a half centuries."

What the . . . ? "Holy shit! You're 250 years old?!"

Dorian gives me a wink of his beautiful eye in response. "Surprised?"

"Um, hell yeah! Ok, that's pretty much disgusting, Chester the Molester. I've been screwing an ancient artifact!"

Before I can even break into a giggle, I am pinned flat against the far end of the couch, unable to move or even comprehend how I got here. My arms are pinioned above my head and Dorian is hovering over me, his lips fixed into a menacing sneer.

"Make no mistake, little girl," he mutters just inches from my face. "I am anything but ancient. And you haven't seen *screwing*. Not *yet*."

"Is that a threat?" I pant, my heaving chest making my hardened nipples that much more noticeable.

"I don't do threats. That's another thing that's not my style." Dorian licks his lips and I have to fight the urge to lift my mouth to his and suck his tongue into my mouth.

I squirm under his sinful gaze. "A promise?"

Answering my question, Dorian lowers his mouth to mine yet doesn't touch me. His cool breath kisses my skin, leaving icy tingles in its wake.

"Is that what you want?" he asks. I nod, completely mesmerized by his closeness and the feel of his body against mine. Dorian then grazes my jaw with a single finger, teasing me like only he can. "I want you to say it. Tell me you want me. Tell me you want me to make you feel good. Tell me you want me to fill you, live deep inside you. Tell me, little girl."

"I want you, Dorian," I nearly sob, taken aback by his intensity. Not to mention my overwhelming need for him in every way imaginable. "So fucking bad it hurts."

I swear I hear a growl erupt from his chest as Dorian meets my lips with his. My mouth opens reflexively, eager to take him in, tasting the depth of his hunger for me. It mirrors my own and I moan at the feeling of his tongue exploring the soft wetness of mine. With one hand grasping the junction of my thigh and backside and the other cradling the back of my neck, Dorian devours each muffled whimper and whine. His passion is alarming and I find myself pulling at his soft, tousled hair and the collar of his shirt, wanting more and more.

Everything about this kiss screams desperation and desire. The thought that I could have lost Dorian, that he could have actually turned out to be some revolting monster that didn't give a damn about me, truly terrified me. Not the Dark or my unknown stalker or even death itself. Losing Dorian is what I feared above anything else. And as we lay here, tongues and limbs wholly intertwined, we still can't get enough. Even if we survive this, an eternity of loving Dorian would never be enough for me.

Dorian pulls away, touching his forehead to mine. Both of our breaths are ragged and anxious to meet again. "I want you to understand something, little girl," he breathes. "What I am about to do to you will be unlike anything you have ever experienced. I want to totally consume you in a way that I was unable to before."

"What are you talking about?" I gasp. *Shit, why are we even talking at all?*

"Trust me, ok. Just don't be afraid of me."

I gently push against Dorian's chest so I can assess his fiery blue gaze. "Dorian, I could never be afraid of you. Ever. Of course I trust you."

Dorian makes a pained groan as if the notion of love and acceptance physically hurts him. Then his mouth finds mine as he lifts me up effortlessly. I wrap my legs tightly around his waist, indulging in the strong softness of his skilled tongue. I don't realize that we are even moving until he lays me on the bed seconds later. Dorian abandons me to stand at the foot of the bed, eyeing my violet satin-clad body writhing with expectation.

"You are so beautiful, Gabriella. I want to love you from the inside out. Will you let me?" he murmurs in his velvety soft voice.

I nod, panting feverishly. *God, I'm on fire.*

"Undress," he whispers.

I feel like I am on display, completely exposed for Dorian's viewing pleasure as I slip the thin spaghetti straps from my shoulders one by one. He's watching me intently, the top row of his teeth pressed into his bottom lip, the pink of his tongue barely visible. His narrowed eyes take in the sight of my bare flesh as I sit up to let the gown fall to my waist, revealing full, aching breasts. Dorian gasps in response, letting his tongue slide out between his teeth. I take his reaction as a compliment and lift my ass up to slide the flimsy garment down further, kicking it off the bed with my foot. I'm completely naked, vulnerable, and his. *All his.*

"*Mmmm,*" Dorian moans. "I need to feel you on my tongue."

Holy shit! Did he just say that?

Dorian laboriously unfastens his white shirt, locking his eyes on mine. I can feel myself getting wetter and hotter with every button. He's making a game of this; he knows what he does to me. He can *feel* it. By the time he lets it slide off his shoulders, my fingers have already found my soaking wet sex. I didn't even realize I had let my hand slip down between my legs.

Dorian smirks devilishly, noting my confused expression. "Don't be shy on my account. Pleasure yourself."

"I'd rather you do that," I reply coyly.

Another growl escapes. "Gladly."

Dorian kneels at the foot of the bed, grabbing me by my hips and swiftly pulling me to the very edge. He spreads my thighs and places them on his shoulders, drinking in the sight of my glistening flesh. Soft, wet kisses decorate my inner thighs, driving me mad with expectation. He runs his teeth along the inside of one thigh then bites down right before reaching my swollen clit, causing me to yelp in surprise. The yelp develops into a moan as I savor the tingles that follow along the path of Dorian's touch. He repeats the ritual on the other leg and this time I groan in ecstasy. Every kiss, every bite leaves a new depth of sensation. Pain evolves into a pulsation; pleasure erupts into prickles. And as quickly as they began, they spread, alighting every nerve with a singeing heat that causes me to cry out, my back arching off the bed.

"Just feel, Gabriella. Just feel what I can do to you with just a kiss."

Dorian laves my throbbing folds with his tongue and I completely lose it. Just one touch with his mouth and I crumble into a mewling mess of whimpers and pants. It's as if I've never been touched before, like my body is raw and utterly open to him. I'm barely able to control my erratic breaths when Dorian covers me with his mouth, sucking and licking me until I am practically choking on my own sobs.

"*Oh God!*" I cry. "Dorian, please!" My body shudders again, my thighs twitching uncontrollably on his shoulders.

"What, little girl?" he says against my swollen clit, sending vibrations to the already hypersensitive flesh.

"I . . . I . . . can't," I stammer.

"You can't what?" Dorian juts his tongue inside me, lapping up my warm nectar. "*Mmmmm.*"

"Ugh!" I nearly scream, unable to come up with anything intelligible. It feels *so good* but *too* good. *Unnatural.* Yet, our insane chemistry just comes naturally.

Dorian buries his face between my legs and consumes me enthusiastically, expressing his satisfaction with my flavor with a stream of deep groans. It's like he can't get enough, and I continually feed him with wave after wave of fresh, silken honey.

"Stop! Please! I can't take anymore!" I beg hoarsely. Tears stream down the sides of my face, my skin flush and burning. "It's too much. It's too fucking much."

Dorian finally pulls away, leaving twin bites on the inside of each thigh before standing. He licks his glistening lips, unwilling to let a drop go to waste. His eyes flicker as he observes my trembling frame amusingly.

"I'm not done with you yet, Gabriella. I still want you." He takes a step forward and rests a knee on the bed, right between my legs. "Don't be afraid."

Dorian holds up his palm and it is suddenly enraptured with a bright blue haze. But before I can even wrap my head around it or question it, he pushes it forward a bit. And somehow, in a way that I can't even begin to explain, my entire body moves to the middle of the bed involuntarily like I am a naked, quivering marionette and he is my puppet-master.

I scream with shock and confusion. "What the hell, Dorian? What are you doing me? Your hand . . ." I can't even begin to rationalize what I'm seeing, what I'm experiencing.

"Don't be afraid," Dorian repeats, taking a few steps back. "Trust me. I won't hurt you." He spreads his fingers apart, and again my body complies, splaying my limbs out flat against the satin comforter. "Look at me."

His hand makes a beckoning gesture and my head elevates from the bed, slightly bending forward so I am forced to meet his eyes. I can't move, my body completely manipulated by the simple movements of Dorian's single hand. And then I see it; I see *him*. His darkness creeps onto his face, masking his once beautiful, exotic features. The creature before me is not *my* Dorian. He is threatening, sinister, and so insanely sexy. And as confusing and frustrating as it is to admit, I am scorching hot for him.

His fingers begin to dance as if they are stroking the keys to an imaginary piano. His movements incite the tiny tingles, inflaming every nerve ending, from my fingertips through my swollen breasts to the apex of my thighs. I gasp loudly, my eyes fixed on Dorian's as he continues to tickle the invisible ivories. His strokes increase, and so do the pleasurable prickles, igniting from a spark to a wildfire, quickly spreading to every inch of my body. I want to scream, writhe, thrash. He is torturing me from the inside out and I am slowly dying a hundred delicious deaths.

Dorian finally steps forward, continuing to pleasure me with his magic fingers, though he has yet to touch me. He steps towards me and kneels on the bed, still keeping his eyes on mine, still keeping a safe distance from my panting, tormented frame. He gracefully brings up his other hand, and I nearly choke on my garbled cries. I don't know if I can take any more. This feeling is already so overwhelmingly good; it's as if he is bathing me with a million tiny tongues. After already enduring multiple mind-numbing orgasms, I don't see how I could possibly endure any more stimulation.

Still conducting the symphony of my body with his right hand, Dorian takes the index finger of his left and slowly moves it up and down. I feel it instantly; it's as if he is raking it against my already raw heat. I can *feel* him there, yet he isn't even touching me. *Holy shit!* I will surely go mad. I am not equipped to even wrap my head around this. I feel myself losing control, fighting against the treacherous waves of my violent climax.

"No," he rasps, an animalistic sound rumbling from his throat. "I need to be inside you."

Dorian lets his right hand fall, yet continues to touch and tease me with his left. His eyes are bright, burning blue flames and I can tell that the words are for his benefit as well. If he can feel what I feel than he must also be battling his own orgasm. He bites his bottom lip, concentrating furiously on his measured strokes. I whimper and whine, wanting to grind against him though I know he is not there. He grins sinfully, painfully drawing out every touch and tease.

Finally Dorian closes his eyes, breaking his hold on my body and restoring his gorgeous face. The darkness has fallen away, his conventional human beauty taking its place. I am a panting, whimpering wreck, yet he is so coldly controlled. I gaze at him admiringly as he undoes his slacks. He steps out of them then comes to me, holding his body over mine. I don't know what to make of this. How could I possibly take anymore? But I want to feel *him*. I want his body on top of mine. I want to kiss him, taste him, feel his warmth living inside of me.

With a tentative hand, I reach up to stroke his chiseled jaw. He nestles into the contact, letting his eyes close and draws in the scent of my palm. *Breathing* me. When his eyes reopen, they are bright and sparkling, like the moon's reflection on dark water. I let my hands roam his shoulders and back, pulling his face down to mine. My tongue tastes his sweet flavor mixed with my own, my hands knotting in his hair.

Dorian lifts his head and stares down at me with cautious, searching eyes. This is not the Dark One who manipulated my body with just a brush of his fingertips. This is not the calculated, controlled killer. This is a man seeking acceptance. He needs to know that I'm okay with all this, okay with his darkness. Okay with *him.*

I look into his baby blues earnestly. "I love you, Dorian. No matter what you are, I love *you.*"

Relief and affection wash over him and Dorian lowers himself to reunite our lips. His hands find mine and he conjoins them over my head, our fingers intertwined in their own embrace. I could taste his lips forever, and I want to. I never want to kiss another man ever again. No other man even exists.

Dorian pulls a hand from mine to guide himself into my warm, soft flesh and enters me slowly, our unified gasps echoing throughout the dim bedroom. He fills me, satisfies my craving for him. Each stroke is measured and deliberate. He finds my hands again and joins our palms as he passionately digs deeper into my middle. I moan and sigh as he bathes my neck and shoulders with kisses before moving back to my mouth to consume my most erotic sounds.

For what seems like hours, Dorian makes good on his promise to love me from the inside out. He fills every part of me in ways that I could never fathom in my wildest fantasies. And for the first time since learning what I am and all it entails, bullshit and denial aside, I undoubtedly believe in magic.

Four

"Are you sure you can't come?" I whine, poking my lip out like a spoiled brat.

It's Saturday afternoon, and I begrudgingly have to go home soon to get ready for Morgan's celebratory barbeque. I love my girl, but I'm not ready to leave Dorian or his arms. There's so much more I need to know. And if we have any chance at surviving this, knowledge is power.

Dorian chuckles and flicks my lip gently. "No, little girl. I told you. Chris and Donna are not ready to see me."

"They know there's nothing they could do to make me stop seeing you. Maybe it'd be good for them to see that you really don't intend to kill me," I say with nervous laughter.

Dorian nods. "In time, but not at Morgan's house. We shouldn't ruin her day. Besides, we need to be sure there are no other witnesses just in case things become hostile."

I look at Dorian quizzically. "You wouldn't hurt them, would you?" After witnessing just a fraction of Dorian's incredible power, Chris and Donna would be annihilated in the blink of an eye.

"Of course not. But I can't say the same about you. You aren't in control of yourself yet."

Huh? Dorian thinks *I* would hurt them? "What are you talking about?"

"Gabriella, you are still so raw. You are completely ruled by your emotions. If things became heated, I don't know how you'd react. *I* could defend myself. They could not."

I think of how I left things with my parents less than a day ago–my hands trembling violently, my eyes burning with unseen frost and every light flickering throughout the house. They were afraid of me, and I *liked* it. Their fear empowered me. My parents wanted to keep me from Dorian and I was ready to strike like an untamed animal. He's right; I am a serious danger to them.

"You're right," I nod solemnly. "The sooner I move out, the safer they'll be. Will the apartment be ready by graduation?"

"It will be. Or you could come here and stay with me."

I choke on my own saliva, hacking into my palm. "Um, are you serious? You just told me you were sent to murder me and now you're asking me to move in with you?"

Dorian shrugs, his mouth twisting into an uneasy, hopeful grin. "I know it seems too soon for us; I understand that. But you need to be protected, Gabriella. I need to make sure that whoever is out there lusting for your blood doesn't get near you."

He lets out a breath then shakes his head. "And I just want you here with me. Always. I know it's selfish of me to request that of you but it's the truth. Having you near mollifies me in a way that I can't describe. I've never felt this . . . *good.* I'm completely addicted to you and I'm not sure how to deal with that."

What happened to the elusive, enigmatic man that totally beguiled me with just a look? Dorian's words leave me speechless; there's not much I can say in response. Of course I feel the same way. Of course I only want to be where he is. I've been battling my own addiction to him, feeling more and more drawn to him with every passing second we're together. Part of me wants to pull back and put some space between us so I could gradually wean myself from my insatiable craving for him. Yet I know that I could never be strong enough to actually stay away. Even as I stared at that photo for the first time, the evidence of Dorian's betrayal looking back at me, I couldn't stay away. And now that I know how he feels, now that I know he loves me too, all resistance is futile.

"Why do you think that is? I mean, I understand why we're drawn to each other; I get that level of crazed need to feel you. But why me? And why does it suddenly feel so . . . *intense*?"

Dorian takes my hands in his, pulling me to face him. "Every time I touch you, every time I *breathe* you, that feeling of frenzy intensifies. I take you inside of me; I absorb your life force. I know you don't understand how deep of a connection that is just yet. But willingly giving yourself for the sake of pleasure is one of the most intimate acts for us, both Dark and Light alike."

He brings my hands to his lips, trailing soft kisses on each knuckle. "Little girl, we, the Dark, don't love easily. It's a notion that is rare for our kind. So when we find it, we don't take it lightly. We fight for it. We *die* for it."

Die for it? Dorian has said that he would gladly die for me yet the words still surprise me. But the nagging reminder that his ravenous lust for my essence could accidentally kill me nudges my sensibility before I give into his request.

"As much as I want to spend every second of the rest of eternity with you, I think there are too many doubts, too many questions for right now. I want to be with you; I know that for sure. But we have to sort this shit out, Dorian. What we have–what I *thought* we had–is in repair. Hell, *I'm* in repair. Plus I want to room with Morgan. We've planned this for months and I won't let her down."

Dorian nods, giving me a tight-lipped grin. "I understand. You're right to be reluctant. And it'd be for the best. The more we are together, the closer we are, the harder it is to resist. We should be smart about this. Our lives are already at stake. No need to make things even riskier."

"Thank you," I smile. "Speaking of Morgan . . . you know about her, right? How she's different?"

"Yes, I know," he nods. Dorian looks at me with a furrowed brow. Something about this topic troubles him. "When I told you I would protect your friends, I meant it. When I tried to make good on that promise, I learned that Morgan already had a protection spell around her. Something that even I could not penetrate. I am Dark, but Dark magic and black magic are two different things. Even still, I am considerably more powerful than any Vodou."

"Mr. Pierre? Could he have done something?"

"No, it wasn't him. He has the gift of sight but he can't use. The only thing I could think of would be if a powerful force of black magic actually was sacrificed for this one spell. But who would do that? Then I did some digging. You know about Morgan's grandmother, right?"

"Right," I answer meekly.

"She was very powerful for a priestess. But her life was short-lived. She died suddenly, a few years back. No one knew what caused her death. Do you know what triggered her sudden demise?"

I shake my head slowly. What is he getting at? "No, Dorian. I don't."

He looks at me with remorseful eyes, and reaches out to stroke my cheek. "Her son and his family moved to Colorado Springs. And her granddaughter instantly befriended another young lady. On the outside, this new friend seemed innocent enough. But her grandmother learned that this girl was very different. Very special. Very dangerous. And she sacrificed herself to give her family one last gift."

Tears pool in my wide, horror-stricken eyes. "Morgan's grandmother killed herself to protect Morgan from *me*?"

"Yes, my love. Do not be saddened. Even Morgan's father does not know the truth and he never will. That form of magic is unnatural, and our kind avoids it all costs. She did us all a kindness, you will see."

I look at Dorian in disbelief. "How can you say that? Her grandmother killed herself to protect Morgan from me! *Killed* herself! Am I that horrible, Dorian? Am I that much of a monster?"

"No, of course not! Don't you dare think that this is your fault. People fear what they don't understand. And you have to remember, you are not an ordinary person. You are a goddess amongst mere mortals. *Shit*, you are a goddess to *me*."

Dorian's words stop me up short. Again, he is right; I am not just some regular person on the street. People will fear me, and rightfully so. But to think that Dorian looks at me in such a high regard startles me. His love is enough. That is all the devotion I need.

"Do *you* fear me, Dorian?"

He looks away, pondering my question before meeting my gaze. "I only fear losing you. The Dark are fearless. We are one of the most powerful forces on Earth. There is virtually nothing to fear."

Dorian brushes my cheek adoringly with the back of his hand, causing me to nestle into his touch. "But you, my love, hold *the* most powerful magic that this world has ever seen. And I am in love with you. You could easily decimate me by simply taking your love away."

I look at Dorian in amazement, taken aback by his admission and wistful expression. I could hurt him? I don't care about the magic I will ascend into on my 21st birthday. I don't care about being the most feared force on Earth. All I want is Dorian. Hurting him–losing him–would crush me just like it would him.

"Dorian, I would never do that. You have to know that. And I would never physically hurt you. How could I?"

Dorian laughs heartily and I can't help but feel relieved at his lightheartedness. "You just don't get it, do you? By linking myself to you, I've made your emotions my own. But I've also allowed you access to my heart. You control it; it is yours. If you stopped loving me, it would literally kill me."

Now I understand; I see why Aurora was so upset with Dorian for creating the bond. I could kill Dorian. If I suddenly decided that I didn't want him anymore, he would die. I would never do that, but the thought that I hold that much power over his life terrifies me to my core.

"Dorian, why would you do that? How could you?"

"I told you, Gabriella. We die for love. It is not something we take lightly. So I really hope you are serious about your affections for me," he laughs.

I look at him in disbelief. How can he take this so casually? "I would never do that, Dorian. I love you wholeheartedly. But I really wish you wouldn't have done that. Don't you know I have a reputation for being painfully indecisive and conflicted about my feelings? Not to mention, my fear of commitment."

"I'm well aware of your human life, Gabriella," he replies gravely.

I sigh and shake my head at my blunder. I really have a way with words. "I don't mean it like that." I reach both my hands out to cup his, squeezing a bit. "I'm not going anywhere. Ever. I'm just afraid of that much responsibility."

Dorian looks at me questioningly, a smirk playing at his lips. "You better get used to responsibility. You do know what the Light have planned for you, right?"

"Is it any different than what the Dark want from me?"

"*Touché*," he snickers.

"Can you . . . tell me about them? The Light? I know virtually nothing about that side of me, other than what Natalia wrote in her journal."

"What is it you want to know?" he asks dryly, his face blank of all emotion.

I shrug. "I don't know. What's their power like?"

Dorian chews his bottom lip then sighs his resignation. "I want to tell you that they are self-righteous, contradicting martyrs. That they are so outspoken and judgmental when it comes to *our* transgressions, yet they have no qualms about committing the exact same crimes in the name of the *Light*.

"But that would just be my very biased opinion. The Light are just as powerful, if not more so, than the Dark. Why? Because they have faith. Not just in the Divine Power; we all bow down to the Divine. They have faith in the Light. Their belief is unshakable. This act of treason resulting in your creation initially stemmed from the Dark's corruption, not theirs. And look at me now, sitting here with you, too weak and pathetic to kill you all because of love." He shakes his head as if he still can't believe it.

"How can you say that?" I mutter. He thinks loving me is

pathetic? Ouch.

"Because the Light have always believed in love. We are a bit more stubborn in that aspect. And since it is not an emotion we know well, when we find it, we hold onto it. *We die for it*."

Again, Dorian speaks of dying for love. This isn't just a figure of speech; it's proclamation. The Dark's deep devotion for their mates is unwavering. Even Aurora, who has been blatantly rejected by Dorian, is still willing to help him deceive his father and save me. Her love for him will never die. But how far does that go? Would she be willing to betray me in order to have Dorian to herself?

I try to shake the reservations from my head, though I know there is more than an inkling of truth to it. Why wouldn't there be? If I were in her shoes, and there was only a powerless girl standing between me and my happily ever after, would I be willing to kill for it? *Could* I kill for Dorian?

I look down at Dorian's hands enraptured in mine. I inspect the insides of them, raking my fingers against his palms. "How did you do that? Can you just turn it on and off at will?"

Dorian gives me his sexy half-smile and spreads his hands out. Suddenly, they are engulfed in what looks like translucent light blue flames. I quickly yelp and recoil, pulling my hands back. Dorian laughs at my trepidation.

"It's okay. I won't hurt you," he smiles. He looks like a little boy showing off his shiny new toy. "Don't be afraid."

I scoot forward cautiously and fold my bare legs in front of me. Slowly, I extend my hand towards his into the mystic blue fire hovering over his palms. Tiny bolts of electricity shoot up to greet me, sticking to my hand like static. It doesn't hurt. It's tingly, like the prickles that coursed through my body the first time Dorian's lips brushed my skin. And it's oddly cold, though it looks like his hands are on fire. I am completely mesmerized.

"How?" is all I can mutter in awe.

"We, both Dark and Light, draw magic from the elements. It is what powers us. I mainly draw from water."

I run my fingers down his hand, and the tickling sparks follow them. I giggle in amazement. "So that's why rain helps you, right?"

Dorian nods. "I can draw from any element as well as manipulate them. Water has always just been easier for me. It's quite fitting, actually. The loose translation of my first name is '*of the sea*.'"

"And what you did to my body–how you manipulated *me*–how did you do that?" I can't even speak the words without blushing. Dorian made me feel as if he had a thousand hands, all caressing me at once, yet he didn't even touch me. The recollection provokes dampness between my legs.

Dorian smirks then inhales as if he can smell the sex on me. He closes his hands, causing the blue fire to dissipate. "I made love to your mind. You only *think* you felt those sensations. I have the ability to plant those thoughts in your head."

Talk about a mind-fuck.

I bite my bottom lip and look down. Just talking about it arouses me but I know I have to go soon. I look outside at the grey, cloudy skies and frown. "I just hope the weather holds up long enough or there won't even *be* a barbeque."

"It will. But it will rain tonight. After dark," Dorian replies. I meet his gaze with question in my hazel eyes. "Gotta feed the beast, baby." He leans forward and plants a kiss on my forehead.

With an agitated sigh, I swing my legs off the side of the bed and stand up to make my way to the shower. I'm wearing only Dorian's dress shirt from the night before with just a few buttons fastened, exposing a good bit of cleavage and a lot of leg.

"Well, since you can't come with me today, there's something you can do to make it up to me," I say, spinning around to face him before I reach the adjoined bathroom.

"And what's that?" he responds with a raised brow. He looks so amazingly sexy lounging on the bed, dressed only in black boxer briefs.

"Hmmm, why don't you meet me in the shower and find out?"

And before I can turn around to tease him with my sultry exit, Dorian appears before me, trails of dark vapors dissolving around his frame. Then he shows me just how incredibly skilled he is at manipulating water, pleasuring me under the shower's jets until my body is too weak and sated to withstand anymore.

"Where the hell have you been, young lady?" Chris barks as soon as I step foot in the house. "You nearly gave us heart attacks. Do you know how worried we've been?"

"Sorry, forgot my phone," I mutter, brushing past him.

"Is that you, Gabriella?" my mom calls out, scurrying from the kitchen.

"Yeah. I'm back. Alive, obviously," I say sardonically. I really don't want to be here; it doesn't even feel like home anymore.

"So? Where were you?" Chris questions, following me into my room.

I toss my purse onto my bed and kick off my sneakers. "With Dorian. And for your information, he told me everything. He was honest about why he came here. And you know what? He's not going to do it; he can't. Dorian loves me, and like it or not, I love him too."

"And you believe him?" Chris is really beginning to annoy me with the third degree.

"Most definitely. He can't lie; he's been spelled. And he's taught me more about who I am than I would have learned on my own. He's helping me deal with all *this*. And he is risking his own life to protect me. I seriously doubt a heartless killer would do something like that."

"It's not that we think he's heartless, dear. We're just worried for you," Donna says, feeling the tension radiating between Chris and I. I will myself to calm down, remembering Dorian's reservations about meeting with my parents.

"Well, don't be. I appreciate you both, I truly do, but this is beyond you. Dorian wants to save me. I know you think he's this bad guy but he's not. He's *good*. He has the ability to love, just like my father did."

"Dorian isn't a bad guy," Donna says reassuringly. Chris rolls his eyes and shakes his head before stalking out of my bedroom and down to his study. Donna's solemn eyes follow his retreat before returning to me. "I just know what he's up against. Even he can't fight it."

"Because he's the Dark Prince. Because his father is the king."

"Yes. No one defies him and lives to tell about it," Donna replies gravely. "He won't win."

I sigh and walk to my door, indicating that I'd like to be alone. I'm tired of talking about this. I just want some peace. I just want Dorian.

"Look, I need to get ready for Morgan's party. I'll be ready to go in half an hour."

My mom nods and exits the room. She turns to look at me with mournful eyes. "I just want you to be careful. That's all we want from you. You can't save him and save yourself too."

Though Morgan and her family also reside in Briargate, their ranch style home is considerably more lavish and extensive. We pull up to the Pierre property nestled in a cul-de-sac in one of the more pricey areas of the neighborhood. Cars line the sidewalk and driveway, indicating that the party is already in full swing.

"Hey Gabs! I'm so glad you finally made it!" Morgan beams. She's got a frozen daiquiri in her hand and is feeling tropical in a colorful maxi dress complete with an oversized flower in her hair. "Where's Dorian?" she whispers, eyeing my parents just a few yards away.

"He couldn't make it," I smile weakly.

"That's too bad. Oh well, Jared and James are here with their mom. And Miguel and his family came too. Oh! Remember those fabulous guys we met at the Luxe grand opening?" She sips her fruity cocktail through a straw.

"Yeah, Carlos, Jackson, and X, right? They came?" Looks like Dorian was right. Carlos and Jackson are both stylists at his salon.

"X didn't. But the other guys came, and girl, they had me dying! I love them; they are freakin' hilarious! We are *so* going out tonight!"

"I don't know, Morgan. It's supposed to rain later." If there's one thing that can put a damper on a night of club-hopping, it's rain. Morgan's weave would resemble that of a wet dog, and mine would frizz up to Diana Ross status.

Morgan looks at me disbelievingly. "What makes you say that? It's not in the forecast; I checked."

I smile and shrug at my little secret. "Hey, I'm gonna go find Jared. I'll let you get back to your guests."

I scout out the crowd of people gathered around tables of food and drinks. The roar of laughter, conversation and music echoes through the crisp mountain air. I spot Jared positioned near the pool by himself, constructing a text message on his cell phone.

"Hey you," I smile as I approach.

Jared's head snaps up as if he's been caught red handed. "Hey Gabs!" He pulls me into his arms for one of his famous bear hugs. Wow, that was unexpected, especially since things have been pretty hot and cold with us. "You look nice," he says, taking in my knee-length floral sundress.

"Thanks, you too."

Jared always looks nice, even in jeans and a t-shirt. Today he sports a fitted polo shirt, designer wash jeans and his favorite baseball cap. Almost something the old Jared would wear. *My* Jared.

"Aurora didn't come?"

"Nah, something came up. But I'm supposed to go over to her place after I leave here."

"So you guys are still going strong, huh?" I would normally know the answer to this question but it seems as if Jared and I hardly speak outside of classes.

Jared nods nonchalantly. "Yeah, we are. I really like her. Like, *really* like her. I never thought I'd feel that way about someone . . . other than you of course. But hey, I guess everything happens for a reason, right?"

I smile at my old friend and former object of my desire. "Right."

Part of me wants to warn Jared, tell him that his entire relationship was orchestrated so Aurora could infiltrate our group. But the other part of me, the rational part of me, knows that I have to let this play out for all our sakes. Because no matter what I feel for Aurora, her secrets are my secrets. We are in this together. Though we feel nothing but disdain for each other, we both have a common goal, a common love: Dorian. And if tolerating her is what I have to do to keep him alive and make it to my ascension, then I'll do just that.

"Hey, I was thinking, Gabs. I really want you and Aurora to get along. Not just that, but actually be friends. I know she irks you; I can tell. But outside of my mom, you two are the most important women in my life. I want to be able to hang out with both of you without feeling like I'm cheating. So maybe you guys could get together and just talk?"

I scrunch up my nose as if the thought of having a conversation with Aurora pains me. In all honesty, it very well could. "Geez, Jared, I don't know. Things are fine how they are now."

"Just think about it, Gabs. It'd mean a lot to me." Again, he gives me a hearty embrace. "Hey, I'm about to get outta here. If you see Morgan, tell her I said bye and congrats, ok?"

"Sure," I reply, a little disappointed, though I have no right to be. I haven't actually been Friend of the Year.

Hours later, after copious amounts of food and drink have been consumed by all, a frightening clap of thunder rips through the sky, signaling the end of the party and the beginning of a violent storm. As the first drops of rain kiss my face, I look up at the sky and smile. My Dorian is at work. I feel close to him in this moment, knowing that he too is standing out in the rain, replenishing his strength. I want to be where he is; I want the rain to wash away my fear and restore my confidence that everything will be alright.

"What the hell are you doing, Gabs?" Morgan yells scampering to shelter.

I look around at all the scurrying partygoers, completely oblivious to their aversions. A day ago, I would have been one of them. I would have run straight for cover as soon as I felt the first drop. But now as I stand in the rain, sopping wet, I realize that I am growing closer to the paranormal side of me. I am becoming what I was intended to be. Even as lightning flashes across the deathly dark skies, I feel contented. Dorian's magic courses through my body. I have nothing to fear.

"So I see *Dorian* didn't bother to show up," Chris sneers as we make our way back home.

I wring my wet hair back into a ponytail and roll my eyes from the back seat. "He didn't think it would be a good idea just yet."

"Humph," he scoffs, earning a stern sideways glance from Donna. "Don't tell me he's afraid."

"He was actually," I say flatly, meeting his gaze in the rearview mirror. "For you two. At what I would do if things became heated. See, he actually *cares* enough about you guys to want to keep you safe. *From me.*"

My parents exchange worried glances and we ride the rest of the way in silence. I am what I am; there's no denying the inevitable anymore. I'm not like them. I was not made for this world. The closer I am to Dorian, the closer I am to ascension, the more powerful I feel. There's no bridging the gap now. As much as I love them, I now realize that they are only my mortal family–a temporary fixture to create the façade of a normal girl. But I am anything but normal. I am the epitome of all that is taboo in their world.

Though I have finals, studying and my last week of work to keep me busy, it seems as if I can't focus on anything other than missing Dorian. Phone calls, text messages and quick kisses during my break at work do nothing to satisfy my craving for him. I need to hold him, smell him. *Feel* him.

By Wednesday, I am nearly writhing with my overwhelming need for him. It's near midnight, I've stashed my textbooks for the evening, and I'm trying desperately to get some sleep. Every time I begin to doze off, I slip into a vivid dream that results in me jolting awake, leaving the space between my legs throbbing and wet.

Finally I flick on my bedside lamp and reach for my phone. Could Dorian still be awake? Of course he is. Just hearing his voice would soothe me; it always does. Yet I don't want him to think I'm totally desperate and helpless. I sigh and toss my cell back on my dresser. No. I have to get through this; I have to get used to not having him around all the time. He's trying to practice restraint. Having me around, breathing me in so often will kill me. I need to stop playing Russian Roulette with my life.

I reach for the remote to my television and turn it on, flicking mindlessly through the channels. Seems like everything either reminds me of him or makes my mind wander into dark territory.

Every song on the radio does the same. Dorian completely fills every corner of my mind.

"*Ugh!* Dorian, why can't you just be here?" I whine into my pillow, giving it a frustrated punch.

"Be careful what you wish for, little girl," a silky baritone mutters.

Startled, I look up instantly, my eyes searching for the source of the phantom voice. There, in the corner of my bedroom, shrouded in the shadows, stands my love. Dorian. Dissipating wisps of dark vapors surround him, and I can see his azure eyes gleaming brightly in the midst of the darkness. He is here. He has heard my cry. Has felt my yearn for him.

"*Dorian*," I breathe. My eyes are wide with excitement and my heart beats furiously in anticipation.

In the next instant, he's beside me, sitting on my childhood bed. Having him here arouses me. I've never had a guy in my room, supernatural or not. I can't resist; I crush my body against his, practically straddling his lap in my oversized t-shirt and pink panties. Dorian instantly reciprocates, palming my behind as our mouths and tongues unite. *God, I've missed him.* It's more than that; I've ached for him.

"How did you get here? What about the wards?" I ask suddenly.

"Yes, those," he smirks. "They only ward off those who wish to hurt you. I must admit, I could not penetrate them at first, not until I was certain that I would not kill you."

I stare at him questioningly, the hint of a frown on my face. "So when did you decide that?"

"I think a part of me always knew I couldn't. But I wouldn't admit it to myself. I still fought against the unknown emotions because I didn't understand them. But now . . . I can't fight anymore. I want you–all of you. I want to own every part of you."

I look up at the man I love, the Warlock who has risked everything for me. I just want to give him all of me. I want him to know just how deep my love flows. I rejoin our mouths, pressing my aching breasts against his chest and grind my sex into his lap. In turn, Dorian grips handfuls of my backside, pulling me deeper into his erection restricted only by his dark grey slacks. I grip the hard mounds of muscle of his shoulders as I begin a slow, erotic dance, the lace of my panties causing delicious friction.

"Do you think you can be quiet?" he asks breathlessly, pulling his head up from mine momentarily. I give him a doubtful expression. I lose all control when I am with him. That kind of pleasure cannot be muted. "I can fix that," he says raising his index finger.

"No!" I whisper loudly. "No, I don't want you to. I want the thrill of feeling you with the chance of getting caught," I say slyly.

Dorian chuckles and shakes his head. "You naughty little girl. I believe I've created a monster."

"Or just unleashed the one that's always been there."

And with that, I push him back onto my bed and show him just how incredibly much I've craved him until the wee hours of the morning.

Five

Graduation

Three months ago, it was the only thing I had to look forward to. It would be considered the most monumental event of my life thus far. But now as I walk across the makeshift stage to collect my degree, it all seems so miniscule. To some, an Associate's degree would be viewed as a stepping stone to higher education. A great accomplishment in which I should be proud. To me, it's just a piece of paper; something Chris and Donna can hang up amongst the countless class photos displayed throughout the house. I will never use it. It will not define me.

Despite the turmoil brewing in my parents' home at my moving out, and the fact that no one has been able to track the Warlock that has claimed several lives of innocent girls in search of me, I am happy. *Incredibly happy*. I have more than just some measly degree; I have love. I have Dorian. That in itself is a reason to live.

As I look out into the crowd, towards the very last row, I see him grinning back at me proudly. He's come here to support me, despite my parents' reservations. And even though Aurora sits beside him, scowling with contempt, I don't care. He's here for *me*.

After the commencement speeches and ceremonial fanfare, I weave through the crowd in search of my love, my Dorian. Still, he stands towards the back, concentrating furiously as he scans the room. He's watching for any sign of trouble. I notice the rapid changes in his expressions, as if he's in deep conversation. He's communicating with Aurora, who has probably gone off to find Jared. They are here to protect us, suspecting my would-be killer would try to strike and slip into the crowd undetected.

"Everything ok?" I mutter when I approach him.

Dorian looks down and smiles at me warmly. "It is now," he breathes. "There's been movement. Someone has been here but we don't know who."

"You can't *sense* them?"

"Not if they don't want me to. But I know something was here. I just can't tell who." He takes a moment of thoughtful silence and I know he's speaking to Aurora. "Aurora can't pick up the trail. *Shit.* I should have been more careful with you."

I pull Dorian's face down to mine and look him in his crystal blue eyes. "You did nothing wrong. It's because you are here that I've even made it this far. Whoever it is probably sensed your presence and got scared. Just you being here protects me enough."

Inching closer, Dorian joins his mouth with mine. When he pulls away a bit, I notice that his expression has transformed into something I can't quite comprehend.

"I can't wait until you ascend. Then I can have you all the time without fear of hurting you. And whoever this is, we could hunt them together," he seethes. "And you would like it. You would love tearing him apart. It would make you feel so good. We would slaughter him together and then fuck like animals."

Startled, and maybe even a bit repulsed, I study Dorian's intimidating leer. His eyes have darkened and his mouth is twisted into a menacing grin. This is the hunter in him–the assassin that sought out to slay my mother. The killer that grew angry with my father, his best friend, for sparing her life. He wants to kill. It's been so long since he has. But the Dark in him craves it. He needs it to feed the beast.

"Uh, Gabriella?" my mom says from behind us. Dorian instantly stiffens, recovering his cool demeanor as I turn around to face them.

"Hey, Mom. Dad." I give them each a warm embrace.

"Congratulations, Kiddo," Chris mutters. I can see his tense jaw flexing as he glares at Dorian. "Dorian. It's been a while."

"Twenty years," Dorian notes in a level voice. He turns to

Donna and gently bows his head. "Donna, you're looking well. You haven't aged a day."

"And neither have you," she replies tersely. "It's good to see you, Dorian."

"Why the hell are you here?" Chris snaps, clearly over the pleasantries.

"Dad!" I screech.

Dorian looks to me and gives me a reassuring half-smile. He's in control. "For her. For Gabriella."

"I know that. But we both know what that entails. We know why you were sent." I can see Chris's hands form giant fists at his sides. *Don't do it, Dad.*

"I'm here to protect her. I love Gabriella. I would never hurt her." I reflexively smile at his admission, despite the tense moment, because I know he's being honest.

"So the rumors, they are true?" Donna asks quietly.

Dorian shakes his head. "I am not sure. But I know what I feel." He looks down at me lovingly. "I've given her me. I've bonded with her. We made the link."

"What?!" Donna shrieks. I look at my mother's bewildered expression. Even Chris looks confused at her outburst. "Dorian, you know what that means, don't you? Why would you do that?"

"To show her how much I love her. No matter the circumstances. She has my heart."

"But if it is true, then what? What will you do then?" Ok, now *I'm* confused.

Dorian furrows his brow, mulling over her question. "That is for Gabriella to decide. My life is in her hands."

We stand in silence, glaring at each other with apprehensive eyes. "We'll meet you at the car, Kiddo. Don't take too long," Chris finally says to break the tension.

"What was that about?" I ask Dorian once my parents are out of earshot.

"What have you done to him?" Aurora interjects before I get my answer. I roll my eyes at her rude interruption.

"Stay out of it, Aurora," Dorian says between gritted teeth.

"No, I won't stay out of it. She's draining you. You look like you're going to drop at any moment!" Aurora puts her hands on her hips and glares at me fiercely. "Gabriella, you have to see what you're doing to him. Someone is going to end up dead."

I look between my visibly annoyed lover and his painfully gorgeous ex as they exchange menacing stares. "What is she talking about, Dorian? Have I hurt you in some way?"

Dorian sighs and shakes his head, turning his gaze to me. "No, you haven't. We have just been spending too much time together. I've been giving you so much of me just to ensure I don't weaken you. It isn't your fault."

I digest what he's telling me. Dorian has given me too much of himself and now he is suffering. Aurora is obviously seeing his *true* self, the part of him that he's keeping from me. My poor Dorian is deteriorating right before my eyes, all because we can't stay away from each other, and I can't even see the damage I've caused. Ever since we discovered that he could penetrate the wards around my house, I've demanded to see him every night. That was only a little over a week ago yet he is already perishing.

"Oh my God, Dorian! Why didn't you tell me?" My hands fly up to his beautiful face, searching for any sign of pain. He doesn't *look* like he's hurting. He looks a little bit older but not much. I just wish I could *see* him.

"I'll be fine," he responds. He nods towards a large window. "It will rain soon."

"Yeah, but that won't be enough. And you know it. You need help, Dorian," Aurora chimes in.

I look to her, suddenly terrified and desperate. "Tell me what to do. How can I fix him?"

Aurora smirks coldly and leans forward. "You could let him breathe you. But for what he needs, it would surely kill you. You are still pathetically powerless."

"No!" Dorian growls. He takes a step forward, his eyes flickering with disgust and hatred.

"Well then, he'll have to drain someone," she remarks simply. She looks at her meticulous manicured nails as if the whole conversation of saving Dorian's life bores her. "A power source. Someone like your adopted mother, perhaps?" Aurora smiles as if the notion is humorous.

"Watch it, bitch!" I spew angrily. A few nearby people look in our direction but the roar of congratulatory cheers has masked our conversation.

"Ok, ok, settle down," she giggles. "There is a way. It's your only other option. But you won't like it."

I look to Dorian, reading the regret on his face. It must be bad. But not worse than losing him. "Anything," I whisper.

"I can transfer to him. He can breathe *me*," she coos wickedly.

"Absolutely not!" Dorian seethes.

"You and I both know there is no other way, Dorian. I am your last hope. Come on, if Gabriella loves you so much, she would understand. She would do anything to save you. I know I would."

I look at my lover's torn expression. He knows this is our only option. He is suffering because of me, because of my intense need for him. I have no other choice but to save him.

"Let's do it. Tonight," I murmur, hanging my head in shame.

"No, baby, we don't have to do this. It's ok," he pleads, gripping me by the shoulders.

And then I see it; there is a crack in his mirage. For just a second, I see what I have done to him. His eyes are flat, sunken in, lifeless. His skin is pale and dry. He is only a ghost of the man that I love. My heart instantly shatters at the sight.

"Yes we do," I croak, through trembling lips. I clear my throat and look to Aurora, shrugging out of Dorian's hold. "We'll do it. I'll be over at 7."

"Great!" she beams. "I'll even let you watch." And with that, she spins around and disappears into the crowd.

"You don't know what you've just agreed to," Dorian whispers. There is pain, remorse in his voice.

"I know that it will save you and that's all that matters." I wrap my arms around him and bury my face in his hard chest. I look back up at him and try to plaster on a reassuring smile. "I've gotta go. I'll see you later. Don't worry, it's gonna be ok."

As I walk out to the parking lot, I fight to hold back the tears that threaten to unravel me. I *don't* know what I've agreed to, but if it saves my Dorian, then I have to go through with it. He needs this, and I need him. If he can defy his father, his entire race of Warlocks, than I can surely give him this. All Aurora is going to do is help him. How bad could it be?

After a painfully awkward early dinner with my parents, I kiss them goodnight, ensuring them that I'll be back in the morning. I've told them a bunch of us new graduates are going out to celebrate though I'm sure they know I'm going to be with Dorian.

As I drive to the Broadmoor, my stomach is tied in a thousand knots. I don't know what to expect. If he is going to breathe Aurora, what does that consist of? Will he just grab her hand and take a whiff? It must be something more if he was so apprehensive. I could tell he was struggling with the idea yet he knows he needs this. I have to be supportive. He would do it for me if it meant saving *my* life.

"So glad you could make it, Gabriella," Aurora leers as she opens the door to Dorian's suite.

Why the hell is she answering *his* door? I see she's changed from the modest wrap dress she wore at the graduation into a tight black pencil skirt, silk button-up blouse and platform high heels.

I step in defensively, preparing myself for the worst. Instead, I find Dorian staring out of the French doors into the dark night. He has a crystal glass of scotch in one hand while his other arm is resting against the glass. He's weak, and it breaks my heart. He turns on my approach, his eyes glimmering faintly behind dark lashes as he smiles. Even in suffering, he is still the most stunning man I've ever seen. He is still wearing his dark dress slacks and shirt from earlier, the top few buttons unfastened exposing his tan chiseled chest. I don't hesitate to wrap my arms around his neck and kiss him, tasting the strong remnants of alcohol. His arms squeeze my waist desperately in turn. I don't want to lose him; I can't. Whatever he needs, I'm more than willing to do what it takes.

"Ok, let's get this over with. The bedroom would be the best place. Like I said, you're more than welcome to watch. I'm not shy," Aurora smiles slyly.

I look to Dorian for direction, and he nods reluctantly. "Fine."

Aurora sashays to the bedroom and I turn to follow her when Dorian grabs my arm, pulling me back to him. "If I feel you hurting, I'll try to stop. I swear, I'll try."

"I know you will. But you need to get better. That's all I care about. If it weren't for me, you wouldn't even be like this."

When we enter the dimly lit bedroom, I instantly want to scream for Aurora to get out. This is the place where Dorian has made love to me countless times; this is *our* sacred place. She has no business in here. But she knows what she's doing. I don't. Now more than ever I wish I could fast forward to my ascension. I wish I could let that magic fill me so I could channel it to Dorian. *I* should be the one healing him. *I* should be the one saving him.

I take the armchair as Dorian sits on the edge of the foot of the bed. We are facing each other, his expression full of pain, doubt and weariness. This is just as difficult for him. Aurora eclipses my view of him, standing directly in front of him nearly between his legs. I literally bite my tongue and dig my fingernails into my palms to keep from tackling her. This moment isn't about me or my jealousy. This is about Dorian. And no matter how much I hate Aurora in this moment, I know that she loves him just as much as I do. She is his savior right now.

"Look at me," she coos in her soft, sensual soprano. She places her hands on his shoulders, beckoning him to meet her gaze.

I hear Dorian sigh deeply before pulling his chin up to meet her eyes with his. The air in the room shifts and begins to shimmer around them. I can hear the hum of a forbidden chant in high pitched soprano, too low for me to make out. Vibrations radiate from their frames, indicating their powerful currents. This is it; Aurora is fixing Dorian. *My* Dorian. I hear him take in a sharp breath. I can't tell if it is out of pleasure or surprise. She moves closer into him, nestling between his legs. I want to scream, tell her to get away from him. I want to slap that smug look right off her face. But Dorian needs her; he doesn't need me. He needs *her*.

"Stop!" I hear him call out, breaking me from my tortured reverie. He peers around Aurora's slender body and looks to me with apologetic eyes. "Gabriella. Come," he breathes with an outstretched hand.

Slowly, I feel myself rise to my feet. I take the seven measured steps to him, grasping his hand weakly. Dorian pulls me down onto the bed next to him. He looks at me, his dazzling eyes searching the hidden pain etched in my face. He knows how I feel; my emotions are his emotions. But I've been swallowing the torment that threatens to eat me alive ever since we stepped into this room. I've been dispelling my agony so he can get better without worrying about me.

After I flash him a reassuring, yet manufactured, smile, he turns back to Aurora and nods, signaling her to continue. She sighs agitatedly at my intrusion, regaining her composure before boring her ice blue eyes into his. Again she begins to chant in their ancient, hidden tongue, her singsong voice wavering with emotion.

Hot tears pool rapidly in my eyes, sliding down my face, as I see Dorian's face transform from affliction to pure bliss. His eyes grow brighter; they are nearly glowing in his euphoric high. He grips my hand tighter, telling me he's still here, he's still with me. Aurora's face is a mixture of carnal desire and ecstasy as she purrs her admission to Dorian, as if I don't even exist in this moment. It's just the two of them. I am nothing more than a pathetic spectator intruding on their intimate moment.

Why am I even sitting here, watching like some perverted voyeur? I should leave; I should run away from their depravity. *Dammit*, I should kick both of their asses for making me feel so weak and disgusting! But I can't. I am a damn fool, a sick puppy. I am trapped in my own self-inflicted misery.

Dorian begins to tremble and a low growl escapes him. He squeezes my hand harder still and though it hurts, I don't dare pull away. The tears flow faster and I choke on my anguished sobs. *When will this be over? Hasn't he had enough?* The blue glow radiating from their transmission grows brighter still and they both begin to pant, their chests heaving rapidly. Soft moans cascade from Aurora's lips as she surrenders decades of lust and desire to her past love. It startles me, hearing her passionate cries for Dorian. I gauge his expression, search it for any sign that he feels the same passion. The answer nearly destroys me. He feels it too. He wants her; he needs her. He said he'd try to stop but her magic consumes him. *He* consumes her.

As if my heart and my pride could take another blow, Dorian releases my hand, replacing it with the taut flesh of Aurora's backside. She gasps in delight, her eyes fixed on Dorian's, her breathing wild with a flood of ardor. He slides her skirt up to her hips, his hands kneading her exposed tight mounds in a black lace thong and pulls her into his lap. She straddles him, leaving only centimeters between their wanting mouths. I can't bear to witness this. I can't stand the torture. Yet I can't look away. I need to see this. I have to see Dorian in his element, even if he is at home with Aurora.

He is visibly aroused; they both are. And I am certain that if it weren't for my presence, he would be inside her. *Why isn't he stopping?* He said he'd feel my pain and he would try to stop. Maybe he can't. Maybe the carnal beast within him has taken over and my Dorian is no longer present. Maybe he really is Dark to his core.

Faster than I can comprehend, Dorian flips Aurora onto her back with a low guttural growl, completely forgetting my miserable existence just inches away. I'm sobbing, drowning in a pool of my own sorrow. He easily pops the top buttons of her blouse and buries his face into her neck and chest, inhaling fiercely. Aurora moans and writhes under his weight as he continues to knead her ass and back, sucking in mouthfuls of her sweet scent. Her hands pull at his slick, black hair as he delves into the apex of her full breasts, the bridge of his nose skimming her round swells. Low groans and ringing moans fill the room, joined by my strained, anguished cries. I should leave; I should run out of this suite right now. But love and devotion hold me prisoner. I am a prisoner of Dorian's love. And right now he is torturing me, killing me. Yet I make no move to run to freedom. I sit and witness my own death.

"Stop!" Dorian shouts hoarsely, his voice full of emotion. He pushes away from Aurora and sits up. "Go," he commands.

Aurora stands on shaky legs, visibly drunk off Dorian's intensity. She smiles at me lazily. "He's all yours," she whispers as she adjusts her disheveled clothing then staggers out of the room and down the hall.

Dorian gazes at me with sorrowful eyes. He knows what he has done. He knows the brutality I have just experienced. In a swift movement, he is on me, caressing my body furiously. He kisses my face, my neck, the tops of my breasts. And being the desperate sycophant that I am, I let him. Even knowing that just moments ago, his face was buried in Aurora's cleavage, his hands grasping her backside. *What am I doing?* What is happening to me?

"I'm so sorry," he murmurs into my skin. "I'm so sorry, my love. I love only you. I want only you."

My sobs grow louder as I hear his words. He loves me yet he has hurt me. Deeply wounded me like no one has ever done. And I've let him. I let this happen; I encouraged it. I deserve this punishment for it was my own doing.

"I know," I cry into his chest. I try to hush my whimpering yet I can't seem to catch my breath. I'm pathetic–a driveling mess of nauseating self-loathing.

"I'm so sorry. I love you. I love you," he breathes, finding my mouth.

His hands wipe away my mascara–streaked tears before knotting in my tresses. The kiss deepens, cutting off my cries and I begin to melt into his arms. Even after his assault on my heart, he is the only one that can soothe me. Only he knows the depths of my depravity, because he is just as dark and twisted. Two equally confused, pathetic, fucked up souls.

I can't even comprehend how I could be aroused after witnessing the sensual exchange between Aurora and Dorian, but I am. And as disgusting and weak as it makes me feel, I am panting as he slides my panties down my legs exposing my dripping wet sex. I want him; I want to show him that I can make him feel good too.

Dorian stands long enough to unfasten his pants and relinquish his hardness. He pushes my dress up to gather around my waist before urgently entering me, burying his shame and apologies in my warmth. I murmur his name repeatedly as he digs himself deeper and deeper, filling me until I choke on my own gasps. His rhythm is rushed and unconstrained. He is running away from his corruption. He is trying to escape his darkness. But no matter how deep he delves, no matter how hard he thrusts, no matter how good it feels, he is who he is. He is Dark. My Dark Prince. And I am just as Dark and twisted for loving him.

Six

"I am so sorry, little girl. So, so sorry," Dorian murmurs into my hair.

It's late or very early, and somewhere between my earth-shattering orgasm followed by more pitiful sobs, I dozed off. Dorian's naked body is lying beside me, tightly twisted around my frame protectively. I know he is full of regret but we both know it was necessary. Aurora had to let him breathe her. I just didn't expect it to be so sexual, so erotic. I can only imagine how sex was for them, and though I try to dispel the thoughts, they keep creeping back up into my mind. I'm not like them, not yet, at least. Everything about them is extraordinary from their physical perfection to the intangible way they move. Of course I can't even begin to wrap my head around it. It is not meant for me. We are from two different worlds.

"Did you sleep at all?" I whisper hoarsely. I am still too ashamed to look at him. Ashamed because after what I witnessed, after what he did to me, I still let him have me.

"No. I can't. Not when your pain cripples me so. I am so sorry."

With a huff, I turn to gauge Dorian's expression. He is clearly anguished though he looks better. Younger. His eyes have returned to their dazzling azure color and I can tell that his skin has returned to its warm olive complexion in the dim lighting.

"It's ok, Dorian. I'm ok. It had to be done. We both knew it'd be uncomfortable. I just didn't expect it to be like *that*," I say, my voice cracking at the end. "Is it always going to be like that? When you need to be *fixed*?"

"Yes. But I hope to not need to breathe anyone else but you. Ever. Do you understand why I was so reluctant to see you every day? I didn't want to *need* that. To need Aurora."

"Yes," I nod. Had I known that our close proximity would result in him needing anyone else but me, especially Miss Painfully Perfect, I would have been less demanding about him spending each night with me. But I needed him. My addiction for him grows stronger every day. "Is there anything we can do? To ease the . . . cravings?"

"It's harder now. Now that we are linked. But I'll look into it. For now, we just have to make every moment together count."

I look at my love thoughtfully. He's right. I can't dwell on something I can't control. "Was it hard for my parents too?"

Dorian shrugs. "Since they were both powerful in their own right, their exchange wasn't as . . . staggering as it is for you and me. You are enticing for all forces, not just the Dark and Light. There will be those that want to harness that power for themselves."

"Is that what you want to do?" I whisper before I can stop myself. I was thinking it; it was not meant to be heard aloud.

Shame flashes on Dorian's face momentarily. "Part of me does. It feels so . . . good. Strong. It's in my nature to want it. And I've only had a taste, only a fraction of how potent you will be. But taking it from you would kill you, and I could not bear that."

"You said that if I stop loving you, you would die. What if I died? What will happen to you?"

Dorian chews his bottom lip as he ponders my question. "I will live."

"And if you die, what happens to me?"

"You will live."

"What if you stop loving me? Will that kill me?"

Dorian looks at me gravely. The talk of death has made him uneasy yet these are things I need to know. "Yes. It will. But I would never do that. I can't."

I shake my head exasperatedly. "Dorian, I don't know how the Dark view the idea of commitment, but you have basically linked us for the rest of our lives. You aren't going to want me forever. And as soon as something or someone better comes along, I will die. Do you understand that? It will kill me if you leave me!"

"Do you plan on wanting someone else? Is my love not enough for you?" he asks in a level voice. How can he be so calm about this? We haven't even defined our relationship, for crying out loud!

"No, Dorian, of course not." It's the truth; no one compares to him. He is my heart and soul. He is my everything. "But you have to know that this scares me. You say that you could never stop loving me, but how do I know that's true? And don't tell me because you can't lie! I know that. You don't know what the future holds for us. What if ascending *changes* me? What if I really do become some freak?"

Dorian chuckles lightheartedly and as always, his laughter makes me smile despite the morbid nature of the conversation. "That won't happen. Ascending will bring out every remarkable quality in you and then heighten it times ten. No, a hundred. You'll be more amazing than you already are. There won't be a force on Earth that could deny your power. They will worship the ground you walk on."

Wow. Could I really handle all that adoration? Not to mention the huge burden of responsibility. "And then what? What would be expected of me?"

He shrugs. "All I can hope is that we will be together, no matter what you choose."

Together. "So *are* we together? I mean, we've just never talked about it." Though he's already bonded me for life. *No big deal.*

Dorian chuckles again. "I should say so! But if you must label it, you are mine and I am yours. Like I told you before, you can be whatever you want to me."

I smile instinctively. He's mine. Dorian-*freakin'*-Skotos is mine. *That's right, bitches!*

"I like being yours."

Dorian returns my amorous gaze. "I *love* it."

Hours later, with the sun bright overhead, we ride the few minutes to Paralia. Dorian has insisted that we stop by before going to my house to pack up my things. He even arranged everything for the move.

"So what is it that you want me to see, Dorian?" I ask as we walk down the short path to the apartment reserved for Morgan and me.

"I have a surprise for you," he smiles. He reaches over and places his hand in mine, then brings it up to his lips to plant a tender kiss on my knuckles. My body instantly reacts to his touch and a flood of tingles sprout from my fingertips and up my arm.

"A surprise? What now?"

Dorian already insisted we take one of the furnished units to save us money on buying furniture. Had I known he would fill it with plush leather couches, dark mahogany high tables, and top of the line appliances, I would have declined. The apartment was already too much, especially since he wouldn't accept any payment from either of us.

We step into the luxury apartment, the smell of leather and freshly polished wood greeting us. I take in the high vaulted ceilings and wrought-iron chandeliers in awe. Living here will take some getting used to. I just hope I do a good enough job at Cashmere to make up for it.

"Through here. In your room," he says leading me past the stainless steel kitchen and down the hall.

Morgan insisted I take the larger bedroom though I assured her she could have it. Her wardrobe alone could fill an entire room. I think she'd feel uncomfortable taking the larger one considering what Dorian has done for us.

We step inside and I am nearly floored at the sight before me.

Dorian has completely transformed the bare white walls and hardwood floors into something that can only be described as utterly astonishing. A light blue color, similar to the cerulean blue that made him look so young and free, bathes three of the four walls. The fourth is painted gunmetal grey, housing a giant sconce fashioned in the same design as the pendant he gave me. It's a large round mirror, adorned with glittering white crystals. Around those crystals lie black ones, equally dazzling. Reflexively, my hand flies up to my beautiful necklace, fingering the diamonds and delicate pearl center.

Below the sconce, lies a modern, simple yet stylish bed. It is *very* Dorian, with its sleek black comforter, crisp white sheets and alternating blue and black pillows. Simple nightstands sit on either side of the bed, matching perfectly with the giant dresser and armoire stationed against the blue walls. Framed black and white prints of famous musicians and artists also adorn the walls. Nestled in one of the corners lies a plush black chaise lounge littered with blue pillows, coupled with what looks to be some kind of sound system. It is extremely streamlined and a far cry from my rinky-dink iPod dock. The speakers are tiny yet I am sure they pump out enough sound to vibrate a concert hall. It's all so overwhelming and more than I could ever imagine.

"Dorian! Oh my God! When did you do this?" I exclaim, crushing my body to his with excitement.

"While you were sleeping," he smiles slyly.

My eyes narrow slightly. "You left me?"

Dorian flashes me a knowing crooked grin. "No."

My face alights with awe. "It's amazing. Thank you." I shake my head in disbelief. "I'll never get used to how well you know me. Better than I know myself sometimes, I think."

"You really think so?" he asks with a raised eyebrow.

"I *know* so. Look at this place," I say, gesturing around the room. "I could have never come up with something like this. And the truth is I *don't* know myself. I don't really know my likes and dislikes. I don't have any real hobbies. I only know what I was spelled to know. That's not a life; that's a mirage. Meeting you, being with you, has given me something *real*. It's made me realize who I was truly meant to be."

Dorian looks down at me lovingly and I think he's about to tell me that he's known who I was all along, that he's loved me for who I was. Instead he scoops me up into his arms and swings me around, causing me to squeal. We end up on the bed, both laughing as if nothing else in the world matters. And in this moment, nothing else *does* matter. It's just me and him. *Forever*.

"I'm pretty sure you know what you like," he notes, hovering over me. He props himself up on one elbow. "See. You like this, right?" And with that, Dorian rubs his thumb over the fabric covering my left nipple.

"Mmmm, yes, I do," I breathe, closing my eyes.

Dorian then moves to the right breast, fingering the area ever so gently. "And this?"

"I like that too. So much," I murmur.

I feel Dorian's hands drift under my shirt, his fingers skimming my bare stomach. His touch sends little shockwaves to every nerve ending and a reflexive moan escapes my lips. In the next moment, I feel the wetness of his warm tongue at my belly button.

"Oh God, Dorian. That feels so good," I say with a strained voice. My hands travel down to take a handful of his hair. Suddenly, Dorian's head snaps up, his eyes flickering white hot. "What's wrong?" I ask with alarm. I sit up and look around me furiously.

"Fuck!" he shouts, his eyes ablaze with anger. He's on his feet, though my human eyes don't detect the movement. I notice the air around him quivering.

"What? What is it?" Oh crap, what did I do?

"It's Aurora. Something has happened. We have to go," he explains, pulling me to my feet.

He tugs me out of the apartment, ignoring my questions as to what could be wrong. Once we're in the car, his fists pummel the steering wheel, shaking the entire car, before looking at me with regretful eyes. Oh shit. It's bad.

Against my better judgment, I reach a shaky hand towards him, resting it on his forearm. "What is it? Please talk to me."

"I am so sorry, Gabriella. We have to go to the hospital."

"Why, Dorian? What is going on?" I plead.

Dorian shakes his head, revving up the car and whipping out of the parking lot at dangerous speed. He still refuses to talk to me, though I know he can feel my questioning eyes burn a hole in the side of his head.

I blow out an agitated breath. "Damn it, Dorian! Tell me!"

Again, Dorian ignores my pleas, causing me to shout expletives and demand he talk to me right this instant. My heart is racing and every alarm bell in my head sounds simultaneously. What could have happened to make his mood shift so drastically?

Dorian races towards Memorial Hospital, turning every approaching streetlight green. He's concentrating, baring his teeth like a vicious animal. I know he must be still in deep conversation with Aurora, and it kills me that it's not *me* he's talking to. Though he refuses to make eye contact with me, I can see his eyes are gleaming with intense rage. I quiet my tirade for answers and try to focus my breathing, feeling the familiar trembling of my hands. I'm about to lose it, and if Dorian doesn't tell me what's going on, he may be in the line of fire.

When we finally pull into a space in the hospital's garage, Dorian looks to me with sadness etched in his beautiful face. The sight pains me and causes the storm behind my own eyes to calm instantly. What could be troubling him? What has Aurora told him?

"My love, I am so sorry," he murmurs, quieting the car's engine.

"Dorian, what is it? Just tell me," I whisper.

Dorian closes his baby blues and turns his head away as if he is physically pained. When he returns his gaze to me, they are dark and solemn. I've never seen him so shaken, so affected, and it frightens me.

"There's been another incident. Another victim," he finally says. "The killer has returned."

There's no worse feeling than knowing that you are directly responsible for someone else's pain. But when it is someone you love that is suffering, and you can't do anything but sit back and watch, that is truly unbearable. No one deserves to die, especially because of me. They didn't ask for this life; *I* didn't ask for it either. But as I run down the long corridor of Memorial Hospital towards the Emergency Department, there's no way I can shake the guilt. I caused this.

"Jared! Oh my God, what happened?" I shriek, running into his arms. He cradles me into his large biceps, holding me close to his chest. His heart is racing, and I know my dear friend is in immense pain. Though I'm well aware that both Dorian and Aurora are watching us intently, I don't care. I can't. Jared needs me and I don't care how it looks.

"Gabs," he chokes out hoarsely. I feel his trembling lips in my hair, and I squeeze him tighter. "I'm so glad you're here."

I look up at my frightened friend. "Just tell me. What happened?" I whisper. Dorian still has not informed me of the latest victim and seeing Jared so shaken is making me think the worst. I usher him over to a row of blue plastic seats.

"We all went out last night. I drank too much. I stayed over at Aurora's though I know I should've come home. I was so fucking stupid! When I pulled up this morning, I could tell something wasn't right. I don't know, Gabs . . . I just don't know what to do."

Jared takes a moment to collect himself, clearly overrun with emotion. Only then do I notice James speaking to a woman at the front desk, flailing his arms wildly. I look back at my distraught friend, placing my arms around him. His eyes are glossy and drained. "We don't know what happened to her! It's like she had a stroke or something. She was just lying there in the floor, her eyes wide open. But she can't talk, she can't move. What the hell, Gabs! Something happened to my mom and even the fucking doctors are clueless!"

I whip my head around to look back at Dorian with wide, horrified eyes. As always, Dorian is perfectly poised and controlled, though I know he is secretly livid. I give Jared another squeeze before jumping to my feet and pulling Dorian down an empty hallway.

"You know what happened to her, don't you?" I whisper fiercely.

"Yes," he replies coolly. How can he be so calm? Just minutes ago, he was furious and remorseful. *Bipolar much?*

"So it's him? Whoever is after me went after Tammy?"

"Yes."

"Then why is she still alive? Why did he leave her like . . . that? Frozen?"

"She was petrified," a singsong soprano interjects. Aurora. "He petrified her so he could suck information out of her. We must've pulled up before he could finish the job." Aurora looks to Dorian and is suddenly filled with regret. "I'm sorry, Dorian. I watched him like you said. I had no idea his mom was in danger."

"I fucking told you! Get control of yourself! How weak and stupid can you be? I'm sick of your shit, Aurora! I swear, if you don't get it together, I will kill you myself," he seethes nastily. He's furious with her, though I'm not sure why. She tried to do everything he's asked of her.

"Dorian, it's not her fault. Just calm down," I say soothingly, trying to diffuse the situation. Aurora looks five shades paler and on the brink of tears. I can't help but feel bad for her. "She tried her best to help."

Dorian looks to me, the remains of contempt etched on his face. He really is angry. "She did nothing but help herself to that boy."

I sigh and shake my head, unsure of what any of that has to do with Tammy's predicament. I can't deal with their complex relationship right now. All I care about is helping my friends.

"Look. Enough about that. Can you help her? Can you fix their mom? Please?" I plead.

Dorian exhales, finally letting go of his anger then looks to Aurora. "What did you find?"

She shrugs before shaking her head. "Nothing. He's deliberately hiding from us. Leaving no trace, not even a scent."

"Do you think you could reverse whatever he did to her?" I ask, looking to a stone-faced Dorian.

"It depends. Petrifications are very specific. They are . . . personal. I don't know what kind of magic was used. But I will try. For you, I will try." He gently strokes my cheek, his way of apologizing for his foul temper and I see a flash of pain in his eyes. Tammy was petrified, just like him. Just the mere mention of his twenty year punishment hurts him.

"Dorian," Aurora mutters. "If you asked the king, maybe he could help. At least tell us what to do?"

"No!" Dorian growls, his eyes suddenly ablaze with hatred. "We will not involve him, do you understand? You will not go to him." Aurora drops her head in shame and nods. Again, I feel bad for her. "I will go now to see what I can find. Aurora, do not let them out of your sight. Not even for a second. Do you think you can manage that task?"

Aurora lifts her head long enough to mutter, "Yes, Dorian."

Before I can protest her harsh treatment or inquire what Dorian plans to do, he is gone, only leaving a dense wisp of grey smoke behind, which also quickly dissipates. I look at Aurora with compassionate eyes, unsure of what to say to console her. It is apparent that Dorian has broken her.

"Come on, we better get back to the boys," I murmur.

I lead Aurora back to the waiting room where both Jared and James are speaking to police officers. We pick a quiet corner to sit, neither one of us wanting to address the tension in the room or the sensual exchange the night before.

"He's right," she finally whispers. "I should have done better. I should have watched all of them."

"Aurora, there's no way you could have known someone would go after Tammy. I know I didn't."

Aurora shakes her head. "He's so protective. So loyal." She isn't talking about Jared. "It was easy for me to fall for him. He just had this pull. I just always wanted to impress him, make him proud of me."

I nod, understanding what Aurora is trying to say. "You still love him."

"Yes. I do. I always will. We die for love, you know. But he never did for me what he did for you. We are bonded, yes. But he never made the link. He never linked his life to mine. He never trusted me like he trusts you." She is so full of anguish, it's hard not to sympathize with her, even if she is talking about my Dorian.

"I never asked him to do that. I never wanted it. It scares me to think I have so much power over his life."

Aurora looks at me, her blue eyes searching mine. "Does it scare you that he has power over yours?"

I take a moment to process her question. Am I afraid that Dorian has control over whether I live or die? Honestly, the only thing that scares me is losing him. If he were to stop loving me, I'd be nothing but an empty shell anyway.

"No. I trust him completely. He could have killed me a thousand times already. But he's only shown me kindness and generosity. And love. If he deceived me, I'd want to die anyway."

Aurora nods, and I know that it's a possibility that she could feel the same way too. Now I can begin to understand her. Maybe even forgive her one day. I know she probably made more of a production of their power exchange than absolutely necessary to get under my skin, but she couldn't help it. She loves Dorian. It was her only chance to be close to him. Had I'd been in her shoes, I probably would have done the same thing.

"I'll have to come back," Dorian's silky voice breaks us from our individual ponderings. Our heads both whip around behind us. How long has he been standing there? Long enough to hear our unexpected heart to heart?

"Didn't you find anything?" I ask. I stand to my feet and quickly close the distance between us. I can understand Aurora, but that doesn't mean I trust her.

Dorian rubs the small of my back, sending tingles up my spine. "Too risky right now. I'll try again tonight." He turns to Aurora, hostility in his glare. "Stay with the boy and his family. I mean it." Aurora quickly nods before bringing her attention to Jared as he approaches.

"Hey, the cops need to talk to you, Aurora."

Reluctantly, I release my hold on Dorian to give my friend a hug. "I'm so sorry, Jared. We're gonna come back later. I need to get home and check in. Keep me posted, ok."

Jared nods. "Good idea. Thanks for coming, guys." Then he turns to usher Aurora towards the police officers.

"Do you think you'll be able to help her?" I ask Dorian as we make our way to my childhood home.

"I don't know. I don't even know what type of magic it is."

"What do you mean?"

"I don't know if it's Light or Dark. Or something else entirely."

"Well obviously it's Dark, Dorian! You think the Light is capable of this carnage? Besides, they want nothing to do with me until I ascend. They vowed to stay hidden until I'm 21."

Dorian shrugs before turning onto the street that houses my parents' home. He parks his Mercedes on the curb, and cuts the ignition. Neither one of us are ready to get out.

"I think you're being too hard on Aurora. I know that sounds funny coming from me, but she didn't mean for this to happen." There. That's my good deed for the day.

Dorian chuckles before removing his shades and looking into my eyes. "Aurora can't be trusted, Gabriella."

"But *you* trust her, right?"

"That's because I *know* her. I know what she is."

"Well, enlighten me," I say folding my arms in front of my chest. The more I know about Aurora, the better.

Dorian sighs before angling his body towards mine. "Ok, Aurora is an Órexis."

Okay. Now what the hell does *that* mean? Though the name does sound familiar . . .

"The meaning of that is *desire*" he continues. "Now the Órexes are known for their ability to manipulate the more carnal emotions. They thrive off sexual depravity. It's what sustains them."

"Oh," is all I can say in response. There really is a lot to learn about the Dark. Not to mention, the Light, whom I know virtually nothing about.

"When I met Aurora, we were both very young and untamed. I was stubborn and eager to become a man. Aurora wanted to aide my efforts. She was incredibly opportunistic, you could say. We did a lot of bad things together, and I'll admit we had a lot of fun. But Aurora was insatiable, just as she is today. She has no self-control. She is completely ruled by her desires."

I get it now; Aurora really *is* a sex kitten. No wonder Jared is putty in her hands. She has clouded his judgment with sex, and because he is so filled with lust for her, it feeds her. Explains why Dorian was so pissed at her. She has been so wrapped up in quenching her sexual thirst instead of doing the job she was instructed to do. And now Jared's mom is in the hospital. So much for thinking I understood her. I don't even know if she has the ability to truly love Dorian.

"Did you ever love her?"

Dorian shakes his head. "No. I lusted for her, and maybe there was a time when I thought I did love her. I did care for her deeply. But she always took things too far. I was rebellious but I wasn't stupid. And there are some lines that you just don't cross." Dorian unfolds my arms and takes my hands in his. He kisses each knuckle gently and I instantly begin to soften.

"Last night, seeing you with her, like that . . . Was that how it was? Between you two?" I mentally scold myself for asking, but I want to know, no matter how much it hurts me.

"You don't want to know that, Gabriella." He places more kisses on my hands, trying to distract me from going into this forbidden territory.

"Yes, I do. I just need to know. Did she manipulate you to act like that or was that real desire for her? Because it looked to me like you wanted her. I know for a fact you did."

Dorian swallows then sighs, letting go of my hands. He leans back in his seat and looks up at the sky as if he's searching for the answer in the clouds. "If you must know, that was just a fraction of the intensity that Aurora and I once shared. Breathing her in was arousing for me because I was taking in her desire. I didn't want to feel that way, but I couldn't help it."

He looks back at me, searching my face for any sign of understanding. "But being with you–loving you–is unlike anything I have ever experienced. It's so much more than sex, Gabriella. It's as if I've been numb these past 250 years. And now, with you, I feel *everything*."

I try to muster an encouraging smile though I am a bit disturbed at the fact that Aurora's desires now live inside Dorian. But he's here, alive and breathing, and though the idea sickens me that they share such a salacious past, I owe her for that. However, the only person Dorian will breathe is me from now on.

"Come on, my parents are expecting us," I say opening the car door. "Ready for this?"

Dorian is already out of the car, giving me one of his famous sexy smirks. *How the hell does he do that?* "If it means getting you all to myself, than I'm ready for anything."

We step into my parents' home, and I announce our arrival. Donna comes rushing to the door, alarmed and flustered.

"Oh thank goodness! Did you hear about Tammy?" she shrieks, embracing me fiercely. Then she takes in the sight of Dorian and her mouth drops. "Dorian? How did you get in here?"

"Hello, Donna. I told you, I do not wish to hurt her. I love her. If I didn't than I couldn't penetrate the wards."

"And how long have you been able to get past them?" she asks tentatively.

Dorian looks down at me and smiles. "For a while now."

"Where's Dad?" I ask, struggling to pull my eyes from Dorian's beauty.

"He went to the hospital to sit with the boys. Did you go see them?"

"We were just there. Mom, something strange is going on." I gesture for us to take a seat in the living room. "Jared said her eyes were wide open but she can't move or talk or anything."

Donna nods slowly then looks at Dorian. "She's been petrified."

"Yes," Dorian replies.

"Any indication of who could have done it?"

Dorian shakes his head gravely. "I'm going back tonight. I have someone watching Jared and his family. They will be safe. In the meantime, I have placed wards around Gabriella's apartment. She will be safe as well."

"I should hope so," Donna mutters. She looks up at both of us with glossy eyes. "She's part of your world now, Dorian. Please take care of her. We tried the best we could. She deserved a shot at having a normal life."

Dorian takes my hand in his and nods. "I know. And I will; I'll protect her with everything I have. You and Chris did well. Alex and Natalia would be proud," he says with a reassuring smile.

The mention of my parents causes a tear to roll down Donna's cheek. A sob escapes her lips and she tries to plaster on a smile. I can feel my own throat tighten with emotion. "I know you love her. I just hope it survives."

"It will, Donna."

Dorian looks at my adopted mother intently, as if he's trying to communicate something to her. For what seems like several seconds, they stare at each other, sharing an unspoken secret. My eyes dart between them; surely they know I'm sitting right here, confusion etched in my face.

"Um, hello," I finally say with a hint of agitation. "We came to get some of my things. We should hurry so we can get back to the hospital."

I stand and retreat to my childhood bedroom, Dorian right on my heels. "What was that about?" I ask as soon as we're alone. I don't like being left in the dark.

Dorian shakes his head, trying to dispel my suspicions. "She's just worried about you. She wants to make sure I'll be there for you no matter what happens."

I look at him questioningly. "Well . . . will you?"

Dorian looks to me as if the answer is obvious. "Of course." He walks over to pick up the small framed photo Jared gave me for my last birthday on my nightstand. "Maybe I should be asking *you* that question," he remarks, his gaze locked on the picture.

"A little too late to be *asking*, being that I *am* linked to you for life," I retort with a hand on my hip.

Dorian tosses the photo into a box, and looks at me quizzically. "Do you want to undo the link?"

Oh crap. "I don't know. I didn't think it was something that could be undone. And I honestly have no plans to be without you." I walk over to him and place my hands on his chest. "Do *you* want to undo it? Can you?"

Dorian shakes his head then leans down to plant a tender kiss on my lips. "No, I don't. And no, I can't. But I know someone who can."

"You do?" I ask a bit too eagerly. Dorian raises an eyebrow in surprise and maybe a little disappointment. "Not that I want to. I'm just curious. Someone can break the link?"

Dorian nods and runs his hands down my back. He gazes down at me lovingly yet there's a hint of sadness in his eyes. "Yes," he nods solemnly. "My father."

I try to retain Dorian's lightheartedness by smiling brightly. "Too bad we won't be needing his services."

My melancholy lover gives me a sexy half-smile. "Go spend some time with Donna. She will miss you. I'll take care of these boxes and meet you outside."

"But won't you need some help?"

Dorian rolls his eyes before shooing me out my childhood bedroom. Donna will be glad to know that it will stay intact for the most part now that Dorian has completely furnished my new room at the apartment. Somehow I think he knew she'd need to have a reminder of her once normal adopted child. I find her in the kitchen, furiously preparing sandwiches and snacks for, I'm assuming, Jared and James.

"Anything I can do to help?" I ask.

"So now you want to help?" she laughs lightly. "I should've taught you how to cook. I'm afraid you'll starve once you leave. But your father was more concerned about you knowing how to defend yourself. Rightfully so."

I take a seat at the breakfast table and grab one of the freshly baked cookies cooling on a wire rack. I haven't eaten much all day and with all the activity, I'm famished.

"So you knew something like this might happen? You knew someone might come for me?"

"It was certainly a possibility, dear," she sighs. "Plus you already had the hunter gene in you. It was only natural you'd be more physical than domestic."

I finish chewing the remains of my cookie, nodding slowly.

“Was my mother, Natalia, was she like me? Not so domestic?”

Donna smiles as she recalls the memory. “She was more like you than me, yet she was nurturing. She was warm. She was a lover *and* a fighter.”

“Will I be a hunter? Like a Dark Hunter?” That is, if I choose to ascend as a Light Enchanter.

“I don’t know, honey. I wish I did. The Light and the Dark are very secretive about their way of life. Unless you are one, they are simply myth. Many myths that we, mortals, read about in history books.”

Now I’m intrigued. “Like what?”

“Mythology. Legends of gods and goddesses that had the power to control the elements, the actions and emotions of mortals. Things of that nature.”

“So all that stuff was true?” *Holy shit!* Could Dorian really *be* a Greek god? I certainly wouldn’t be surprised.

“No, not necessarily. Supposedly they were more like bedtime stories than anything else. You should ask Dorian. I’m sure he’s pretty well versed in his kind’s history.”

“Yeah, probably.” I smile warmly at my mother, realizing that it is time to go. I’m not ready to say goodbye though I know I’m simply fifteen minutes away. “You know, I really appreciate all that you and Dad did for me. And you’ll always be my parents in my heart.”

Donna’s eyes cloud with a fresh wave of tears. “I know, honey. And you’ll always be our baby girl. No matter what happens from here. We know you’ll make us proud. Just promise me you’ll be careful.”

“I will, Mom. And I’ll be fine.”

We embrace and after reassuring Donna that I’ll come over for dinner as often as possible, I head outside to find Dorian leaning up against his Mercedes. Of course the boxes were probably loaded with a snap of his fingers. I’ll never get used to how ridiculously alluring and fascinating he is.

"All packed up? You don't look like you even broke a sweat," I jibe.

"Maybe because I didn't," he smirks seductively.

He opens the passenger side door for me and I slide in. But before I can even get both legs inside and close the door behind me, he's in the driver's seat, the remnants of grey smoke swirling around him.

We cruise out of Briargate and head towards my new home. Morgan had planned to move in throughout the weekend as well but with the news of Jared and James's mom, her parents talked her into staying home for another night. I don't blame them; Tammy's sudden affliction is more than a little disturbing. And I wouldn't be surprised if Mr. Pierre had a hunch about what happened to her.

"What are you thinking about?" Dorian asks after flashing his identification at the Paralia guard shack.

I shake my head. "Just trying to wrap my head around all this. This crap is seriously pissing me off."

He gives me a slant of his eyes. "There's nothing you could've done. Whoever this is . . . whatever it is . . . he's completely eluding us. I was wrong before. This isn't someone who is just striking blindly. We're dealing with a professional."

"The Shadow?" I ask with wide eyes.

"Possibly. Or a hunter. There are more out there than just Dark Hunters," Dorian replies, whipping into my assigned parking space.

"Like what?" Do I really want to know?

"Another time," he replies, shutting down my curiosity. "I need to feed you." Dorian takes in my playfully offended expression. "Food, Gabriella. I need to feed you some food. For *now*."

I follow Dorian into the apartment, kicking off my shoes and settling onto one of the stools stationed at the marble-top breakfast bar. Dorian busies himself in the kitchen, opening the refrigerator and cabinets and removing packages of food and dishes. Of course the kitchen is stocked with food, though neither Morgan nor I are great in the cooking department. Dorian, however, seems comfortable and confident behind the stove.

"What are you making?" I ask after a few moments of ogling him.

"You'll see. Hope you like lamb."

I nod. "So what, no *abracadabra* and lunch is served?" I ask, tapping my fingernails against the cool, smooth marble countertop.

"Nah. Sometimes I like to mix it up. I thought I'd cook for you," he says rummaging through the fresh produce.

"Cook for me? Since when do you cook?" I ask with a raised eyebrow.

Dorian smiles slyly. "Oh my dear, Gabriella, you have so much to learn about me." He grabs a couple beers from the fridge, popping them open and setting one down in front of me. "I found a little Greek deli and grabbed a few things for the fridge. Thought it was time I got you in touch with your roots," he winks taking a swig of his beer.

"My roots? You mean, I'm . . ."

"Greek? Yes, in part. Alex's father is Greek though most of his family was from Egypt." Dorian turns around just in time to take in my astonished expression. "There are Dark and Light forces all over the globe. We look just like regular people," he winks. He turns on some kind of indoor grill unit he's installed in the kitchen. Probably for times like these.

"But do they look like you? With . . . the eyes?" Dorian's ice blue eyes are an anomaly; too beautiful not to be extraordinary.

He pulls out a little container of stuffed olives and places them in front of me, nabbing one for himself before returning to the grill. "The Dark do, though most of them change them to blend in. Or hide." He pulls out some seasoned meat skewers and places them on the hot grill.

"So . . . are all magical forces from Greece?" I ask, picking up an olive and popping it in my mouth.

Dorian moves around the kitchen as if he is at home. He pulls out a cutting board and begins to assemble a salad. "No, not at all.

Mostly just the Dark families of nobility. The Light royals are mainly from Rome."

Rome? "So the Light have royalty too?" This stuff just keeps getting better.

"We all have laws; hierarchy. If we didn't, we'd all go around slaughtering each other for power."

"And my mom? Was she from Rome?"

"I believe her family was from Spain originally but settled in Italy. Why the sudden interest?"

I finger the feta-stuffed olive I'm holding before popping it into my mouth and chewing slowly. "Just never knew what I was," I shrug.

"You're Light and Dark. That goes far beyond nationality, Gabriella," he smiles.

I smile back at my equally exotic lover as he moves around the kitchen with grace and ease. I feel selfish as I relish this moment. In light of all that's going on with Jared's mom, I shouldn't be allowed to enjoy this. I shouldn't *be* this happy. But I am. Having Dorian makes it hard not to be.

"I'm happy too," he suddenly remarks. He places our plates on the bar in front of me then walks around to join me.

My mouth drops in aggravation. "Thought you said you weren't a mind-reader."

"I'm not. But I can feel what you feel. The link, Gabriella. Your emotions become mine."

"Why can't I feel what you feel? Doesn't seem fair to me," I smirk, picking up a forkful of salad dressed with a yogurt sauce.

"You will but not until you ascend. You're still a somewhat normal girl." He chews a bite of skewered meat. "After that, you could probably infiltrate any mind you please and plant all sorts of crazy ideas."

Infiltrate any mind? How can he discuss something so intrusive and insensitive so casually?

"But . . . how? How do you get into my head? It's freakin'

infuriating to know that you can just mess with my thoughts whenever you please." I sigh before taking another swig of beer. Suddenly I'm not as hungry as I thought I was. "You did that before, didn't you? You messed with my head, making me doubt all the signs, all the hints that you were Dark. Why?"

Dorian chews his lip nervously. "I thought I wanted you to know what I was. To make it . . . *easier* for me. But then I'd change my mind. I wasn't ready to let you go." He picks at his food, obviously uncomfortable with discussing another layer of his betrayal. "I apologize for confusing you. I thought if I removed those thoughts from your mind, soothed your qualms, we could have more time."

I understand; Dorian wanted to hang onto the beautiful illusion just as much as I did. Ignorance truly was bliss when we both could mask the truth of our identities. But that doesn't excuse him from altering my thoughts. There has to be some boundaries.

"Just promise me you won't do it again. I mean, the stuff in the bedroom is fine," I blush, looking down at my plate, "but no more messing around in my head. My thoughts and feelings are mine. You might be able to feel them and influence what I think, but they are mine, Dorian."

Dorian puts down his fork and turns to me with a furrowed brow. "You're angry."

"You're damn right, I'm angry! I mean, I get why you made the link; it's for my own safety. But I have to be honest with you–if you had given me a choice, if I would have known what was in that vial, I would have said no." I let out a breath, and grab his hands, trying to make him see my point without hurting his feelings. "I thought I was going crazy, Dorian. I felt stupid as hell ignoring all the signs pointing to what you were. Don't take that away from me. Don't take away my ability to think for myself. You don't want a puppet for a girlfriend."

Dorian stares at me for what seems like several minutes, his ice blue eyes unblinking and unreadable. "You're right," he finally mutters. "You are absolutely right. I'll never make you feel like that again."

I nod and return to my plate. It really is delicious and the fact that Dorian has prepared it makes it that much more scrumptious. "Thank you."

Dorian doesn't budge; he's still staring at me intently. "You want to break the link. You wouldn't have chosen that for yourself."

I wash down my bite of food with the rest of my beer. Something tells me I'm going to need a few more. "I get why you did it, Dorian. And I appreciate that you trust me that much. But if you haven't noticed, I'm not exactly easy to love. I say the wrong things, I'm too aggressive, and I have a habit of hurting the people I care about. One day you'll realize that, and I'll be dead."

He frowns at me like I have two heads, and I swear I hear a low growl vibrate from his chest. "Don't ever say that," he mutters between clenched teeth. His eyes spark with heated electricity. "I would never, ever do that, Gabriella. How many times do I have to tell you? You are everything to me. Maybe that depth of devotion is hard for you to understand being that you still have this silly notion that you are human and need to conform to human standards of commitment. But I absolutely, unconditionally love you. That will never change, little girl."

I nearly flinch at his intensity, unable to tear my eyes away from his. I believe him; every fiber of my being believes him. And because I feel that same gravity of devotion for him, I can understand why he made the link. Part of me is glad that he did it. He chose me, not Aurora, not some other equally gorgeous, powerful force. He chose *me*.

My mouth curls up into a smile, and a giggle erupts from my lips. "You know, you could have just sent flowers."

Dorian matches my jovial expression, stowing his ominous scowl. "No. You don't want flowers."

"You're right. A six pack then? Nothing says I love you like booze." I return to my meal, hoping it isn't too cold. "So what time are we leaving for the hospital?"

"*We?*" he scoffs. "*We* aren't going anywhere, Gabriella."

I sit straight up, no sign of good humor to be found on my face. "Why not?" Dorian shakes his head and chuckles a bit, causing me to grow furious with his amusement at my expense. "That's bullshit, Dorian and you know it. I'm coming!"

Before I can blink, Dorian is in my face, only mere inches separating us from contact. His eyes are fiery bright blue, alight with anger and lust. He bares his teeth, a low, guttural growl rumbling his chest. I reflexively recoil in surprise, taking in a sharp breath. Just like that, Dorian's darkness has crept back in with a vengeance.

"No," he seethes between gritted teeth.

My breath is ragged with anxiety and I know I shouldn't push him when he's like this, but my stubbornness overrides my sanity. "Why not? Jared is *my* friend."

"I said no. I cannot protect you and try to . . . *fix* his mother at the same time," he replies stonily. This whole issue has him riled up.

"I never asked you to protect me; I asked you to protect my friends. I can handle myself. I'm going!" I say with a bit more fervor. I won't let him intimidate me. He's trying to scare me into submission. And while I'd love nothing more than to run and cower in a corner, I can't let him bully me.

Some fucked up relationship we've got, eh?

"Don't you get it, Gabriella?" he spews. "This could very well be a trap to lure you. The first place you're expected to be is the hospital. Don't let your pride cause you to act recklessly."

"But I need to be there! You don't know Jared like I do. He is my best friend and I-"

"I. Said. *No*!" Dorian growls.

With a huff, I hop down off of my barstool and stalk to my room–the room that Dorian so lovingly decorated for me. But before I can reach the entrance of the hallway, he's in front of me, blocking my path.

"Get the hell out of my way, Dorian!"

His expression is softer, and a smirk is playing at his lips. He enjoys rattling me, making me feel inferior. *Pompous asshole prince.*

"Don't be angry, little girl. It's for your own good," he coos.

"I'm not your little girl," I retort, my arms folded tightly in front of my chest, my hands balled into hard fists. "And I don't give a damn what you say. You can try to scare me with your little tricks, but I'm still going. I'm not afraid of you."

Dorian stands straight up, his bright eyes transforming into a dark smolder. He cocks his head to one side, as if he is trying to decipher a cryptic message. "You know, there are ways I could *make* you stay here."

My own eyes narrow menacingly. I feel my fists begin to quiver and instinctively squeeze them tighter. Icy cold prickles rouse the rims of my eyes and it feels like they have been touched with dry ice. Hot and cold all at once. Shit. Dorian has pissed me off and I'm about to go ape shit.

"Careful, little girl. You wouldn't want to hurt yourself," he says coolly. He's provoking me, mocking me. It just pushes my rage to the brink of no return.

"Scared?" I retort through tightly pursed lips.

"Not at all. But I don't want to hurt you either. But I will. And I'll enjoy it."

"You wouldn't," I hiss.

This is it. Eventually Dorian and I would not see eye to eye and it would get volatile, no matter how much we love each other. We're not just two separate sides of a coin; we're two different currencies completely. I just didn't expect to go from a pleasant meal to a supernatural showdown.

Dorian bites his lip stiffly, exhaling sharply. Then he grabs me, flinging me over his shoulder. Before I can even open my mouth to protest, I am on my new bed, laying on my back with Dorian standing over me. I knew it wouldn't be a fair fight being that he is considerably stronger than me, but I wasn't going to back down. I won't let him control me. He might be used to getting his way among his kind but I'm not Dark. He is not *my* prince.

"You asked for this," he mutters. Dorian raises his palm, letting the blue fog envelop it. Then my body completely betrays me.

"What the hell, Dorian!" I shriek. My arms and legs stretch themselves wide, fusing me to the bed. I have no control over the movements; I can't even move. He is literally manipulating me with the slightest wave of his hand. "Stop it! Now!"

Dorian ignores my pleas and makes another slight movement, tearing my shirt into ragged shreds. I try to thrash and fight but resistance is futile. He looks back at my brand new sound system and suddenly it purrs to life, pumping out a seductive, carnal tune.

What the hell? Now he wants to add mood music to his tirade? *Sick bastard.*

I feel the fly of my jeans begin to unzip and I scream with contempt. He's undressing me. He wants to splay my body on this bed and watch me writhe. My jeans roll down over my legs and drop to the floor, and Dorian licks his lips at the sight. I am completely vulnerable and at his mercy like a helpless lamb. The more I squirm, the wider he grins. It's maddening, sickening even. Maddening because he is taking advantage of my body and my tragic love for him. Sickening because I am dripping wet and panting with desire.

Dorian inhales deeply, closing his eyes in ecstasy. "Mmmm. I love it when you fight."

"You are fucking crazy, you know that, Dorian? Why are you doing this to me?" I seethe.

He ghosts to my side, the eerie way he does when he's in his element. He takes one long finger and lets it glide the length of my jaw. "I haven't done anything to you, baby. Not yet," he says with a sinister smile. "But don't worry. I plan to show you just how fucking crazy I can be."

God, he's so repulsive and terrifying right now. *And so damn hot!* I look up at him with lust and desperation etched in my face. I don't know what he plans to do with me, if he plans to do anything at all. I just wish he'd get it over with and put me out of my misery.

The look of pleasure and excitement on his face tells me that he wants to make this last. He wants to torture me slowly like the efficient assassin he is. He licks his lips and lets his fingers travel down to my bra-clad breasts. He brushes the swell of my cleavage, causing a moan to betray me. I bite my bottom lip in frustration at my weakness for him, but I can't help it. I want him. I'll always want him.

Reading my body language and my emotions, Dorian murmurs, "You have no idea how bad I want you right now."

"Let me go and you can have me," I pant. Though he already has me *now*. Secretly, I don't want him to stop. I want to see how this will play out.

"I don't think so, little girl," he says shaking his head.

Dorian lets his hands roam freely over the tops of my breasts. His cool touch causes shivers to rack my entire body. He fingers my nipples through the fabric, causing them to strain and ache. I gasp, trying to hold onto the last ounce of my resolve. I want to feel his skin against mine, want to feel the prickles that ignite every time he touches me. Yet, he continues to tease me through the cotton bra cups, no matter how fiercely I beg him with my wanting eyes.

Dorian touches the front clasp of my bra. "Want me to take it off?"

I bite my tongue, refusing to answer him. Instead I give him a cold, sharp look. He smiles then eases his fingers into it, caressing my bare nipple. I moan appreciatively, and he moves to the next one, rubbing the swell between his fingers. He continues his measured tease until my sighs evolve into moans. Finally he relieves my aching breasts by unclasping my bra, my nipples hardening under his lustful gaze. He dips his head down and samples my hardened nodes, and I cry in pleasure.

"So you want to play it like that, huh?" Dorian continues to bathe my breasts with his tongue, suckling them gently. He then commences to flick my stiff nipples with his tongue, one at a time, before taking them between his teeth. I moan and pant wildly. It feels too good not to give in. His dark tendrils graze my face as he continues his delicious assault. He smells of clear blue waters and eroticism, and I want to dive head first into both.

Dorian shifts his body onto the bed and eases between my legs easily without missing a beat. Only the thin cotton of my panties clothes my damp sex and I can feel the bulge of his erection through his pants. Slowly, he begins to grind, still licking and sucking and nibbling. It feels heavenly, and my swollen heat throbs against him.

"*Ooooh*," I sigh.

His head snaps up, his ice blue eyes boring into warm hazel depths of mine. "What was that, my love? You want me to stop?"

I shake my head furiously. "No. Don't stop," I beg before I can stop myself. "No. Stop. Let me go. I want to touch you."

Dorian smiles slyly and shakes his head. He then returns his attention to my swollen mounds and I gratefully sigh. He begins to kiss a path to my belly button, letting his tongue swirl my navel then back up to my breasts. I'm on fire; his touch is like feeling a hundred tongues all at once. I feel his fingers at the waist of my panties as he begins to peel them off. Once I am stripped bare, he abandons me to stand at the foot of the bed. I want to beg him to stay with me, to pleasure me, to fill me, yet he just stands there, gazing down at my nakedness.

His hand reaches to undo the buttons of his shirt and I finally get a peek at his magnificent body, adorned only by the small tattoo on his side. I want to be free of his restraint so I can feel the smoothness of his chest. I want to kiss my way from his tiny nipples through the rippled valley of his abs down his amazingly sculpted hip muscles. I want to run my tongue down the shaft of his hardness and taste the sweet drops of nectar that tell me that he's ready too. I want to feel him all over me yet all I can do is devour him with my eyes.

I pant expectantly once Dorian stands before me gloriously naked yet he makes no move to climb inside of me. Instead he makes a movement with his finger, causing my legs to spread farther apart and bend at the knees. He licks his lips before kneeling onto the bed, eyeing my scorching, wet sex like a hungry lion. Oh no. *No!* There's no way I could maintain any sense of composure if he does that. I struggle to move without prevail. I can't relinquish this kind of control to him. Temporarily paralyzed, spread eagle and completely naked, I lay exposed for Dorian's enjoyment. Yet, if he tastes my wetness, I will surely surrender to him in every way possible. I would do anything he wanted.

"No, Dorian, no!" I urge. "Please don't."

Dorian gives me a sexy half-smile. "What is it that you don't want me to do? This?" And with that, he lowers his mouth down into my blazing heat and takes a slow, laborious lick. I cry out with pleasure and Dorian brings his head back up to gloat.

"Yes!" I pant. "That. Please. Don't."

Dorian cocks his head to one side and looks at me quizzically. "But what about this?" Again he brings his head down and lets his tongue explore my fleshy folds. His mouth gently sucks and teases while I squirm and sing his praises.

"Oh. My. God. Dorian," I say between gasps. "Don't. No."

"See, Gabriella, you're saying one thing but I know for a fact that you feel differently. Don't you want it?"

"Yes! Of course I do, I just . . . I . . . I can't lose control. I won't," I stammer.

Again, Dorian smiles devilishly. He licks his lips, tasting the remnants of my juices. Everything about him is so erotic, so hot. I want him here, between my thighs, sampling my pleasure. But I want to be able to rub his shoulders, grab fistfuls of his hair in my state of euphoria. I'm completely helpless tied up, and that's exactly how Dorian wants me.

"I'm sorry, little girl. But you've already lost control. You never had it."

Dorian buries his face in the apex of my thighs, and I instantly cry his name. His slick tongue dives into every crevice and swell. He's ravenous; it's as if he hasn't eaten in days the way he consumes me. Every time I think he has devoured every ounce of my wetness, a fresh wave greets his hungry lips. It's so carnal, so salacious and it arouses me to no end. Though his deep, throaty groans are masked by my shrill cries, I know he's affected too. His hands fly up to finger my nipples, never straying from the rhythm of his firm, wet tongue. The sensation is . . . *magical.* Pure pleasure personified. It brings me to my brink, pushing me over the edge and I release a flash flood of sweetness.

After Dorian has consumed every drop, he sits straight up on his knees. My lust is still glistening on his full lips, and surprisingly, I urge to taste them. Again, hearing my thoughts in the uncanny way that he does, he leans forward and kisses me, letting me sample my own sex. The act is so ridiculously kinky, something I would have never dreamed of doing, yet I relish my flavor. Dorian leans back onto his knees again, his hard erection tapping me on my inner thighs. My eyes widen at the sight of it; it's beautiful, generous, and perfect in every way.

"What should I do now, Gabriella? Do you want to feel me?" Dorian says, biting his bottom lip. His eyes are aflame with concentrated sex and desire. He looks every bit like the Greek god that he is.

"Yes. *Hell yes*, Dorian!" I groan. I want him so bad. I don't think I've ever wanted anything more.

Dorian shakes his head playfully. "No, no, I don't think you do. Make me believe it. I need to hear you say it."

Why is he doing this to me? I'm lightheaded from panting so much and my skin is sizzling. *Can't he see how hot I am for him?* Can't he *feel* it?

"Yes, Dorian, I want you!"

"I don't believe you, baby. Scream it." Dorian's eyes are suddenly glowing, ablaze with an inferno of hedonism. They illuminate in the dimming sunlight streaming through the cracks of the curtains, revealing the savage Dark One.

"I want you! Please! I want you inside me!" shouts a desperate, agonized voice that I don't even recognize.

With a carnal growl, Dorian rocks into me, filling my depths with his long, probing sex. A garbled cry escapes me, utterly shocked at the jolting impact. His hips rise and fall, thrusting fervently as he grips the sides of my ass, elevating me off the bed. I can feel his fingers digging into my soft flesh, pulling me into him to meet his hard, measured strokes. Farther and farther he delves, each thrust proving to be deeper than the last. They meet every pleasure point, every secret dwelling that provokes my pivotal downfall. My cries are a harsh, expletive, shrill song of praise; his, a chant of torturous restraint and control. Just when I think I cannot take anymore, Dorian's hand travels down to my swollen clit, and he begins to gently massage, aligning it with the rhythm of his thrusts and the provocative music.

"Oh God, you feel so good," I moan. And he does; so good I want to cry.

"Yeah? Has anyone ever felt this good to you?"

I shake my head furiously. "No, baby. Never."

"I am going to own every part of you. *Only me*," he grits. "Tell me no one else will have you. Tell me I own *this*." He stirs my sex, pinching my swell. It's enough to make me erupt violently, and all coherent thought and speech escape me.

Dorian digs into my core harder, pressing my button, rubbing my own slickness into the delicate bud. "Tell me I fucking own it!" he growls.

"Yes–*oh God*–yes, Dorian! You own it," I sputter. "All of it. It's yours."

As if hearing my admission flipped some internal switch, Dorian increases the pace and ferocity of his strokes. Every time he slams into me, the Earth shifts a bit. The air around us shimmers and glows. This isn't natural; this isn't how sex is supposed to be for ordinary people. But we are anything but ordinary, and even if I were, I wouldn't want anything other than the sheer animalistic bliss that Dorian delivers. He is all-consuming; I feel him stimulating every part of me all at once. *Owning me.*

Dorian squeezes my ass tighter, his fingernails breaking the skin and I feel him begin to quiver his demise. With a strangled groan, he submits into me, and we drift out into the dark waters together. Just my Dorian and me lost at sea, and the monsters within us that feed off our carnality.

EIGHT

My eyes flutter open only to be met with complete darkness. *Where am I?* I feel around frantically for any sign of familiarity, realizing that I'm alone in my new bed. I'm disoriented and naked. *Shit. What time is it? Where is Dorian?* I don't even remember falling asleep.

The lights flicker on and I raise my hand to shield my adjusting eyes. I look around me frantically to find the source of light and see Dorian sitting on the chaise lounge. He's slouching, his elbows resting lazily on his knees, a drastic change from his usual poised stance.

"Dorian? Is everything ok? Are you alright?" I ask sitting straight up. I think to climb out of bed and go to him but my muscles are still stiff with exhaustion.

Dorian doesn't budge. He still has not raised his head to meet my gaze or even acknowledge my presence, though I'm certain he is the one who turned on the lights as soon as he realized I was awake.

"What's going on? Dorian, please talk to me!" I shout with urgency. I'm afraid; has he been hurt?

Dorian lifts his head and reveals the reason why he was reluctant to show himself to me. His eyes are dark and menacing. Cold. Yet there is pain and remorse in them. Something has surely transpired while I was asleep and I automatically begin to think the worst.

"What happened? You can tell me," I say just above a whisper.

Dorian's expression is desolate and unreadable, giving nothing away. His mouth opens just a fraction before closing shut. He wants to tell me, he needs to, but he's . . . frightened? No. He could never be scared of anything. I couldn't imagine a force more powerful or terrifying than he. However, something has surely shaken him and I am writhing in the unknown.

"I apologize, my love," he finally whispers.

What? Oh no. Has he gone to see Aurora? Did he breathe her? *Shit!*

Dorian shakes his head a bit, dispelling my trivial worries. "I was unsuccessful."

"What are you talking about?"

"It didn't work. I couldn't . . . I didn't," he stammers. He takes a deep breath then lets his ice blue eyes meet mine, emanating hurt and regret. "I couldn't fix her, Gabriella."

I take in a sharp breath, trying to digest what he's telling me. "What does that mean?"

Suddenly, Dorian is next to me, wisps of charcoal smoke surrounding him before quickly dissipating. He turns to me urgently, seething with contempt and rage, his eyes burning deadly blue fire. His hands fly up to cup my face, bringing it up to meet his intense gaze.

"It means she is stuck, a pile of nothingness. Just. Like. Me. Forever petrified, frozen like a fucking corpse until we can find another way. Or until I kill the fucker who did this."

"Dorian, please calm down," I whisper, reaching a tentative hand up to stroke his face. He instantly recoils, scooting away to put space between us.

"Calm down? Ha! What world do you live in, Gabriella? Because that's where I wanna go. Where everything is just fucking ponies and gumdrops," he spews angrily.

"That was uncalled for," I mumble casting my glassy eyes down to my knotted hands on the comforter.

"Yeah it was. And you know what? That's the reality. All of this is uncalled for." Dorian's breathing is rapid as if he's just run the length of the apartment complex. But I know he is not physically winded. He's enraged and trying to get his emotions in check before he explodes.

He looks back up at me with remorseful eyes, searching for understanding. "You have no idea what it's like, Gabriella," he whispers.

I gaze at my Dark lover, equally pained at his erratic desperation. "Then tell me."

Dorian shakes his head a bit, trying to dispel the memories that still haunt him. He can't bring himself to say it. We sit for several minutes in silence, him looking out into the night through the window, me looking at him, trying to beckon him to talk to me. Finally Dorian turns his head to me, and his icy cold guise has thawed. My Dorian has come back to me.

"When my father summoned me, I knew there would be consequences for my omissions. No one defies the king. I was certain that I would be put to death and I was accepting of it." Dorian looks away for a bit as if he can't look his truth in the eye. "But as he stared down at me, so cold and callous–*deadened*–I became afraid. I didn't want to die. I hadn't even lived yet. Over 200 years and I still felt like something was missing."

He runs a hand over his solemn face. "I was a coward, Gabriella. I should have chosen death. But as I looked up at my father, as I saw the contempt, the disgust, the sheer hatred he had for me, I was afraid. I couldn't do it."

The thought that Dorian could be afraid of anything brings me up short. He is so strong, so confident. To me, he's invincible. Yet, every time he has mentioned his father, he has been visibly disturbed. How could he be frightened of his own father? What kind of monster is he?

"What happened to you?" I whisper, understanding just an inkling of Dorian's grief.

Dorian shakes his head, refusing to speak about the terrors that plague him.

"Please," I beg. "Please don't shut me out."

He turns to me, his face twisted with disgust. "What if I told you that my own father is the epitome of evil? So revolted by his own son that he personally carried out my sentence? That he took pleasure in stripping away my power, leaving me a pathetic, lifeless shell? And if given the chance, would be more than happy to end me for good?"

I bite my bottom lip to keep it from trembling. My eyes water but I refuse to acknowledge the tears. I need to be strong for Dorian. This moment isn't about my agony, it's about his.

"Then I'd say that he is the worst kind of monster that ever existed. And that you are so much better, so much stronger than he is," I croak with a wavering voice.

Dorian shakes his head, refusing to believe my words. "I have taken dozens of lives. Death meant nothing to me. I've sucked the life out of more people than I can remember. I've enjoyed the brutality. I was addicted to it. The thrill of the hunt, chasing them down only made me want to slaughter them more. I was like a bloodthirsty animal. Tell me, does that sound like someone that deserves love or death?"

Slowly, I extend my hand towards him, holding my breath and preparing for his rejection. He remains still, and I let my hand rest on his. "Everyone deserves love, Dorian."

"Really?" he asks incredulously. "Serial killers? Terrorists? Rapists? Do they deserve love? Because I am no better than them."

I mull over Dorian's question in my head. Could I love a serial killer or a rapist? No, absolutely not. Those people deserve nothing but a slow, torturous death. Dorian is not like them. He is not even a person at all. He is the Dark Prince, a supernatural magic force of evil. And he does deserve love. Who he is expected to be and the man before me, the man that I love, are not aligned, regardless of what he's done.

"You are not them, Dorian. You are *good.* I don't care what you did before. The Dorian I know is *good.*" I let my hand stroke his beautiful, forlorn face. "Dealing with this, trying to help Tammy, brought it all back to the surface for you, huh?"

"Yes," he nods slowly.

"I should have never asked you to get involved. I was desperate and I wasn't thinking straight. I'm sorry." *Shit.* I should have been more sensitive instead of just assuming Dorian could do it.

"No," he shakes his head. "It is not your fault. I should have been stronger."

I scoot closer to him and awkwardly try to wrap my arms around his tense, rigid body. "Don't say that. You are strong. It's okay to be afraid, Dorian."

His glazed eyes focus on nothing in particular. "When I saw her, staring blankly, unable to talk, move, anything . . . it reminded me of myself. It was like looking down and seeing your worst nightmare. But your worst nightmare is you."

"You don't have to live that anymore," I whisper gently, rubbing his back. I begin to feel him release some of the tension that binds him so tightly. "You're not that person anymore. You're free."

Dorian turns his body towards mine, his eyes searching for something in my mask of a reassuring smile. Because he knows the truth; he knows how I really feel. I'm just as afraid as he is. No one is really free, not until the killer is found. And even then, we are all slaves to our alliances, our heritage. We are slaves to the magic that flows through our veins. Whether we are taught to kill or taught to heal, taught to love or taught to hate, we have to choose a side.

And as I squeeze Dorian tight, I know that my own choice will annihilate me. I can't lose him by aligning with the Light, pledging to go against the Dark that threaten to extract their power. Yet I could never side with the Dark, abandoning everything my parents, both biological and adopted, taught me and become a ruthless savage. I am stuck, frozen in my own petrification, just like Dorian. And right now, not even his love can fix me.

"Hey Carmen, I'll be back in the office doing some paperwork. Think you can hold it down out here?"

"Sure, Gabs. I've got it!" she beams proudly.

It's been two months since I've started my new job as manager at Cashmere. Two months of rooming with Morgan in our plush new apartment at Paralia. And two months since Tammy, Jared's mom, was petrified by an evil, sadistic Warlock who lusts for my blood.

Luckily, running a high end boutique is a lot more time consuming and distracting than I initially thought, but I enjoy the challenge. Anything to stifle the immense guilt I feel for what happened to Tammy. And to get my mind off of Dorian, who has thrust himself into hunting the vicious predator, and as a result, has been keeping a little distance between us. I can't stand it, but I know it's for my own good. Being so close, breathing me, is dangerous for the both of us. Not to mention the insatiable sexual need we have for each other. It's nearly impossible to think of anything else, or resist drinking in too much.

Though we talk daily, our conjugal visits have been limited to only a few times a week. I can't help but feel somewhat disjointed from him. I know he loves me but my body craves him just as much as my heart does. Maybe even more.

I open my email and skim through the countless messages from designers, vendors and other business-related matters. Surprisingly, I've been doing well with staying on top of it all, especially since I hired Carmen, Miguel's style savvy sister, as my personal assistant and right hand. She's been a huge asset and without her, I think I would have been as lost as a whore in church with all the fashion terminology.

My face instantly brightens when I come across an email from Dorian. I open it with haste, wondering if it's one of the more risqué notes we've been exchanging during our days apart. They've been hot enough to torture me into the late hours of the night yet the promise of reenacting each scenario upon our next encounter has been more than worth it.

Subject: Tonight

Gabriella,

My love, an urgent matter has arisen and I won't be able to see you tonight. I will call you as soon as I can, but I cannot say when that will be. Be especially careful and diligent until I see you. Understand what I am saying, Gabriella. I will contact you when I can.

I love you,

D

Damn it! What the hell is going on? I know Dorian needs me to read between the lines. Something is going down and he wants me to be careful. I have to trust him in this. I read the cryptic email again just to be certain that I'm not missing something. Should I reply? Should I call him? No. He said *he'd* contact *me*. Before I can worry myself into an early grave, my cell phone chimes to life. I nearly break my neck trying to answer it, praying that it's Dorian, yet discover that it's Morgan. I try to swallow the feelings of disappointment before answering.

"Hey Morg, what's up?" I say, trying to muster a few ounces of enthusiasm.

"Just working, girl. I wanted to hit you up real quick to see what's up for tonight. I was thinking . . . we should have a little housewarming dinner at the apartment, just our close circle, as a way to maybe get Jared and James out for a little while. They've been so stressed; I think a Friday night of fun would be good for them."

"Good idea!" It really is; the guys have both visibly lost weight from eating so much hospital food when they do eat at all. With their mom still in her fixed state, their entire lives have been turned upside down.

"What'd you have in mind?" I ask, genuinely excited to hang with my friends.

"Let's make it a fiesta! Tacos, nachos, and, of course, Senor Tequila! I can make a mean margarita."

"Cool, let's do it." I could use a good distraction and tequila has proven be a great coping mechanism in the past.

"So I'll call Miguel, the guys, and I'm guessing Dorian and Aurora will be there?"

Just the mere mention of his name makes my heart sink, causing a twinge of grief to attack my chest. "Ummm, not Dorian. He has a business matter to tend to this evening."

"Oh. Ok, I guess. Well, then I'll see you later. I'll stop by the store after I get off at 7 so I can get everything together. I'll even have Miguel come over to help so he can make sure I don't muck it up. What time will you get home tonight?"

"Eh, around 9:30. Save me a margarita?" *Lord knows I need it and then some.*

We say our goodbyes and I continue to sift through my inbox. I receive one from an email address I don't recognize and the subject field is blank. Probably just junk mail but my curiosity gets the best of me.

Subject: (none)
Dark Light,
8 months
Align with the Dark or Die

Ugh! Seriously? So now messages at my job? I get the freakin' point. A bunch of threatening messages is not going to sway my decision. And can they *be* any more predictable? First, Dorian cancels our plans for some unknown reason and now I get some asinine cyber threat? Just not my day.

Out of sheer annoyance I hit the 'Reply' button and begin to fashion my own email.

Subject: Real original

Dear Dark Assholes,

I get the point. Showing me that you know how to log onto a computer and utilize Google must've taken some pretty keen strategizing on your part. Really, *really* cool trick. Now leave me the hell alone.

-The DL

I hesitate before pressing 'Send,' knowing that I am just provoking them and asking for trouble. But hell, I don't care. If they want to harass me for simply living, then they can get a taste of their own medicine. Soon after I have sent the message, I receive an 'Undeliverable' notice in response. Oh great. Seconds later, I get another email from Dorian.

Subject: STOP

Gabriella,

Don't ever do that shit again. I'm serious.

-D

The fuck? How did he know? It doesn't even surprise me. Something obviously has crawled up his ass and his attempt at reprimanding me just makes me even more annoyed. I power down my computer without responding and rejoin Carmen on the sales floor for the remainder of the evening, desperately trying to forget all forces of Dark, Light or other.

As I am counting the register after closing, I receive a text message from Morgan, asking me to swing by the grocery store and pick up another package of taco shells. I lock up the store for the night and jump in my trusty Honda and head for the nearby market, which lucky for me, stays open late. The aisle housing the Mexican cuisine features an array of products and brands. I choose one at random, and when I turn to head for the register, I nearly collide with a broad chest clothed in navy blue pinstripes.

"Uh, um, excuse me," I stammer, taking a step back to gather myself.

"No, excuse me," a deep baritone croons.

I look up to give the gentlemen an apologetic smile and am struck senseless by the mere sight of him. Smooth tan skin with not even a shadow of stubble, dark slicked hair, and striking blue eyes. He's tall with broad shoulders, draped in what I can only imagine is an expensive designer tailored suit. I can tell he's a good bit older than I am, maybe mid 30s at the most, but as handsome and dashing as he is, no man 10 years his junior could compete. Now I know what the term *'debonair'* means; he is the living embodiment of it.

From what I can see in the few seconds our eyes lock, the man emanates class and elegance, causing an unwelcomed pulsing below to break me from my musings. I quickly flash him a nervous grin and all but run to the checkout to mask my flushed cheeks. Wow, I must really be craving Dorian. Other than him, I've never been so sexually affected just by a simple glance.

I race home, trying to escape my embarrassingly erotic reaction to the painfully handsome stranger and the image of his enticing smirk as he watched me exit. *Shit!* Something was off about that man. Something I've seen before. *Felt* before. I can't be certain but a deep-seated instinct is telling me that whoever–whatever–he is, he's dangerous. And I was dangerously drawn to him. I shake my head, trying to dispel my guilt-mixed desire, and make my way inside to my friends and many needed shots of tequila.

"Gabs! You're home!" Jared slurs, enrapturing me in one of his famous bear hugs. Looks like he's already beat me to it.

"Hey, Jared! I missed you, buddy!" I greet him, equally enthusiastic. I make it a point not to bring up Tammy's condition. This night is about fun, and anguish mixed with hard liquor is not a good combination. "Where's Aurora?"

"She couldn't make it but this really isn't her thing anyway," he shrugs nonchalantly. "Definitely *our* thing though." He gives me a little nudge of his elbow and returns his attention back to loading his plate.

Platters of tacos, nachos, salsa, guacamole, and condiments crowd our dining room table along with a pitcher of margaritas. I toss my purse and head to the kitchen to stow the taco shells. When I return to the fiesta, I see that Morgan has on a giant sombrero, a margarita in one hand and is about to belt out a tune on the karaoke machine. *Wow*. Even Dolce, her pretentious Chihuahua, has on a brightly colored outfit and mini sombrero. Jared, James and Miguel are all lounging on the couches, munching, laughing and talking.

As I grab a plate and a family-sized margarita, I smile at the sight of my friends. It's just like old times–the five of us hanging out, acting like rowdy college kids. We were carefree, only worrying about the prospect of getting lucky that night or not being too hungover at work or class the next day. This is how it *should* be. We should get the chance to be young and dumb instead of being bogged down by supernatural crises.

My mind wanders to the photo that is now housed in the drawer of my nightstand. Chris, Donna, Natalia, Alexander and Dorian. They were not unlike us, just five friends that wanted to enjoy every minute together. They only wanted love, acceptance and understanding. They only wanted to *live*. And they deserved to, no matter what world they were birthed into. They didn't get the choice that I was given. All of the trivial worries that plagued me months ago seem so ridiculous now. The five of them fought to live. *To love*. Privileges we take for granted. I want to honor their memory. I want to prove to my parents, both human and otherworldly, that I *can* do this. I can and will live up to my destiny.

"Hey Gabs, get over here! You'll miss the show!" Jared calls to me, breaking me from my reverie.

I smile at him brightly. "Well, line 'em up, because I've got some catching up to do."

After Morgan belts out her tipsy rendition of Madonna's "Like a Virgin," we all take turns wearing the giant sombrero and singing our favorite songs. We even do a few duets, complete with ridiculously dramatic dance moves. I laugh until my stomach hurts and tears sprout in the corners of my eyes. I've missed this. As much as I love being with Dorian, there's nothing like an outrageously fun night with your best friends.

I'm not sure when we all pass out for the night but somehow I make it to my own bed. Sleep comes easy with the help of one too many libations and I quickly fall into a vivid, colorful dream.

I'm on a white-sand beach, the bright sun bathing my body with warmth. There isn't a cloud in the sky and the ocean waters are so clear you can see straight to the bottom. An array of vibrant multicolored fish and coral inhabit the crystal blue waters, and I gasp in awe.

In the distance I see lush green hills. Atop of them sit hundreds of little houses, all sandstone white with rust colored roofs. Very European. I look to the other side of me and find magnificent stone structures. Nature's statues. Everything is perfect, and I am content, even alone.

I look down at myself and am amazed at the beautiful white bikini I'm wearing. It makes me feel so sexy, so uninhibited. I lay down right onto the bare ground and the warm sands welcome me. There's a nice breeze, just enough to cool me from the sun's rays. I spread my arms and soak it all up, completely relaxed and contented. This must be heaven.

Suddenly a dark figure stands before me, gazing down at me, blocking the sunlight from reaching me. My eyes adjust to the unexpected shade. I look to see who my mystery visitor could be and gasp at the discovery.

It's him.

The strikingly handsome man from the market dressed in the navy blue suit. He looks down at me, giving me the same seductive smirk from earlier, admiring my body in the scanty bikini. His eyes dance with delight at the sight of me, and it makes me feel . . . sexy, desirable.

I don't try to cover myself. I let him marvel at my curves. I even make a show of it, slowly letting my hands caress my thighs, my bare stomach, the tops of my breasts. I lick my lips for him and my eyes narrow as I look up at his approving grin. I continue to gently fondle myself, hoping that he will find pleasure in my erotic display. I want to impress him. I want to show him that even though I may be young, I can please him. I want him to touch my body. I want to feel his skin on mine. But he makes no move to appease me. His restraint is maddening and only intensifies my hunger for him.

Letting my fingers slip beneath the bikini bottoms, I find my scorching hot sex. I stroke it once and brace for his reaction.

Nothing.

I do it again, hoping to rouse him, yet he remains still, quietly observing. I continue to touch and tease myself in an attempt to show him how confident and alluring I can be. My eyes stay on his as I imagine that it is his hand that pleases me. I want him. And I want him to want me.

"I can make you feel this sexy, this free every single day," he says suddenly, his voice seductively smooth. Just the sound of it causes me to quiver uncontrollably until I can't hold it anymore. I want to give him every ounce of my pleasure. I want him to feel the overwhelming throb that consumes me. And I explode, dripping

sweet sap around my own fingers.

I jerk awake and sit up in my bed, breathing heavily, the heat between my legs pulsing wildly. I feel the dampness on my panties. *Holy shit!* What the hell was that? Did I just . . . ? No, I couldn't have. But the proof is right here, saturated into white lace. Suddenly, the brightness of my bedside lamps flicker on and I nearly scream with fright, shielding my eyes from the intensity.

"Have a nice dream?" a deep voice murmurs solemnly.

Dorian.

He's across the room, sitting on the chaise lounge. He has on a dark charcoal grey suit, crisp white shirt, no tie with the top few buttons undone.

"Dorian," I breathe. I want to tell him to come to me but I need to get to the bathroom. "Hold on, I'll be right back." I race to my private restroom and discard my panties in the hamper. I also take the liberty to gargle to get the icky remnants of tequila out of my mouth. After I have freshened up, I walk back out, sans panties.

Dorian is sitting on my bed, still looking somber. "Is that all you wore to bed?" he asks after I've settled back under the covers.

I look down at my short cotton nightgown. "Pajamas?"

Dorian sighs, obviously annoyed. "Pretty inappropriate considering there are three other men sleeping only feet away from you."

I shrug. "Well, they're all out in the living room, right?" It's really no big deal. I'd much rather them crash here than drink and drive. And it's not like we've never passed out after a night of partying before.

"The brothers are," he replies. *Oh.* Miguel must've found his way to Morgan's room.

"Well, they are out cold. They had a lot to drink; we all did. It was good for them to get out of that hospital and let loose a bit."

"Yes. Their mother," he nods, looking towards my window, out into the night. "She will be fine. They should be able to see her later this morning."

Huh? "What are you talking about, Dorian." I let my hand reach out and pull his chin towards me. His eyes are bright and dazzling yet he looks so . . . distraught.

"She will be . . . *fixed.* The petrification will be reversed."

My eyes grow wide with glee. "Oh my God, Dorian!" I exclaim, wrapping my arms around him and squeezing tightly. "You did it? You found a way?"

Dorian shakes his head sadly. This is the best news we've had in weeks and he's upset? "Aurora? Did she find something?" I ask. Again Dorian shakes his head, breaking away from my embrace. I frown. "Then how, Dorian? Why don't you seem happy? Who could have reversed it?"

Dorian remains silent for several seconds before turning his head to look at me with cold, desolate eyes. Something about his gaze is disturbing, as if he is dead inside. Every bit of life and love appears to have been drained right out of him.

"My father."

My eyes widen in horror and a scream catches in my throat, causing me to choke on a gasp of air. "*Your father?* What?" I rasp in disbelief. I must still be drunk. There's no way I could have heard him correctly.

"You never answered my question," Dorian murmurs.

I huff with frustration. "What? What question, Dorian?"

"Did you have a nice dream?"

Sheer horror washes over my face at the remembrance of our link. He can feel what I feel. *Shit*. So he knows I was aroused. Hell, I was more than aroused. I freaking came in my sleep.

"Yeah . . . um. It's just been a few days since we were together. And I wanted you so bad. That hasn't happened to me in a while, I swear."

"I don't care about you having a wet dream, Gabriella," he says exasperated. "That shit means nothing to me. I'm more concerned about who you were dreaming about."

I am utterly shocked. He *knows* I was dreaming about somebody else? No! Crap. How do I explain this one?

"I'm sorry, Dorian. I can't choose who I dream about. It's not like I did that purposely. I don't even know who that was!"

Dorian nods and chews his bottom lip as if he's concentrating. "I do."

"What? Hold up, what's going on? What do you mean?"

Dorian turns his head and lets his ice blue eyes meld into mine. "My father, Gabriella." With a tentative hand, he brushes my cheek and his face cringes in pain. "That was my father."

Suddenly the air becomes so thick I can't breathe. My head is swimming, my insides sloshing around like a whirlpool. "Oh my God, Dorian. Oh my . . . I'm so sorry. Oh shit," I stammer.

He strokes my hair, caressing me lovingly. "It's ok, little girl. It's not your fault. You did nothing wrong."

My eyes dart around wildly and I am breathless. I feel flush, clammy. I struggle to swallow down the bile rising in my throat. "I'm so sorry. I didn't know. Oh shit, I think I'm going to be sick."

I turn to try to make it to the toilet but Dorian stops me before I make it off the bed, placing his hand over my stomach. His hands ignite fiery blue momentarily then the intense wave of nausea ceases, and I strangely feel completely coherent.

Holy shit! Could this night get any more bizarre? Hell, am I still freakin' dreaming?

But I can't dwell on Dorian's amazing ability to cure me of the consequences of excessive amounts of tequila. His father is here. And he knows who I am.

"How? Why did he come here? How did he know about Tammy?" I am just so confused, the questions just keep pouring out.

Dorian's expression darkens to one of violent contempt. "Fucking Aurora. I told her not to involve him. I told her I would find a way. Her affections for that boy . . ." He shakes his head angrily. "She deceived me. She *will* pay for her misdeeds."

"But Dorian, she did it for Jared. Maybe she really does care for him and got scared? He came to fix Tammy. He came to help. Why?"

It would make more sense if I already didn't know that he was a murderous tyrant. And to think I was dreaming about him? Desiring him? Even in the market earlier, I was *drawn* to him. I don't get it. Why? How could I be so . . . *attracted* to someone like him?

"I don't know. Get under my skin. Insult me. Provoke me. See you. Take your pick," he shrugs. He assesses the confusion and fear etched in my face and eases me back down onto the bed, laying next to me. "Hey, don't worry about it. I won't let him hurt you. You are safe, little girl."

I nuzzle into Dorian's arms, letting my head rest on his firm chest. "How did he know who I was?"

"He knew when I knew, baby," he coos. Right. His curse, his inability to lie.

"But he looks so . . . young. Too young to be your father at least." Yeah, he's got a few extra years on me, but he and Dorian look more like brothers than father and son.

"One of the benefits of killing for your own personal gain," he remarks.

"Is he going to kill *me*?" I whisper meekly.

"No. He won't get his hands dirty. Not with something so . . . high profile. No one wants to be known as the one who slaughters the Dark Light, the savior of the Light Enchanters," he says sardonically.

I lift my head to look at him with question in my eyes. "Huh? Is that what I'm known as?"

Dorian shrugs. "It was just always assumed that that's the way you would go."

"So you thought I'd align with the Light?" Again, Dorian shrugs, looking impassive. "Dorian, if you thought that, then you knew you'd have to kill me."

Dorian shakes his head sternly. "No. I would not have done it. I can't."

"But if you didn't, then they'd kill you! All this time, you were prepared for them to murder you? Were you even going to tell me?" I can't believe it. Dorian felt he was playing a losing game yet he continued to act as if everything would be fine. He made me believe that we could potentially survive this together.

Dorian looks at me, refusing to answer my questions, and I know my suspicions are true. He was willing to die for me. I knew that we would face adversity, and with the annoying messages from the Dark, I figured I could fool them somehow, make them believe I'd side with them. I never imagined that Dorian's death was already in the works.

I bring my head back down to his chest, letting the sound of his heartbeat soothe my troubled mind. "What did he do to me? Why did he make me . . . *feel* that way?" I whisper after a few silent minutes.

"He got inside your head. He planted the seed; played to your desires, your aspirations. Your insecurities. Made you want him."

"But I don't!" I state fervently. At least I think I don't. Even before the dream, in the supermarket, I *was* intrigued by him. *God*, I'm so confused!

"It's okay. Seriously. He is very charming. Women are instantly beguiled by him. He is the epitome of sophistication and class," he says thoughtfully. Dorian's face then transforms into something terrifyingly vile and imperiling. "I fucking hate him."

"You don't mean that, Dorian. He's your dad. And to be honest, you are not unlike him." I instantly feel Dorian stiffen and I know I've struck a nerve. "Other than the evil, coldhearted dictator part, of course. You are extremely charming and gorgeous and fascinating, Dorian. I wanted you the moment I saw you. And you still take my breath away every single time I'm with you."

Sheesh. I am definitely still drunk. I am *way* too loose with the lips.

I feel Dorian shift as if he's shaking his head. "But his power . . . he has abilities that I don't possess. He likes it that way. He keeps us all beneath him so there is never a chance that anyone would ever challenge him. And those who have been stupid enough to try have never lived to tell about it. He gets whatever he wants, no matter the cost, no matter who he destroys in the process. Women love him; men fear him."

"But *I* don't love him, Dorian. I don't even *like* him."

Dorian lets his hands dance in my hair, massaging my scalp gently. "But you want him," he states somberly.

"What? Hell no! Absolutely not!" How can he even say that? I only want Dorian, and I always will. For me to desire his dad is just downright . . . *gross.*

"You do," he states simply. "He couldn't have planted the dream if you didn't. Even if you opened yourself to him for just a second, that is all he needs. Then he has access to the deepest depths of your subconscious."

If there was ever a time where I wanted to press rewind, it's now. I would have never stopped at the market. I would have gone straight home and told Morgan that they were out of damn taco shells. How can Dorian be so calm about this? Doesn't this wound him? Knowing that even for a fraction of a millisecond that I *allegedly* lusted for his dad?

"I'm so sorry, Dorian. I have missed you so much. I swear I have no interest in your father."

I stretch my neck to look up at my lover, only to find him smiling down at me adoringly. "I know, little girl." Again he strokes my hair and I go back to listening to his heartbeat. "Did he speak to you?" he asks after a while.

"Huh?" I reply sleepily. Anytime Dorian plays with my hair, I am instantly relaxed to the point of unconsciousness.

"In the dream. Did he speak to you?"

Oh. "Um, yeah. But only like one sentence." *And it was one helluva sentence.*

"What did he say?"

I take a deep breath and try to recall what Dorian's father, the Dark King, said to me verbatim. "He said *'I can make you feel this sexy, this free every single day.'* What the hell does that even mean?" I say with a nervous, strained chuckle.

Dorian doesn't return my humor. "I see," he responds flatly. "It means that he knows that you feel trapped, confined and uncomfortable with yourself. And he can . . . he can make you feel free and sexy. It means he'll give you what you want."

"But all I want is you!" I exclaim whipping my head around so he can see the conviction in my eyes.

Dorian gives me a wistful half-smile. "I know you think you do, little girl."

He eases my head back down onto his chest and commences to play in my hair. I snuggle into him, letting my own hand stroke his abdomen. Even through his dress shirt, I can feel the hard, taut ripples.

Dorian nuzzles in closer to me and I feel his lips in my hair. "But the king always gets what he wants. And what he wants is you."

Ten

"I am just overjoyed that the boys have their mom back. I know they are beyond relieved," Donna says pulling the roast out of the oven. It smells delicious, and my mouth instantly begins to salivate as the aroma wafts throughout the kitchen. I set three table settings for our traditional family dinner.

"They are. When they found out yesterday, I was afraid they'd kill themselves trying to race to the hospital!" I don't have the heart to tell her that I had learned of Tammy's miraculous recovery in the wee hours of the morning before. Or the Dark King's impromptu visit to our unsuspecting town of Colorado Springs.

"Well, Tammy looks like she'll be fine. She doesn't even remember the attack. It's as if nothing happened at all," my mom remarks, setting the meat, potatoes and vegetables onto a serving platter. She looks at me skeptically. "So Dorian found a way?"

I shrug, returning my attention to folding the napkins into neat triangles to avoid eye contact. "I guess so."

"Here, this should do," Chris interjects as he enters the kitchen. He holds up a bottle of red wine that he's retrieved from the wine rack in his study. Things are still strained between us though we are both making an effort to rekindle our relationship.

"Looks good, dear," my mom remarks. "Ok, dinner is served."

We all sit at the kitchen table, ready to dig into the sumptuous meal that Donna has prepared for us. It's nice to enjoy a normal family dinner together. I've made it a point to at least be here on Sundays, especially since Dorian insisted that Cashmere close early on the conventional holy day so I can spend as much time with my parents as possible. I think he knows how much more difficult it will be to maintain my once carefree, human life after my ascension. He knows Donna and Chris; he likes them. They may have all even been friends at one time. He knows losing me will break their hearts and sympathizes with them. He values my human relationships, causing me to appreciate my family and friends just a little more while I still can.

"So things are going well with Dorian, I presume," Chris states flatly, filling our glasses with wine.

"Yes," I say tersely. Looks like he wants to jump right in with the questions. I grab my glass and take a lengthy sip, preparing for battle.

"Humph. So I'm assuming you'll be aligning with the Dark upon your ascension." Chris cuts into his meat, and places a portion into his mouth. Disappointment and judgment is written all over his face.

I finish chewing my bite of food then gently place my silverware on the table. Looks like I can forget about a nice, relaxing family meal. "I haven't actually decided. And I don't really understand why I have to. I am equally Dark just as I am equally Light. Why should I have to choose one side and shun the other?"

"This isn't about being fair, Gabriella," he says. "It's about believing in something and devoting yourself to it. Natalia lived her life for the Light. And she died because she fell victim to the Dark allure." Chris shakes his head as if to dispel any false speculation. "Now I'm not saying that your father didn't love her; I know he did. Alex was a good man. But I can't say the same about the rest of them."

I look over at Donna who is silently picking at her meal and nod weakly, not quite agreeing with Chris but not totally disagreeing either. I get what he's saying. Other than Dorian, I can't fully trust any Dark One as far as I could throw them. But the same could be said about the Light. I know nothing about them, and they've chosen to keep it that way. Why should I place my devotion in their hands?

"But you once knew Dorian too. He sacrificed so much to protect my parents and their secret. He protected me before he even knew me. Why do you hate him so much?"

"I don't hate him, Gabriella. It's *because* I know him that makes me so cautious. It's what he's capable of that worries me. He's Dark. That's not going to change no matter what you do. A tiger can't change its stripes."

So what is he saying? That no matter what, Dorian will never be good? That he'll always be a cold, callous assassin? I don't want to change him; I never have. I love him for who and what he is. I just want to show him the good that's already there, that's been there all along. I don't ever expect him to be anything less than Dark, just like he can't expect me to be anything less than the indecisive, irrational, hot-headed Dark Light that I am.

"I understand that I could never bring Dorian into the Light, if that's what you're implying. And I honestly don't want to. It was you who told me that there is no absolute evil, just as there is no absolute good. Just because Dorian was born into a family that does not value the man that he is, that doesn't make him a bad person. He's proved that more than once already."

I take a deep breath and try to reflect just how deeply I feel for Dorian. I have to make them understand. "I *see* him, Dad. I know that sounds crazy, but I do. I know who he is and I'm not going to turn away from him just because of some ancient feud that isn't even my fight to begin with. And if I did, that makes me no better than the ones that slaughtered my birth parents and left me an orphaned half-breed. They acted out of fear, out of hatred. I want to act out of understanding, acceptance. *Love*. Like Alex and Natalia did. Like you and Mom did when you took me in and raised me as your own."

Chris chews his food and swallows laboriously. He then picks up his glass of wine and downs it in one quick gulp before turning to me. *Uh oh, here it comes.* I down my wine as well, ready for the onslaught.

"When did you get so smart, Kiddo?" he responds, pride and affection twinkling in his brown eyes.

I smile at my dad, the man who cared for me from birth. The

man who dried every tear and bandaged every scraped knee. "I had some really awesome parents. They taught me everything I know."

When I arrive home late that evening and have stowed the insane amount of leftovers packaged lovingly by Donna, I find Dorian is in my room waiting for me. I hadn't seen nor heard from him since early the morning before when Jared and James had received a call from the hospital, informing them of their mom's recovery. He dashed out of here, muttering something about tying up loose ends. I wasn't about to beg him to stay. I needed to be happy for my friends and let them enjoy their moment of triumph. And as perturbed as I was by not hearing from Dorian, seeing him now, looking every bit as deliciously sexy as he always is in jeans and a dark knit V-neck tee, I can't be mad at him. I know he had a good reason for staying away. At least that's what I have to believe.

"You're back," I remark, kicking off my sandals and tossing my purse onto my dresser. He really hates when I do this. He's always so meticulously neat. Oh well, *I* can't wave a finger and have my room magically transformed into a showroom. I trot into my conjoined bathroom to freshen up, knowing that it will be tidied when I emerge and secretly grin to myself.

After brushing my teeth and throwing on an oversized tee, I find Dorian at the large window next to my bed. I've realized looking out into the darkness helps him think, gives him clarity. He's holding a glass of scotch from the stash he keeps here for his visits. I think to wrap my arms around him and rest my head on the firm ripples of his back but I need answers before getting distracted by his body.

I flop down onto my bed and pick up the tiny remote to my stereo system, looking for something mellow and cathartic. I opt for Coldplay; I have a feeling it's going to be a long, emotional night.

"I had to make sure he was gone," he says after a few strained minutes.

Oh. I don't dare ask him to clarify; I know who he means. His father. The dashing, charming, yet disgustingly manipulative Dark King.

"And he is, I presume." I try to sound unbiased, unaffected but I just can't seem to wash away the aggravation from my voice.

Dorian finally looks to me, a mixture of remorse and relief in his eyes. He takes another sip of his potent poison then hands it to me. I purposely take a sip in the same spot that his succulent lips have just kissed before setting it on my bedside table. I look up at him in expectance of his explanation for his disappearing act.

"I needed to be certain that he would not come for you. Occupy him, entertain him with . . . other things." Dorian picks up the crystal glass and downs its contents as if to wash away the vile memory of spending quality time with his dad.

I have a pretty good idea of what Dorian means. The Dark King is a known philandering murderer. Who knows what kind of disgusting, kinky activities he's into? And what could that mean for Dorian? Was he expected to engage in the same? I can't bring myself to even entertain the notion.

"And he was . . . satisfied? Enough to leave?"

Ick. No matter how handsome, refined or alluring his father is, imagining him getting his rocks off by causing someone bodily harm is revolting. I physically cringe at the thought of the brutality.

"I'd say so. But I know what you're thinking. He is a little more tactful than you would expect. You'd be surprised. The women are just as depraved and immoral. They like it. They beg him for it." Dorian takes a single finger and lifts my chin up to meet his gaze. "I don't do any of it. Ever. I don't want to and I never have."

"I know," I murmur, refusing to meet his gaze. And I *do* know. Dorian could have any woman in the world. *Any*. But he came here. I'm not overly confident in myself, yet I am not stupid or insecure enough to pester him with trivial *girl* worries.

"Do you? Because I feel like there's something else. Like something you're keeping from me. You're uncomfortable."

"I'm not uncomfortable." I whisper, wringing my hands.

Dorian gives me a knowing look accompanied by a skeptical smirk. *Shit*. Can he feel *everything*?

I take a deep breath and look up at the gorgeous creature before me, hoping like hell that I don't offend him. "Ok, ok. It's just . . . I'm trying to understand what happened. I know you say you hate your father and he is . . . disappointed with the choices you've made. But being Dark, the things you've rejected, the things that you dislike in him, don't they just come natural for your kind? I know my father, Alex, was different, but so are you. If there are more that feel like you do, and I'm sure there are, why is consorting with the Light so forbidden? And why am I the only one of my kind?"

Dorian's gaze darkens a bit yet I don't feel it is in anger or even desire. No, this is something else, another layer to the enigma that is the man I love. Maybe shame? Regret?

"You are perceptive, little girl."

With a sigh, Dorian sits beside me, kicking off his shoes before scooting himself upward so he is reclining on the mound of pillows. Usually he would have somewhat manifested in the spot but I notice that he hasn't used since he's arrived. Did he overexert himself during his father's visit? Is he weakened?

He pulls me into his arms, placing my head on his hard, warm chest. *Ahhh*. This is heaven. Feeling him, having him close to me, makes me feel like all is right in the world, and there are no murderers, no sociopathic fathers, no Light, no Dark. Just us.

"First of all, we didn't start out as evil. When the Divine Power created us, we were literally made to rule the dark, the night. Just as the Light were made to control the day. Sort of like nature's guardians.

"But as time went on, the worldly temptations that were shrouded in the dark hours of night grew undeniable to our kind, and the Dark became consumed with lust, greed, power. They wanted to rule the night and everything else, and would stop at nothing to obtain their desires. Even kill to sate the thirst for omnipotence. Thus spawning the idea that darkness is synonymous for evil."

"So it's true? There is no such thing as absolute evil?" *I knew it!* Dorian could never be completely immoral, even if he tried. There truly is good in him.

"No. Not originally. But over time, our power evolved into something else. Something dark and destructive. We lost our ability to heal, our ability to help others unselfishly. Our ability to love and show compassion naturally. We were completely corrupted."

I nod against his chest, trying to formulate a way of tactfully asking my next question. "So, um, if the Divine Power created you, the Dark, why couldn't he, you know, end you? I mean, I'm glad that didn't happen for obvious reasons, but it seems like the logical solution."

I feel Dorian's lips in my hair then hear him swiftly inhale, breathing life back into his weary body. He needed this contact for more than the comfort of our close proximity.

"We were created to be complementary to the Light. Two separate yet equal powers. We are the Yin and Yang. Without one, the other cannot survive. To destroy us would also end the Light."

Oh. That makes sense. Also keeps the Dark from completely annihilating the Light. Driving the Light into extinction would be suicide.

"There were other consequences." Dorian gently lifts me off of his chest to lift his shirt. A sharp breath reflexively catches in my throat at the sight of his smooth, delicious torso. "The tattoo. We, the Dark, are marked. Only other supernatural creatures can see it as a way to warn them of our treachery, to shame us for our transgressions. You've heard of the Mark of the Beast?"

I furrow my brow in confusion. "From the book of Revelation? But I thought that was 666? And wasn't that, like, towards the end of the world or something?"

Geez, this is getting creepy.

Dorian shakes his head before sliding his shirt back down to cover his magnificence. *Dammit.* But I can't be distracted with my carnal desires, not when he is sharing so much with me.

"Each is the name of our clan, or our family. The Skotos, the Órexes, and even your father's family, the Polemos, are all branded. There are many others, though the Skotos have been the ruling family for thousands of years, long before even my father was created. However, it has been said that there will be one that will wear the true Mark of the Beast."

Dorian strokes my cheek with back of his hand, letting his touch linger for a long beat at my chin. "Some believe it will be you."

"*What?!*" I scream, with no regard for courtesy or modesty. *Oh hell no!* Did he just say what I *think* he said? Of all the bizarre conversations, this has to be the most asinine, ridiculous, sacrilegious one yet. I look at Dorian with wild, horrified eyes. "Are you trying to say that I'm the freakin' antichrist?!"

Dorian chuckles before shaking his head. "No, no, calm down. Of course not. But you are a unique breed, so to speak. People will try to breathe truth into any fable they don't quite understand. It is not you; only the Divine Power knows who and when. You are quite the opposite. Your birth was considered the coming of a new dawn. A savior . . . to the Light, that is."

Whew. Disaster averted. I don't even feel comfortable discussing the end of days, let alone contributing to it. "How so?" I ask, thankful for the change in direction. I let out a deep sigh of relief and nestle back into his arms.

"Their hope is that you will restore the balance, bring peace amongst the Light and Dark. While most of the Light are hopeful that you will succeed in this by aligning with them, there are others who fear your power."

"And the Dark? How do they feel about my presence?" I ask meekly. Whatever it is, it can't be good.

Dorian shrugs. "Obviously, there are those of us who don't want peace. They don't want to restore the natural order. Then there are some who feel that your power could be . . . *useful*."

"Your father," I whisper. He wants to use me, keep me as his little pet to attack those who defy him.

"Yes." Dorian's hands find their way to my scalp, and he begins to massage. I instantly feel all the tension drain from my body. Dorian and those magic fingers.

"Is that why you hate him? Because he doesn't want peace? Because he likes this corrupted regime?"

"That's not the only reason. The Dark, especially the Skotos, were corrupt long before his rule. And sadly, so was I. I'm no boy scout but honestly, it was just getting old. Decades of killing, sating my wanton desires without regard, straying from our true purpose. I wanted something else, something *more*. I knew it was out there but I never truly felt it until I found you." I feel Dorian's soft lips kiss the crown of my head lovingly. I squeeze my arms tighter across his waist in response.

"And he wanted to keep you from finding it, from finding happiness," I say, trying to piece together the scattered remains of Dorian and his father's strained relationship. Every child wants love and acceptance from their parents, even when the parents are degenerate villains. There has to be another reason. The Dark King must've personally hurt his son in some awful way. A pang of sorrow strikes my chest and I stifle a pained gasp.

"Yes." I feel Dorian's body become rigid with apprehension but before I can excuse him from his painful account, he takes a deep breath and continues. "I was very young, not even a century old. I wanted the world. Ambitious, strong, stubborn. Aurora was in my life then. We had plans for the future, and I really thought she was what I wanted."

Oh. Aurora. The stunning, seductive sex goddess. *The fancy slore in expensive shoes.* His first love.

Her intrusion into our intimate conversation makes my throat tighten and I fight the urge to groan my disdain. I know they had a very colorful sex life. After seeing how sensual their power exchange was for myself, how could I deny their intense chemistry? He *wanted* her. And even though I know his feelings for her have changed dramatically since they were young, I can't help but feel a little twinge of jealousy at the history and connection they share.

Dorian lifts my chin up a bit to meet my mouth with his. His taste revitalizes every nerve in my body. He is sustenance; I need him like I need air. He must feel my irrational resentment and wants me to know that he is here for me and me alone. I'd be a fool to doubt his intentions after all he's shared this evening.

"My father had a different view of who I was to be. The thought that one day I could sit on his throne secretly frightened him. He likes the authority; he likes to feel as if he should be worshipped as a god. It was never what I wanted, and he feared that one day I would succumb to my . . . humanity. So he thought if he could break me, could unleash my inner demons, I'd either embrace his way or run away from it altogether."

Dorian gives my arm a little squeeze as if he's trying to brace himself for the painful memory that he's kept hidden all these years. "As I told you, Aurora is an Órexis. And if there is one thing that the Órexes cannot deny it is sexual desire. I thought my affections were enough to sustain her. I was wrong."

I look up at the strong, beautiful man before me. Though his voice is level and unaffected, I know he has been hurt. How could *he* not be enough for any woman? And not just in the sexual sense either. Dorian, the kind, mesmerizing, mysterious, sexy, humble man I fell head over heels in love with is *more* than enough. He is everything.

Dorian sighs, letting go of the tension that has bound him in his solemn recollection. "My father's method of seduction to lure Aurora was not unlike what he has tried to do with you. Once he knows your deepest, darkest secrets, he manipulates you into thinking that he can provide anything you want, anything you need.

"Aurora went to him willingly unbeknownst to me. She offered herself to him; she *wanted* to pleasure him. And as they were engaged in the heinous act, he summoned me so I could see for myself just how insanely depraved and wicked he really is. Aurora couldn't say anything. She had no explanation for what she had done. And I can't fully blame her. He took advantage of her weaknesses, her fears, her desires."

My already aching heart completely splinters at Dorian's divulgence. How could his own father, the man who gave him life, be so revoltingly vicious? Not to mention, sleep with his girlfriend and then call his son in to witness it? I want to cry, scream, fight for my scorned lover. Yet I hold in my pained sobs, knowing that feeling my grief will only bring him more torment.

"You know, I'll never forget the smug look on his face. He was so . . . satisfied with himself as if he had done me a favor. He said to me, *'See son, a true king always gets what he wants.'*" Dorian sucks his teeth, his jaw tight with contempt. "Arrogant fuck."

Dorian releases the grip on my arm and massages as if he has just realized he was squeezing it. "After that, I joined the Shadow and buried myself in hunting and killing to fill the massive void that he strived to make even broader. I didn't see nor speak to my family or Aurora until I was summoned. When they discovered your parents."

"Oh Dorian," I croak. My throat is rough and dry with emotion. I clear it then look up at him with glossy eyes. "I would never do that. *Ever*. I don't care what he thinks he knows about me. There is nothing he could give me that I don't already have in you."

Dorian gives me his boyish, dazzling half-grin. He is simply so breathtaking, it literally makes my heart sputter. His smile makes me smile, and I do so widely. I lean forward a bit and gently touch my lips to his. Just a simple gesture to show him that he is not alone, and that my love for him is tender and sincere. He doesn't want pity. He doesn't want mourning. And I won't give him that. I will give him me. I have to fix Dorian, the Dark assassin that I love so much it hurts, just as he has fixed me in my time of need. And there's only one way I know how.

I let my hand move from his jawline to his disheveled black hair, grabbing soft handfuls. The other stealthily yet shakily reaches for the hem of his shirt. I slide it upwards, revealing defined cuts of muscle under smooth, olive skin and I gasp at the feel of it. His body truly never ceases to amaze me.

"I want it off," I murmur, pulling away from him only to relinquish him of his shirt. I marvel at the sheer splendor before me, struggling to pull my eyes away. *God, he's marvelous.* I could literally look at his body all day.

Hastily, I rejoin our lips, swinging my leg over his lap to straddle him. My tongue explores the sweet softness of his mouth as my hands grip his silky locks with fervor. I could never get enough of kissing him. The taste of his tongue is downright orgasmic. I moan against his lips, enthusiastically feeding my hunger for him.

Dorian's hands are on my ass, squeezing, kneading, pulling me into the growing stiffness of his middle. Luckily I am only sheathed in a sleepshirt and panties, giving him easy access to my already tingling erogenous zones. But this is my show; I want to show him how much he is desired and loved. Tonight is not about him giving me yet another earth-shattering, hair-pulling, lip-biting orgasm. Tonight is about pleasing *him*.

Reluctantly, I pull my lips away from his only to leave a trail of soft kisses from his lips to his neck. I inhale his mouthwatering scent, all the while grazing the tiny stubble of his chin and throat with my tongue. I kiss a path to his marble-like chest, so smooth and hard to the touch. My lips find his right nipple, where I tease and suck and kiss tenderly. I hear him groan at the sensation, and his compulsory reaction encourages me to continue, moving to his left where I repeat the routine. His sighs develop into low hisses, and I know he is affected. He is aroused, and hearing him so exposed, so vulnerable, causes the flame between my thighs to erupt into a raging combustion.

"*Shit*, Gabriella," Dorian moans, motivating me to repeat my slow, torturous attack.

My hands find the fly of his jeans, and I eagerly unfasten the top button and unzip them, unveiling the strained bulge constricted in denim. It feels so strong and vital, I just want it to live inside me. My hungry mouth leaves his skin so I can focus on the task of unleashing the pulsing, raging monster begging to be freed. I maneuver his jeans down to his ankles, where he aides me in my efforts by hurriedly kicking them off. I take in the magnificent man before me clad only in dark boxer briefs. As much as I want to just capture this moment and commit it to memory, I want him. And a simple eye-fuck will just not do.

I tug at the waist of his underwear, eager to discover just how deep his desire goes. As always, he doesn't disappoint. Dorian gives me a front row viewing of his rock-hard length, causing my eyes to grow wide with delight. Impulsively, I lower my mouth to it, kissing the tip gently. I can hear a surprised breath catch in Dorian's throat. He wants this, and so do I. And I give it to him, hungrily devouring his beautiful hardness with vigor.

Deep, baritone moans harmonize with the music, creating a melodic symphony of sex. Despite his pleas to slow my pace and show him mercy, I continue my oral assault, relishing in the involuntary trembles of his legs. I challenge myself to take him deeper and deeper into my mouth, wanting to taste every inch of him. Not because I have to, but because I want to. Pleasing him is all the motivation I need.

Dorian's light trembles transform into jerking quivers and I know the end is near for him. Yet I don't let up; I continue this delectable torture until I feel his intense shudders cease when he releases his sweet sap. I consume every bit of him before looking up at his sated expression through hooded eyes. He is completely bewildered at my spontaneity and I mentally pat myself on the back for being able to thoroughly blow his mind.

With my eyes still fixed on Dorian's staggered, beautiful face, I pull my sleepshirt up over my head, exposing my full, perky mounds and satin panties. He bites his lip, eager to put his mouth on me but reigning in his usual plan of attack. He wants me to take the lead, and that's exactly what I plan to do.

I make a show of slipping my panties off, my eyes never leaving his as I bite my bottom lip in seductive verve. With a catlike slink, I make my way to him so our faces are just centimeters apart and I am hovering over his still-hardened rod. I tease him, lowering myself so that his impressive length just barely grazes my flesh then pulling away. It's torturous for me too, but I love seeing Dorian so eager and ready to feel me.

Finally I give in, easing myself down onto him with a garbled moan. How can he feel this *good*? How can it still surprise me? This type of pleasure shouldn't even be legal.

Dorian fills every deep cavernous space with authority as I rock back and forth onto him. We become one, an all-consuming tangle of moans, kisses and sighs. I keep with the rhythm of the music, careful not to go too far into shaky ground, though I want to so, so bad. I've wanted this, dreamt of this for too long. I want to release this flood of passion onto him but I know it will completely unravel me, surrendering the control that I now possess in this moment. I want to prove that I crave only him, I love only him. I want Dorian to feel it emanating from me. I not only want him to live within my soft, warm dwellings, I want him to *own* it entirely, just as he owns my heart.

I lean forward, bringing our faces together again, aligning our eyes so that he can clearly see the immense desire burning within them.

"Don't," Dorian whispers urgently. "You shouldn't do it."

I grind my flesh onto him even further, causing him to groan mangled expletives through clenched teeth. "But I want to," I whisper. "I'll be ok. I promise."

And before Dorian can object any further, I channel every ounce of passion, strength and love within my heart and soul, and yield it to him. All of it. I give him me. I let him feel, smell, hear, see, and taste all the ways I love him. And with a sharp huff of air, Dorian receives me, bringing him to his momentous brink, and taking me along with him down his journey into euphoria.

Eleven

"Take the day off. Rest. I don't want you to feel weak or disoriented."

"Dorian, I am perfectly fine. I feel good, really," I respond, applying my mascara in the vanity mirror of my bathroom draped in a terry-cloth robe. Dorian's hips are wrapped only in a fluffy white towel, showcasing his hard, taut body, making it impossible to focus on the task at hand. I've already nearly poked my eye out twice.

Running his hand through his messy, damp locks, Dorian twists his lips to one side, making him look unbelievably cute and boyish. "I don't know, Gabs. It worries me to have you out there right after you've used. The exchange of power between two forces is extremely draining. Especially for you. I loved it–hell, it was incredible–but you shouldn't have done it."

I spin around, completely taken aback by his comment. "What did you just say?"

"Uh, it worries me to have you out after you've used and you shouldn't have done it?" he recalls with a raised eyebrow.

I shake my head, cocking my head to one side. "No. What did you call me?"

"Oh, yeah. Gabs," he smiles sheepishly.

I smile back at my beautifully buoyant lover, relishing in our lighthearted banter after weeks of distress. Tammy is healed, his father is gone, and there has been no sign of my paranormal stalker. For now, all is right in the world.

"You've never called me that before. My friends are the only ones that call me that," I remark, returning my attention to applying my light makeup.

"Am I not your friend?"

I put down my eyeliner and gaze at Dorian's reflection in the mirror. "I'd say you are much more than that."

Dorian closes the distance between us and places his hands around my waist from behind. "But we're friends. That's one of the things I love about you. Even if there was nothing sexual between us, even if I didn't love you as deeply as I do, I'd still *like* you."

He turns my body around to face him, guiding me by my hips. I gaze into his bright blue, twinkling eyes, noticing how youthful and carefree he appears. "I've never had that with any woman, and it is seriously blowing my mind. I don't just like holding you, feeling you, making you come until you cry . . . I like talking to you. Knowing you."

I fight the urge to burst into a fit of girlish giggles and settle for a sweet, tender kiss instead. I like Dorian too. Besides Jared, he's the only other guy that I've opened up to. I've peeled back all my complicated layers and revealed the scared, stubborn, crass girl that I really am. I've let myself *feel* with him. And the fact that even after he's learned all those things about me, bullshit and baggage included, and still wants me, reconfirms my decision. I will love Dorian until the day I die. And even if that day is tomorrow, I will fight for this love–for *him*–because he is worth it.

"Well, other than just being a cool ass chick, I know exactly why you like me." I press my lips against his for a quick peck before turning back around to finish primping. "I am my father's daughter, Dorian. Maybe you see a piece of Alexander in me. You miss him."

Dorian takes a step back, visibly shaken by my observation. *Oh shit. I guess I can add 'tactless' to my list of attributes.* Yet, he's not angry or saddened by the memory of my deceased father and his best friend. He's thoughtful, surprised.

Finally, he nods, and flashes his ridiculously sexy half-smile. "I do. I miss him. And I guess you do favor him in some ways."

I move into the bedroom to dress. Though I'm not ready to leave him, I have to be at Cashmere in thirty minutes to open. "Tell me about him," I say with a gentle smile. I know that revisiting this part of Dorian's past could potentially hurt him.

He flops onto the bed and sighs, looking up toward the ceiling as if he is recalling a distant memory. "I have to admit, at first Alex hated me. Being the spoiled, entitled eldest son of the king, I thought I could flex my so-called authority even after I joined the Shadow. I was wrong. We were all equal, all brothers. Alex quickly kicked my ass and I never forgot it."

What? My dad kicked Dorian's ass? How is that even possible? Dorian is invincible. No one could physically hurt him. At least *I* couldn't.

"He taught me the ropes, whipped me into shape. He wasn't much older than I was, yet he was so much more grounded, humbled. Disciplined. Being that he was the illegitimate son of a nobleman, he had to work for what he achieved. He knew what it meant to be a man. And he taught me more about that than even my own father."

I slip on my modest red floral shirtdress, accenting it with a tan belt, all the while beaming with pride at the thought of my father having a positive impact on Dorian, the man that I love. To know that he helped shape and mold the compassionate, decent Dark One that stands before me today makes me feel somewhat close to him. And proud to be his daughter.

"My father's family . . . you said their name last night. What was it again?"

Dorian nods. "Polemos."

"What does that mean?" I ask, slipping into my wedge sandals.

Dorian is still sprawled out on the bed, only a towel covering his tantalizing nether regions. He seems so comfortable in his skin, so self-assured. He looks at me, his eyes filled with nostalgia. "War. He was a great warrior. All the Polemos are."

War. He was a fighter, just like me. And my mother was a bad ass in her own right. Now it all makes sense. Learning about my parents is more than just an education. I am learning about *me*, the girl I never really knew. The girl that was spelled to appear mundane and insignificant.

Dorian tugs at the hem of my dress like a child trying to summon his mother. “Don’t go,” he whines playfully. “If you stay, I’ll tell you anything you want to know.”

“You’ll tell me anyway. Besides, the boutique can’t run itself. Can’t make you much money if I close up shop every time you want to play hooky, boss man.”

Dorian shrugs. “What do I care? I have no need for any of it.”

“Then why do you own all this?” I say waving my hand around the room to indicate the luxury apartment complex. “You have all these businesses but you don’t care?”

My spirited lover laughs heartily, even going as far as to throw his head back with glee. “I thought you would have figured it out! It’s all a front, all constructed to lure you. I present a convenience so you never have the need to look elsewhere.”

“*What the hell?*” I shriek, placing my hands on my hips.

Dorian lifts his palms in feigned defense. “Calm down, killer. It was for your own good. I had to ensure I kept you near. To protect you. And I wanted to make you happy, honestly. I want to give you everything you could ever want and need. I’m extremely wealthy, Gabriella. Every business I’ve acquired has been for you. It’s all for you.”

His heartfelt admission successfully stops me up short, causing me to release my tightly clenched fists. “Oh. So what . . . you want me to be a kept woman?” Barefoot, pregnant and in the kitchen comes to mind if only I could cook . . . or even conceive children.

“Not at all. You would never allow it anyway. I get the feeling you have an aversion to authority, not to mention your inability to relinquish even an ounce of control.”

“Damn right!” I smile.

“Plus, I like your spunk. Your independence. Your refusal to take any of my shit. And I like that you make me feel young. *Free.* You are sincere and real. My entire life I’ve been surrounded by women who felt like they hit the jackpot as soon as they met me.

They were ready to let me walk all over them just as long as they could say that they were connected to me somehow. And I did just that. I'd get what I wanted and move on without a second thought. But women like that bore me. I like a challenge," he winks.

"I hardly think I was much of a challenge, Dorian. I showed up at *your* hotel room, remember?"

"But you knew what you wanted. And it wasn't money or status or even the exterior. There was something else there. Other than you being so horny you nearly came the first time I touched you," he chuckles.

What the hell? What's gotten into him?

Oh. Me, of course. Just as Aurora emitted her lustful desires into him, Dorian has received my good-humored crudeness. Just like the first time I transferred my amorous feelings into him. The next day he was different–witty and teasing. Sheesh, so I guess my tacky sense of humor is my superpower.

"Well, sorry, I hadn't been around the block as many times as you, old wise prince," I jibe. "Besides, you don't fight fair!"

"I never said I did, little girl. Now . . . about you going to work. You might as well undress and get back in this bed with me or I'll be forced to be very undiplomatic with your body. Again. And this time, I'll make it hurt."

My eyes grow wide with shock and excitement at the memory of Dorian completely immobilizing me and manipulating each of my pleasure points. And as much as it scares me to admit it, the prospect of seeing him in his darkness, unleashing the vicious beast inside of him that completely shatters every ounce of my resolve, arouses me.

"No! I really have to go to work! Carmen will be waiting outside!" I plead. "Why don't you just come with me? And if you see that I'm weak or moody, we'll come straight home. I promise."

Dorian smiles and nods at the idea. "Home," he murmurs thoughtfully. He sighs then stands to his feet, letting the towel around his waist drop to the floor. His impressive semi-hard length instantly makes my mouth salivate. "Like what you see?"

"I do. But I've got to get to work, Mr. Skotos. My boss can be a real hard-on," I giggle. "Now get dressed so you can see your hard-earned money at work."

We opt to walk the few minutes to Cashmere to enjoy the bright, warm sunshine. There isn't a cloud in the sky, and I instantly lift my head to let the sun's rays kiss my face. *Ahhh.* It feels divine. Almost as good as Dorian's kisses.

"You channel the sun," Dorian notes, as I skip ahead, swinging my arms like an actress in a ridiculously cheesy tampon commercial.

"Huh?" I ask, spinning around to gauge Dorian's beautiful face. He looks stylish and dangerously sexy as always, dressed in linen pants and a crisp button up shirt rolled up to his elbows.

"You feel rejuvenated in sunlight, right? Stronger?" He awaits my baffled expression. "Hmmm, maybe you are more Light than Dark," he remarks with a smirk.

He's right. The sun does put me in good spirits. But I thought everyone had that reaction when it was sunny versus rainy and gloomy. "True," I respond. "You don't feel that way?"

Dorian shrugs, strolling gracefully as if the pavement is his runway. "I don't have an aversion to it. I won't burst into flames," he chuckles. "But it does nothing for me."

I nod, recalling the loose translation of Dorian's first name. "I bet you're an amazing swimmer."

Dorian's eyes twinkle as a nostalgic smile creeps onto his face. "I am. Skiathos has the most beautiful, crystal clear waters. I wish I could take you there."

"Maybe one day you will," I reply, taking his hand in mine. I don't have the heart to tell him that I'd already been there very recently. In the dream his father gave me.

We approach the storefront just as Carmen is parking her car and I quickly unlock our fingers to avoid any skepticism, earning a pointed glare from Dorian. I'm sure Miguel informed her of my relationship with him, the now full owner of Cashmere, yet I feel it would be tasteless and unprofessional to make it obvious on the job.

The look of shock and adulation sketched on Carmen's face as she takes in Dorian's startling splendor makes me giggle internally. *Poor girl*. He still has that effect on me, especially when his eyes are smoldering with licentious desire and danger.

"Carmen, this is Mr. Skotos. He'll be checking up on us today," I say, unlocking the front door and ushering them inside.

Carmen extends her trembling hand. "N-Nice to meet you, Mr. Skotos. Um, uh, I've, uh, heard so much about you."

Dorian smiles warmly, obviously trying to dispel any stuffy feelings of formality. "Please, call me Dorian. And I'm not here to check up on either of you. I know you're doing an excellent job here." He places his large hand in Carmen's and she instantly recoils.

"Ack! Sorry! I didn't mean to shock you," she says stroking her palm.

Dorian looks at me quizzically for a beat then returns his gaze to Carmen where he waves off the strange occurrence. "No worries. Good to meet you Carmen." He looks to me and says, "I'll be in the back office. I have some paperwork I'd like you to sign when you have a moment."

Something has surely ruffled him, though he's doing well at masking it from Carmen. She seems none the wiser, shuffling off to prepare for the morning's opening. Dressed in high-waisted harem pants, a white tank and jeweled heeled sandals, Carmen's keen eye for fashion is definitely a strong selling point. I don't require anyone to buy or wear the clothing at the boutique. All I ask is that the staff strives to promote similar styles that we carry and be creative with making it their own. So far it has worked with women both young and old. I want the store to exude individuality and personal diversity, rather than what's just hot for the season.

"Carmen, I'm going to grab the cash drawer. Holler if you need anything, ok?"

I head to the back office where our safe is kept to find Dorian lounging thoughtfully at the desk. I close the door behind me, well aware that there's something he needs to tell me.

"What was that all about?" I whisper, though I know there's no way Carmen can hear me all the way back here.

Dorian shakes his head. "You never told me Carmen and Miguel practiced Santeria."

I give Dorian a skeptical look. "Uh, probably because I didn't know, not to mention, even know what *Santeria* is. So what . . . you felt something with Carmen? Is she *something*?" *Geez*, first Morgan, now Carmen too? Do I have any *normal* friends?

Dorian shakes his head. "No, not Carmen, exactly. Or even Miguel. Someone in their bloodline. A *Bruja*, a witch. Could be nothing, or could be . . . bothersome."

What? This just keeps getting more bizarre. "So you can pretty much sense any other mystical being by touch, right?"

"No, I can sense any power source around me. Carmen sensed me by touch, and I got a glimpse of her bloodline. She doesn't know what I am though. That never happened when she's touched you, I presume."

I shake my head. "So there's like . . . forces all around us? Like you?" *And me.*

Dorian chuckles a bit, folding his hands behind his head. "Of course. We, as well as the Light, have the ability to deflect. But if we're deflecting, we can't detect what's around us." Dorian turns the swivel chair to follow my movements as I walk over to the safe to retrieve the cash drawer. "We're everywhere, Gabriella. You'd be surprised."

I finish concentrating on the combination lock, biting my lip in determination before looking at him skeptically. "So since we've been together, we've come across *others*? When?"

Dorian shrugs and flashes me a crooked grin. "A few times. Our first date actually. The waitress at the sports bar was Light. Do you remember?"

How could I forget? Our conversation was so seamless, so fluid. I couldn't believe someone so inexplicably sexy could be so down to earth. And there *was* something off about the waitress. She was visibly shaken just at the sight of him, afraid even. After Dorian confirmed that she wasn't just some scorned ex-lover, I chalked it up to poor service.

"I remember that! She was damn near scared of you. But you left her such a large tip. What was up with that? I thought you guys all hated each other."

"Relations aren't as volatile as they used to be. We can't very well go around killing each other, can we?" Dorian's eyes flash to the door. "Carmen is coming. You better get out there and make me some money," he says jokingly.

I go to leave the office and nearly collide with Carmen just as her hand is raised to knock. "Oh crap, I'm so sorry, Gabs! I was just seeing if you needed any help. It's a few minutes to nine."

"Here I come." I look back at my playful lover once Carmen retreats to the front of the store. "I'll be back to check on you. Try not to break anything, ok," I say with a wink.

The morning zips by and we are surprisingly busy for a Monday. Word must've gotten out about the delicious Greek god observing quietly, causing most of the shoppers to lose their bearings, along with all intelligent thought. I spy Dorian slyly while ringing up an older woman, probably mid to late 50s, who is nearly drooling while fishing out her credit card. I don't mind her ogling eyes; she spent nearly $3000, scoring Carmen a sizable commission.

By noon, Amy, another one of our sales clerks comes on shift and I am thankful for the help. Her reaction is as staggering as Carmen's when she lays eyes on Dorian, and a little grin creeps onto my face. After the lunch rush, I send Carmen on her break, even though we are still pretty busy.

"I'll help," Dorian says after I assure Carmen half a dozen times that we'll be fine for an hour without her.

I look at him with a questioning brow. "Um, you? Have you ever done retail? Or even worked a regular job? Ever?"

A wide, animated grin spreads across his gorgeous face. "Nope.

But I think I could handle it. I'm a *very* hard worker," he breathes seductively. *Mmmm, very hard, indeed.*

I am painfully aware of Amy's eyes on us, puzzled by our casual exchange. She doesn't know about our relationship and I intend to keep it that way.

"Ok, Mr. Skotos. Let me know if there's anything I can help you with."

I try to put some distance between us, diverting my attention to a new display of edgy, skull-adorned baubles from a local designer. I know he's probably scowling at my back right now, but he doesn't get a chance to stew for too long before he is bum-rushed with a barrage of hopeless female consumers who buy any and everything he touches.

Once Carmen has returned and sales have slowed a bit, Dorian requests to speak to me in private about some paperwork. As soon as we enter the office, he locks the door.

"So what the hell was that about?" he questions, leaning casually against the door.

"Dorian, please don't tell me you're seriously upset. I don't want people to think that I got this job just because we're fucking. That's tacky."

Dorian's face suddenly twists up in a violent sneer, his eyes darkening into a menacing glower, yet his eyes are bright and raging. *Oh shit.* I've offended him.

"*Fucking?*" he hisses. "I tell you that I would lay down my life for you and that translates as just *fucking*?" His body slowly lurches towards me in an inhuman way, as if he has no bones or joints to constrict his twisted movements.

Shit. I really have a way with words. "I didn't mean it like that! *I* know what we have, but it will be perceived as just me screwing my way up the ladder." Tentatively, I reach my hand towards him, letting my fingertips stroke the base of his jaw. I'm not afraid of the monster inside of him anymore. I know it's a part of who he is and I'll never be able to change that. Not to mention that my own inner demon could be substantially more venomous. "I hate it as much as you do. I've wanted to touch you all day."

Dorian cages the vicious beast, letting the charming, alluring man I know and love resurface. "You have no idea how hard it has been to keep my hands off you." He bites his bottom lip, nestling into my touch before pulling me towards him by the small of my back. "I don't like you hiding what you are to me. I don't give a damn what people think."

"But I do," I say against his hard chest. "I want to be taken seriously. I want to earn their respect."

"Hmmm. Noble. Yet not good enough for me. I want them to know. And because you've made me so angry, I can only think of one way for you to pay for your misdeeds."

My head snaps up to meet his smoldering gaze and I register exactly what he means. Before I know it, I am bent over the desk and my dress is raised over my ass.

"Hey! Dorian, what the hell are you doing?" I whisper fiercely.

"I'm going to fuck you, little girl," he grits, kneading my backside. "Since that's what you think we've been doing all this time."

"I didn't mean it like that! Oh God, Dorian, they'll hear us!" Even with the store's stereo system blaring, there's no way we could be discreet, considering how *spirited* we both can be. Sex with Dorian is always so dynamic. I wouldn't have it any other way.

I hear the familiar sounds of his belt and zipper, and heat instantly pools and pulses between my legs. *Dammit!* His lips are on my ear, nibbling gently, his cool breath sending shivers down my spine.

"That's the point. I want them all to know just how good I make you feel. Just how much your body craves this." He nudges his hardness against my ass. "Just how hard you come when I live inside you."

Holy shit! As if my body could betray me any further, I am suddenly dripping wet, panting feverishly as I steady myself against the desk. I feel the hard thickness of him slap the top of my lace-clad ass as he slides his slacks down to his ankles. He quickly relinquishes me of my panties and I hurriedly step out of them.

"Please," I beg in a breathy voice. "I don't think I can be quiet. I want you too bad."

Dorian strokes the searing fire between my legs and I unsuccessfully muffle a moan. "Good. I want to hear you. I want you to scream my fucking name," he says between gritted teeth. "You need to remember who I am. Remember who *owns* this."

Dorian parts my legs wider by inserting his knee between them, still stroking my throbbing swell with precision. He slips a finger inside of me, and I bite my lip to refrain from crying out his praises. He stirs my insides, fingering my walls, feeling them contract and quiver around him.

"Baby, you are so wet for me." To my dismay, he removes it and I hear the sounds of sucking. "Mmmm, you taste so sweet." Again, Dorian slides the finger inside of me, repeating the delightful torment, causing me to grind against his single digit. He removes his finger, and places it in front of my face. "Suck," he demands.

The fuck?

I look at his long, agile finger, glistening with my own nectar. I bite my lip apprehensively before Dorian urges his finger into my mouth. *Oh what the hell*. I devour it, eagerly sucking it like it is Dorian on my tongue. Tasting my own juices only rouses me more and I begin to rub against him, yearning for him to fill me until I burst.

"Greedy little girl," Dorian mumbles in my ear as he takes his hand away. He brings it to my front, stirring my clit as he eases me into position. I feel his knees bend behind me as the head of his penis finds my soft slit.

With a penetrating thrust, Dorian is inside me, stretching my pink walls, digging into my core. As always, we moan in unison at the feeling, me relishing in the intense fullness, he stunned by the gloriously snug warmth. Dorian delivers deep, deliberate blow after blow, causing me to resort to biting my bottom lip to muffle my cries. My knees buckle and tremble with every impact yet Dorian steadies me by holding my hips, refusing to show me any mercy or restraint. I can't contain my moans any longer; I let them spill out in strained, garbled expletives and pleas to a higher power.

"That's right, baby. Tell me you love it," Dorian growls, quickening his pace. "Give it to me. Let go."

With a surprising roar of my own, I buck against him, the desk screeching with each powerful thrust. I want to give it to him. I want him to feel my insides shiver and become slick with my own lustful essence.

I feel his cool breath on my shoulder as a rush of foreign babble falls from his lips. It's Greek. Freakin' Greek. *Holy hell!* Though I can't understand him, it's incredibly erotic and only heightens our carnal frenzy. A hand releases my hip and I feel it around the base of my throat, applying more and more pressure with every hard stroke while he continues the foreign chant in my ear. The room is spinning and my eyes roll to the back of my head. My limbs are like jelly yet I still meet him thrust for thrust, encouraging him to take me even harder.

"*Don't stop don't stop don't stop*," I croak through the tightness at my neck, gripping his hips behind me to motivate each thrust. I'm so close I can taste it. And I want it hard, rough and wonderfully brutal.

"Ah! *Fuck!*" Dorian calls out loudly, releasing my neck and pounding me from behind ruthlessly as he succumbs to his own overwhelming orgasm. Feeling his heat spurt into me takes me over the edge and I unravel instantly, calling his name with reverent praise and adulation.

"Shit," I mutter as we crumple to the ground, both of us spent and sated from our ear-splitting orgasms. Regrettably, he slips out of me but I'm too weak to protest. "I know they heard us."

Dorian chuckles at my horrifying humiliation. I weakly turn my head to scowl at him. "It's not funny, Dorian! Customers probably heard us! *Oh God oh God*!"

"Relax, Gabriella," he chortles.

"Relax? How the hell can I relax? *Shit, shit, shit!* How could I have been so stupid?" I cover my face with my damp arm in shame. *I might as well take a bow and accept the award for Slore of the Year.*

"Hey," Dorian coos, gently pushing my arm away and pulling my face towards his. His eyes are filled with warmth and ardor, immediately comforting my troubled ego. "Seriously. I took care of it. The room is spelled to be sound proof. They didn't hear a thing."

I look at Dorian in disbelief, unsure if I should be upset or elated. Before I can decide on an appropriate reaction, he's on his feet, tugging me up onto mine. My legs are still quite shaky balancing on my wedge heeled sandals so I steady myself on the desk which has been scooted at least six inches from its original spot. Dorian bends down to grab my panties, holding them out so I can step in them carefully. He then tucks in his shirt and fastens his pants.

"Now that's out of the way, I do have some paperwork for you to sign." He picks up a packet of papers from off the desk and points to a field requiring a signature. "Sign here," he says handing me a pen.

"What's this?"

Dorian shakes his head nonchalantly. "Just some documents renegotiating your position here now that I own it in full. Nothing you need to ultimately worry about now." He flashes me a dazzling smile and I nearly melt at how insanely beautiful and happy he looks. Reluctantly, I tear my eyes from his face just long enough to scrawl my name. "And here and here," he says flipping through a few more pages.

I do as he requests then look up at him and shake my head. "Always business and pleasure with you, huh?"

"Why have one or the other when you can have both?" he winks. "Now let's get you fed."

We walk down to a little old-fashioned diner about a block away and indulge in burgers, fries and milkshakes. Of course, the milkshakes are Dorian's favorite part and I giggle jovially at his attempt to suck down the thick froth without getting a brain-freeze.

"Geez, all that power, and you haven't figured out a way to combat *that*?" I laugh.

Dorian presses his hand against his forehead and squints his eyes tightly. "You're right. Pretty damn pathetic."

After lunch, Dorian asks me to walk down to Luxe with him so he can check on something. I gladly oblige, more than happy to get a chance to see Morgan as well as Carlos and Jackson. Those guys are always a riot and I make a mental note to invite them to our next tequila-inspired karaoke night. *Oh, the costumes!* I can only imagine. As we turn on the street that houses the salon, Dorian stops me in my tracks.

"Shit. There's someone in the salon." His brow furrows in annoyance. "*Fucking Light*."

"Do you know who?"

Dorian shakes his head, his eyes narrowing in concentration as if he's trying to pick up some unknown signal. "No. Stay by me. Don't touch anyone."

"Should I just stay outside?"

Dorian looks at me incredulously, all of the good humor he exuded just seconds ago nowhere in sight. "Hell no. Absolutely not. I am a Skotos. *We* are to be feared. We never back down or run away from anything. Ever."

He intertwines his fingers with mine and gives me a stiff tug towards the salon, his body humming, almost vibrating with tension. A low murmur escapes his lips but I can't make out what he's saying. I can tell Dorian is furious, maybe even a little nervous, but his pride won't let him show it. It's the first time I've ever seen him embrace the weight of his family's credo.

We enter the salon with the usual flourish that accompanies us whenever I am with Dorian. It's impossible for anyone, man or woman, to not stop and stare at his exotic splendor. My stomach is snarled with apprehension and uncertainty, yet I am oddly elated at being in the presence of the Light, though I would have no idea who it could be. Would they be ridiculously beautiful like Dorian, and even Aurora? I wouldn't be surprised, considering how stunning Natalia was.

"Gabs! Dorian! What brings you two here?" Morgan exclaims as we approach. Sitting in the sleek stylist's chair at her station sits a middle aged woman who I see has requested a severe, trendy cut with blunt, straight bangs. Her eyes are glued on Dorian, her mouth forming an 'O' in admiration.

"Just hanging out. How's everything going?" I try my hardest to seem passive but I am anxiously scanning the large room for any sign of the Light. Dorian squeezes my hand gently, noticing my distraction. He still appears impassive though the tiny furrow of his brow tells me that he is deep in concentration.

"Oooh, *mija*, I know you better come over here and speak to me!" I hear from behind us. We turn around to see Carlos, a hand on his narrow hip, smiling at me brightly.

"Carlos!" I beam. We cross the room to greet him but when I try to advance further to give him a hug, Dorian stops me before I can take another step.

"Mr. Skotos, good to see you," he says with a nod. Dorian returns the gesture politely before returning to the task of scanning the room with cold, trained eyes. When he isn't looking, Carlos mouths gestures between us with enthusiasm, mouthing, *"You're together?"* I blush scarlet and nod gracefully, receiving a sassy snap and a head swing from Carlos in response.

Jackson joins us, looking statuesque in platform heeled boots to accompany the all-black attire that is the salon's dress code. His platinum blonde hair is radiant and makes him look devilishly angelic. *Omg, is he Light?* He is certainly attractive enough. I stealthily give Dorian a sideways glance, only to see a subtle head shake in response. *Of course not.* Dorian would know.

Jackson gives me a brilliant smile, showcasing his gleaming white, perfect teeth. He has got to be the prettiest man I've ever seen aside from Dorian. "I just want to come over and say hi, babe," he purrs. "X is back at my station; stop by. I know he'd love to see you."

I see Jackson whisper something to Carlos and look at me. Carlos nods excitedly, causing Jackson to flash me a wink. He grabs a pair of shears from Carlos's station before waving at both Dorian and I and returning to his task.

"So, anyway," Carlos says hands still propped on his hips. "My birthday is this Friday and we're having a little party down at that new club Aria. I really want you to come. Both of you," he smiles.

I look up at Dorian hopefully, and am pleasantly surprised when he nods his approval. "Carlos, we'd love to," I say. I would have gone without him, but having Dorian by my side doesn't hurt.

"Great! Bring whoever you want; the more the merrier. And be ready to party because you know how we do!" he cackles.

Dorian hurriedly ushers me to his back office, giving me only a few seconds to stop and greet Xavier as Jackson cuts his chocolate brown hair into a stylish yet conservative style.

"So anything?" I ask once we are alone.

Dorian shakes his head and purses his lips in frustration. Other than Morgan, Carlos, Jackson, and Xavier, I didn't recognize any of the other stylists or clientele. And most of them were too obviously enraptured with Dorian's beauty to seem put off or defensive.

"But are you sure about Jackson? I mean, look at him. *That* can't be natural."

"No, Gabriella. He's human."

I tap my foot, trying to remember the faces of each client. "Oooh! Maybe the lady with the miniature dog. Aren't the Light supposed to be animal lovers or something?"

Dorian shakes his head once again, walking to the desk to rifle through a pamphlet of papers. "No."

"Or what about-"

"Dammit, Gabriella! I don't fucking know who it is!" Dorian shouts before I can complete my thought. He glares at me through cold, wrathful eyes, obviously infuriated by my line of questioning. "Just shut up so I can think for a second. *Shit*."

I do as I'm told and am compliantly silent, disgusted both with myself for obliging to his demands without resistance, and with him for treating me like a misbehaved delinquent. I would never take this from anybody else. Not even Jared. So why am I backing down now? Why am I letting Dorian disrespect and belittle me without even so much as an eye roll? What is happening to me? Has Dorian finally sexed me into stupefied submission?

The walk back to Cashmere is painfully quiet and tense, only making me more aware of my dejected spirit coupled with Dorian's intense rage. Hard to believe that less than an hour ago, Dorian had me bent over my desk, showing me just how deep his love goes. Now there is only disdain and aggravation etched in his face.

"I think you should go," I say to him a few storefronts down from Cashmere.

Dorian exhales his irritation in a sharp huff and looks away, shaking his head in disbelief of my pettiness. "Don't be ridiculous. I'll stay until the end of your shift."

"No. You should go," I insist. "We'll talk later."

Dorian slightly softens his rigid expression, hoping to coax me into seeing things his way. "I need to be here with you. I need to protect you."

"Protect me from what?" I snap angrily. "Because all I see is you chasing a ghost and treating me like shit because you feel inadequate. How can you help me when you can't even help yourself? Hell, your own dad wants you dead. Maybe *you're* the one who needs protection. Go home, Dorian. I don't want or need you here."

I turn on my heel and march to the boutique and don't stop until I'm nestled safely inside the solace of my office. I flop into the swivel chair and let my ragged shoulders fall in defeat. I'm angry, frustrated, and hurt, yet I have no one to blame but myself. Only Dorian can wound me like this, stripping me bare of my strength and rebellion, because I've let him penetrate the parts of me that I've kept safeguarded for so long. Only he can push me to that place that causes me to speak so cruelly out of hurt and anger, revealing just how extremely immature I truly am.

What the hell is wrong with me? What have I just done?

Dorian confided in me and I didn't hesitate to use his deepest secrets as ammunition. He'll never forgive me; *I'll* never forgive myself. He must think I am just some petty, selfish, reckless child, and he wouldn't be far off. He will see me for what I truly am, not the person I have wanted to be since the day I met him. Someone that is worthy of his affections. Even without the link that ties our lives together, his disapproval kills me.

I come home later that evening, half expecting to find Dorian waiting in my room but come up disappointed. Part of me is relieved; I'm not ready to face him or admit the power he has over me. Yet the honest part of me is suffering inside, feeling weak and depleted. I still want him, even though he has demeaned me, and I hate myself for feeling that way. I need him to feel safe, to feel whole. But why would he come here after what I've said to him? I pretty much told him that he's failed me, making me just another person in his life that sees him as a disappointment.

Once again, my big mouth has hurt someone that I love. And even if Dorian hurt me first, there's no excuse for what I've said. I am no better than his father. No, actually I'm worse. I knew how to hurt Dorian, I knew what triggers took him to his dark place, and I did it anyway.

TWELVE

The next few days pass excruciatingly slow, a little piece of me dying with each day without Dorian. I know I should call him but my pride–well, what's left of it–along with sheer humiliation, won't let me. If he wanted to see me, he'd be here. The looming truth that Dorian has finally seen me for what I really am and would rather do without the headache is unbearable. But I can't fault him; he deserves so much more than me. Regardless of what he is, regardless of his past, he is perfect in every way.

After a tortuous sleep that I eventually aided with an entire bottle of red wine, I awaken Thursday morning feeling confused and anguished. My head is pounding and my body feels like it's been dipped in cement. Dorian still hasn't called nor texted and my mind is beginning to sprout painful musings of him running to Aurora's waiting arms and warm bed.

Maybe this is it. Maybe Dorian has had enough of me and my childish ways. He didn't deserve that considering he's devoted his life to protecting me. Yet, because I was feeling irrational and scorned, I had to have the last word. I had to make him feel as demoralized as he made me feel. Right or wrong, I took it too far, and I am dreadfully afraid that I've pushed him away for good.

Luckily it's my day off, so I slowly nurse my hangover, watching bad TV and eating junk in bed. I'm in a dark place; I can feel myself slowly ticking towards self-destruction. Even with the faint remains of my alcohol-induced headache, all I want to do is drink until I can't feel anymore. It's only noon but I head to the kitchen to pour myself a shot of tequila and grab a cold beer to chase it.

With Morgan at work, the apartment seems cold and desolate,

yet I feel like I'm suffocating, the feelings of loneliness and remorse tightly gripping my chest. I have to get out of here; the longer I stay, the more I'll have to *feel*. I down my shot, letting the hot, burning liquid scorch my aching chest. Then I pick up the phone. There's only one person who could begin to ease my discontentment.

"Hey Jared, what's up, buddy?" I say after he picks up after two rings.

"Gabs! Didn't expect to hear from you! I'm glad you called," he says cheerfully.

Jared. Always a breath of fresh air. His sincerity instantly begins to soothe my troubled soul. "I wanted to see if you were busy today. It's my day off, and I was hoping we could hang." Translation: *I was hoping you could help me forget what a massive screw up I am.*

"Really?" he replies incredulously. "You want to spend your day off with me? Not Dorian?"

Crap. Of course he'd bring him up, causing the tightness in my chest to return with a vengeance. I take a deep breath, trying to level my shaky voice despite the large lump in my throat. "No. I want to spend it with you," I say, hoping he can't detect any sign of suffering.

"Ok," he says cautiously. He knows there's more to it than what I'm giving away. "Where do you wanna meet up?"

"Um, actually, would you mind coming to pick me up? I've already been drinking."

A long beat passes before Jared speaks again. "You ok?" He knows me better than anyone else and I can't hide from him. Yet, he also knows when not to press the issue with a barrage of judgments and questions.

"I will be. See you in half an hour?"

After downing my beer, I rummage through my closet in search of something to wear. I don't even feel like getting dressed at this point but I couldn't subject Jared to the embarrassment of having to be seen with me in pajama pants and a t-shirt. I decide on jeans, a charcoal grey tank and black flip flops. It's not much better than my

PJs but at least I've taken the time to comb my unruly hair. Before Jared arrives, I take another shot of tequila to ward off the threat of melancholy that keeps trying to creep its way to the surface. He's punctual as always, and I instantly notice the worry etched in his face when I open the front door.

"Don't," is all I say shaking my head. I don't want his concern; I don't deserve it. I grab my purse, and we head for his car in tense silence.

"Where to?" Jared asks once we are on the road, headed towards Academy Boulevard.

"Just drive. I'll tell you when I see it," I respond.

I see Jared's CD booklet, housing his music collection. I flip through until I find what I'm looking for before ejecting The Script, singing a heartfelt melody. I can't hear this, not now when I am trying so hard to hold it together. I pop in Eminem, knowing that only he could relate to my afflicted state of mind.

I instruct Jared to pull into the first tattoo parlor we see. He looks over at me with hesitation and question in his eyes.

"My treat," I say opening the passenger side door. Lord knows I can afford it since I started working at Cashmere. Thanks to Dorian, my salary as a store manager rivals that of a CEO of a major corporation.

Dorian. Just thinking about him causes me to gasp in agonized desperation. I can literally feel my heart splintering, sharp little shards poking me in the chest.

"Gabs, I just hope you know what you're doing," Jared says, opening the door to the shop for me. *Always a perfect gentleman.* Even though I am far from a prim and proper lady.

"I do too," I smile weakly.

Jared and I flip through dozens of giant photo albums in search of body art. He has a few random pieces already and has taken me up on my offer for some new ink. He's chosen to get a tribute piece to mark Tammy's miraculous recovery. I honestly have no idea what I want which is no surprise.

“So things are kinda rocky with Dorian?” Jared casually asks about thirty minutes into our search.

“You could say that,” I sigh. “We got into a fight. Well, he said something that upset me and I let him have it. I really went too far. Now I’m afraid he’ll never speak to me again.”

Jared nods, knowing the routine all too well. I don’t let myself just hurt; I get angry. And when I’m angry, I see red, unable to control whatever venom falls from my tongue. Then the damage is done. And rather than trying to mend the broken relationship, I simply punish myself for my misstep, too ashamed to face my mistakes and the real issues festering within me. Unfortunately, the people that I love the most are usually in the line of fire. If it weren’t for my family and the few friends I actually do have refusing to give up on me, I would have pushed them away years ago rather than reveal just how insecure and broken I really am.

“You really do love him,” Jared remarks.

I take a deep breath, feeling a swell of emotion rise in my chest. “Yes. So much.”

“Then it will be ok. He’ll forgive you. You’re worth it, Gabs,” he smiles warmly.

I struggle to return his sentiment then return my attention back to the book. A grouping of eight photos grabs my attention and I nearly drop the album.

“What’s wrong, Gabs?” Jared asks, gauging my startled reaction. “You look like you just saw a ghost.”

I shake my head, unable to verbalize my shock and horror. Just then, the tattooed receptionist walks by and I wave her down.

“Excuse me, who received these tattoos?”

The young lady, who looks more like a 50s pin-up girl with her jet black hair and red lips, takes a closer look at the collection I’m pointing to with a shaky finger. “Uh, I think it was a group of some Emo kids a while ago. I remember because they were really odd, kinda freaked me out. Since then, not too many people have asked for them. Is this what you want?”

"No, thank you," I respond. "Just wondering."

Once she returns to her station, I pull out my phone and take a picture of the page. I take a long look at each word, fashioned in what I assume is ancient Greek. I touch each one, feeling somewhat drawn to them, connected to the exotic scrawl. Under each photo of foreign characters etched on pale skin is the phonetic translation.

Algea
Apatē
Thanatos
Mīsos
Oinos
Polemos
Órexis
Skotos

"That looks like Aurora's last name. And isn't Skotos Dorian's last name?" Jared asks casually while orchestrating a text message on his cell phone. Luckily, he's been so wrapped up in his task that he still hasn't caught on to my anxiety. I nod and quickly flip to the next page to avoid further questions. I couldn't explain it even if I tried.

Once Jared and I are each in an artist's chair, I mentally prepare myself for my first tattoo, a lotus blossom accented with feminine filigree extending from the nape of my neck, down my spine and ending at the middle of my back. It's a beautiful piece and though I've opted to do without the vibrant pinks and greens in the photo, it still evokes feelings of serenity and peace, exactly what I so desperately want to channel. Reluctantly, I remove my shirt and unsnap my bra, then carefully shield my breasts as I turn to sit backwards on the reclining chair.

"Pretty big piece for a first timer," the bearded artist warns before touching my unmarked skin with the buzzing needle of the tattoo gun. "This'll hurt."

I turn my head a fraction to look him in his eyes, demonstrating my absolute certainty. “Good.”

Hours later, we emerge from the shop bandaged, sore and starving. We stop at a drive thru to grab some fast food before heading back to Paralia to eat. I am anxious to get home, hopeful that Dorian is finally ready to make amends but am once again disappointed when I discover my empty bedroom. The stinging on my back pales in comparison to the radiating ache in my chest. Being without him is unbearable. The only inkling of hope I have to hold onto is the fact that I’m still alive. He still loves me.

Morgan surfaces from her bedroom wearing a spicy red minidress and heels, her long weave fashioned into a bun atop of her head.

“Hey, I got you some food, but looks like you’ve got plans,” I remark from the carpeted living room floor where we’ve decided to eat our chicken strips and fries.

“Yeah, I’ve got a date. Don’t wait up,” she winks, grabbing her clutch purse and heading out.

“I can stay,” Jared says once we are alone.

“No. I’ll be fine.” He’s been texting all day, surely with Aurora, and has already given me so much of his time. There’s no telling what plans he had to bail on to come rescue me from myself.

After repeatedly assuring him that I won’t go off the deep end and drink myself stupid, Jared leaves to meet up with Aurora. I’m alone once again with my overwhelming guilt and remorse. I head to the cabinet to pour myself a drink and down three shots without blinking, desperately trying to squelch the rising urge to cry. Then I carefully bathe before climbing into bed and praying for the crippling pain that reaches to the depths of my core to subside.

I feel the soft, white sand between my toes, little granules glistening like tiny diamonds in the sunlight. The sun feels heavenly, heating my bare back like a warm, feather-light blanket. The sounds of crashing waves combined with the fresh, salty smell of seawater piques my memory. I've been here before. My eyes are closed, heavy with relaxation but I know where I am.

Skiathos.

I'm alone again, but I don't feel lonely. I'm not afraid of this unknown, exotic land. I feel oddly comfortable here. I feel at home. I want to turn over onto my back so I can look up at the clear blue skies, but my body is so heavy and fatigued. And the sand is so soft and warm, I just can't bring myself to disturb this perfect moment.

Suddenly, a cool, tingling sensation runs up and down my spine, causing me to lightly shiver. The contrast of the hot sun coupled with the coldness is delightfully titillating. I moan reflexively as the tingles spread out towards every nerve ending, igniting my carnal senses.

"I love you, little girl," a velvety smooth voice murmurs in my ear. It's a voice I know, a voice I want to hear for the rest of my life.

Dorian.

I force my heavy eyelids to flutter open to find the source of the angelic voice but am greeted with darkness instead. I am no longer on the beach. I am in my bedroom. However, I can still feel the icy tingles kissing my back and I lift my head in response. He's here, tracing the outline of my tattoo with a single cool finger. I can't see the expression on his face, only the twinkling depths of his azure eyes. Emotion instantly floods my chest, erupting into a strained sob.

"Dorian," I choke, feeling hot tears pool in my tired eyes. The response startles him and he quickly kneels to meet my gaze.

"I'm here. Are you hurt?" he questions worriedly.

I don't say a word. I'm afraid that if I do, he will disappear. I simply turn from my stomach onto my side and pull him onto the bed with me. He willingly obliges and we lay face to face, silently relishing the comfort of closeness. I let the cool freshness of his scent envelop me, the soft pads of his fingers wiping away my tears.

Having him here now makes me realize just how broken I was without him. Now I can *breathe.* Each of his touches strips away the anguish that was strangling me, draining the life right out of me. It's now more apparent than ever that I can't live without him.

"I'm sorry," I finally say, once I am certain that I can contain myself.

I feel Dorian shift as if he's shaking his head. "Don't be. I shouldn't have spoken to you in that manner. Forgive me. And you were right."

"No, I wasn't. I was absolutely wrong to say those things. I hate myself for it." I lift my hand to stroke Dorian's stubble-laden cheek. He nestles into the touch and inhales, breathing my essence. He needs me just as much as I need him. "I never want to fight again. I never want to be without you."

"You won't," he breathes. "I'll never leave you, Gabriella. I never did."

Dorian's fingers drift from my face down the curve of my side, making me remember that I've gone to bed topless to allow my tattoo to heal. My free hand flies up to my breasts reflexively yet Dorian quickly pulls it back down.

"Don't ever hide from me. I love you, every inch of you, inside and out. You never have to shield your body. Or your heart."

Dorian can see right through me, straight to my core. He knows the insecure, scared feelings I harbor deep inside. He knows my darkest secrets, my deepest regrets. He lives in me.

"I'll never forgive myself for what I've done." I whisper. "I hate myself for hurting you."

I feel Dorian smile against my hand. "I've lived through worse, little girl."

"But not from me. I never want to be the source of your pain. I don't want to be that person anymore–always so defensive, expecting for someone to hurt me. I don't want to push you away."

"You won't. You can't. I've been waiting my entire life to love you," he says before placing a soft kiss on the inside of my palm.

My heart warms at his admission, carefully falling back into place, jagged shard by shard. And with that, I close the small distance between us and nestle into his arms, the only place I'll ever want to be.

When we awaken Friday morning, I am still tightly secured in Dorian's arms, chest to chest. We spent the entire night talking, kissing, and feeling the warmth of each other's bodies. I wanted to feel him entirely, wanted him to make love to me but he refused until my back healed a bit. Plus it was nice just being together again, knowing that more than sex binds us. Along with his incredible body, he truly has the most beautiful soul.

"Good morning, little girl," Dorian murmurs in my hair.

"How do you always know when I'm awake?" I giggle against his skin. It always smells so wonderful, so refreshing.

Dorian leaves a kiss on the crown of my head. "That beautiful brain of yours."

Reluctantly, I wriggle out of his hold to trot to the bathroom. I'm dressed in only yellow striped flannel boxer shorts and can't help but blush as Dorian watches me cross the room with desire burning in his smoldering eyes. After relieving my bladder of last night's tequila and brushing my teeth, I reemerge and giddily flop back onto the bed. Dorian inspects my back in the daylight, though I'm certain he could see it perfectly fine in the dark.

"Do you like it?" I ask timidly.

"I do. It suits you." He leans forward and kisses the tender skin around it, his cool lips soothing the soreness. "Very sexy."

"*Mmmm*," I moan. Even the slightest touch makes my body quiver.

"Don't do that. If you start making those kinds of sounds, I won't be able to stop. I know you're sore. I don't want to hurt you."

I look up at Dorian solemnly. "That pain is nothing in comparison to how I felt these past few days. Not because you hurt me, but because I hurt you. I want it to hurt. I want to suffer for what I've done."

He cocks his head to one side and gives me a crooked smile. "Gabriella, the only pain I felt was the agonizing feeling that I had lost you. Nothing else matters to me. Knowing I could only watch you as you slept, knowing I couldn't touch you, kiss you, be inside you . . . It destroyed me. Last night, I couldn't stay away. I was too weak for you. I had to touch you, feel your skin against mine."

I sit up and straddle his lap, pressing my lips against his. Dorian instantly responds, pulling me closer into him by my backside. His skilled tongue delves into my mouth, massaging, tasting, teasing. My bare swollen breasts ache against his chiseled chest, longing to be touched and fondled. I can feel the swell of his erection under his slacks jabbing my sensitive flesh. I want him now, and I don't care if it hurts. Just as my hands fumble to undo his fly, I feel an unwelcomed vibration in his pants pocket. *You've got to be kidding me!*

I ease back just far enough for Dorian to fish out his cell. He hits the Talk button and gives an exasperated greeting then listens contently. I suddenly remember the picture I took with my own phone and hop off his lap to retrieve it despite his puppy dog faced plea for me to stay.

"Look what I found at the tattoo parlor," I say, handing him the phone once he's done with his call.

Dorian studies the picture for a beat then his unreadable eyes meet mine. "*Humph.* Humans."

"The lady there told me that some random guys each got them. How would they know? And what are these other names?"

Dorian sighs and rubs his eyes as if he's suddenly grown weary. "There were 8 original Dark families, supposedly the very first clans of the Dark which spawned all other clans. Over time, of course many more were birthed, but it is believed that we are the purest, most powerful of all the Dark. Each family is influential in their own right, the Skotos obviously being the most dominant."

“So these eight families, are they the noble families in Greece?” I sit up on my knees, totally engrossed in the subject, hanging on to Dorian’s every word. This is my heritage too. My father was Polemos.

“Yes. It is rumored that they are responsible for the corruption of the Dark.” Dorian runs his hand through his sexy disheveled hair. “I’m not entirely sure how humans got ahold of this information, but I’m not surprised. Myths can easily reflect truth. I’ve been . . . out of the loop, so to speak, for the last twenty years. Apparently, changes have been made.”

Right. Dorian’s petrification was only reversed so he could hunt and kill me. Who knows what he awoke to find. “What do you think this means?”

Dorian shrugs. “I can’t say. There’s been a breach, that’s for sure. Whether or not it was intentional is the question.” I can see the subject has aged him, his brow furrowed in deliberation. I smile at him brightly and plant a kiss on his soft lips, hoping to restore his pleasant mood. It works. “Get dressed. I’m going to take you to work then I have some business to attend to. I’ll be back in time to take you to lunch.”

Business at Cashmere is steady, and I happily jump into helping customers and rearranging displays, a welcomed change from my melancholy demeanor in the past days. Once it slows a bit, I take a moment to peruse the racks for something hot to wear for Carlos’s birthday party later tonight. I had totally forgotten about it until Morgan mentioned it over coffee this morning. She, too, seemed oddly chipper, indicating that her date the evening before was successful. I wanted to ask her who the mystery man was but didn’t want to put her on the spot in front of Dorian. Before I can think too much about it or complete my search for a dress, Carmen asks me to sign for a delivery.

“It’s addressed to you,” she says, observing the black jacquard box adorned with an elaborate red bow.

I shrug my shoulders and take the small package back to my

office to inspect. Probably a few sample pieces from a new designer who wants a little extra credit for flair. After I've successfully unraveled the bow and open the box, I find something else entirely. An all-white jeweled string bikini sits amidst a sea of black tissue paper. It's absolutely gorgeous, yet I already knew that it would be. I've worn this bikini before. In my dream. The dream the Dark King gave me.

Resting on top of the sexy swimwear is a white note card. I take a deep breath and turn it over to read.

The lotus flower–a symbol of sacred beauty through adversity. Purity. Rebirth.

Congratulations on embracing the true goddess within you.

-Stavros

"How very convenient," a voice mutters from behind me.

I spin around, clutching my chest, the note still gripped tightly in my hand. "Dorian!" I shriek. "When did you get here?" He obviously didn't come through the door.

He holds his hand out, requesting the notecard and ignoring my question. I look back down at it, contemplating scrapping it to save us the drama but reluctantly hand it over. Dorian studies it with an unreadable expression, showing no signs of discontent or irritation. The momentary flash of his crystal blue eyes is the only sign of reaction at all. He sets the card on the desk then mutters something in Greek, *'Stavros'* being the only word I'm able to decipher in his heavy accent. Even in this heated moment, it arouses me fiercely.

"Your father?" I finally mumble after a few tense moments of silence. Dorian's eyes meet mine, and I receive the answer to my question, his irises icy and cold with ire. *Crap.* Can we go one day without him losing his shit about something?

I force a stiff smile of reassurance. "I'll get rid of it. Not my style anyway."

"No. It was a gift," he mutters. "You should keep it. It would look incredible on you." His cool hand strokes my cheek delicately. He's trying desperately to reel in his anger.

"Thanks, but no thanks. I do feel like I should send him a thank you note though. Do you know where I could send it?"

Dorian's brow furrows a bit, unable to mask his surprise and confusion. Then something else reads across his beautiful face. Resignation. He nods in defeat.

"Good!" I beam. I pull out a sheet of stationary and begin to fashion my letter of gratitude to Dorian's persistently vile father.

Stavros,

Thank you for the swimsuit; it is beautiful. However, I can't and won't accept gifts from you or anyone else. I am pretty crazy in love with your son, Dorian. Him and only him. And there is nothing that you could ever give me that I don't already have in him. So please, don't waste your money or your time.

Sincerely,

Gabriella

I fold the piece of paper in half and place it in the box followed by the elaborate box top. "Please be sure he gets this," I say handing it over to Dorian, who looks somewhat bemused.

"You don't have to do that. I'm serious," he insists. "I'm sure this will make him very angry. Probably provoke him to do something rash."

"And would that bother you?"

Dorian takes a beat to think about it before giving me a sexy half-smile. "Not in the least."

THIRTEEN

By 10 PM, I am dressed and ready to head out to Carlos's birthday celebration at Aria. I'm literally running on fumes, having worked a full day from opening to close at Cashmere, not to mention extremely sexually frustrated. Dorian still has not put out the flame burning deep between my thighs, and I'm starting to think he's still punishing me for our fight earlier in the week. I can't think like that; the immense guilt may creep back in, causing me to tumble back into a state of depression. And I have so much to be thankful for right now.

Dorian shows up at my apartment, eyes alight with the same carnal craving that's eating me alive. He looks devilishly dashing in charcoal grey designer jeans, a white dress shirt with sleeves rolled to his elbows, skinny silk tie and a black vest, all tailored to accentuate his remarkable build. He is by far the best dressed man I have ever seen, looking more male model than ruthless assassin. His perfectly chaotic black locks and the bit of rugged stubble scream bad boy meets business, making my ache for him even more unbearable. I want him now, and won't hesitate to pull up my strapless silver and black foil shirred dress for easier access.

"You look incredible, baby," he coos in my ear, placing a soft kiss just below my earlobe. It's enough to drive me absolutely mad.

"You too. Is it a coincidence that we match?" I ask with a raised eyebrow. Sheesh, who knew we would be one of *those* couples?

Dorian gives me a wink of his smoldering eye, and bites his bottom lip. Yes, he must be just as affected. The prospect of actually making it to this birthday party is looking slimmer by the second.

"Either you're going to take me back in that bedroom and give me a proper ruining or we need to leave," I say with a hand perched on my curvy hip. I would skip the affair altogether had I not promised Morgan I would be there before she left with Miguel.

Dorian grabs my hand, intertwining our fingers, and leads me out to his gleaming black Mercedes. As we cruise east towards Powers Boulevard, the sensual sounds of Usher radiating from the speakers, the pulsing down below becomes amplified in the confined space. I need him like I need air. Just something to ease the intense yearning for him.

"I know, baby," he breathes.

That's it. I can't take this anymore. With lustful fervor, I undo my seatbelt then lean over to anxiously unfasten his belt buckle, causing Dorian to nearly yelp in surprise at my spontaneity. I hurriedly undo the fly if his jeans, feeling the heat radiating from the hardened bulge begging to be relinquished. My eyes grow wide with excitement as I unleash his rock hard erection, feeling it pulse in my hands. I'm so *hungry* for him, I can't wait any longer. I take him in my mouth, hearing a grateful sigh at the feeling of my wet tongue. I pull back, sucking, swirling it with my tongue before sliding back down to the back of my throat. I wish I could savor every luscious inch of him, yet his substantial size makes it impossible. Over and over, I suckle and lick, letting my hands stroke the sensitive parts of him that my mouth can't reach. He moans approvingly, his fingers gently massaging my scalp. They slide down to my breasts, slipping inside of my dress, flicking and tugging my aching nipples. I moan against his flesh in my mouth, vibrating his swell, adding an extra element of pleasure.

"Ah, shit, baby, you're gonna make me . . ." Dorian breathes. He's panting, struggling to keep his eyes on the road, though his driving hasn't faltered in the least.

"No, don't," I command, coming up for air for just a second before resuming my relentless tongue-lashing and savoring the tiny trickles of sweet sap collecting at the tip.

"You're gonna make . . . Fuck, I'm gonna come, baby," he rasps, his breathing wild with sweet agony. His fingers continue to strum my hard nipples and I moan again, letting the vibrations shudder through him. I slow my pace, to avoid his unraveling, refusing to bring him to the brink that he so desperately needs, just like me.

Pleasing him only intensifies the burning inside me, the throb evolving into an uncontrollable quake. I squeeze my thighs together, fighting the urge to touch myself while I pleasure my impassioned lover. This is about him. This is my redemption.

Dorian swells and pulsates in my mouth, warning me that release is near. Reluctantly, I pull away, and sit up, leaving his burning hot, distended member standing upright in his lap. Dorian looks over at me incredulously, completely taken aback at what has transpired. Not only did I completely catch him off guard, which is not an easy feat by any means, I've left him hard as a rock and ready to explode. He's speechless, unable to articulate a single word now that every ounce of blood has traveled south of the border.

Wow. Dorian *flustered*? Now there's a first!

I casually pull the passenger side mirror down and fluff my hair, scooping it all to one side to hang over my shoulder before looking over at my disoriented lover.

"I'm sorry but you'll just have to wait until later. Sucks, doesn't it?" Pun *definitely* intended. "Here, let me help you with that."

I gently maneuver his still stiffened manhood into his pants with the very tips of my fingers, making it painfully clear that playtime is over. Carefully tucking in his shirt and refastening his pants, I flash him a naughty smile, catching a wicked look of his own.

"Oh little girl, you're going to regret that," Dorian mutters, pulling into the crowded parking lot.

I finish applying my shimmery nude lipgloss before smacking my pouty lips together and gazing back at him. "Bring it on."

Aria is a multi-level warehouse turned nightclub boasting raucous fun for the young and beautiful of all walks of life. It's not as posh and upscale as Shade, Dorian's restaurant and lounge in Breckenridge, but with its white couches, polished stainless steel tables, and pastel colored strobe lights, it definitely gives off a euphoric, almost angelic vibe. The DJ in the main room is spinning all the latest dance hits and the dance floor is already packed with girls showing too much skin in too high heels. Carlos has reserved a VIP section with a large white sectional and a long table packed with spirits, gifts and even a cake.

We approach the party hand in hand, a first for me in such a public place, and receive a barrage of surprised looks and smiles. How could people *not* react? Dorian looks even more drop dead sexy tonight, and knowing what has just transpired in the car ride just minutes before makes him that much more irresistible.

"Gabs! You guys came!" Carlos beams. He is in full diva mode with fire engine red tight leather pants, a matching leather vest adorned with small silver spikes, and heeled black boots. Even his red faux hawk seems to sparkle, going perfectly with the glittery black and silver makeup covering his eyelids. Carlos looks like some type of rock star superhero, and he is stunning.

"Of course! Happy birthday, Carlos!" I say giving him a hug and handing him a gift bag. It's a gold bottle of champagne that I'm sure rivals my monthly salary–courtesy of Dorian, of course–and a gift certificate to Cashmere. Though it's a women's clothing store, Carlos could and would work those threads better than most women.

"You are one lucky bitch!" Carlos whispers in my ear as we embrace. I laugh nervously as I look over his shoulder at Dorian who rolls his eyes playfully. Of course he heard; he hears everything.

We settle in with glasses of champagne, greeting our friends and mingling with party guests. Morgan looks ravishing in a metallic champagne colored halter dress, showing off her fabulous cleavage and long, gorgeous legs. She and Miguel are dancing intimately when she spots me and strolls over.

"What took you guys so long?" she shouts over the thumping bass-lines.

"Ugh, traffic totally blew," I say with a smile. I look over at Dorian and give him a wink. Let him hear *that*!

Everyone is having a great time drinking and dancing, even Aurora, who is oddly pleasant and not as annoyingly shrill. When Carlos and Jackson–who is rockin' the hell out of a tight tank and even tighter pants–pull all the girls on the dance floor for Beyonce's "Single Ladies," we all giggle and dance like best friends. The combination of champagne, positive vibes, and having Dorian gazing at me in admiration has got me on cloud 9. And for a moment, I pretend that we're just two normal people hanging out with friends and having fun. The thought brings an involuntary smile to my face. This is how life should be. I strut back over to him, eager to be back in his arms.

"Hmmm, this is fitting," Dorian murmurs, handing me a fresh glass of champagne just as Rihanna's "S&M" comes on, spinning a salacious tale of bad girls who like it rough.

"How so?" I ask, downing half my drink.

Dorian places his hand on the small of my back, letting his fingers slide up to meet my bare skin. I instantly feel the titillating tingles accompanied by his touch coursing through my body. "Because you like it. You like pain with your pleasure."

He's right, but I still play coy, hoping to prolong our little game. "And how would you know that?"

Answering my question, Dorian lets his hand travel farther north to the nape of my neck, right above the beginning of my healing tattoo. With a sudden jerk, he knots his hand in my hair, brusquely pulling me towards him so his mouth is on mine. I gasp in shock and at the sharp pain ripping through my scalp, giving his forceful tongue the leeway it needs to command my mouth. To an outsider, it looks like we are just two lovers sharing a tender kiss. However, the tight grip Dorian has on my hair, causing my head to snap back violently, actually hurts, feeling like tiny daggers attacking my strained hair follicles. His other hand flies up to my exposed throat, cradling it tightly. He gives it a firm squeeze, and I moan into his mouth.

"Careful, little girl. Your Dark is showing," he murmurs against my lips. Then he bites my bottom one hard enough to deliver a sting before letting me go.

I'm panting, my chest heaving as if I've just danced through ten songs straight. My sex throbs with a vengeance, infuriated with the constant tease of release. I'm burning hot for Dorian, and his little stunt has just upped the ante.

Just as I'm beginning to collect my bearings and settle into normalcy, Xavier comes over with a tray of tequila shots for everyone. After all are distributed to the crowd of party guests, we toast to Carlos's birthday, singing the Happy Birthday song loud and obnoxiously. He beams brightly, his brown eyes twinkling with unshed tears. It warms my heart that we were here to commemorate this day with him. I look over at Dorian, a mixture of curiosity and nostalgia playing on his features. Maybe birthday celebrations are something the Dark don't engage in. Or maybe he is missing the friendships that he once had and lost. I put his hand in mine and give it a squeeze. If it's up to me, there will be many more celebrations like this together.

We're chatting it up with Carmen when Morgan pulls me away to meet some of her friends and fellow stylists from Luxe. I look over at Dorian, standing yards away, his bright blue eyes locked on mine. I vaguely hear Morgan making the introductions, unable to tear my eyes from his. I'm completely mesmerized, damn near hypnotized by his gaze as if I've never seen anything like them before. It feels like lava is running through my veins, warmth radiating all through my body. The heat begins to travel through my breasts, stinging each nipple. Then it's in my belly, slithering further south combining with my slippery wetness. The sensation is so agonizingly good; I can feel it pushing me closer and closer to the edge of my downfall. Then Dorian's delicious lips part a fraction, forming a small 'O' as if he is blowing out a candle, and it happens.

I come. *Hard.*

Right there in the middle of Morgan and three other people whose names I could not remember if you paid me, I climax, unable to contain the tragic cry of defeat and attracting a number of questioning stares.

"Excuse me, something is caught in my throat," I cough, trying to mask my guffaw. I grab Morgan's glass of champagne and down its contents in record time, excusing myself to the ladies room. I swear I hear Dorian's baritone voice laughing behind me.

When I emerge from the bathroom stall, I nearly run right smack into Aurora draped in skintight gold sequins. She stares at me intently, almost fascinated with our near collision. The bathroom is empty apart from the two of us, and I instantly know something isn't right.

"Hey Aurora, everything ok?"

"Everything is fine, Gabriella," she purrs in her sweet soprano. "Having a good time?"

"Yeah, I am. How about you?" I maneuver around her stock still body and head for the sink, keeping my eyes fixed on her through the mirror. *Awkward.*

Finally Aurora saunters over next to me, so close that our arms are almost touching. I can feel the static between us, sending tiny bolts of electricity up and down my extremities. She tears her brazen, blue eyes from my reflection in the mirror and turns towards me.

"He's happy with you. I've never seen him like this. He really does love you."

Of course. This is about Dorian. "I love him too, Aurora," I say tentatively. *Where is this going?*

"And Jared? Do you love him?" her expression is completely unreadable. I can't decipher if she's being aggressive or simply curious.

I flash her a nervous smile. Not because I'm afraid of her, but because I'm afraid of what I may do to her if she steps out of line. "I'll always have a special place in my heart for Jared. He and I have been friends for a long time."

Aurora nods her head slowly. "He loves you. I can see it. I

didn't quite understand it before but . . . ," she trails off, lost in her own thoughts. "Have you ever thought of how it would be to have both of them? At once? Pleasing you simultaneously? I know I have."

The fuck? Where the hell did that come from? And why am I just standing here, my eyes wide with shock, unable to verbalize my disgust?

Aurora bites her pouty pink bottom lip seductively, her eyes sweeping the length of my body. I suddenly feel as if I am butt naked in the middle of rush hour traffic.

"You know, Jared is a very good lover. Very generous and attentive. Very . . . *big*." A wicked grin spreads across her face and her ice blue eyes meet mine. "And Dorian . . . oh my. He's still the best I've ever had. He's so . . . intense. Domineering. Just all-consuming. Don't you agree?"

What the . . . Did she just say what I think she said?

"What are you getting at Aurora?" I say, finally finding my voice, though it's shaky and weak.

She moves in close enough to bathe me with her sweet, cool breath. Close enough that I smell the scent of her perfume mixed with the tang of alcohol. And something else . . . Pure sex and sin.

"We should all get together, the four of us. Jared and Dorian, pleasuring you simultaneously–could you imagine? Both of them devouring you at once? We could . . . *share*." She skims her tongue across her top teeth suggestively. "I know I wouldn't mind having a little fun. Like I said, I'm not shy."

Aurora lifts her perfectly petite manicured hand and lightly strokes the top of my cleavage with her fingertips. I am mortified, not only at her action but because shamefully, her soft touch is . . . enticing. Arousing, even. *Shit.*

I finally take a step backward, confused and ashamed at my body's betrayal. "Aurora, I don't think that's a good idea," I stammer. *What the hell is wrong with me?* Why am I *not* knocking her on her ass?

Aurora shrugs nonchalantly. “Suit yourself.” She takes a step toward me, closing the small distance between us and leans in. Her lips brush my earlobe, igniting a sizzle in my veins. “Just remember, only a girl knows what a girl wants,” she whispers, sending an icy shiver down my spine.

Before another lust-laced word is spoken, a group of intoxicated young women burst into the bathroom, cackling and singing, causing me to take a reflexive step backwards. I fade into the commotion until I have escaped the women’s restroom, finding Dorian leaning against the wall a few feet away.

“Are you okay?” he asks gauging the flustered look on my face. “I saw Aurora follow you in.”

“I will be. Aurora . . . *what the hell?* I think she just propositioned us for a foursome with her and Jared. She even made a pass at me! It was . . . *weird.*” I shake my head as to dispel the heated encounter and try to ignore my own wayward hormones.

Dorian chuckles a bit then shakes his head solemnly. “She’s affected.”

“Affected? What the hell does that mean?”

Dorian strokes my cheek with the back of his hand. “My love, I’m not the only one who finds you irresistible. Especially the closer you are to ascension. With Aurora being an Órexis, she can manipulate your desires. Confuse you.”

You can say that again.

“So what? Should I expect her to keep trying to get me in bed?” *And will I be able to resist?*

Dorian shakes his head. “No. She just needs to replenish. She’s about to get what she needs.” He nods his head towards the women’s restroom, where Aurora still has not emerged even with the intrusion of rowdy girls.

Horror washes over my face and I take in a sharp breath. “Dorian! She’s not going to kill them, is she?”

Again, Dorian chuckles and shakes his head. He pulls me to him by my hips, wrapping his arms around my waist. “No, she won’t.

But those girls are about to get *very* bi-curious."

Sheesh. Talk about sex-crazed. Not to mention Aurora's description of Jared's *generous* sexual abilities. How the hell do I wipe *that* from memory? And do I even want to?

Ugh, FML.

Dorian places a gentle kiss on my forehead, causing me to abandon my worried expression. "So what do you want to do? Do you just want to leave?"

"No," I answer thoughtfully. "Right now, I need a strong drink. Then I want you to take me on that dance floor and make me remember just how straight I am."

We bound to the bar, where Dorian orders two glasses of the best overpriced scotch they have. I sip the poison slowly, letting its warmth slide down my throat and spread to my hips, my thighs, my moist apex . . .

Holy shit, chill out, Gabs. Overly sexual is just not my thing. Or is it?

Right on cue, "Moves Like Jagger" resonates from the speakers, causing a stampede to the dance floor. I set my glass down and grab Dorian's hand.

"Phase 2, let's dance," I say as he looks at me quizzically.

"I don't dance," Dorian replies yet lets me pull him anyway.

"Is that right? Because I clearly remember someone once telling me that if you can fuck, you can dance. And you *can* fuck, right?" I smile, reminding him of the very words he spoke to me when he wanted me to strip for him. And anyone that can move like him in the bedroom can definitely dance.

Dorian rolls his eyes and smirks naughtily, giving me all the answer I need. I lead him to the dance floor where his graceful, fluid dance moves draw quite a crowd along with more than a few admirers, men and women alike. With liquid courage coursing through my veins, I hold my own, grinding against him seductively and rolling my hips to the beat.

After he wows the crowd, I am swept away by my friends when

one of our favorite songs blares from the speakers. Being here with them, remembering simpler times where warding off hangovers rather than evil mystical beings was our biggest worry, pulls at my heartstrings. In this moment, we're the only ones in the expansive, crowded club, singing our hearts out about youth and recklessness. Because this is what it's all about–having fun, conquering the night, suffering the next day, and doing it all again.

We shouldn't have to grow up. We shouldn't have to be mature. But that's our reality; we can't go back to how things once were. So all we have is tonight. Tonight, we'll be as ridiculous and juvenile as possible. Tonight, we'll make bad choices that we may regret tomorrow. Tonight, it's all about us. Because our nights like this are numbered. *My* nights are numbered.

Large, soft hands caress every inch of my naked body, alternating wet kisses on every erogenous zone. My neck. My shoulders. My nipples. My belly bottom. The back of my knees. The sensitive skin of my inner thighs. One hand grasps the satin sheets while my other reaches out to the source of my pleasure. My fingers weave through silken strands of hair, tugging gently. He brings his head up to mine, a sexy half-smile on his full lips. Dorian. Naked and utterly beautiful.

"Do I make you feel good, baby?" he murmurs as he nuzzles into my neck, licking and sucking a trail to my earlobe.

"Mmmm, yes, Dorian," I coo, letting my eyes close.

"How good?" His teeth graze my skin, sending prickly heat down to the pit of my belly.

"So. Good," I gasp.

His hands are still all over me–rolling my nipples between those magic fingers, teasing my swollen clit. I pull him down, unable to resist not feeling his lips for a second more. Dorian sucks my tongue into his mouth, nipping and tasting until I feel I could explode from his kiss alone. Another set of hands joins his yet I am too caught up in Dorian's flavor to even be startled. The hands are large, strong yet soft. They are moving up my thighs, replacing Dorian's fingers as he moves to cup and fondle my aching breasts. When he pulls away, our erotic intruder comes into view.

Jared. Holy shit! Jared!

He's all hardened muscle, sun-kissed skin and a smattering of sexy, dark tattoos on his chest and biceps. Shit, he's gorgeous and my body instantly responds to him. He grins seductively while swirling my sex with long, adept fingers. I look to Dorian, awaiting the onslaught of his wrath yet he gazes back at me with nothing but pure unadulterated desire as he continues to flick and caress. As if it were choreographed, they switch places–Dorian between my legs and Jared at my torso. He licks his lips, taking in the sight of my naked body for the very first time.

"God, Gabs, I want you so bad," he rasps. "I've wanted you for so long. Too long. Do you want me?"

Do I? Hell yes!

I feel Dorian's wet tongue on my inner thighs, his teeth nibbling the sensitive area. I moan, unable to overanalyze an appropriate response.

"Yes, Jared," I breathe, just as Dorian slowly inserts a finger inside me, making it impossible to backpedal.

Simultaneously, their tongues are inside me–Jared in my mouth and Dorian in my dripping wet heat. My body shudders at the sensation and I moan into Jared's mouth as his hands find my heavy mounds. I know I won't be able to hold on. It just feels too good. So. Damn. Good.

When Jared pulls his mouth away, I see that we are not alone. On the other side of me kneels Aurora, clad in only a pair of lace panties. She smiles at me lustfully, biting her bottom lip. My traitorous breath catches in response. She is absolutely beautiful.

Sexy and perfect. I hate that I don't find her presence revolting. I find her so damn enticing.

Jared leans over me and pulls Aurora's mouth to his, causing a slight twinge of jealousy to stiffen my body. Dorian sucks my flesh into his mouth hard, making all bitter thoughts abandon me. As Jared and Aurora continue their lip-lock, they each begin to caress my breasts. The combination of sensation is sheer torture and bliss and I come with a hoarse cry. Dorian laps up my release, refusing to show me any mercy though my flesh is almost achingly sensitive. It's too much. I don't know if I can take anymore.

Jared and Aurora break their kiss then look down at me. Jared grasps my hand, placing it on Aurora's thigh. Her skin is so soft and silky, her scent involuntarily making my mouth water. I can't help myself; I slowly let it move up her body, feeling the heat of her sex against my hand. She parts her legs, allowing me to cup it through the lace of her panties. Hearing her moan in response, along with Dorian between my thighs still strumming my own sex, only encourages me. I let my fingers stroke her wetness, the thin layer of fabric our only barrier. She leans over and places her pink lips around my hardened nipple as we both cry out our satisfaction in lustful harmony.

With hooded eyes, I look over at Jared as he grips his massive erection in his hand. I gulp, my eyes widening with shock and delight at his size. He smiles at my reaction.

Well, shit. Aurora wasn't lying.

As if she heard her name in my salacious thoughts, Aurora licks a path up from my breasts to my mouth. Feeling her small, soft tongue in my mouth, her warm lips working against mine and smelling her scent drives me absolutely mad. My hand knots in her long hair, while the fingers of my other hook inside her panties.

When she lifts her face from mine, completely overcome with ecstasy and whimpering, I see that Jared and Dorian have switched places once more. Dorian is beside me, wearing his usual wicked grin as he watches Aurora and I touch each other. Jared's long fingers are inside me, preparing me, while he spreads my legs wider. And just as his insanely large length begins stretch me open, Dorian grabs Aurora by the back of her head and crushes her mouth to his . . .

I thrash awake, gasping for air, nearly naked and disoriented. *The fuck? Did I just . . .* No. It was just a dream. A ridiculously freaky, tempting dream, but just a dream. *Whew.*

Where am I? I can't remember anything past . . . being on the dance floor? *Shit.* I look around me, taking in my surroundings. Dorian's bedroom. I'm in his bed, dressed only in boy shorts and a sheer cami, the slick satin cool against my slightly stinging back. I look up to see Dorian hovering over me sitting on his knees, his hands alight with cold, blue flames touching my bare stomach. His eyes rapidly meet mine, too quickly for any human.

"Better?" he asks. He's shirtless, wearing only low-hung jeans around the severe cut of his hips.

I mentally assess my sudden coherency. Moments before, I didn't even know how I had arrived here, indicating that I was too inebriated to make it here on my own. What happened back at the club? *Oh crap crap crap.* Did I make a fool out of myself? I obviously blacked out and Dorian took care of me. But when?

"Yes," I respond. And I do; somehow I feel absolutely fine. A bit shaken by the dream, but fine nonetheless.

"Good" he replies solemnly. Dorian removes his hands from my abdomen, closing them to extinguish the mystical flames and sits up. I steadily do the same.

He must have felt my arousal. He must've sensed I was dreaming about more than just his body on mine. Shit. Oh well, might as well face the music.

"Did you feel . . . ?" I whisper, more than a bit ashamed at my colorful imagination.

"Yes."

Crap. "You didn't . . . I mean, you didn't plant that dream, right?"

He shakes his head. "No, little girl. I didn't."

I furrow my brow. "If not you, than who? Aurora?"

The corner of Dorian's lips twitch in amusement. "No, Gabriella. That was you. That was all you."

Me? *Oh hell no!* I would never even think of having an orgy, let alone participate in one. I mean, Dorian and Jared at the same time is the fantasy to top all fantasies, but Aurora . . . No, that'll never happen.

"I thought you said the Dark couldn't heal," I say, hoping to steer the conversation onto something a little less sexually immoral.

"We can't. I simply absorbed the alcohol in your body."

So *that's* what he did for me that night after our tequila-filled fiesta. The question had been gnawing at me for a week. *A week?* That's all it's been? Only a week since I saw *him*, dreamt of *him*. Only a week since I willingly touched myself in hopes to entice him on the beach. The Dark King. *Crap.* Get outta my head! I'm like a horny teenager on Red Bull and Viagra!

"Thank you. I would have been no fun." My eyes grow wide with terror. "Please tell me I didn't do anything embarrassing. Oh God . . . I didn't get on the stage, did I?"

Dorian laughs, and the sound is music to my ears, despite my anxiety. "No, little girl. Though you did give everyone quite a show. Sure you weren't an exotic dancer in a past life?" he chuckles.

I smack him on the arm and feign offense, eventually giggling at my own expense. Yup, that sounds like me.

"Jared and I had quite the relentless task of warding off young defenseless suitors."

"Jared?" I respond too quickly.

"Yes. He cares for you deeply. Wouldn't let a guy get close enough to touch you the entire time."

The sentiment makes my heart swell. I told Aurora the truth; Jared will always have a place in my heart. "Dorian, I don't want him to get hurt in all this."

He gathers me into his arms, and rests my head on his chest, reclining back onto the pillows. "I know, little girl." I am all too aware he hasn't assured me that Jared won't get hurt; he's just told me he understands.

"You said my Dark is showing tonight," I say after a few contemplative moments. "What'd you mean by that?"

I feel Dorian smile against the crown of my head. "You are drawn to Dark elements–eroticism, alcoholism, aggression, masochism. It's who you are. It's what sustains you. But you are unlike any of us. You want it *all.* And you have the power to manipulate it all. You invoke them in me often."

What? Hell no! Dorian feels the tension building in my body and squeezes me a bit tighter to soothe me.

"But you draw from Light. The sun strengthens you. You're compassionate, loving, nurturing. You're a natural protector. You see the good in people even when they don't see it in themselves. Even when there's none to be found. *You're* good. And you make me want to be good too. For you."

I take a moment to digest Dorian's assessment of the anomaly that is *me*. So many things to him, yet I don't even know who I am. Am I good? I hurt the people closest to me, the people I love, whenever I lose control. Nurturing? Compassionate? I've never considered myself either of those things. I still don't have a tight grasp on who I truly am. I'm still Unknown, still Nobody. Because even with the discovery of my paranormal heritage and the prophecy of what I was meant to be, I'm just not there. I'm just regular old Gabs. The girl who was never good enough.

"Do you want me to align with the Dark?" I say to break the deafening silence.

"Part of me does. Yes."

"Why? If you hate what you are so much?"

"So we can be together." Dorian rests his hands on my shoulders, looking me in my bewildered hazel eyes. "And I don't hate what I am, Gabriella. I *know* what I am. I accept it. You just still have not accepted that the same darkness that lives in me also lives in you."

He's right. I refer to his darkness as something foreign, unlike me in every way. But I harbor the same Dark element. It's in me. But because it has been a part of who I was for the past twenty years, I never deemed it as alien. Maybe I was built to be Dark. I didn't fall in love with someone from the Light. I didn't build an unbreakable bond with that side of me. It was the Dark who accepted me, while the Light chose to forsake me. Maybe my destiny is to rule the Dark with my Dark Prince.

"Now, little girl, if you are feeling better, I believe we have a score to settle," Dorian says sitting upright.

"What are you talking about?" I turn to him, a question in my hazel eyes.

"I think you know exactly what I am talking about. I told you that you would regret that little stunt. And after tonight, you will think twice about playing games with me." Dorian licks his lips and the pink of his tongue causes my breath to hitch.

"What are you going to do?"

"I'm going to give you what you need. What you crave," he responds with dark hooded eyes. He bears his teeth and my heartbeat quickens in response. "And when you think that you can't take anymore, when your body trembles with the intense waves of pleasure, and you cry because ecstasy completely overwhelms you, I'm going to do it again. And again. Until you are blissfully ruined. Until the only thing you see when you close your eyes is me."

And without further explanation, Dorian does just that.

FOURTEEN

"Just give it to me straight. How bad was it?"

Morgan pulls at a lock of her now honey blonde hair and cringes at the memory. "Well . . . it wasn't *horrible*. I've seen worse. Shit, I've *done* worse!" she giggles. She abandons her hair-of-the-month and commences to stabbing her overdressed salad. "But it was pretty shocking. Even for you, Gabs."

Shit. I've really done it this time. It's late afternoon on Sunday, two days after Carlos's birthday celebration at Aria. Morgan and I both have the day off, a first since we moved in together, and made a promise to catch up and have some girl time.

"That bad, huh?" I say, trying to piece together the foggy memories of Friday night. "It just seems like a blur to me. What was the worst part?"

Morgan's eyes turn towards the sky and she chews her lip as if lost in silent deliberation. "Well, when you pulled Dorian on the dance floor and sang along to *Bad Romance*, I think even *I* was a bit uncomfortable. It was like GaGa gone wrong. *Terribly* wrong," she laughs.

Bad Romance? I *sang* to him? Oh no, no, no! "And then what? He got me out of there?" *Oh, please say he saved me from further embarrassment.* Singing is bad enough, but me trying to be sexy at the same time? That is just cruel and unusual punishment.

Morgan shrugs. "Actually, no. He thought your crazy ass was funny. Maybe he was even a bit endeared by the whole thing. But you had to leave before you were thrown out for fighting."

Fighting? "What? I was in a fight?" I sure as hell didn't feel like I was, unless Dorian . . . no, never mind. He can't heal. Not that I would need healing.

"No, thank God. He pulled you away before anything escalated. Apparently, some girl was getting a bit too up close and personal with him while he was at the bar getting you some much-needed water. I would have checked her myself if I had seen it, but I guess you did."

Morgan puts her fork down and peers at me with cautious eyes. "Gabs, you walked over, grabbed the girl by her hair and nearly yanked her across the room. Dorian wasn't even giving her the time of day and you were ready to commit murder! It was unreal! He had to literally carry you out of there, kicking and screaming like a psycho.

"Gabs, I love you, girl. You know I do. But when you get drunk, it's like balls to the wall, sorority girl, *Hangover*, spring break, Girls Gone Wild drunk. And it just seems like you're going down that path again. I know you had a rough week and all, but these past few days were scary for me. I'd come home every night, and you'd be drunk, listening to sad ass music. Seriously, if I have to listen to your breakup playlist one more freakin' time, I will shoot myself. And then the tattoo? What's going on, Gabs?"

I study my half-eaten chicken sandwich before meeting Morgan's questioning eyes. What can I say to her? Yeah, we all have our demons, but how do I explain that my demons are a part of *me*? That I *am* the demon?

I'm sorry," I say shaking my head. "I didn't mean to embarrass you. I didn't even mean to get that drunk." My mouth twists into a pained grimace. "The past few days were really bad for me. I just got carried away."

Morgan's hand flies to mine, and she rests her palm on the back of it gently. "Hey, Gabs, you are not an embarrassment. I'm just worried, you know, of what to expect," she says, her voice cracking towards the end. She picks up her iced tea and takes a sip. "You are so wrapped up in Dorian, I feel that if things were to end, it will completely crush you. I don't want to see you lose yourself. I know you love him and I know he is your first real boyfriend. And I do like him. But the hold he has on you worries me. I know you are this bad ass, tough chick, but I really do believe that Dorian has the ability to break you. He may be the only one who can. You manage his store, you live in his apartment . . . what happens if you two break up?"

I swallow, clearly disturbed at the course this conversation has taken. The question is one I've pondered at length yet have not come up with a reasonable response. Where *would* it leave me? Back at Chris and Donna's house, *broken* and utterly despaired? And my friends . . . if Dorian and I split, will he undo the wards that protect them? Will he . . . *kill me*?

"I can't say what will happen, Morgan. I can only hope that we never have to find out." I look up at my best girlfriend and try to give her a confident smile, yet fail. "But I will try to do better. I promise."

Morgan nods and smiles back before picking up her fork and stabbing a piece of grilled chicken. "I know, girl. I just don't want to see you hurt. You have so much to offer, so much to live for. I don't want you to throw all that away for a guy. No matter how ridiculously rich and handsome he is," she winks.

I spend the rest of the evening contemplating my conversation with Morgan. She's right, and admitting that truth has put me in a bad head space. Not to mention the rainy, gloomy weather but I know it is a necessary evil. Dorian made good on his promise to give me what I craved and then some. After dragging me out of Aria and relieving me of the copious amounts of alcohol in my system, he slowly tortured my body with crippling pleasure for hours. The term 'multiple orgasms' simply does not measure up to what he gave me, making me eat my words from our racy car ride.

But of course, our passion has a price. He gave me so much of *himself*, and regrettably has had to stay away because of his own craving for me. *For my power*. The thought that his attraction to me is somehow biologically engraved in him still daunts me, yet I can't be certain that my yearning for him is any different. Of course I'd be attracted to him, even without the supernatural pull. But Morgan's words still echo in my head.

Dorian can *break* me.

I've never put too much stock into *any* guy, Jared included. I could have lived with solely his friendship. *But can I live without Dorian?* When both of our lives are so expendable in the eyes of the Dark, and even the Light, could living without him be an actual possibility?

By Monday night, I am overwhelmed with the discouraging thoughts that have plagued my mind every second Dorian and I are apart. I *need* him. I've become an addict, completely strung out on the feeling he gives me. But it goes beyond that. Dorian tantalizes every part of me. His passion, his intellect, the mystery that hides behind those startling baby blue eyes–I want it *all*. My first instinct is to reject the intense hunger for him, to run away and hide my true desires. But I *can't*. He consumes me completely.

Suddenly the fortune teller's haunting words resonate in my head as if her ghost can read my forlorn thoughts.

"Darkness approaches you from many angles. It eclipses the light around you, pulling you further and further into a world of great pain and tragedy. It seeps into you. Alters you. Soon it will consume you completely. Yet, you will allow it. You will welcome the darkness. Because you are the darkness."

I am the darkness. And it seems as if Dorian is pulling me deeper into the curse of my bloodline. I am going further into the Dark. It's what he wants. He wants me to align with the Dark so we can be together. But wouldn't that be like selling my soul to the devil simply for *love*?

I arrive at Dorian's hotel suite late that evening after texting him the four dreaded words that make a guy's balls jump into his stomach.

– We need to talk.

I use the key card he's given me and let myself in, finding him out on the balcony, staring blankly into the night. A crystal glass of scotch is in his hand, his other resting on the railing. Even shrouded in darkness, wearing only dark slacks and a black sleeveless undershirt, he takes my breath away. This is going to be harder than I thought.

"You're worried," he says on my approach without turning around.

I go to him, sliding my arms around his firm waist. He smells heavenly as always, causing me to nestle my face into his hard back.

"With good reason," I reply. "We should have had this conversation months ago. But you always seem to *distract* me."

Dorian finally turns to face me, looking down at me with a sexy half-smirk. His eyes are dancing with wild possibilities, causing my heartbeat to quicken at just the sight of him. "Can I distract you now?" he breathes seductively.

Yes, yes you can.

"Maybe later," I respond, stowing my body's carnal requests. If I give him my body now, then I might as well surrender my will. I have to stand strong, no matter how bad I want him, which is pretty damn bad.

Dorian sighs reluctantly and leads me back inside. He stops to refill his drink, pouring one for me as well.

"Have you eaten?" he asks, handing me my glass as I take a seat on the black and gold couch.

I shake my head. "Later for that too." I take a much needed swig and meet his icy glare.

Dorian nods stiffly and sits on the adjacent loveseat, not bothering to hide his irritation. Neither one of us relishes the thought of going into such sensitive territory, especially since we only recently kissed and made up. But the longer we put this off, the murkier our future seems.

I take a deep breath, steeling myself as to not seem meek or uncertain. "I think I made a mistake when I said I'd work for you and live at Paralia."

Dorian sips his poison and looks at me with a blank, unreadable expression. I don't know if I've offended him or if he agrees. "Why do you say that?"

"Because I've made myself completely dependent on you. If you leave me, I'm homeless, jobless, and completely clueless. I'm broken, even more so than when you met me. I think we rushed into all this and maybe we should slow down."

"Slow down? Is that really an option for us?" he asks incredulously. "Gabriella, we don't have all the time in the world to fool around. All we have is now." He takes another hefty gulp and sets down his glass.

I take a sip and nod in agreement. "I know. I know tomorrow isn't promised for either of us. But I shouldn't abandon common sense and be blinded by my feelings for you. Why should I trust that you'll never abandon me? That you really won't . . . *kill* me?"

Before I can blink, he's beside me, evaporating swirls of grey surrounding him. Dorian grasps my face between his hands, his eyes searching mine intently. "What do I have to do for you to understand that I would never leave you? Would never hurt you? I've given you my heart, my life. *Shit.* What else do you *want*?" he says just above a whisper.

The desperation in his voice, the earnest look on his face pierces the depths of my resolve. He's given me *everything*, yet I still question his devotion. But it's not him who I doubt. It's me. I know that I could never be worthy of such a beautiful creature. I'm selfish, irrational, brash, and unstable. I'm everything he's not. It's only a matter of time before the other shoe drops and he realizes it for himself.

Dorian lets his fingers wander into my soft tendrils, wrapping a curl around his finger. "Gabriella, you're all I've ever wanted. I don't care what you decide upon your ascension, I just want you. *You* are enough," he whispers, answering my secret anguished concerns.

Gazing into his bright blue eyes, something stirs within me at his sincerity. My chest tightens and a knot forms in my throat, causing warm moisture to sprout at the brim of my eyelids. *Shit.* I'm going to cry.

"Dorian," I choke, fighting back the building sobs threatening to erupt at any moment. "I'm no good for you. And I know sooner or later, you'll figure it out. And it will *kill* me. It will literally *kill me*," I say just as the first hot tears escape.

Dorian crushes me to his chest, his arms squeezing out a barrage of whimpers. "Shhhh, little girl. Don't you say that. Never say that," he whispers into my hair over my strained sobs.

He holds me for several minutes, letting me empty my tears onto the front of his shirt. When I finally regain my composure, I look up at him, apology in my eyes. This wasn't about him and his ability to completely dismantle me with his rejection. It was about me shoving my pathetic insecurities onto him. Whether or not we conquer our relationship full speed ahead or reduce to a snail's pace, I'll never feel worthy of him. He sees past all the fighting, cursing, drinking and tough talk. He sees me for what I truly am. A little girl who has never known her place in this world, was never picked first, has never fit in. *His* little girl, the Light-Dark abomination.

An hour later, we sit cross-legged on the floor, munching on room service, and listening to the soulful sounds of Adele. After Dorian kissed away my tears, we sat in silence, holding each other as if it were our last night together. It made me think of how it must've been for Natalia and Alex as they waited for death. How do you begin to prepare for that? How do you say goodbye? How *can* you?

"There is something I need to tell you," I say as Dorian refills our glasses.

He gives me a pointed look. "Oh?"

I nod, giving myself a moment to formulate my thoughts. "The fortune teller, the one that was killed. You know she was murdered because of me, right?"

"I do," he responds without blinking.

"What she told me that night, when she touched me. She said that darkness would consume me, and I'd accept it. That I was the darkness." An involuntary shiver creeps up my spine as if the soothsayer's ghost has arrived along with my morbid reflections.

Dorian wipes his delectable mouth with his napkin and nods yet doesn't respond. So she must've been right. I *am* becoming consumed by darkness.

"Dorian, do you think our relationship is pushing me into the Dark? Are you trying to make me . . . *like you*?"

I watch Dorian as he takes a long sip of his wine then sets his glass down on the coffee table. He finally gazes at me with mournful eyes, indicating that my worst fears are reality.

"Little girl, I don't want you to be like me. I've never wanted that for you," he says softly. "But darkness does consume you. It consumes me too. But it isn't me; it isn't my darkness." Dorian reaches his hand towards me tentatively to brush the line of my jaw. "It's yours."

Huh? "What are you talking about? How can *I* consume *you*? I am powerless, Dorian. Remember?"

"It's in you. I feel it every day, beckoning me to antagonize the beast in you. I *try* to resist. But as I told you before, you are drawn to Dark elements. It arouses you, *feeds* you. I find myself losing control when we're together. It's another reason why I try to stay away."

I absorb Dorian's words, trying to piece together a logical explanation. The darkness within me wants to be unleashed, and it's manifesting in Dorian as a result. There is immense evil within me pushing me into the Dark. Somehow, I'm not surprised. Nothing surprises me anymore. I just have to make the conscious decision to fight even harder to stay in the Light for both our sakes. I have to resist my Dark urges that want to surface and wreak havoc on all those who choose to stand against me, my friends and family included.

Luckily, the song changes and I shift my attention to the melodies emanating from the sleek stereo system nearby, hopelessly trying to salvage the evening and what's left of my sanity. It's a song I know and love, and I perk up into a thoughtful smile.

"What?" Dorian quizzes with a sexy raised eyebrow. *God, I love it when he does that.*

I smile sweetly. "Nothing. Just thinking."

"About what?" When I answer with a shy grin, Dorian playfully presses me for answers. "Aw, come on. You can tell me."

"No, it's . . . embarrassing," I say with a blush of scarlet. "You'll laugh at me."

Dorian feigns surprise. "Don't tell me the big bad Dark Light is *afraid*," he teases. "Seriously, I want to know what has made you smile, so I can ensure it happens again and again."

I sigh and channel what's left of my steely nerves. "Ok. This song. It reminds me of you. Was kinda like my song for you when I first started having real feelings for you. When I admitted to myself that I sorta . . . loved you."

I can't help but cast my eyes downward in mortification as the beautiful sounds of guitar echo throughout the suite. My cheeks are hot and I get an unwelcome tightness in my chest, indicating the swell of restricted emotion. And as Adele belts out the first notes, I know that I won't be able to hold the tears much longer.

Every lyric coaxes the unspoken realizations that I find it so hard to verbalize. So many years of being lonely and discounted, no one ever truly seeing *me*, the person that I really am. The Gabriella I so desperately wanted to be. Yet somehow he broke through the walls and barriers and penetrated my frail, dejected heart. He loves me for all that I am and what I will become, even though it scares us both to death. He accepts the darkest parts of me and doesn't try to change me, in all my shattered complexity. Meeting him has given this façade of my life new meaning. He's given me purpose, strength. He's given me *love*. Dorian has given me everything and, in turn, is everything to me. Designed by the Divine Power especially for me.

I feel cool fingers brush my cheek before pulling my head up to meet a pair of dazzling azure eyes. Eyes so full of adoration that it causes a poignant gasp to catch in my throat. Dorian smiles tenderly and appears amazed and grateful at my silly, romantic gesture.

"No one's ever dedicated a song to me. Thank you," he says before placing a sweet kiss on my lips. He sweeps a loose curl behind my ear, still cradling my face in his hand. "I love you, little girl. So much it astounds me."

Dorian is on his feet faster than I can see and he pulls me to mine. He ushers me to the bedroom where I find dozens of flickering candles illuminating the room, filling the space with the scent of jasmine. Of course they weren't here before and I gaze up at Dorian and smile brightly. He flashes me a wink in response then turns his smolder upwards, indicating that I should do the same.

Miraculously, the high vaulted ceiling is black as night and glittering with hundreds of twinkling stars. They appear as luminous and radiant as the ones that inhabit the sky and I am completely beguiled. I look back in awe at the gorgeous creature before me. The Dark One I've surrendered my heart to. The man who taught me to live and love despite our twin imminent deaths.

"Dorian," I gasp. "It's amazing. What is all this about?"

He leads me to the grand four poster bed shrouded in satin, looking at me adoringly. He strokes my cheek gently with the back of his hand and I reflexively turn into his touch.

"Loving you is and will always be my greatest honor. You've done the impossible; you've opened me, Gabriella. And despite what the future may hold for us, I will carry that with me forever. My heart will always be yours, in life and in death."

In life and in death.

I absorb Dorian's amorous proclamation, emotion swelling in

my chest. But there is something else in his beautiful words. An edge of remorse, a hint of sadness. I try to squelch the creeping doubt and enjoy this moment despite the subtle double entendre.

Dorian holds up a single finger then makes a whirling motion, the room falling away from us, dissipating before my eyes. Four walls no longer contain us. Plush carpeting is replaced my soft, white sands between our toes. There are no dressers, no bedside tables, not even an inkling of the gold and black room that has housed our intimacy countless times. The sounds of crashing waves flood my ears. The only light besides the twinkling stars is produced by the enormous iridescent moon stationed above us. The scents of water, fresh rain and seduction surround us, and the aromatic memory instantly stirs something within me.

Skiathos.

"*Dorian.* How?" I gasp, unable to produce any other words to describe my awe.

"I told you I wanted to bring you here. And while I still hope to one day, this illusion will have to do." He leans forward and kisses me tenderly. "I want to make love to you under the stars. I want to become one with you, create a new memory in the place where I was birthed. I want to bring you *home*."

Dorian's hands roam my bare back, making me painfully aware that I am suddenly naked. He too is nude and it instantly distracts me from my own insecurities. Seeing his luscious body illuminated only by the moonlight is a glorious sight. His olive complexion and those ice blue eyes contrasted by his jet black ruffled locks seem to glow in the most startling, ethereal way. He is so remarkably gorgeous and content here in his element. He pulls me into him, our warm bodies mingling, reacting to the familiar static that occurs every time we touch.

Dorian gently pulls my face up to meet his, and envelops my mouth with his soft lips. His agile tongue strokes mine, tasting and teasing with leisure. There is no rush. He's taking his time with me, making this intimate act last. This is different. So full of emotion and wonder, as if it's our first kiss. We want to commit every taste, every sensation to memory.

Dorian's hands gently caress my back, my backside then moves back up to knot in my tresses. In turn, I knead and massage the defined cuts of his shoulders, in awe of how hard yet soft his body feels against mine. It literally makes me weak in the knees and I buckle and sway. Dorian cradles me lovingly, easing me down onto the warm sand.

He's hovering over me, his mouth still on mine, still exploring unhurriedly. Dorian's hands softly fondle every surface of my body as if I am a rare, cherished jewel. His lips break away from my mouth and move to the curve of my jaw, leaving warm, feather-light kisses. He moves down to my neck, gently licking and sucking, causing my body to instinctively bow and quiver at the sensation. His large hands palm the mounds of my breasts, caressing each nipple until they ache, longing to be kissed. He appeases me eagerly and I moan in appraisal, grabbing soft handful of his silky black hair. Dorian then licks a trail to my navel, where he also is delightfully attentive. He then commences to kiss every inch of my torso, careful not to miss a spot. His tongue, his lips, the light grazing of his teeth, it's all too much to bear, and my sighs and moans add a new element to the harmony of crashing waves.

Soft kisses and caresses travel down through my thighs, to my knees until I feel Dorian's mouth on my toes, suckling and nibbling gently. *Oh God.* The feeling is incredible and I gasp in surprise. His teeth graze and nip the soft pads of each digit before his tongue bathes my instep. Then Dorian moves up to my calves, paying special attention to the sensitive space behind my knees. I moan my enjoyment to the moon, shudders overwhelming my body.

"Do you like that, baby?" Dorian finally says, looking up at me. I gaze at him through hooded eyes and bite my bottom lip in response. Dorian smirks before returning his attention to pleasuring my hidden erogenous zones. His tongue travels farther north and he eases his face between my knees, leaving tingling kisses on the insides of my thighs.

"Mmmm, Dorian," I breathe, panting wildly.

Hearing me say his name instantly excites him and he gently bites down on the sensitive flesh of my thigh then sucks. It feels so good; I moan his name again, and he repeats his assault on the other. Then I feel his fingers massaging my swollen clit, completely overwhelming my senses. I cry out and am startled by the tortured sounds of pleasure escaping my lips. The combination of the tiny nips on my inner thighs and his fingers stirring my throbbing heat begins to unravel me and I feel the beginning quivers of climax building within me.

"That's right, baby, let go," Dorian murmurs. Then he places his succulent mouth where his fingers once were and sucks my swell, pushing me over the edge. Violent ripples consume me and I shudder uncontrollably as I release a river of my pleasure. Dorian hungrily laps it up, moaning his own appreciation of my flavor.

Still not entirely in control of my body, Dorian delves deeper into my wet, trembling sex, refusing to end the waves of orgasm that have pulled me under. I grasp the soft granules of sand, furiously trying to regain my faculties but the search is futile. My back bucks and bows off of the ground, knees shaking violently on either side of Dorian's head. I can't take any more. Feeling this good is abnormal, clearly ethereal.

"Please, baby. I can't. I can't, Dorian," I pant. What is he doing to me? There's no way I can come again.

"Yes, you can. And you will." Dorian nibbles my hypersensitive sex and the action brings me to my brink once more. I cry out, convulsing, pulling handfuls of his black soft hair. He is right as always. I could, and I do. *Hard.*

Finally showing me an ounce of mercy, Dorian climbs on top of me, holding himself up by his elbows as he watches me fight the tremors of orgasm with tightly closed eyes. Once I've salvaged an inkling of self-control, I open my eyes to peer at his beautiful face looking down on me. He's smirking, partly amused at my display, and satisfied with himself for stripping me of all sensibility. I quickly try to plaster on an impassive guise, mentally scolding myself for being so dramatic.

"Oh please, don't stop on account of me. I love seeing you like this. So unrestricted and raw. So beautiful."

Beautiful. I'll never get tired of hearing him say that to me, especially considering how extraordinarily gorgeous and perfect he is. The fact that he even exists and wants me is a mystery in itself. I don't reject the smile creeping onto my face and pull his face down to kiss his succulent lips. The kiss instantly deepens, Dorian grabbing a soft handful of the base of my backside and beginning a slow grind. I feel him pulsing against me and though I've already come twice, I want to feel him. I *need* to feel him. This is where he belongs. *He lives in me.*

I reach down and guide him to my slickness and he gladly eases in slowly, gasping at the warmth and comfort. I take a moment to study his expression, his brows knit together, eyes squinting in sheer ecstasy. It is me who makes him feel this way. Me who makes him bear his teeth as he strokes unhurriedly. He's concentrating, trying to hold on and enjoy this ride. But as I kiss and nibble his hard shoulders, pull his hair, rake my nails up and down his back, he knows he can't fight much longer. It feels too good. I want him just as afflicted as he makes me. I want his submission just as much as he wants mine. I squeeze my walls around him, hug his hardness and refuse to let him go. Dorian's eyes widen and his mouth forms a tight '*O'*. A low, guttural groan vibrates from his chest and I know I've got him exactly where I want him.

Dorian slows his already measured pace and looks down at me with love and wonder in his eyes. "Little girl, you wield powerful magic," he whispers. He uttered those same words to me the first time we were together, the first time he gave me so much mind-numbing pleasure.

"I could say the same about you," I breathe.

Still thrusting slowly, he runs his agile fingers through my tresses before bringing up a lock of hair and inhaling. "I want you to remember us like this," he says, looking intently in my eyes. He's searching them, pleading for understanding. For what, I am not sure. "No matter what, I want you to know that my love for you is real. And I will die loving you. Live in this moment with me, Gabriella. Let it carry us through the storm."

What is he trying to tell me? Before I can fix my lips to ask, his mouth is on mine, swallowing all feelings of anxiety and doubt. His kiss is so urgent and passionate, it completely consumes all questions and I do just as he wishes. I live in the moment with him. Just me and Dorian, my Dark Prince.

He plunges into me deeper and I sigh against his lips. The rise and fall of his hips, stirring my insides in a sensual rhythm ignites the telltale quivers of my approaching orgasm. *How?* This has to be an illusion too, right? No, absolutely not. The pleasure that Dorian gives me is undeniably real. His love is *real.*

Dorian intensifies his strokes signaling that he too is on the cusp of release. He pulls his lips away and gazes down at me with a strained yet contented expression, pushing himself deeper still. His eyes are a burning blue inferno of ardent desire and I can't bear to look away. He's even more captivating and beautiful in this raw moment.

"Come with me, baby," he urges, his brow furrowed.

Glints of spectacular blues, reds and greens pop and sizzle overhead, crackling, glittering, raining sparks down upon us. *Fireworks.* Two remarkable forces of nature colliding. Breath blissfully ragged, limbs tangled and weak. Delightfully shattered as we float back down to Earth from our orgasm-induced high.

This all-consuming, inexplicable pleasure dispels reality yet transcends my most intimate fantasies. Fantasies I didn't even know inhabited my subconscious until I met *him*. Dorian. For he is my fantasy. And he is all mine.

"Does it hurt?" Dorian asks, his gloriously nude body lying on his side atop of the comforter. We are back in the suite, having had to abandon our paradise.

I shake my head before resting my cheek on top of my crossed forearms, lying on my stomach while Dorian traces the scabbing outline of my tattoo. "No, not really. Just a little sore. Itches more than anything."

"What I wouldn't give to take away your discomfort." For a moment he looks somber, even a bit pained at his inability to heal. I reach out and stroke his cheek, offering my essence to him. Dorian quickly indulges in my scent then gives me a dazzling half-smile. "I really wish you would have let me do it. There would have been no healing process. Plus I don't like another man's hands on you. I was tempted to kill him out of sheer jealousy. I've never felt so *irrational* before."

Dorian jealous? Now that's a thought! "It was totally innocent and I covered up as best as I could. And what do you mean, '*let you do it*'?"

"Little girl, I am a man of many talents. I believe I have proven that abundantly," he smirks. I giggle at his racy insinuation and shake my head. "It isn't difficult. It would be my honor to mark you. It would truly be the best birthday gift I could ever receive."

"Dorian, it's your birthday? Why didn't you tell me?"

My beautiful lover shrugs and leans over to kiss my bare back, his cool lips easing the healing flesh. "After a century or so, you don't even bother to acknowledge it. But being here with you has already been more than enough, so I can understand if you are reluctant to let me." There's a hint of sadness in his voice but I can't see his face to assess the source.

"Wait. First off, of course, I want to know it's your birthday.

We could have celebrated or something! And I would have bought you gifts. Geez, Dorian, now I feel like an ass." I roll over to my side so I can gauge his reaction. "And what do you mean by *mark me*?"

"I can mark you, Gabriella. Much like the mark I wear but of course I would never bestow that curse on you." Dorian lets his fingers dance in the loose curls cascading over my shoulder and down to my breast. "Our kind has the ability to mark others as a sign of deep devotion and commitment. And love. Just something to show that you are mine. Forever."

"Geez, sounds a lot like getting married." Dorian's eyes are suddenly wide with shock and horror and I instantly regret even thinking the words. "Not that I want to get married, of course," I say hurriedly trying to erase the unease from his expression. "Tell me about this mark. Like, will regular people see it or just people like *us*?"

"It depends. Do you want everyone to see it?"

I think back to when I was reluctant to show the employees at Cashmere that we were together and the look on his face every time I pulled my hand away in public. It angered him, though part of me feels it hurt him more than anything else. He's been rejected his entire life by his own father. Centuries of feeling like a disappointment, an outcast. I want to prove to him that this is where he belongs. *With me.*

"Yes, I do," I nod, smiling. "I'd like that. You're not gonna scrawl your name on me or something, right?" Crap. Maybe I should have asked that *before* I agreed.

"No, not unless you want me to. I can give you anything you want." Dorian scoots forward, closing the small distance between our bodies. "Once you ascend, it's very possible that you will be marked. Whether that is the mark of the Dark, or something else entirely, I want to be etched in you first. I want you to see it every day and let it remind you of the immense love I have for you, little girl. Because there will be a time where I may not be around to tell you. Do you understand what I'm saying?"

I slowly nod though I am unable to fathom having to live without Dorian. I know better than to ask further questions, questions that could reveal the truth that we are both trying to conceal in order to save our lives.

"I'll do it. But only if you do it too." I want Dorian to be mine just as much as he wants me to be his. I want him to know that my love is with him always, in this life and the next.

Dorian perks into a sly smile. "So what did you have in mind?"

I bite my bottom lip and shift my eyes towards the ceiling as I try to imagine a symbol of our complicated love. Our need for each other, the hunger to constantly be in one another's presence is so intense, it's as if there is some unseen magnetic pull that keeps us conjoined. I can't even describe it; it goes beyond all things natural and logical.

"Anchors." When Dorian gives me a perplexed raise of his eyebrow, I continue. "I've always felt that we were anchored to each other in some uncanny way. No matter how we try to deny it, we can't fight the impulse. And I know it's more than some deep-seated, ancient attraction between the Light and the Dark. I *need* you." I look down, a bit embarrassed at my earnest admission but it's the truth. "Plus I think it's fitting considering the meaning of your name."

I feel a single cool finger on my chin, pulling my face up. Dorian's glittering baby blues meld with my hazels and his delicious lips spread into a broad smile. "I love it. And I feel the same way; I need you too. Whenever we're apart, all I can think about is holding you again. How I would give anything to be in your presence, even if it could very well kill me. We *are* anchored, little girl. We were made this way, made for each other. This is our destiny."

I try to stifle the swell of joyous emotion that tightens my throat. I honestly don't know what I have done to deserve the amazing creature lying beside me. *Dorian is my destiny.* Even with my impending ascension and the assassin trying to snuff me out, I feel so fortunate because I have him. If it weren't for my parents' unshakable love for each other, if it weren't for Dorian's defiance of his father, we would not be here now. It was destiny that Dorian was sent to kill me. Destiny that kept me uncertain of who I was and what I was meant for. *Everything happens for a reason.*

"So little girl, where should we place them?" he asks with a bright smile. Dorian looks so youthful and exuberant.

"Why don't you choose? I'm only good for one awesome idea a day," I jibe.

Dorian cocks his head to one side and runs a hand through his already disheveled after-sex hair. *Geez, if he gets any hotter, I'll spontaneously combust!*

"Right here," he says pointing to the spot below his thumb, right before the back of his hand meets his palm. "That way, whenever our fingers are intertwined, our anchors will be side by side. Forever anchored to the other."

I break into an amorous smile and nod, offering my right hand. I can hardly wait to wear Dorian's mark, to literally have him engraved in me forever. He takes my hand and kisses every knuckle sweetly. Then in an inconceivably swift movement, he's sitting upright, still holding my hand with his left. He holds up his right index finger and suddenly it is alight with electric blue flames. I am instantly captivated by it, unable to look away. Dorian's magic completely enthralls me.

"Be still, little girl. It won't hurt much but it may be a little jolting," he says.

"Have you done this before?" I ask meekly.

Dorian cocks his head to one side before shaking his head, a sexy grin playing at his lips. "No. I have never wanted to mark anyone. Just like you are the first I have ever linked my life to. These acts are incredibly rare for my kind."

A frown creeps onto my face. "Why?" I sit up as well, my long waves dangling at my breasts.

"We don't love easily. You can imagine how difficult it is for us to commit our lives to merely one person, to give and love unselfishly. I never thought I could, honestly. I never had any interest in that level of commitment. But then I found you . . ." he trails off, lost in his own memory. "You have permanently altered me. Two and a half centuries and it takes a twenty year old girl to change my life." He shakes his head, smiling disbelievingly.

His words, so earnest and heartfelt, spark the intrusion of doubt unexpectedly. If I were just an ordinary girl, not an immortal magical being, not expected to be the most powerful force ever created, would he still want me? Would he love me if I were human? *Are* we only anchored by our love? Is it actually me, Gabriella, that he desires, or is it the Dark Light?

Dorian reads the anxiety on my face and his brow furrows. "You don't have to do it if you don't want to," he mutters.

I try to mask my unease with a smile and nod. "No, I'm ready. Mark me, baby," I wink.

Amused by my playful banter, Dorian brings my hand up, turning it gently to the side. I hold my breath as he carefully lowers his ignited finger to my creamy skin. It initially shocks me and I struggle to maintain my composure. It doesn't hurt yet it isn't exactly pleasant either. It is . . . jolting, like he said. The sensation can only be best described as burning cold.

Dorian concentrates on making even, level strokes with his finger against my skin. His touch leaves behind visible bluish ink etched deeply into my flesh. When he is finished a mere few seconds later, a small dark blue anchor no larger than a quarter rests on my right hand. It's simple, beautiful and profound. Perfect.

"Do you like it?" Dorian asks, almost timidly. I finish assessing my new piece of artwork before launching myself into his arms and joining his mouth with mine. It's virtually painless and I let both my hands roam his hard bare back and shoulders passionately. Dorian cups the soft flesh of my backside in response and I instantly feel his manhood awaken.

I pull away, smiling brightly at my beautiful lover. "I love it. And thank you for letting me spend your birthday with you."

After Dorian has marked his own hand, he joins it with my right, intertwining our fingers. Our twin anchors are identical in every way and I am overjoyed at the prospect of carrying a piece of Dorian with me for the rest of my life, though he has shown that he is dreadfully opposed to more conventional shows of commitment. I frown at the memory.

"What's wrong?" he asks me, noting the aggravation on my face. *Shit*, I really need to learn to control my emotions. I shake my head, not wanting to ruin the moment, or his birthday. My trivial *girl* worries will have to wait.

"Oh, come on. Don't be shy. You know I'll find out one way or another."

Again I just shake my head, not wanting to delve into the murkiness in my mind. *Live in the moment, Gabs.*

Dorian reaches out and strokes my cheek gently. "Please, little girl. Tell me," he whispers.

The sentiment and yearning in his voice catches me off guard and I look up at him, startled. So much emotion that I can't even begin to comprehend washes over him. What happened to keeping things light and casual? His intensity is staggering.

I take a deep breath and look down at my hands, resting on my naked thighs. "When I mentioned marriage, you looked like you were horrified, disgusted at the idea. I'm not saying that's what I want. I've never even put much thought into it. But it just kinda caught me off guard, how upset you looked. Like you could never imagine marrying someone like me."

There. I said it. When Dorian doesn't respond, I take the liberty to finish my sullen thoughts while I still have the courage. "It's probably for the best anyway. No one will ever want to marry me, considering what I am. Especially since I can't have children."

I shrug, hoping to make light of the situation and convince myself that I'm alright, that I'm only imagining the aching in my tight chest. When I finally will myself to look back up to meet Dorian's eyes, I see that his expression is one of anguish and sorrow.

Shit. I must've hit the nail right on the head. That or he feels sorry for me, the pitiful little girl who sits stripped and naked before him. Either conclusion is unbearable.

Dorian swallows then looks down as he formulates the most tactful way to confirm my fears. When his eyes meet mine, there is something in them. *Regret*. But why? "Gabriella, I could never marry you."

Ouch. Though I expected that reaction, I can't halt the debilitating ache radiating in my chest, making its way up to my throat in the form of an agonized knot. I try to steady my breathing, trying to reel my emotions in, but I can't mask the pain that I know is surely engraved on my now pale face. I turn my head to look away, too pained and afraid to look this truth in its ugly face.

"I wouldn't do that to you," he continues, shaking his head. "I would love nothing more than to spend my life with you. You know that. But marrying you is something else entirely. For my kind, that is."

"Is it?" I whisper, my throat tight and raw.

Dorian nods solemnly. "I am in succession to the throne. One day I will be king, if I live to see that day. Marrying you will make you queen. It will completely thrust you into the Dark. You don't want that. *I* don't want that. You deserve a normal life. You deserve a *choice*."

Huh? A life without Dorian? That's not a choice; that's a death sentence.

"Then why did you make me think we'd be together forever? If you wanted me to lead a normal life? You want me to choose someone else?"

"I don't want it, but it's not fair of me to expect you to settle for this," he says with a wave of his hand. "For *me*." *Settle for Dorian?* He thinks I'm settling? What the hell? "And I will always be with you. Even if it's merely watching you in the shadows. I have no choice in the matter. I am completely addicted to you."

"So this has nothing to do with me not being enough for you?

Enough to sustain you?" I look back down at my hands. "And not being able to give you children?"

"Absolutely not!" he suddenly shouts, causing my head to snap back up to gauge his furious expression. "Stop saying that! You are *enough*, Gabriella! I know you can't conceive; I've always known. And I don't care. You are all I want, do you understand me? You and only you!"

Dorian's passionate declaration causes tears to prick the rims of my eyes. I blink furiously trying to dismiss them, yet one solitary hot tear escapes and slides down my cheek. I look up at him through glassy eyes, too overwrought with emotion to say anything in response in fear that more tears will quickly follow. Seeing me desperately trying to maintain my composure, Dorian pulls me into his arms, burying my face into his chest as he strokes my hair. I breathe in the freshness of his skin and let the euphoric scent soothe my aching heart.

"You are enough, little girl. You are everything," he whispers into the crown of my head. And I cry silent tears into the warmth of his smooth, bare chest.

Fifteen

With the falling of the first leaves of autumn, I fall deeper into the life that was set out for me, deeper into my destiny. With Dorian. Things have been oddly normal, a feeling I used to despise about my once mundane life. But now it's something that I crave, something that I haven't felt since I was nineteen. I have finally begun to accept that this is my *new* normal. My life will never go back to the ordinary charade it once was. Not to mention, waking up to the mouthwatering supernatural being beside me is *anything* but ordinary.

"Good morning, beautiful girl," Dorian murmurs in my hair. His eyes are still closed and his body is tangled with mine in a tight embrace.

"Good morning. Sleep well?"

"Mmmm, I'm not sure I'm done sleeping yet. I was having the most magnificent dream."

"Oh? About what?" I reach my hand up to play in his black tousled locks. His bed head is extraordinarily sexy.

"If I tell you, than it won't come true. And I so desperately want it to be true," he says, inhaling the fragrance of my hair.

I feel the hardness of his morning erection against my thigh and reflexively rub against it. "Sure there's no way I can persuade you to tell me?"

Tap, tap, tap.

"Hey, Gabs, it's me, can I come in?" Morgan calls out from the other side of my bedroom door.

"Pretend like you're asleep!" I whisper furiously to Dorian. He smiles and buries his face into the pillow. After I ensure his naked body is completely covered and slip on my robe, I open my bedroom door to greet my best friend and roommate. "Hey Morg, what's up?"

Morgan peers into my room and spies Dorian lying in my bed, pretending to be asleep. "Oh shit, Gabs, my bad. I didn't know he was here," she whispers. "Just really quick . . . I am in need of some '*lady products*,' if you know what I mean. I just ran out. Got any to spare?"

"Sure." I wave let her in, waving her towards my bathroom. Once we enter, I close the door and search for my stash of tampons under the sink. "Here. You can have them all," I say handing her an unopened box.

"Are you sure?" she asks with a bewildered look. "If I'm on mine, then you should be on yours too." She nods her head towards the door, towards the beautiful naked man sleeping in my bed before her face turns into a combination of disgust and amusement. "Ew! You dirty whore!" she shrieks playfully.

I gasp at Morgan's heinous insinuation. "Morgan! Keep your voice down!" I whisper furiously. "And no, I'm not on my period!" *Shit!* I know Dorian can hear every word and I am utterly mortified.

"What? How is that possible? We've been synced up since high school, Gabs. Like clockwork." Morgan's eyes suddenly grow wide with sheer horror, her jaw nearly hitting the tiled floor. "Gabs, when was your last period?"

"What? I don't know." I rack my brain, trying to recollect the date, chewing my lip until it hurts. "Um, a couple months, I guess." Yeah, that's right. Dorian was trying desperately to convince me that he didn't care, that the blood didn't bother him. As extremely difficult and physically painful it was to deny him, I refused, opting to engage in . . . other activities to keep us both satisfied.

"Oh my God, Gabs! You're pregnant!" she exclaims. I instantly shush her but her shocked expression and flailing arms say it all.

"No, I am not, Morgan." *Right?* Shit. Has it really been that long since my last period?

"Holy fuck, Gabs, I think you are! Come on, I think I have an emergency pregnancy test in my room." She exits in a flourish to find said test and I dash to the bed where Dorian is already sitting up, wearing only a solemn expression.

"Did you hear what she just said?" I whisper almost embarrassed at the thought.

Dorian nods. "You aren't though, little girl. I'm sorry."

"Don't be. I'm glad. I didn't really think I was anyway," I mutter, a hint of sadness in my voice.

I'm definitely relieved yet part of me grieves for the babies that will never grow in my womb. The realization that I will never be a mother, will never share life with another being, pummels me. I never truly thought about having children until I found someone I wanted to spend my life with. And accepting that I will never give Dorian sparkling blue-eyed, raven-haired babies knocks the wind right out of me. Will my love be enough to placate him? Knowing that I can never give him an heir?

Dorian leans forward and leaves a single chaste kiss on my forehead as I try to fight a wave of fresh tears. Before he can invoke any further emotion, I flash him a manufactured smile and quickly exit the bedroom, hoping to mollify Morgan with a negative pregnancy test and put all talk of motherhood and babies to rest.

By Sunday, I am over the pregnancy scare but deem it necessary to discuss my dilemma with Donna, the only mother I have ever known. She has prepared a roasted chicken with spiced sweet potatoes and sautéed green beans for our weekly family dinner and I have opted to watch her cook in hopes that some of her culinary skills will rub off on me. No use in making myself totally un-wifely.

I take a sip of the crisp white wine that Chris has poured for us before escaping to the living room to watch football. This is as good a time as any to broach the sensitive subject. "Hey Mom, can I ask you something?"

"Sure honey," Donna replies, basting the golden brown bird.

"Is it normal for me to not have a period? I mean, without being pregnant?"

Donna looks up to meet my awkward gaze. This is the first time

I've ever alluded to being sexually active, though I'm sure she knows that I am no angel. "I'm so sorry, Gabi. It's starting. The process. The curse is changing you. To ensure you don't procreate."

"So it's final? I'll never have children? There's nothing that can be done?"

Maybe I wasn't over it entirely. Not only has the man I love professed to never marry me, I can't even have a child of my own. And though I honestly have no plans of starting a family any time soon, the revelation that I will *never* have one truly breaks my heart.

"Nothing that we can do, no. As far as any other forces, I'm not entirely sure." Donna drops the utensil in her hand, realization setting in. Her face becomes frighteningly pale. "Is this about Dorian? Does he want you to give him a child?"

I shake my head furiously, hoping to ease her worry. "No. He knows I can't have children and he's fine with that." I look away to hide my unresolved sorrow. "It's not like he'd marry me anyway."

Donna reaches over and sets her petite hand on my shoulder. "Oh honey. He can't. Not if he wants to save you. I know it doesn't seem like it now, but he's doing you a favor, you'll see." She cradles my face in both of her small hands. "One day you will find a wonderful young man that will love you for who you are. And you'll be happy. And lead a long, wonderful life full of love and laughter."

I try to find the words to tell her that Dorian *is* my happiness. That he and I are anchored for life. But what does that mean exactly? That I am aligning with the Dark? That I will pledge my allegiance to them, vow to fight for them? I try to squelch my confusion with a swig of my wine.

"What's that?" Donna asks, pointing at my hand.

"What?" I ask, though I know exactly what she is referring to. The mark Dorian gave me.

She takes my hand, inspecting the little blue anchor. "You got a tattoo? When?"

"Um, a while back. I'm surprised you hadn't seen it." Crap. Though I hadn't gone so far as to wear gloves whenever I came to visit, I wasn't exactly trying to flaunt it either. "Dorian gave it to me," I tack on as an afterthought.

"You let him mark you?!" she shrieks. "Oh dear, what have you done?"

Sheesh, melodramatic much?

"It's no big deal. Just a little tattoo. He has one too."

Donna chews her lip, something obviously eating at her. She drops her eyes and steps forward a bit. "Honey, I think there's something I should-"

"Ok, it's halftime. Please tell me dinner is ready. I'm starving!" Chris stampedes in, appearing to have had a couple beers. Judging by the roars and jeers, his team is winning. I give him a bright smile, genuinely thrilled to see him so laidback. Finally things are headed in the right direction with us and I long for the closeness we once shared.

"Sure is, Dad. Let's eat!" I exclaim beaming. And while I am not totally ignorant of Donna's doubts, I can't find the strength to ingest any more revelations.

The next afternoon, Carmen informs me that Dorian has left a message for me to come to Luxe to see him right away. I quickly slather on a fresh coat of lipgloss, eager to see Dorian and curious as to what has brought him to the salon. He hardly ever goes there and truly has no interest in the cosmetology industry. I walk the block or so towards Luxe, the brisk mountain air causing me to pull my leather jacket around me. Many of the shops and restaurant are displaying whimsy Halloween decorations and I make a mental note to pick some up for Cashmere at a party supply store.

As I approach the salon, a chilling sensation rips through me, causing me to shiver violently for a spilt second. Goosebumps prick every inch of my skin and I pull my jacket tighter around me, unable to shake the unexpected, gripping cold. I can feel the tiny hairs on the back of my neck stand to attention. *Sheesh, talk about a case of heebie-jeebies.* Could someone be watching me? I quickly scamper into the salon, anxious to find solace in Dorian and inform him of my suspicion.

"Hey Gabs, what's up?" Morgan inquires, looking over her shoulder as she finishes up with a client.

"Dorian called me. Said he needed to see me." I glance back over towards the door, still feeling on edge.

"Dorian? He isn't here today." Morgan then removes the black cape from her client and spins the chair around. "There you go, sir. Now you look even more handsome, if that's even possible," she gushes.

As my eyes fall on the dashing man sitting before me clad in a dark tailored suit, I fight the blood-curdling scream building in my throat. He smirks, his gleaming blue eyes scanning the length of my body hungrily.

"Hello, Gabriella. How lovely to see you again," he says coolly. His words sound muffled, muted by the rapid pounding of my heart vibrating in my ears.

I open my mouth to fashion a response, aware that Morgan is looking between the two of us clearly perplexed. *Shit*. What do I say?

"Hello, Stavros. What brings you to Luxe today?"

The Dark King smiles menacingly, and as devilishly handsome as he is, I can't help but feel nauseous with terror. "Oh, just thought I would stop by. And I wanted to see you." His voice is smooth yet assertive, not unlike his son's. *Dorian.* Where is he?

My eyes flicker to Morgan who is bursting with confusion. Noticing the anxiety and alarm etched on my face, Stavros casually holds up his hand, causing everyone and everything in the salon to abruptly freeze before my eyes. I can't believe it; every person is unmoving, totally frozen in time where they stand. Morgan is still staring at me, her eyes narrowed in puzzlement. She looks like a wax statue of herself, along with the other stylists and patrons of Luxe. *Unreal.* My eyes grow wide with horror, and I open my mouth to scream, praying that someone somewhere will hear me.

"Careful, young lady. I wouldn't do that if I were you. Snap of my fingers is all it would take to end everyone in here. I do not wish to harm you or your friends. I only want to talk."

"Where's Dorian?" I croak mustering every ounce of courage left in me. I am trembling yet I give him a steely gaze, refusing to let him see me ruffled. I am screaming, fighting within, struggling to maintain my composure. *Oh my God! What the hell is happening?*

"My son will be along shortly." Stavros stands, buttoning his suit jacket, his smoldering eyes never leaving mine. "I only wish to speak with you. If you would do me the honor of taking a walk with me, the humans in this salon will not be harmed." He extends the crook of his arm to me.

"And they'll go back to how they were?"

"Yes. You have my word." Stavros drops his arm and instead extends his hand. "Please." I look down at it then back up to meet his eyes, my glare hard and unforgiving. "You know you want to. It'd make us both feel better," he smiles, flashing a row of gleaming, white teeth.

"I'll walk with you. But keep your hands to yourself."

Turning on my heel, I stalk out of the salon, willing my shaky knees to keep me upright. His footsteps are silent yet I know he is right behind me. I can *feel* him. *Where the hell is Dorian?* Can't he sense my anxiety?

I lead Stavros away from the salon, my arms wrapped around me tightly. It suddenly seems much colder than it was just minutes before and I am overly aware of the pulsing current crackling in the space between us. Once we have reached a grassy clearing hosting a few park benches, I stop and turn to him abruptly.

"Ok, you wanted to talk. So talk," I say tersely.

"Relax, Gabriella. Have a seat," Stavros says, unbuttoning his suit jacket and gracefully folding his tall, broad frame onto a bench. He looks up at me and smiles, looking mouthwateringly suave. I sit at the other end of the bench with a huff, knowing exactly what his game is. "Now, first thing's first. You sent back my gift. Why?"

My head snaps to him and I frown, despite the flutter deep down in my stomach. Now that I see him up close, I notice that he looks younger than I initially thought. Glossy raven hair, glittering blue eyes, and tan olive skin. A more refined, polished version of Dorian. Classically handsome yet sinfully sexy. *Shit.*

"I didn't want it," I mutter.

"Oh but I think you *do* want it. Don't let your affections for my son dissuade you from the things you really want in life. Things that I can and will provide." I see the pink of Stavros's tongue as it glides across the top of his teeth, causing my breath to hitch involuntarily. "And unlike my son, I won't make you work for it. If you were mine, I'd give you anything you wanted. Not hire you as my employee," he scoffs.

"But I like to work. It keeps me busy," I say meekly. I clear my voice and try to square my shoulders. *Stay strong, Gabs.* "And besides, I think you *do* want me as your employee. Just in a sick, twisted way."

Stavros's full lips curl downward as if he is considering the validity of my statement. "Believe what you wish, but you don't recognize the real villain here. I won't deny my intentions, as depraved as you may view them, but at least I am honest. Can you say the same of your beloved?"

Is he serious? "Are you trying to say that I shouldn't trust Dorian? Knowing that he can't lie? And weren't you the one who cursed him in the first place?" I glare at him through the narrow slits of my eyes. He has successfully pissed me off. "I trust him wholeheartedly. He could have killed me months ago. And *he* hasn't tried to mind-fuck me without my consent."

Stavros blinks rapidly, his gaze heating with rage. I can literally feel the inferno brewing under his impassive guise. I've hit a nerve.

Just as I think he is about to unleash his darkness on all of downtown Colorado Springs, he smiles. "Gabriella, you slay me," he remarks, obviously amused. "Judging by your most recent show of devotion, I'd say he has most certainly earned your trust."

"What are you talking about?" I ask with a raised eyebrow.

The Dark King reaches towards my right hand and I quickly pull it back, refusing to let him touch me. He smirks and cuts his eyes at me. "I won't hurt you, Gabriella. I don't like repeating myself. I was referring to your *tattoo*. You let him mark you."

Reflexively, I rub the tiny blue anchor and hold it close to my chest. "Yeah, so what?"

Again, Stavros flashes his dazzling, heart-stopping smile. "Maybe I've underestimated my son. Maybe he is living up to his potential." He makes a bemused face at the notion and shakes his head. "Moving on. I've come to inform you that I have lifted the order. Dorian is no longer obligated to kill you."

What?! "You have?"

Stavros nods. "Yes. I want your allegiance more than anything I have ever wanted to acquire, I must admit. But I want it sincerely. You will be free to choose."

"Seriously?" I shriek, failing to mute the sheer elation in my voice. "And you won't kill Dorian for failing to assassinate me?"

"No. I don't relish the idea of murdering my own son, Gabriella," he replies with an edge to his voice. Remorse flashes in his eyes. Maybe the Dark King isn't as monstrous as I initially thought.

I take a deep breath and ask the question that has been gnawing at me since we sat. "And if I choose the Light? Then what?" I whisper.

Stavros shrugs nonchalantly as if he is bored with the notion. "Then I suppose that we will belong to opposing forces. You must know what that will mean for you and Dorian. How that will affect your relationship. Especially now that you are marked."

I digest his words but refuse to give anything away. "Thank

you, Stavros. I really do mean that."

"It is my pleasure, Gabriella. Also, I am aware that there is murderer on the loose. I can assure that I have nothing to do with it and would like to provide a bit more protection for you. My son is efficient enough but I don't want to be careless with your life while you are still so vulnerable."

"Is that right?" I ask unconvinced. "And what's in it for you?"

"Nothing at all," Stavros replies. "I only want to keep you safe. Being that you are half Dark and I am king, it is my duty to ensure that my people are taken care of. Now shall we head back?" he says, suddenly standing, again extending the crook of his arm. "I know my son will be anxious to see you."

I stand and exhale with relief, appeasing the Dark King by linking my arm through his, careful to avoid contact with his skin. "Yes, please."

"Ah, Gabriella. You are quite a gem. Your essence is simply hypnotic. How does my son resist you?"

I let myself smile genuinely for a beat. "He doesn't. I let him . . . breathe me . . . sometimes."

"Oh? *Interesting*," he remarks as we make our way down the shopping district.

"Can I ask you a question?" I say, finally deciding to bite the bullet. When Stavros nods, I continue. "You came and helped Tammy. You reversed the petrification. Why?"

The king cocks his head to one side, just like his son does when he is lost in deliberations. "Because it needed to be done. She needed help."

"But . . . why? Considering what you are? Why risk it for a human? There's got to be something in it for you."

"We are not demons, Gabriella. I see the Light influence has already poisoned your mind. They, too, could have intervened and done the very same thing. Yet, where were they? Where have they been the last twenty years?"

He stops walking and turns to me, regarding me intensely. It is the first unguarded show of emotion he's allowed me to witness. "We've been there, Gabriella. The entire time. Through every fight, every disappointment, every night you stumbled home in a drunken stupor, we were there. We've protected you when the Light chose to abandon you, and we protect you now. They see you as an abomination. We see you as the goddess that you were meant to be."

His earnest admission stops me up short. His words seem so sincere; have I been wrong about the Dark all along? Are the Light truly as self-righteous as Dorian believes?

"Then why did you want to kill me?" I whisper. I clear my throat, hoping to appear more aloof. "And why would they ignore me all these years if they are hoping I would help them?"

Stavros shrugs and shakes his head, proceeding to make his way towards the salon. "We are all somewhat ruled by our fears, our irrational feelings. I acted callously. Forgive me. And while I cannot speak for their motives behind abandoning you, I would assume it was for the same ignorant reasons I felt you needed to be destroyed."

I choose to ignore his apology, somewhat skeptical of his candor. "Do you know who spelled me? Who made me . . . *this way*?" I ask weakly.

"I do not." Stavros looks at me quizzically.

"So there is no way to reverse the curse?"

Before Stavros has the chance to answer, we both glimpse Dorian flying out of the salon's doors. The look on his face is beyond seething mad and he is tense with anger, his hands rigid and stiff at his sides. The air visibly shimmers around him and I can almost feel the heat of his rage though we are several feet away. He gives his father a murderous stare and an audible growl rumbles from his panting chest. I hurriedly unlink my arm from Stavros's and stuff my hands in my jacket pockets. *Shit, busted.* Dorian quickly closes the distance between us in the blink of an eye and forcefully pulls me to his side, away from his father, his vengeful eyes never leaving the smug look on Stavros's face.

"Temper, temper, my son. We would not want to put a damper

on this joyous occasion, now would we? Besides, she could do worse," he says winking at me. "I bid you farewell, Gabriella. Thank you for spending time with me today." The Dark King then turns and walks away.

Suddenly I am repulsed at myself for being so naïve. This had to be a setup, just a ploy to get under Dorian's skin. And my gullible ass played right into the king's plan.

We stand there for several minutes, gazing at Stavros's retreating back. Dorian never looks down at me, never utters a word. He still has a tight grip on my arm and I suspect I'll have a distinct bruise showcasing each fingerprint. Yet, I don't protest. I deserve much, much worse for being such a complete imbecile and disappointment to Dorian.

Once Stavros is out of our line of vision, Dorian spins me around and tugs me towards Cashmere, not even bothering to look at me or slow down to alleviate my much shorter legs. Once we enter the boutique, he lets go of my arm and grabs my hand, leading me back to the office without so much as a nod in anyone's direction. His touch is searing–scorching dry ice. I smile uncomfortably at the array of confused faces. *Crap.* So much for being discreet.

Once we are in the small, contained space of my office, Dorian locks the door and whips me around to face him. His face is still venomous and I brace for his wrath.

Fuck. I've really done it this time.

Instead he crushes his mouth to mine, gripping my backside and pulling my body into his. In a swift movement, he spins our bodies around, pressing me against the wall with a *thud*. Once I've registered what is happening, my hands clutch the hardness of his shoulders, feeling the tense tendons flex as he kneads my back and ass. His kiss is urgent and harsh, his strong tongue conquering my mouth and his teeth deliberately nip my lip. I flinch at the momentary sting and moan in Dorian's mouth.

Before I know it, I am in the air, my tan knee high boots dangling at Dorian's hips. I lock them around his waist. His hands are under my sweaterdress and with a quick pull, my panties are in shreds on the floor. My fingers tug at Dorian's soft locks and I don't hold back; I pull *hard*. He groans his response, refusing to cease his relentless tongue-lashing.

I am so caught up in the intensity, so consumed by the desperation in his kiss that I don't even notice that he has unfastened his slacks until I feel the tip of him touch my pinkness. Then with a hard, unforgiving thrust, he is deep inside me and I cry out. He pauses for just a second, relishing in the feel of my tight walls contracting around him. Then he really punishes me. Showing me not an ounce of mercy, Dorian pounds me with fast, brutal strokes. His fingers dig my soft flesh as he holds me up, pushing into me feverishly. I revel in the ache, and it sends me to my glorious end with a cry of pleasurable pain.

"*Fuck!*" he grunts through clenched teeth, spilling his fury into me. We crumple to the ground, both deliciously spent, our ragged breaths the only sounds filling the small, humid space. Dorian pulls me into his arms, cradling me tenderly. I take the liberty of nuzzling into his neck and breathing in his cool, fresh scent. Even with the sheen on sweat blanketing his skin, he still smells wonderful. I resist the urge to jut my tongue out and lick the saltiness.

"I almost tore this town apart today, little girl," he says quietly.

"Why?" I murmur against his skin, though I know exactly what riled him.

"I couldn't find you. He deflected the perimeter around the two of you. I thought he . . ." Dorian trails off, unable to finish the heinous thought. His lips are in my hair and I hear him inhale, hoping to quiet his fears. "I got a message from you, asking me to meet you at your apartment. When I arrived and you weren't there, I waited. After a while, I called your cell but it went straight to voicemail. Then I called the store and Carmen told me that you had left to meet me at the salon per my request. Then I knew."

"I'm so sorry, Dorian," I whisper, my lips moving against his collarbone. "Had I'd known, I would have never gone. But when I got to Luxe, he was . . . persistent. He somehow froze them, all of them. He said he would kill everyone if I didn't go with him."

"I know," he mutters. "Morgan said you came in but when she couldn't remember you leaving or who you left with, I knew. *Shit, Gabriella.* I was ready to fucking kill him, I was so angry. And you let him *touch you.* Why?"

"I don't know. I guess I was grateful. He said he wanted to protect me. And he told me he relinquished you of your duty. He said my allegiance was my choice, that he wouldn't punish either one of us. I just wanted to be appreciative, I guess." Even I'm a bit appalled at my reasoning. "But he never touched my skin. Not once. I wouldn't let him."

He exhales and I feel Dorian release a bit of the tension that is binding him. "Gabriella, I swear . . . I almost lost it. I guess I am at least relieved that some traditions are still honored," he mutters shaking his head.

I raise my head, meeting his beautiful face with my questioning gaze. "Traditions?"

Dorian's fingers slide up to my right hand and he turns it gently, rubbing the little blue anchor. "I've marked you."

"What does that mean? I mean, Donna kinda flipped about it and then Stavros seemed overly interested in it as well. Am I missing something?"

He brings my tatted hand up to his lips and kisses it before inhaling the scent of my palm. I pull it back, discouraging his attempt to stall. "You are mine, just as I am yours. However, by marking you, I have forbidden all other supernatural forces from trying to acquire you, my father especially. You are mine and mine alone."

My jaw nearly drops to the floor. Dorian truly has marked me. He has performed the equivalent of lifting his leg and pissing right on me. And while I am somewhat flattered by his show of commitment, I can't help but feel angry that he chose not to disclose this information until now. And if it had not been for Stavros's impromptu visit, he may not have ever let it slip.

"What the hell, Dorian, how could you keep this from me? How could you make such a permanent decision for me and not even ask me? *Again?*" I sit upright and turn my body so I am facing him, giving him a full view of my enraged expression. *Unbelievable!*

My beautiful, yet currently idiotic, lover looks at me puzzled. "Did you not say you wanted to be with me forever? That you wanted *only* me?"

Shit. He's right. But that's not the point, so I maintain my severe visage. "Of course! But your trust in me should have been enough! I shouldn't have to subject myself to yet another ancient, paranormal ritual just so you can stake your claim." I shake my head and chew my bottom lip. "You know, for someone that will never marry me, you sure have fucked up views of commitment."

Dorian lets out an irritated sigh. "Are we back to that, Gabriella? I already told you why I won't marry you. It is meaningless; just a way to build alliances. A business transaction. I have pledged my devotion to you in the most profound way possible for my kind. Weddings are trivial, ostentatious parties highlighting overindulgence and pageantry. They are ridiculous human nuisances."

"And how would you know that? You aren't even human!" I feel hurt, angry tears spring in my eyes, and I quickly blink them away.

"And neither are you!" he shouts, his voice nearly vibrating the room.

I stare at him blankly, unable to move, speak or even blink. *I am not human.* I'm still trying to fit into this world, still trying to keep up the charade of my normal life. I still want to belong, be liked, fall in love, have a family. I still want my happily ever after. And that just isn't possible for me. I told myself that it would be alright, that Dorian would be enough for me to leave my hopes and aspirations behind. But all the while I had been trying to be enough for him, I never truly considered if he, and all that his presence represents, would be enough for *me*.

I stand on shaky legs and Dorian quickly flies to his feet to aid me. I gather my torn panties and stuff them in my purse then busy myself in fixing my hair and makeup in my compact mirror. Anything to keep from facing the torment of my reality.

"Gabriella," Dorian breathes. I remain silent, too hurt and confused to acknowledge him. "I would give you everything your heart desires if I could. I would marry you. I would have children with you. I would do anything you wanted me to. But that life is just not possible for either one of us. You have to stop believing that there is a place for us in this world. It will only bring you heartache. This isn't where we belong."

I slam down the tube of mascara I am holding and it shakes the steel desk. "Ok, Dorian, I get it! I'll never fit in. I'll never have a normal life. Come on, I haven't for the last twenty years, why start now?"

I shake my head apologetically at my foolishness. "You know, I used to think that I wanted to be extraordinary. That I wanted something more than the whole cookie cutter American dream. I wanted to be special. And now that I am, so much so that there is a killer after me, I just want to press rewind and enjoy my old, boring life. Take extra time to appreciate Chris and Donna, and all my friends."

I feel Dorian's strong hands on my shoulders and he lightly kneads away the tension. *Those magic fingers*. "You still have time, little girl. Don't give up just yet."

I reach my hand up to touch his fingers with mine, spinning around in the swivel chair to face him. "Thank you. I know you're trying to help, trying to make the transition easier for me." I give him pensive smile. "What will happen afterwards? Once I ascend? I'll have to leave, huh?"

Dorian strokes the line of my jaw with the back of his hand, igniting tiny tingles throughout my entire body. "Not right away. Most likely you'll be summoned to either Rome or Greece, depending on what side you choose. Ordinarily, they would appoint your . . . job, per say, based on the skill set you were birthed with. Then you are assigned a region. However, with your unique circumstances, I can't be certain what would happen. I'd imagine that you could ultimately write your own destiny."

I nod. "I don't want much to change. I want to stay here. I wanna come to work every day. I wanna go out with my friends. I wanna have Sunday dinner with Chris and Donna every week." I wrap my arms around his waist and bury my face in his white dress shirt. "And I want you here. I don't want you to leave."

Dorian squeezes me tight, resting his chin on the top of my head before kissing my hair. "I know, little girl. I want to stay with you too."

My head snaps up with alarm. "So you have to go? Wait, I thought you were assigned here?"

Dorian gives me an apologetic half-smile. "I'm royalty, baby. I'm only here to oversee your ascension. Then I go back to Greece. Back home."

Before I can protest, Dorian's face transforms to one of pure disgust and hatred. He closes his eyes and stands upright, his body vibrating with anger. When they reopen, they flash white hot, a low growl rumbling in his chest.

"What? What's wrong?" I question with alarm.

"Stavros. *Shit!* I have to go." Dorian stiffly kisses my forehead then brings my hand to his face, where he gently brushes my knuckles against his lips, his eyes never leaving mine. Then he takes a step backwards and dissipates before my eyes, only leaving behind plumes of grey.

I stand in my tiny office, speechless and disheveled. *What the hell just happened here?* First the Dark King tricks me into meeting with him resulting in Dorian's erratic, yet pleasurable, reaction, then he just disappears?

"*Fucking Warlocks,*" I mutter under my breath before heading back out to the sales floor to finish my shift.

When I arrive home that evening, I receive two text messages, one from Dorian and the other from Jared, the two most important men in my life. *Oh, the irony*. I open Dorian's first, hoping for some type of explanation for his sudden departure. Unfortunately, I come up disappointed.

From Dorian, 9:36 PM

– I must go to Greece immediately. I should be back by the end of the week but I will try to email you to confirm. I love you, little girl. In life and in death.

What the hell? *No!* Something serious must be going down for him to run off so quickly. At least there better be. Before I follow through with my plan to throw my phone against my bedroom wall out of sheer annoyance, I open the second text message.

From Jared, 9:40 PM

– Hey Gabs, think you can meet up with me sometime this week? I have something I really wanna talk to you about and I need to say it face to face. Cool? Can't wait to see you.

Well, *that's* interesting. What is it with the men in my life being so cryptic lately? I take a deep breath and hit reply, shaking my head.

To Jared, 9:41 PM

– Sure, just let me know what time, k?

To Dorian, 9:42 PM

– I love you too, though I wish you weren't leaving. What's going on? Please email me as soon as you can. And be safe. Come home soon.

After getting ready for bed, I stay awake for as long as my heavy eyelids can stand, hoping for the reply text from Dorian that never arrives.

Sixteen

"That's all you're eating?" Jared asks with raised brows.

I look down at my lightly dressed chopped salad. "Just not really hungry, I guess," I shrug.

"Don't tell me you're trying to lose weight. You already have a smokin' bod. Does Dorian like his women boney or somethin'?" Jared asks, letting his eyes fall over the length of my body draped in tight jeans and form-fitting sweater, revealing more cleavage than usual.

"No," I reply shaking my head. "I just haven't had much of an appetite." It's true. Whenever Dorian is called away to Greece, which happens a lot more frequently than I'd like, I can hardly function, let alone eat. I know it's downright pathetic to be so dependent on him but it's the truth. Thank God it's finally Friday and he is expected to get back some time tonight. I need him like I need air; I've been suffocating without him.

Jared shrugs. "Well, anyway. I'm glad you could come tonight. Seems like we never get to hang out like we used to. So what's up? What's new?" He takes a big slug of his soda, regarding me with questioning green eyes. "Holy shit, Gabs! When did you get another tattoo?"

I look down at my right hand, at the little blue anchor that now occupies the space under my thumb. "Oh, that. Yeah. Just a little something I got a while ago. Has it really been that long since we hung out?"

"I guess so," he replies with another shrug. And it has been. The man that sits before me hardly resembles my best guy friend. His auburn locks are styled much like the young heartthrobs featured on magazines and in music videos and his wardrobe has gotten a major style upgrade. Jared has always been a looker but in his designer jeans, fitted tee and leather Moto jacket, he looks more GQ than soccer jock. And as much as it pains me to admit, Aurora has good taste. Jared is looking hotter than ever.

"How's life at UCCS treating you these days?" I ask, hoping to distract my mind from the obvious weirdness lingering between us.

"Great. I really like it there. Everyone is really cool. Obviously I've been busy as hell with soccer but it's been awesome." He bites into his massive bacon burger, chewing slowly before grabbing his soda to wash it down. "And the store? How's it going?"

"Good. Sales are better than ever now that I've incorporated some different styles and local designers. And Carmen is doing great. She's a huge help."

For the next hour, Jared and I try to make idle chitchat to fill the uncomfortable distance between us. I just want to press pause and rewind to a time when things were seamless and easy. We were once so close, kindred spirits even. We could talk for hours about absolutely nothing and when we'd run out of things to say, we could be comfortably silent. As long as we were together, everything made sense. But as I stab my salad at our once favorite restaurant, I realize that I've lost my best friend. Jared Johnson is a stranger to me.

"Well, I guess I better get to why I asked you to come meet me tonight," Jared says after our empty plates and glasses have been cleared. He pulls a navy blue velvet ring box out of his pocket and sets it on the table in front of me. I look up at him with shocked, unblinking eyes.

"Jared . . . is that what I think it is?" *Holy shit!* Is Jared about to propose? My heart is beating out of my chest, and I'm not sure if it's from excitement or immense fear. Maybe a mixture of both.

"It is." He reaches over and opens the tiny box, revealing a glimmering princess cut diamond fixed on a white gold band. "Dealing with what happened with my mom and realizing that our loved ones can be taken from us at any moment, I decided to stop delaying the inevitable. I know what's important to me now, Gabs.

And I'm not afraid. I'm not afraid to take that step."

I try to swallow, but my mouth is suddenly bone dry. I reach over and grasp my iced tea with a shaky hand, downing it in seconds. "What are you saying?" I whisper as soon as I've regained my voice.

"I'm saying that I'm ready. I'm ready to take a leap of faith and start my life with the woman that I love." Jared smiles at me brightly, his emerald eyes gleaming brightly with adoration.

This is it; he's going to say those words. I hold my breath in anticipation.

"I'm going to ask Aurora to marry me."

What. The. *Fuck?* "Jared, what are you talking about?" I sputter. "Are you crazy?" *Aurora?* He wants to marry *Aurora*? Hell no!

"No, I'm not. For once in my life, I'm completely certain about this. Gabs, you should know better than anybody how difficult it was to almost lose my mom again. I'm tired of playing it safe. I want to make Aurora my wife." Jared snaps the top of the ring box down and slides it back towards him.

"That's ridiculous, Jared! You can't marry Aurora!"

Jared recoils as if I've just slapped him across the face. "Why not? We're in love. She gets along with my family. I want to be with her. What's the problem, Gabs?"

What is *the problem?* Is it the fact that Aurora is a sex-crazed Dark One that thrives on the depraved desires of others? The fact that her relationship with Jared was manufactured so she could get close to me? Or that she is admittedly still in love with Dorian and always will be? Or could it be that Jared was the guy I once thought I was truly in love with and hoped to spend my life with? But without even voicing my endless questions aloud, I know that the answer is a combination of all my concerns. Not only is Aurora merely preying off of Jared's undeniable sexual magnetism, she is only sticking around to appease Dorian. The man that we *both* love. The man that I am certain we would both kill and die for. Love that runs so deep it frightens me.

"Jared, she's just no good for you. She isn't who you think she is." No matter the reason, the look on Jared's face tells me he's not buying it. There's no way to make him understand and protect myself, Dorian, and even Aurora at the same time. But I have to try. "You may think she feels the same about you but you're wrong. She can't be trusted."

"And you know this, how?" he says, his brow furrowed in frustration. "Look, Gabs, I get that you and her have problems. But don't sit here and try to say she doesn't care about me. That's really low. Even for you, Gabs."

Even for me? What's that supposed to mean?

"I'm sure she cares about you," I say with a huff. "But there are things you don't know about her, about who she is. And I don't want you getting caught up in her lies." I gaze down at the little blue box and am suddenly repulsed by the sight of it. I try a different angle, hoping to tap into Jared's rationality. "Not to mention that you are no way ready for marriage. You're only 20, for crying out loud! And you haven't even finished school!"

"I'm not saying that we'd get married right away, Gabriella. But Aurora is a few years older than me, and women like her aren't single for long. I need to show her that I'm in this for the long haul. I mean, who *wouldn't* want to marry her?"

Ouch. "Jared, if she really loved you, she'd wait until the time is right. It's only been like what, 5 or 6 months? Give it time. You have your whole life ahead of you."

Jared exhales noisily. "Don't you think I know that? I'm not stupid." He grabs the velvet box and stuffs it back into his pocket. "But after the summer I had, I can't afford *not* to live every day to the fullest. Playing it safe is no longer an option for me."

I nod, hoping that my show of understanding will soften Jared's annoyed expression. "I know. And maybe one day, you'll both be ready for such a monumental step. But I have to say, I don't think that time is now." *Or ever.*

"So you mean to tell me, if Dorian popped the question you'd turn him down?" Jared questions with a raised eyebrow.

I look down at my knotted fingers, trying to force down the swell of agony rising in my chest. I feel my bottom lip begin to quiver and I bite down on it to keep my emotions at bay. *Why the hell does this subject keep coming up?*

"That will never happen," I whisper. "Dorian will never ask me."

"Humph," I hear Jared snort. "Well, looks like Aurora was right about him. But just because your boyfriend has serious commitment issues, you shouldn't try to bring everyone else down too. Our happiness isn't always based on you, you know."

Hold up. I know Jared is *not* going there with me. "And what the hell is that supposed to mean?" I snap, unable to hide my agitation.

Jared runs a hand through his messily styled auburn locks. "It means that misery loves company. Your outlook on love, relationships, life in general . . . you're so fucking pessimistic. All because you are unhappy. So we all feel guilty for wanting what we want and try to downplay our happiness to accommodate you. But you know what? *Shit*, I'm tired of watching *The Gabriella Show*. I'm tired of rushing to your aide every time you've got another shit storm coming your way. I want a life. Not an obligation."

I gaze at Jared blankly, unable to process the razor-sharp words that have just fallen from his lips. How can he say these things to me? *How dare he!* All this time I thought that the friendship Jared and I shared was based off of mutual trust, respect, and even affection for each other. And now he's telling me he felt *obligated* to stick around throughout the train wreck that is my life?

Before I know it, I'm on my feet, my chair screeching against the floor, causing nearby diners to cringe. I am only just aware that I am rummaging through my purse to retrieve my wallet where I grab a twenty to slap down on the table. It is a feat considering the violent shudders rolling through my body. My hands are shaking fiercely and I know that if I don't get out of there, Jared will very easily become the target of my unpredictable rage.

"Oh, so you're leaving? You finally hear the truth and you're running? Instead of staying and talking this out? I thought you never backed down from a challenge, Gabs," he snorts, playing a dangerous game at provoking me.

My eyes snap up to his, icy tingles stabbing my eyelids. "Go fuck yourself," I spew between gritted teeth.

I turn on my heel and stiffly make my way towards the exit of the restaurant, only too aware of the heat radiating from my fingertips. Shudders of white hot anger encapsulate my frame while a deep, agonizing ache grips my chest, causing me to struggle for every breath. I need air, but I can't seem to make it to the door fast enough.

As I approach the refuge of the double doors, a cold gust of air rips through me, blowing them wide open and startling a group of patrons waiting to be seated. I'm too angry and hurt to even question it. I just will my legs to keep walking until I reach the solitude of my little car.

I slide robotically into the car and start it up as the tremors finally begin to subside. *What the fuck just happened here?* How could Jared, of all people, take it there with me? And he really feels that way; he sees me as a liability. The pain plaguing my chest grows in intensity with every unanswered question. I've loved him for years, only to play second to all his dumb-as-a-box-of-rocks girlfriends and fuck buddies, yet he feels that *I'm* the one who's got issues? That I have been too selfish and wrapped up in my own bullshit to be happy for him or anybody else? This is ridiculous. Utterly fucking ridiculous.

Beyond his heinous insults, I try to shake the most staggering occurrence this evening. Jared had a ring. A ring that caused my breath to hitch and my heart to swell at the sight of it. And though it kills me to admit, for one fleeting second, I thought that ring was for me.

What would I have said if it was? I am undoubtedly in love with

Dorian but neither one of us could say what the future holds. And he's made it brutally clear that he has no intention of ever making me his wife. It had never been important to me before but I guess knowing that it could never be a possibility for us has made me somewhat crave matrimony. Plus he said that he wanted me to try to achieve a normal life, a life that didn't include him one day. What does that mean? That his promise of forever means absolutely nothing? Why doesn't he understand that there is no *me* without him?

Not quite ready to go home and face Morgan's questioning glare, I decide to head to the Broadmoor. Dorian had said that he would be in later and would call me when he got in. Right now, more than ever, I need his comfort, his reassurance. His validation. He is the only person that makes me feel like I am more than just a floundering, pathetic girl with no real goals or aspirations. He makes me feel strong and resilient. I need him right now, and not merely for his encouragement. *I need to feel him*. I need to feel his skin on mine, pushing away the dreary clouds darkening my fragile heart. He's the only one who sees just how delicate and broken that I really am. Even through the tough exterior, he knows I am just a little girl. *His* little girl. Frightened and lonely in a world that rejects what I am. That dispels my entire existence.

As I approach the elaborate double doors of Dorian's suite, removing my key card from my purse, I get an overwhelming feeling of unease. Dread sweeps over me, causing the hairs in the back of my neck to stand at attention and my stomach to churn the tiny bits of food I was able to eat at dinner. I put some pep in my step and book it to doors, anxious to surround myself in Dorian's space until he returns.

"What the hell?" I sputter as I enter the living room. I don't even realize that I've lost the grip on the strap of my purse until it tumbles to the ground, splaying its contents on the beige carpet. My heart races at an immeasurable pace yet I feel like I'm in a slow motion sequence of a really horrible movie. And this would be the climax when shit gets real.

"What are you doing here? And you . . . what the hell is going on?" I ask looking between Dorian and Aurora, each of them wearing a mix of shock and horror. It's evident that I walked in on a very heated, intimate conversation. "Um, hello? Somebody better start talking. NOW!"

Aurora puts a hand on her very narrow hip and walks over to me, donning a curve-hugging sheath dress and her signature ridiculously high heels. "Oh relax, Gabriella. We were just talking. It figures you'd be the first to congratulate us."

I look to Dorian, who still is wearing his alarmed expression. He's dressed in a dark suit, white shirt without a tie, the top few buttons unfastened to expose a small patch of smooth, hard chest. His hand grips the crystal glass of scotch he's holding and I'm afraid he'll shatter it any second now.

"Dorian? What the hell is going on? I'm not going to ask again." He licks his lips nervously, the pinkness of his tongue catching my eye and almost distracting me. *Oh hell no!* That shit is not working today!

Aurora steps into my line of vision, holding out her perfectly manicured left hand. On it lies the biggest diamond I have ever seen, gleaming brightly on her ring finger. "Gorgeous, isn't it?" she beams.

I look back to Dorian, still clutching the glass at his side. "Explain. Now."

He lets out a ragged breath, his broad shoulders falling with resignation. "Something happened. Something out of my control. I'm so sorry, Gabriella, but-"

"We're engaged!" Aurora interjects, wriggling her fingers in my face. "We're getting married!"

I stagger backwards, the air exiting my chest so quickly that it leaves me completely breathless. I can sense movement in front of me, but my clouded eyes are unable to focus. Muffled voices and the jingle of feminine laughter echo in the distance. I'm sinking, falling away from this hell.

Snap the fuck out of it, Gabs.

"What did you just say?" I say snapping back to the here and now. There's no way I heard that right. First Jared and now Dorian? *My* Dorian? Un-fucking-believable!

"I said Dorian and I are engaged. Beautiful ring, isn't it?" Aurora snickers.

My head jerks to Dorian, who is wound so tight, he looks like he's about to have an aneurism. "You bought it yourself, Aurora. Stop acting like a child," he grumbles. Tentatively, he closes the distance between us, his eyes cautiously searching. "Gabriella, have a seat so we can talk." He motions with his hands but makes no attempt to touch me.

"I don't want to sit. I want you to tell me what the fuck she's talking about. You're . . . *engaged*?" I quell all feelings of sorrow and let my rage take the reins.

"It's not what you think." Dorian looks back at a smiling Aurora and a frustrated growl quakes his chest before turning back to me. "She made a deal. It was the only way to keep you and your family safe."

"What do you mean, *'she made a deal'*? What kind of deal? And since when has my safety been guaranteed?" I take a step forward into the room, eager to get to the bottom of this.

"Aurora deceived me. She deceived all of us," he grits, trying to ignore Aurora's wind-chime laughter behind him. "And the only reason why she is even allowed to fucking breathe is because I would do anything to keep you safe, my love. I had to. Your life was threatened and I had to."

"Threatened by whom?" I ask placing an attitude-fueled fist on my hip more forcefully than I intend.

Dorian lets out an exasperated sigh. "Everyone."

"*Everyone?* Who the hell is *everyone*?"

He shakes his head. "I didn't know . . . there have been changes. The Light, the Dark . . . relations have been less than cordial. And once the Light caught wind of our relationship, they grew worried. They thought we–that *I*–would influence you. That I would fill you with so much of myself that you would have no other choice but to choose the Dark. These tensions have threatened certain agreements between Light and Dark forces. And some of the Dark families are worried that you could make things difficult for them."

"But that's not my fault!" I shout, feeling the makings of fresh tears. I blink them away. Hell no, I refuse to cry.

"I know that. *We* know that. Then Aurora came up with the asinine idea that if she and I were to marry, that it would be enough to placate the Light. My father agreed. Plus he saw this as a good opportunity to join houses; to create a new elite breed of our kind by joining the Skotos and the Órexes."

I cringe, understanding exactly what Dorian means. Join houses, create a new breed . . . The Dark King wants them to have children. To spawn a new type of power. I swallow down the quickly rising bile, rejecting the urge to vomit. I will not give that bitch the satisfaction of seeing me sick and depleted.

"Don't do it," I croak, shaking my head. "Please. I won't let you do it."

Aurora sashays towards us, a disgustingly pleased look on her face. "It's already done. The deal has been made. And there's no going back now. Plus, I've already started shopping for dresses!"

"Why are you so fucking spiteful?" I snarl, taking a step forward. The room suddenly begins to hum, the floor vibrating under our feet. "You did this purposely to tear us apart! You are so miserable with your own existence, so . . . pathetic that Dorian doesn't want you anymore that you had to go pull some backdoor shit like this!"

"Me? Miserable?" Aurora scoffs, holding her left hand to her chest, the gleam of the massive diamond catching in the light. "Why would I be miserable, Gabriella? Dorian is marrying *me*, not you. He chose me!"

"But you know he doesn't love you!" I scream.

"Oh really? Well, guess what?" she smiles.

"Aurora! Enough!" Dorian barks.

"He doesn't love you, either, sweetie." She pauses for reaction, letting her sickly sweet smile spread even wider, making her look like the Joker in drag. "Aw, don't look so surprised. It's not in his nature. You can't change him, Gabriella."

"I said enough, Aurora! Shut the fuck up and sit down or I swear I will rip you to shreds!" Dorian commands, his voice taking on its ancient, guttural timbre.

Aurora shrugs and goes to sit on the couch, crossing her legs with an air of satisfaction. Dorian looks back to me with apologetic eyes.

"What is she talking about, Dorian? What is she saying?"

Dorian opens his mouth as if he is trying desperately to relay something, anguish plaguing his beautiful face. An internal battle brews behind his crystal blue eyes.

Aurora sighs from behind him. "His curse," she calls out.

I walk past him and stalk towards her. "What curse?"

Aurora admires her ring, her eyes never meeting mine. "He was spelled to love you. His father wanted him to know what it felt like to have to kill the woman he loves. Loving you is merely a facet of his punishment," she giggles. "I mean, really. Why else would he want someone like you? You can't be that dim."

I whip back around to Dorian, hoping, *praying*, for him to dismiss her claims. He just stands there, tortured and defeated.

"I am so sorry, Gabriella. I *do* love you. I know I do. Don't listen to her. It isn't true," he mutters in a low voice.

"You were spelled to love me? All this," I wave around the room, "is a lie? A fucking joke?"

Dorian shakes his head, walking towards me and cupping my face. I want to pull away from him so damn bad but his touch feels so good. I crave his contact.

"I don't believe it; I never have. I know what I feel. No one can tell me differently." His glossy eyes burn into mine, eagerly trying to make me understand. "I love you. I want only you. And I know that is real."

"So this is it. You're getting married." I break his hold on my face and spin around to jab a finger just inches from Aurora's perfectly pink pout. "To her!"

"Oh, gag. Get over it," she says with a wave of her hand. "It's not like you two could've stayed together anyway. He would have never married you even if I didn't suggest the arrangement. Besides, you could never give him an heir."

Fury explodes in my veins, my chest heaving out pure wrath with every breath. My hands ball into tight, hot fists while trembles wrack my frame with a vengeance. Icy cold prickles assault the rims of my eyes before spilling into my irises. The vibrations evolve into a full on quake, every light in the suite flickering violently. Everything not nailed down rattles and shakes causing glasses and knick knacks to fall to the ground.

"Get up! Get the fuck up so I can knock you on your ass! Now! Get up!" I scream taking a step back to give myself more space. She's right; I could never give Dorian an heir, but it's none of her damn business.

She giggles again and stands, swinging her dark locks over shoulder. "Is that so? I'd love to see that." Her hands are suddenly engulfed with a dark red haze at her sides, though her stupid grin doesn't falter.

"Aurora, step away," Dorian commands, standing between us. He places his hands on my shoulders in an attempt to soothe me but instantly cringes and recoils as if he's been shocked with an unseen current. "Gabriella, calm down. Please calm down, little girl," he coos.

"Get out of my way, Dorian," I mutter through clenched teeth. The violent shudders coursing through my body make it an almost impossible feat.

"Oh, please! What did you expect?" Aurora chortles from behind him. "Dorian is a prince. He could never truly be with you.

And you . . . you are an abomination. An inbreed. Your own father wasn't even a pure blood royal. You aren't worthy of him!"

Glass and mirrors shatter as bright auburn flames ignite from my fingertips, engulfing my hands and forearms. And though my eyes are locked tight on Aurora, looking past Dorian's blinding beauty, I know they are there. I can feel them. I can feel the power blazing bright and hot surrounding me. And it feels amazing.

"Come closer and say that shit again. I dare you," I growl. *Hell yes, I growled.*

Aurora laughs again, her sing-song voice piercing my eardrums like nails on a chalkboard. "Aw, how cute! You really are like your mother. She was just as naive and hopeful as you! Not to mention stupid. Aw, poor, poor pathetic Gabriella."

That's it! I. Am. Done.

I push Dorian aside, somehow launching his hard, muscular body across the room with ease. He goes flying several feet towards the dining room, skidding to a stop before smashing into the grand table. As I take the few quick steps towards Aurora's shocked expression, he reappears beside me, calling my name repeatedly yet avoiding contact. I don't hear him; I can't. My frenzied temper won't let me.

Pulling my fist back, I conjure every ounce of strength, anger and revulsion at Aurora's words and thrust it directly into her face, propelling her into a mahogany hutch standing yards away against the wall. She flies into it, breaking the glass doors and splintering the wood with a loud *crash*. Before I know it, she's on her feet again and in my face, though her clothing has been ripped to shreds and her hair is all over her face, chunks of broken wood and glass sprinkled in her dark waves.

"You bitch! I will enjoy watching you die! Just like your whore of a mother!" she screeches, spewing strings of saliva. Her delicate features begin to morph into something monstrous, her eyes ablaze with white flames. Her tan skin melts into a gruesome pale, almost skeletal form and I instantly recognize my parking lot phantom.

Aurora's darkness.

"Enough!" Dorian shouts, the authoritative tone of his voice demanding both our attention. I hadn't even noticed that his own darkness had overcome him, transforming him into something almost unrecognizable and even more frightening than Aurora. I suck in a breath and give him my attention though my fists are still ready to strike.

Dorian shouts an order in their shared secret language, telling her to leave. Reluctantly, the Dark seductress pulls her shoulders back after taking a long, menacing glare at my violent expression before stalking out of the suite. I've won this round but I highly doubt it will be our last standoff.

Slowly, Dorian's beauty falls back into place, confining his demon. Piece by piece he returns to me and I will myself to release the teeth-clenching anger that binds my own body. Only then do I become aware of throwing him several feet into the air and causing him to narrowly miss the dining room table. I can't even begin to explain how I was even capable of that, let alone almost launching Aurora through the wall. Had they been regular humans, I would have surely severely injured, if not killed, them. And the thought of that, realizing just how powerful I will be, doesn't repulse me. I can't help but feel somewhat strengthened by it.

Finally the tremors begin to cease and the lights return to normal as we both cage our inner monsters. Dorian looks to me warily, the tiny lines around his eyes indicating how much this ordeal has aged him. He reaches his hands towards me but still doesn't touch me.

"Gabriella, I . . ." he begins, unsure of how to begin and maybe a little nervous. "I'm sorry. This isn't what I wanted."

"Isn't it?" I gasp, the tightness of my chest constricting my labored breaths. I try to swallow but my mouth feels like sandpaper. "Isn't this what all of you wanted from the beginning?"

He shakes his head, his shoulders slumping in defeat. "No. Not me. But I had no other choice."

"You had a choice, Dorian. I'm the one who wasn't given one. You took it upon yourself to choose for me."

Again, Dorian reaches towards me, finally resting a hand on my shoulder. The contact instantly soothes me but I hold on to my steely expression. He tries to meet my gaze with his ice blue eyes, desperately trying to extinguish my rage but I refuse him access.

"I know you're upset, but-"

"Upset? You think I'm *upset*?" I shriek, shrugging out of his touch. I won't let him distract me with head games this time. "Dorian, you are getting fucking married! I have completely put my life in your hands. I am linked to you. Hell, I let you mark me for Christ's sake!"

"I know," he murmurs, dropping his gaze to the floor. He runs his hand through his tousled black locks. "And I am grateful. But you have to know that Aurora means nothing to me. And we can still-"

"We can still, what? Mess around? Hook up whenever you need a fix? Hell no! I am not like that! And how dare you think I'd be cool with something like that!" I take in a sharp breath of air and close my eyes trying to reel in my temper.

"How can you stand there and act like I did this for any other reason but to protect you?" Dorian scoffs. "I don't want her, Gabriella! I don't want any of this! But I can't–I won't–be without you. It is physically impossible for me. And don't you pretend like you don't feel the same."

"You don't mean that, Dorian. You only think you do, remember? You. Don't. Love. Me." Just saying the words nearly brings me to my knees and I fight to keep the hurt, angry tears at bay. No. I won't let him hurt me. Not again. "I've ignored a lot of shit–you not telling me who you were, you breathing and nearly fucking Aurora right in front of me–because I thought that what we had was destiny. I thought we'd get through it all together. But *this*–you marrying Aurora–I can't ignore. I can't be your fool anymore. I won't let love make me weak."

"This is destiny, Gabriella. Your destiny is with me. We were meant to be together. I love you," he urges.

"Stop it! You don't think this shit is killing me right now? Just stop! You don't love me, Dorian!"

"Don't fucking say that," he grits angrily. "Don't try to tell me what I feel."

"Come on, Dorian! Call a spade a spade. You played me. All of you did. And I'll admit, I was dumb as hell for choosing to see past your betrayal. But I'm done! I. Am. Done! Do you hear me? I asked you to kill me before because I was too weak and blinded by stupid, fucking love. Not anymore. I'm done with being a victim."

Dorian flinches, taking a step back. "Why are you acting like this? You know I did this for you. For us."

"I didn't ask you to!" I yell, my voice cracking with unshed emotion. "You know, I'm pretty sure I lost my best friend tonight. And I come here only to find that I lost the man I love too. All because of shit that just had to be done to save me. I'm so fucking done with losing. I'm done with needing to be saved all the damn time!" I bend down to collect the scattered contents of my purse that has been strewn about during the scuffle.

"What are you saying?" I hear Dorian whisper above me.

I stand and face him, even though it feels as if every bone in my body is breaking just to look at him. I love him so much it destroys me from the inside out. Agony paints his face, his eyes gleaming with his own stubborn tears. The sight causes me to shudder and a radiating ache attacks my chest.

"I'm not *trying* to say anything, Dorian. I *said* I'm done. I won't be your dirty, little secret. Your little abomination to breathe whenever you see fit."

"You know damn well I don't see you like that! Don't be callous, Gabriella," he warns sternly. He rakes his fingers through his mussed black locks.

I divert my eyes from him, fighting the overwhelming urge to fold my body into his arms and let him make it all better. But I know

I can't do that. Not now. Not ever. "It's not about being callous, Dorian. It's about being honest. Aurora was right; I'm not fit to be with you. I've realized that from the jump. Maybe it's time you did too."

"Don't say that," he growls, his lips tightening into a scowl. "Your place is with me. It's our destiny. We need each other."

I shake my head, my eyes wincing with my pained realization. "No, Dorian. You only think you need me. And what you truly want isn't *me* at all. It's my power you want." I reach my hand out to him and rest it on his cheek. Dorian nuzzles his face into the touch and kisses my palm, letting his lips linger on my skin. "All I have left is me. No Jared. No you. I can't let you break me, Dorian. Because if I do, it will sincerely demolish the tiny bit of strength I have left. And I need that to survive. I need it to survive the catastrophe that is my life. To survive without you."

He shakes his head furiously. "No. No . . . just don't. I . . . I . . ." A single, glistening tear rolls down his cheek and soaks into my hand. Knowing Dorian as the composed, stoic man that he is, the sight of his pain causes my own tears to fall rapidly down my flushed cheeks. I have to go; I have to get out of here before I change my mind and surrender to him.

"I'm sorry, Dorian," I whisper through a sob. "But we can't do this."

"No . . . please," he begs hoarsely. "I need you. I've waited for you for so long." He brings his hands up to cup my face, wiping away my tears with his thumbs. "I love you so much, little girl. So much."

"I love you, too," I choke out.

"Then stay. Don't leave me. I won't be without you, Gabriella. I can't be without you."

I shrug out of his touch and I let my hand fall from his cheek. Then I step back from him, drinking in Dorian's beautifully anguished face before forcing my legs to carry me away from him completely. This is it; the end of us. The end of what I thought would have been the most epic love story ever told. I truly thought Dorian was my destiny. I thought the Divine created us to overcome all these obstacles and be living examples of love and resilience. And now that I see how easily Dorian folds when things get tough, how quickly he runs away from adversity, I know that he is not the man I thought he was. Yet, that revelation does nothing to ease the strangling pain assaulting every part of me. It doesn't make me love him any less.

Seventeen

There is an inexplicable peace that comes with numbness. There's no hurt, sorrow, or anguish in it. No reason to cry or scream. No more fear. No more fight.

No more *him*.

I've tried like hell to get here and stay here with a bottle of tequila. Feeling simply hurts too damn much. And though I used to relish the pain, this time, knowing that this particular brand of hurt will swallow me whole, I've pushed it into the dark corners of my mind and refused to acknowledge it.

Just keep drinking. Just keep breathing. It's the only two things I can manage right now.

Tap, tap, tap.

I hear it but I am too far gone for its meaning to register in my clouded mind.

Tap, tap, tap.

"Hey, Gabs?" Morgan says softly, cracking open my bedroom door. She spies me lying on top of the bed, unmoving and dazed. "Holy shit, Gabs, are you ok?"

My lips part reflexively to fashion a response but the numbness takes over, leaving me speechless. I can't answer that question without feeling. Because I am anything but ok.

Morgan makes her way towards me and sits on the edge of my bed. The bed he bought me. For the room he furnished. In the apartment he owns. Shit.

Breathe. Drink. Repeat.

I take a hefty gulp to drown the anxiety trying to claw its way to the surface and look at Morgan blankly. My throat doesn't even suffer the burning affects.

"Gabs, um, I'm worried about you. You've been in here since yesterday. And it's been so . . . quiet. Like eerily quiet. Miguel got a call late last night from Jared. He told him about what happened. Do you wanna talk about it?"

My eyes are on her but her face is unfocused. I force myself to look past her, not able to meet her worried eyes. If I do, I know I'll crumble.

Breathe. Drink. Repeat.

I take another swig, my eyes still fixed on my best girlfriend but not really seeing anything at all.

"Ok . . . well, I can see you're not going to work today. But at least call Carmen. She's been blowing up the house phone all morning. At least let her know you're not coming in today or something. And damn, open up a freakin' window. How much of that shit did you drink? It smells like you took a bath in it."

I smirk, looking away, the first crack of emotion I've shown since last night. Since I left him.

"Anyway, I got a client coming in at 11 so I gotta go. Try not to drown, ok. And call me when you're feeling up to it." Morgan stands and makes her way out of my room, stopping before she leaves the doorway. "It'll be ok, Gabs. I know it doesn't seem like it now, but it will be ok."

After I am once again alone in my dejection, I grab my cell phone and turn it back on, only to be met with a chorus of alerts and chimes. I ignore the missed calls, texts, and voicemails, unable to muster the strength to return to the living just yet.

To Carmen, 10:42 AM

– Sorry about that. I've been sick. You should call Mr. Skotos if you need anything.

Just typing his name makes me want to curl up into a ball and cry until I'm too weak to move. I take a gulp of tequila.

From Carmen, 10:43 AM

– K. All good. Y would I call him?

– Cuz he's the boss.

– Um, no, Gabs. He told us last week that U R now the new owner of Cashmere. He sent us all letters w/ the deets. Did you forget?

What the hell?

No . . . this can't be true. There's got to be some mistake. How the hell can I be the owner of a store when I know absolutely nothing about running one? And how did he manage to do this behind my back? And the most obvious question–Why? A consolation prize for leaving me for Aurora?

Wow. What a considerate fucker.

I sigh and tap out another text, pushing the questions into the farthest, darkest corners of my mind, packing it away with the rest of my confusion and pain.

To Carmen, 10:50 AM

– Oh yeah, sorry. Been out of it. Just call the girls to see if they can take on an extra shift this weekend. You're in charge 'til I get back Monday. Sorry again, Carmen. I owe you one.

– No prob, Gabs. Feel better. I'll take care of everything.

With a huff, I toss my phone on my comforter just as it lights up with another message. Thinking it's Carmen, I pick it up to look. I am so very wrong, and the dull ache in my chest overrides my alcohol-induced numbness. It hurts so bad that I gasp for my next breaths, the ache evolving into a staggering stab. My eyes fill with agonized tears while I read the blurry words on the small screen.

From Dorian, 10:52 AM

– I love you so much, little girl. More than my own existence. I would do anything for you, even lay down my own life. I need you to breathe.

I close the text, seeing that there are several more. Knowing I am just torturing myself, I open the first at the bottom of the list. Maybe there will be an explanation somewhere in it. A reason for this pain.

– Please come back to me, Gabriella. We need to talk. I can't let you go.

– At least let me know you made it home safely. I am trying to give you space but I am worried about you.

– Little girl, I need to see you. I need to hold you. Let me make this better. I love you.

– Please at least send me a text to let me know you're ok. I am going out of my mind.

– I did this for you, my love. I couldn't bear the thought of a world without you. Even if you don't want me anymore. All of this is for you.

– Dammit, Gabriella! Answer your phone! Your voicemail is full and I need to talk to you! Don't shut me out!

– I'm fucking losing it! You don't want to see what I am capable of. You have no idea what I would do to get through to you. Call me, dammit!

– Gabriella, please.

– I'll never stop loving you. I'll never stop needing you. YOU. It's

YOU that I want. I love you, in life and in death.

Unable to control my trembling hand, I let the phone slide out of my grasp. My throat has been completely consumed by the large knot of emotion lodged in it. I can't do this; I can't shed one more tear for fear that I won't be able to stop. Snatching the nearly empty bottle of tequila off my dresser, I down every drop. Then I race to the kitchen for more, grabbing the first thing I see and screwing off the cap. I don't even taste it. I just pray the toxic elixir burns away that horrid knot so I can breathe again and take me back to oblivion.

When I stir awake, it's dark outside. My alarm clock displays that it is after 9 P.M. I've slept the entire day away. Good. Better than living it.

A knock at the door startles me and I realize why I awoke in the first place. Before I can get up to answer it, it creaks open, streaming light into the pitch darkness of my bedroom. A tall, masculine shadow steps in and closes the door behind him.

"You know, you really should answer your phone," Jared says, flicking the light on. I shield my tired eyes, my aching head throbbing at the intensity. "Holy shit, Gabs, you look how I feel."

Jared walks over and sits at the foot of my bed, assessing my ragged appearance. I haven't bathed since yesterday morning, let alone looked in a mirror. I can only imagine what kind of rat's nest sits atop my head.

I shrug, unable to formulate a response. I'm not even sure I can talk after downing so much of the searing liquor and my mouth tastes awful. Then I remember vomiting before passing out this morning. I hold up a finger and stagger to my bathroom to freshen up. No need to kill Jared with my breath just because I feel like death.

"So I take it you found out," Jared murmurs once I reemerge.

I nod, clearing my throat. "Yeah," I reply hoarsely.

"Guess you were right." He runs his hands through his messy hair and snorts, shaking his head in disbelief. "I can't believe I didn't see what was going on right in front of my eyes. They were messing around this entire time. And here I thought *we* had unresolved feelings," he says gesturing between the two of us.

I shrug, still at a loss for words. He's right. Even after meeting . . . *him*, I never stopped caring for Jared. I think I'll always be attracted to him. However, after last night and the way he dug into me at the restaurant, I don't think he and I will ever be the same. He said I was a miserable obligation, a burden to him and the rest of our friends.

"About what I said last night," he begins, reading my mind. "I'm sorry. I shouldn't have said those things."

"But you meant it," a hoarse, rough voice says. I hardly recognize it as my own.

Jared looks at me with apologetic eyes, shame written on his face. Yes, he meant it. He thinks I'm a selfish bitch. And honestly, I'm fresh out of fucks to give.

"It's fine. *I'm* fine. You don't need to feel responsible for me," I say standing up and walking to my bedroom door. "I really need to be alone right now."

Jared takes the hint and makes his way to me. "I really am sorry, Gabs. For everything. You were right about . . . Aurora," he says cringing. That's when I really get a good look at him. His eyes are sunken in with dark circles around them. He's unshaven and his clothes are wrinkled. Jared has been hurting. Maybe as much as I have.

"And I guess you were right about . . . You were right too," I stammer, my eyes casting down. I look up to find his gaze on me, overflowing with unshed pain. It mirrors my own.

After I walk Jared to the door, I pop into Morgan's room just to show her I'm still alive. Then I make a sandwich, realizing I haven't eaten since the salad over 24 hours ago. Still, I can hardly choke it down, and grab a beer instead. After showering and throwing on some ratty old pajamas, I climb into bed and desperately try to close my eyes without seeing . . . *him.*

One day down, eternity to go.

EIGHTEEN

The next day passes in the same excruciating manner and by Monday I am all too happy for the distraction of working. I try my hardest to make myself presentable although my raging headache from my 3 day binge is making it almost impossible. Carmen keeps looking at me with pity in her eyes and by early afternoon, I'm sick of it. I know she's heard and she most likely suspects I've been lying about being sick. I make up an excuse about paperwork and opt to hide in the office.

"Hey, Gabs?" Carmen says, poking her head inside.

Busted. I lift my head from my desk, my sleepy eyes giving away my cat nap. "What's up, Carmen?"

"Someone is here to see you." Her eyes grow large with excitement and she waggles her eyebrows.

My thoughts immediately go to . . . him, but Carmen shakes her head to dispel my unspoken question. "I've never seen him before but, O-M-Geeee! So hot! I think he might be a new designer."

I sit up straight and nod, trying to hide my twinge of disappointment. Why should I be upset that it's not him? I told him we were done. He's engaged; there's no reason for him to come see me.

"I'll be right out. Thanks, Car."

I fluff my hair and give my cheeks a few light smacks to wake up. Then I slather on some lipgloss, hoping I look somewhat professional, seeing as I am now the freakin' owner of Cashmere. How the hell did that even happen? And what the hell am I supposed to do to keep it afloat? I sigh, shaking my head in frustration then head out to greet our guest.

"Hey Gabs, I mean, Gabriella," Carmen stammers as I approach.

The mystery man's back is to me and her eyes once again widen with delight to indicate her approval. I muster up a tight grin, meeting my daily smiling quota. Yeah, that shit won't happen again.

As the man turns to face me, my breath catches in my throat. Perfectly styled dark hair, light blue eyes, and tan skin. And so impossibly gorgeous it makes my eyes hurt. This isn't a man at all, and every alarm bell in my head is telling me, screaming for me, to run like hell.

"Hello, Ms. Winters. I am Nikolai. So lovely to finally meet you," he smiles with an outstretched palm.

The very sight of his dazzling smile causes me to tremble with a mixture of unexpected desire and fright. So freakin' beautiful it's scary and I instantly know that he is Dark. He has to be. And if there is one thing I have learned about the Dark, especially in the last few days, is that they are ruthless, vile bastards with no regard for humanity. I look around me at the innocent, human shoppers and employees in my store. I have to do something; I have to get him away from them without raising suspicion. It's not only my life that is at stake.

I look down at his hand, still extended for me to take in mine. Hell no, there's no way I'm letting him touch me. "Good to meet you too. Sorry, just getting over the flu. Wouldn't want to get you sick," I say with a strained smile. He nods and places his hand behind his back in response. "Let's go back to my office so we can speak comfortably, Nikolai."

With a nervous wave, I turn to make my way to the back office on shaky legs, Nikolai right on my heels. What am I going to do once we get back there? And what could he possibly want? Surely he wouldn't do anything stupid to draw attention to himself in a store full of bystanders. Once I usher him into the tiny room and click the door closed behind me, I glare at Nikolai with cautious yet threatening eyes.

"Who the hell are you and what do you want?" I growl.

Nikolai perks into a wide smile, his white, sparkling teeth

looking more like razor sharp fangs. “I told you; I’m Nikolai. But please, call me Niko. I came to formally introduce myself,” he explains as if I should know this already.

“Nikolai who? And what is that supposed to mean to me?”

Nikolai laughs and shakes his head. “He didn’t mention I’d be coming by? Typical. Well, this is as good a time as any.”

“Mind telling me what the hell you’re talking about? And what are you doing here?!” I nearly shout with clench fists.

“Dorian sent me. He asked me to keep an eye on you during this . . . rough patch you two seem to be having. So here I am.” Niko gracefully folds himself into my swivel chair and props his hands behind his head.

Dorian. Just hearing his name causes my heartbeat to stutter. I try to slow its pace with a series of deeps breaths, feeling a wave of tears prickling the back of my eyes.

“Wow. He really has you affected, doesn’t he? Interesting.”

My cold gaze snaps to Niko, casually lounging in my chair. “I don’t need looking after. Especially not by some strange, Dark asshole who looks like a High School Musical reject. So run along now and feel free to tell him that,” I say, turning to open the door.

“Skotos,” I hear a voice say behind me, causing my hand to drop from the doorknob. “My last name is Skotos. Dorian is my brother.”

I whirl around to look at him again, the beautiful Dark One who looks more boy band than evil Warlock with his frosted blown back coif and trendy clothes. I see it–the familiarity in his face. They share the same perfect nose and chiseled jawline. Niko’s lips are a bit fuller and he’s an inch or so shorter, but he’s definitely Dorian’s sibling. “You’re his brother?”

“Yes. He’s all fucked up in the head over you. It’s downright depressing to watch. And since you won’t speak to him, he sent me.” Niko offers a warm grin, and I see flickers of sincerity in his bright blue eyes. “Things could get complicated for you in the coming months. You’re going to want my help.”

"And why do you say that?" I ask with a hand on my curvy hip.

"I'm sure my father informed you that Dark forces would be moving in for your protection. Don't you think there's a reason for that? And where there is the Dark-"

"-there is the Light," I say finishing his thought, understanding washing over me. Of course. There's got to be a reason why I all of a sudden need more protection. "What's going on? What's happened?"

"You know, you're not what D usually goes for. I mean, don't get me wrong, you're hot as shit. Even with that brooding, emo girl thing you got going on, I'd definitely hit it. And your scent! Holy fuck! I've only been around you for 5 minutes and I already wanna bend you over and fuck you 'til you can't see straight," he chortles, ignoring my question and pissing me off in the process.

I blink rapidly, taken aback by his crudeness. "Wow, asshole. I can see you didn't inherit the Skotos charm. No wonder Dorian didn't mention you. They don't let you out much, do they?"

Niko laughs again. "There she is! I've heard stories about you. And what you did to Aurora . . . I commend you. That bitch has been itching to get her ass whooped for decades!" He rakes his fingers through his styled strands. "And while I love to get the ladies hot and bothered, you should really watch your temper. Especially if you want to live until next week."

"Why do you say that?" I say crossing my arms in front of my chest.

"He didn't tell you?" I shake my head and Niko continues. "When you lose it, when your emotions are heightened, you're easier to detect. I was just fucking with you and look how quickly you were roused." He leans forward and rests his elbows on his knees, his eyes narrowing as they bore into mine. "Except for the bending you over part. That part I would love to do."

I roll my eyes and shake my head, unable to even formulate a response. What else has been kept from me?

"And you keep some really interesting company," he remark,

leaning back in the chair. "Your friends don't know what you are? Even Morgan?"

"How do you know Morgan?" I snap.

Niko smiles and I swear I hear angels singing from above. Gag. "Mmmm, that Vodou blood makes my dick hard. Especially that spicy little piece you got out front," he says with a wink.

Ok, I've officially pegged Niko as a world-class jackass. How can he and . . . *him* be related? They're like night and day. "Touch any one of my friends and I'll kill you myself. That is a promise," I say sternly. I don't want to lose my shit with him, especially if it only makes me more susceptible. Again, the asshole smiles and I feel a familiar burn between my legs. *No!*

"Relax, Gabs. D left strict instructions when it comes to your friends. Not like I could touch them anyway," he shrugs. "You know, he did that for you. He's got them all protected. You've really got him pussy-whipped, huh?"

I look away, my face flaming with emotion at the mention of Niko's brother. *God, I miss him.* I don't think I will ever stop missing him. The thought of ever moving on and being happy just doesn't exist in my mind.

"He doesn't really care about me," I mutter staring blankly at the door. "And don't call me Gabs. Only my friends call me that." I hear Niko chuckle and I turn to scowl at him. What is it about Skotos men that make them want to wreak havoc on my life? Not to mention, my hormones?

"We may not be friends now, but trust me, we will be soon. I mean, come on; look at me. I'm every girl's wet dream plus I'm pretty fucking awesome. You'll see," he grins, winking a blue eye behind incredibly long lashes.

"I highly doubt it, but you just keep telling yourself that, dumbass," I reply with a wink of my own.

Niko shakes his head in playful disbelief and is on his feet faster than I can see, his hard body pressing me into the edge of the desk. With balled fists, I push against his rigid chest but he doesn't budge.

He flashes a crooked smile before leaning into me, close enough that his cool, intoxicating scent fills my nostrils like noxious fumes.

"Back. Up," I say between pursed lips, refusing to breathe through my nose.

"Don't fight it, Gabs. It just makes me want it more." Then he's gone, nothing but writhing grey smoke left behind in his place.

"Ugh!" I scream, pounding my fist on the desk. No one can hear me anyway. "*Fucking Warlocks!*"

The excruciating drilling in my head and the desperate need to seek water and painkillers pulls me from my warm bed the next morning. I stumble to my bathroom and gulp down handfuls of tap water along with a few aspirin before slumping against the sink. The morning routine has become somewhat of a constant in the past few days. It's a mystery that my liver hasn't checked out yet. Luckily, I am not due to work until the afternoon so I nurse my hangover with some food to alleviate my queasy stomach and more water. Then I open up my laptop, forcing myself to face the inevitable.

Just as I suspected, my inbox is completely full. And only one name stares back at me: **D. Skotos**. A spasm assaults my chest and I gasp for air, gripping the front of my shirt. I know I have to do this but, but dammit, I can't. Yet I can't bring myself to hit Delete. It's too much like permanently erasing him from my life. I know that I will have to do it eventually, but there's no way I am strong enough to face that realization today.

Before I know what I am doing, the cursor is hovering over the last message he sent. Then I'm right-clicking. Morbid curiosity is a bitch.

Subject: (none)

Gabriella,

If there was any way I could fix this for you–for us–I would do it without question. Meeting you, falling in love with you, has given me purpose. It's given me a life that I never thought existed for someone like me. I am forever indebted to you for opening me & filling the emptiness that consumed me for centuries.

I never told you this, but that night in the club was not the first time I laid eyes on you. I watched you for weeks in the shadows. I told myself it was solely to acquaint myself with your schedule and rituals, but honestly, I became so enthralled with you that I couldn't stay away. I'd watch you while you worked at the mall, trying hard to seem happy and joyous when I could see the annoyance in your eyes. I'd see you with your friends, how protective and caring you were with them. I could even see the love and admiration you had for Jared, though you tried to mask it.

I have to admit, I found myself wishing you would one day look at me the way you did Jared, though you didn't know I even existed. I'd lie in bed for hours, dreaming of how it would feel to touch your skin. I'd imagine the taste of your lips, the smell of your silken hair. I wanted you long before I ever met you. And in some way, I knew that my desire would grow into something else. Something *more.*

I need you, little girl. I need to see your smile, hear your laughter. I need to see the way your eyes light up and your lips curl reflexively when you hear your favorite song. I need to see how you turn your head up towards the sky and close your eyes in the sunlight. I need to feel your body next to mine, molded so perfectly. I will never stop needing these things. And every second without them–*without you*–is torture.

Please talk to me. I just need to know you are ok. I know I've hurt you and I would gladly endure that pain for you. And if you give me the chance, I will shoulder that burden. I will take it all away.

I love you,
D

I close my eyes for a few moments, replaying the written words in my head. As painful as losing him is, knowing that he still cares for me, genuine or not, warms my insides. But I know I am just tormenting myself. He isn't mine, not anymore. He made his choice and he chose Aurora, no matter what his motives were. He gave up on us. I wasn't enough for him to fight for.

I highlight the emails and place them in a separate folder. One day I will either read them all or simply delete the entire folder. I do the same with the text messages on my phone. I have to get over him and seeing his name pop up on every screen isn't helping. Then I get ready for work, eager to let the monotony distract me from that email, and the overwhelming urge to run straight to the Broadmoor and never leave.

After an uneventful, Skotos-free day at Cashmere, I am rummaging through my closet in search of my favorite flannel pajamas when music suddenly fills my ears. Morgan must be home from work. However, the sound seems closer than her bedroom as if it is playing only a few feet away from me. I shrug to myself before grabbing my pjs and stepping out of the closet. Then my ragged heart plummets into my stomach, causing me to drop my garments.

He's here.

Sitting on the chaise lounge, his elbows resting on his knees, Dorian is here in my bedroom. I freeze where I stand, unable to do much more than breathe, and even that is a feat. The sound of my rapid heartbeat drowns out the music, blood rushing my ears and painting my face with a scarlet flush. How? Why? The questions are on the tip of my tongue yet I am unable to speak. I just drink him in, completely captivated and rendered senseless.

Dorian's sad eyes lock onto mine and a pained grimace flashes across his beautiful face. He's dressed in a simple tee and jeans and he's unshaven. Even with the bit of scruff and his hair a bit more unruly than usual he is still the most perfect being I have ever seen. He stands and cautiously makes his way towards me. When only a foot stands between us, he stops, his eyes never leaving mine. His scent surrounds me, permeating my skin and hair, and I take a deep breath before I can stop myself.

Little crinkles around his eyes and the paleness of his skin tell me that he's weakened. I just want to wrap him in my arms and hold him tight. I just want to make him better. Because having him here, seeing him after days of barely living on autopilot, I feel whole again. Dorian fixes me in a way that I could never put into words. His presence scoops up those jagged little shards of my heart and, piece by piece, puts it together again.

As if hearing my internal admission, Dorian sighs and opens his mouth to speak. But before any sound escapes, I am pressing a finger to his soft lips and shaking my head.

"Please. Don't. Don't say anything," I whisper. "Because hearing your voice will break me again. I won't be able to come back from that. I will crumble right here in front of you."

With pain and regret etched on his face, Dorian nods. He brings his hand up to my finger still on his lips and holds it to his face, nuzzling into my touch. Electric warmth ignites at my fingertips, crawling up my arm and to every nerve ending. His lips brush the inside of my palm before he rests it on his cheek and I gasp at the intimate contact, a sob building in my throat. Then he reaches out and strokes the length of my jaw gently.

We stand there for the remainder of the song–each of us cradling the other's cheek, silently reading the grief in the other's face. Just the simple, chaste gesture is enough to begin to heal the gaping wound in my chest. I could stand here and gaze at him all day without saying a word. Just enjoy the closeness of our broken bodies and the tenderness of his touch.

Dorian takes a tiny step forward, close enough for the heat of his body of mingle with mine. I look up at him with hopeful eyes, my hand still cupping his face. A tiny, sad smile plays at his lips before he presses them to my forehead. I instantly melt into his touch and my entire body hums with appreciation. But before I can respond, he's gone. And I am left standing there, my hand extended into plumes of grey, cradling the space where he was just seconds ago.

The song starts again, bringing me back to the here and now. Unable to make sense of what just happened, I walk over to the chaise lounge and try to piece it all together. Now that every sense is not clouded with all things Dorian, I let my mind focus on the emotion-filled words pouring from my sound system. My eyes quickly fill with stubborn tears and spill down my face as Bruno Mars belts his heartfelt plea to the moon. I realize why he chose this particular song for me and it could not be any more perfect. For countless nights, I watched Dorian stand at the window, looking out into the darkness contently. Sometimes he'd be completely silent and unmovable for so long, I would be bursting with curiosity at what the pitch-black sky could reveal. And he's telling me right now. He's telling me that he hasn't given up. He's still waiting for me.

I don't know how many times the song replayed or how many hours I stood at my bay window, gazing out into the night contently because I knew Dorian was doing the same. But as I crawl into bed, my body stiff with standing in the same position for so long, I realize it is the first night in four days that I didn't need to drink myself to sleep. I no longer need the numbness that is found at the bottom of a bottle. Because now, I have hope.

Nineteen

"Bitch, I don't give a damn what you say. You. Are. Going!" Morgan roars into the phone.

"Come on! I really am tired. It's been crazy busy at the store today. Besides, I don't have a costume," I plead into the receiver.

"Nope, not gonna work. I already have a costume for you. And don't give me that tired crap. All you do is freakin' sleep and, dammit, I want my friend back!"

"Morgan, seriously. I really need to start packing my stuff up and figure out where the hell I'm going to live. I don't have time for frat Halloween parties." I slump into my swivel chair and let my forehead hit the desk. Just the thought of leaving the lavish apartment at Paralia depresses me. Nothing I've found is even half as nice. But I can't see a reason to stay, considering that Dorian owns it.

"Gabs, I told you that Dorian doesn't want you to move out. He said so himself. Just call him. I don't want to lose my roommate and I damn sure don't want to move. There's no way we will find anything better."

I sigh, knowing deep down that Morgan is right. But ever since Dorian showed up in my room and played that song for me, I haven't been able to stop thinking about him. I'd wait up for hours every night, praying he'd reappear. But after weeks of failed optimism without his return, that spurt of hope quickly vanished leaving me empty once again. I was back to my miserable existence: sleeping, working, eating, drinking.

"Look, you know it isn't right for me to stay there. He's getting married, Morgan. And I'm his ex-girlfriend. Technically, I'm not even his employee. I have no right to stay."

An exasperated grunt resounds from the phone. "You know good and well Dorian wants you to stay. Shit, you two need to talk this out yourselves and stop playing games. Between him asking me about you on the sly and you moping around like the walking dead, I have had just about enough! Now, listen, trick. You're going to this party. And you will have a good time. Do you hear me, Gabriella Winters? I need you to snap out of it!"

I make a pained noise, knowing I won't be able to get out of this one. I had been able to dodge social gatherings and weekend club-hopping for the past month with my usual 'I'm tired and depressed' excuse, but I've pretty much run that one into the ground. And I've been a terrible friend to Morgan, leaving her to slay the boy toys of Colorado Springs all by herself. Not to mention, I haven't seen nor heard from Jared since that day in my room.

"Fine! Fine! Fine! You want me to go? I'll go, dammit! But I must warn you: I will get drunk. And if anyone–man, woman or child–comes at me crazy, I won't hesitate to slap a bitch." I slam my palm on the desk to drive my point home, even though I am alone.

"Yay!" Morgan squeals. "And I promise there will be no drama! Just good ol' fashioned fun!"

"Yeah right," I snort. "So what am I wearing for our night of douchery and debauchery?"

"I figured I'd be an angel and you could be a devil. Fitting, right?"

I shake my head to myself. "You have no idea."

The Kappa Sigma house at UCCS looks as if Party City's Halloween aisle threw up on it then sprinkled in some skanks for good measure. Of course, just about every chick here has used the holiday as an excuse to wear lingerie outdoors, adding a pair of bunny ears, a wig or fairy wings to justify it as a costume. Morgan and I are no better, wearing itty bitty tube dresses, hers in white and mine in red, of course. I wanted to wear jeans but could not bear another Morgan whine-fest.

I head straight to the keg situated on the back patio and help myself to a plastic cup full of watered-down beer while Morgan goes to greet some friends of hers. As I'm chugging away on my second cup, I spot Jared weaving through the crowd of festive party goers.

"Hey Gabs!" he calls out to me. He then stops to chat and talk to a group of frat guys before strolling up to me with a wide grin.

"Damn, girl! You look hot!" he shouts over the music, eyeing the red sequined minidress and heels, complete with glittery red horns. It's obvious that Jared's had too many, considering his lustful gaze.

I shrug. "It's Morgan's. She made me wear it. And what are you supposed to be?" I ask with a raised brow.

Jared turns around to reveal a red cape. "Superman?"

"Nice," I remark with a smirk. "So what's been up? Been a while since . . ."

"Since we got kicked to the curb simultaneously?" he snickers. "Yeah, it has." Jared's words sting and I know he's just trying to make light of a bad situation. Still, I'm not ready to start making jokes just yet.

"You ok?" I ask, hoping he'd drop the act and be real with me.

Jared shrugs then looks away at nothing in particular. "Of course, Gabs. Why wouldn't I be? Aurora's not the last chick on Earth. You live and you learn."

"Yeah, but you loved her. You just don't heal from that type of heartache overnight." Why am I even explaining this to him? Why is he trying to act like it doesn't even matter? That he wasn't hurt like I was? Like I still am?

"Actually, you do. You get over it and move on. It's not that hard. Maybe you should try it," Jared replies with a hint of disdain.

I look at my old friend as if he's sprouted two heads. What the hell happened to him? "Move on?"

"Yeah, Gabs, move the hell on. They don't want us; maybe they never did. Maybe we were just convenient little play things. Either way, they got over us so why not get over them?"

I look down at my red plastic cup of lukewarm beer, hoping to find the answer somewhere in the foamy brew. "It's just not that easy."

"It is, Gabs. It really is. You are just still too hung up on that asshole to even try. I mean, look at you. Yeah, on the outside, you look good. But you've got this scowl on your face and this rigid, withdrawn stance," he says, waving the length of my body. "No one is gonna want to talk to the girl that's got '*Baggage*' stamped on her forehead."

My jaw drops and my eyes narrow in pained shock. But before I can lay into him, a blonde Playboy bunny stumbles up to us and pulls Jared's arm.

"Come on, Jay! You owe me a dance, baby!" she whines in an annoyingly shrill baby voice. Gag. Jared turns to her and tells her he'll be right there before turning his attention back to me.

"Wow, well, don't let me keep you, *Jay*. Looks like the frat boy lifestyle has rubbed off on you." I shake my head, hoping to reject the sting of his words and my irritation. It doesn't help and I find myself scowling at his handsome, albeit arrogant, face. "When did you become such an insensitive dick?"

Jared smirks at me mockingly, and I have to squelch the urge to slap him. "Geez, I don't know, *Gabs*. Probably around the same time you decided to hook up with a rich, pretty boy prick over the guy that's been there for you since the 9th grade." Then he reaches over to flick the pearl and diamond pendant fixed around my neck and snorts before casually turning his back to me and rejoining his group of soccer jocks and half-dressed slores.

"There you are!" Morgan calls walking up to me. She follows my line of vision and spies Jared's retreating back. "So you saw Jared?"

I nod then bring my cup to my lips, downing it all. "Yup. And now I need to see the bottom of a bottle of tequila."

We make our way inside to the beer can littered kitchen where the hard booze awaits. Normally it would be reserved for the brothers of the fraternity, but since we are girls, and Morgan has made friends with most of them, they welcome us with shots. I take the first two with ease and by the third I am bobbing my head to the music, laughing as one of the guys tries to woo Morgan with corny pick-up lines. I turn away in search of more when a frigid sensation rips through me, causing me to shiver.

"Sure you can handle another, baby girl?" a velvety voice coos in my ear. I whip around only to be momentarily stupefied by the sight of ice blue eyes beneath long, dark lashes.

"What are you doing here?" I sputter, nearly dropping my glass.

"I came to see you. And I am so glad I did," Niko replies undressing me with his magnificent eyes. "A devil, huh?"

"Yeah," I reply rolling my eyes. I take in his grey tailored suit and tie, and while he stands out like a sore thumb in a place like this, he looks ridiculously sexy. "And what are you supposed to be? A pretentious tool?" I down my shot and chuckle to myself.

Niko smiles and I force myself to look away. "No, not exactly." He pulls out something from behind him and slaps it into his hand. A riding crop? "I am dressed as a certain billionaire playboy with a fetish for pain. And something tells me that you're into that sorta thing," he winks.

My head snaps back to him, my eyes wide with a mix of horror and embarrassment. However, Niko stows his intense gaze and breaks into hysterics, slapping the riding crop against the counter and successfully drawing quite a few questioning stares. I have no other choice but to join him in his fit of laughter. He looks ridiculous–in a hot and sexy kinda way.

"Heeeyyy, Gabs," Morgan slurs, sidling up to us. "Who's your friend?" She smiles sweetly at Niko, a hand on the curve of her hip.

Crap. How do I explain this one? "Oh, uh, this is . . ."

"Niko," he smiles, saving my ass and dazzling Morgan.

"Hi, Niko, I'm Morgan," she gushes. *Sheesh, get a grip, girl.*

"Nice to meet you, Morgan. Wow, Gabs didn't tell me she had such gorgeous friends. But I would expect no less." He smiles again and I swear Morgan's panties melt right down her legs. Luckily,

Miguel enters just as Morgan leans into Niko, successfully grabbing her attention. Thank God. I really didn't want to bear witness to the famous Skotos mind-fuckery.

"Ok, I'll ask you again. What are you doing here?" I whisper once Morgan walks away.

"I'm here for you," he says simply.

"What? Are you following me?"

"Honestly? Yes. Dorian asked me to. Plus it *is* Halloween. Supernatural energy is at its highest and this would be the perfect time for someone or something to strike. I need to make sure you're safe."

I nod, understanding exactly what he means, and am a bit thankful for his presence. I grab another shot glass and fill it along with my own. "Well, no one likes to drink alone," I say handing him the shot of tequila. "To not getting killed!" I hold up my own glass and clink it with his before downing it.

Niko smirks then gulps down the liquor. "See, Gabs, I told you we'd be friends."

"Yeah, yeah, you're still a dumbass. A stalking dumbass, at that."

After a couple more shots, Niko pulls me onto the dance floor. I am too tipsy to even resist him, plus he smells oh so damn good as he pulls me into his strong arms. It feels good to be held after so many lonely weeks without contact from anyone. Just being in his presence soothes my dejected soul.

"He misses you," Niko whispers in my ear as we sway to a slow song. His cool breath tickles my neck, sending a shiver to every erogenous zone.

"I miss him too," I find myself admitting.

Niko assesses my blank expression. "Then why are you here? Why aren't you with him?"

"He's the one getting married," I frown. "And I haven't seen nor heard from him in damn near a month! He doesn't want me."

"How could he not? How could anyone not want you?" he

whispers, fire burning in his ocean blue eyes. The intensity in them causes me to halt all movement, completely captivated by the pure desire they emanate. His gaze slips down to my lips, and I am only too aware where this is headed. But when Niko leans in, his lips just inches from mine, he stops. It's as if some unseen force is compelling him not to go any further. The frustrated furrow of his brow tells me that whatever is keeping him from advancing is unwelcome. The pause gives my intoxicated brain just enough time to wake up and I pull away from him.

"Shit, uh, I, uh, gotta go to the bathroom," I stammer, nearly sprinting and leaving him on the dance floor.

Luckily, the bathroom isn't crowded and a second stall has been installed. I lock myself in one and try to get myself together. *What the hell was that? Was I really about to kiss Dorian's little brother? What is wrong with me?* I take a few deep breaths then head to the sink to splash some water on my face, hoping it will sober me up. As I am reaching for a paper towel, my hand collides with another, causing a jolting current to crawl from my fingertips and up my arm.

"Oh shit! Sorry!" I say pulling my hand back and rubbing it with my other. I smile apologetically at the blond staring back at me with wide, horrified eyes. Then I see it. Her brown eyes momentarily flash bright gold, shining like luminous stars. Familiarity sets in and I realize that I know who she is. And what she is.

"You!" she whispers, taking a step back.

"You!" I repeat, taking a step towards her. "From the sports bar. You are-"

"Don't!" she commands, cutting me off. "Don't you dare say it. Stay away."

"Why?" I ask, standing straight up, feeling a bit offended.

"I cannot consort with you. It is forbidden!"

Just then a group of giggling girls stumble in, startling us both. The blonde peers around me and scowls. "Leave us!" she commands in an ominous tone. The group quickly complies without question.

The girl, who I now see as startling beautiful, something I didn't notice before, looks back to me. "I cannot speak to you, Dark Light. Especially now that you have chosen to associate yourself with *them*."

"That's because they are the only ones who will talk to me! And I am not *with* them. Please, I just have so many questions. I just want to talk."

She shakes her head, and I notice that she grows lovelier by the second, as if she was purposely masking her beauty. Yet, slowly but surely, I can *see* her. Even the brown façade of her eyes falls away, revealing remarkably golden irises.

"I cannot. It is forbidden for us. You will get us both killed if you do not forget about me." She holds her hands up as if the thought of contact repulses her.

"Fine! Turn your back on me then. But isn't the Light supposed to help and heal? And what if I choose wrong? What if you could be the deciding factor in which side I was destined to align to?"

The Sorceress sighs with exasperation, shaking her head. "Fine. Tomorrow. There is a coffee shop in the strip mall on the corner of Union and Academy. Meet me at noon. I'll give you ten minutes then you will forget you ever saw me."

I nod enthusiastically, gripping her shoulders before I can stop myself. "Oh, thank you, thank you! I won't tell anyone I saw you. I promise."

Her eyes widen with disgust at my touch and she pushes away from me. "Control yourself, child. It would do you good to refrain from touching people. Do you *want* to live?"

I open my mouth to apologize when a shrill scream rings out behind the door, followed by more screams and what sounds like a stampede. We both rush to the door, knowing that something terrible has happened. When I swing it open, I nearly collide with Niko. His eyes widen as he gazes over my shoulder, a low growl rumbling his chest. I look back at the Light Enchantress, her expression matching his. The air around us shifts, an iridescent current indicating their pulsing energies. The confined space around us buzzes with electricity. Oh no. Shit is about to get real.

The woman bears her gleaming white teeth, her gaze locked on Niko. “Get her out of here. Now,” she seethes. Then she takes a step back into the bathroom and evaporates before our eyes.

“Come on,” Niko says, grabbing my arm. I stumble through the hysteria, tripping over my heels. Seeing my struggle, Niko tucks me under his arm, holding me close to his torso.

“What’s going on?” I ask into his ear.

He turns his face to me, yet his eyes dart everywhere, looking for a safe exit. “Another girl. Upstairs.”

“Another girl was killed?! Morgan!” I shriek.

“Not her, but I have to get you out of here now.” He forcefully thrusts through the crowd, shielding me from all contact.

“I can’t leave without her.” I try steeling myself but he still pulls me along like a ragdoll. “Niko! I am not leaving my friend!”

“Shit!” he grumbles. His mouth begins to mutter something in what I notice as the language of the Dark. He is saying, *‘Find her humans and ensure their safety.’* Yet it is hardly loud enough for even me to make out.

“Who are you talking to?” I ask as we finally step outside.

“My car is this way,” he says, ignoring my question. “You can text your friend once you are there.”

I slip off my heels as soon as I am inside Niko’s luxurious sports car, my ankles sore from stumbling. He is next to me in seconds, revving it to life.

“What the hell was that back there?” I ask once we are speeding away from the scene.

“I’d like to know the same. How long have you been involved with the Light? Does Dorian know you’ve been seeing them? Who else knows? Answer me, dammit!” he yells, switching lanes and weaving between cars.

“Jesus! Will you slow down?!” I screech, grabbing ahold of the dashboard. “I haven’t been involved with them. That was the first time I have ever spoken to one that I know of, I swear.”

"What did she want?"

"Huh? Nothing. I wanted to talk to her but she refused. Seriously, Niko, slow the fuck down!"

Niko whips into an empty parking lot and throws the car into Park before smacking the steering wheel with his palms. "Fuck!" he shouts. When he turns towards me, I see that almost all the color has drained from his blue eyes. The sight would have scared me shitless if I hadn't seen the same happen with Dorian.

"What's wrong?" I whisper.

He lays his head back onto the headrest and lets his eyelids close, taking a few deep breaths to calm the storm brewing within. "Gabriella, that was too close. You can't just run off whenever you feel like it. And then the Light girl . . . do you know what I would have done if things became hostile? And what my brother . . ."

"Hey," I coo, reaching out to him. I let my hand rest on his, our bare skin igniting a sudden feeling of euphoria. Niko immediately relaxes, sighing his relief.

"What are you doing to me?" he whispers, turning his head to look at me with questioning eyes. I notice that they have returned to their beautiful blue color. He flips his palm towards mine and we intertwine our fingers.

"I don't know," I answer truthfully.

We sit in silence for a while, holding hands and enjoying the contact. It isn't sexual–at least for me it's not–yet there is an indescribable feeling of blissful companionship between us.

"What happened earlier," Niko says quietly. "I apologize. I shouldn't have tried with you. And I knew you were marked. It's just . . . there's an impulse. Something I can't control. Like I am compelled to touch you in a way that I have never felt before."

"I seem to have that effect," I mutter. Me and my supernatural mojo. *Pffft.*

"I better get you home."

Niko pulls his hand away reluctantly and puts the car in Drive. The feelings of fear and confusion begin to crawl their way back to the surface yet they are bearable. We ride in comfortable silence, and I hardly notice when Niko pulls up in front of my apartment.

"Your friend should be home soon. She's safe."

"Thank you." I know not to question him. For some reason I can't understand, I already trust him.

"So . . . friends, right?" Niko says, flashing his brilliant, cocky smile.

I shake my head and a giggle slips out. "Fine. We're friends. Just stow your inner asshole and we're good."

"But you like my inner asshole," he jibes.

I squint my eyes and wriggle my nose. "Ummm, maybe a little." I let my hand touch his again and give him a genuine smile. "Thank you, Niko. I appreciate you looking out for me."

"Goodnight, Gabs."

"Goodnight, Niko."

He doesn't pull away until I am safely inside the apartment and dropping my heels beside the door. I go to the fridge and grab a bottle of water, downing its contents in just a few gulps. I'm already stripping out of my dress when I enter my bedroom and kick it across the room. Yet it doesn't fall to the ground near my bathroom where I flicked it off with my foot. Instead someone catches it, someone that has been waiting for me, lurking in the dark shadows.

TWENTY

"Dorian?" I say just above a whisper.

"Yes, little girl," he replies, stepping into the stream of light coming from the hallway. The mere sight of him, the sound of his voice, nearly unravels me.

"What are you doing here?" I wrap my arms around my body, realizing I am wearing only a strapless bra and thong. I'm tempted to turn around and let him get an eyeful of my curves but my nerves override my boldness.

Dorian closes the distance between us, his eyes scanning the length of my body. Slowly, he brings his hands up and pulls my arms down to reveal my bare skin. He then gives me my favorite crooked smile in appreciation.

"I had to see you. I had to see for myself that you were safe." He lets his fingers graze the pendant he gave me months ago, the pendant I have yet to take off. Then his hand travels down to the soft skin of my bare stomach, leaving behind a trail of goosebumps. "I've missed you . . . so much. I feel like I haven't breathed since the last time I saw you."

"Then why did you stay away?" I frown.

Dorian tilts his head to the side. "I thought that was what you wanted. I wanted to respect your wishes. You said you no longer wanted to be with me."

"Yeah. I know, but . . ." I begin, feeling that familiar tightness in my chest whenever I think of what we had and lost. "I've missed you too. And I don't think I'll ever stop. It isn't getting any easier."

"So what do you want to do?" Dorian never takes his eyes off me. They roam my pouty lips, my neck, the swell of my cleavage, the flat softness of my belly. His gaze makes me feel desired and cherished.

I chew my lip to keep from saying what I really want: him. All of him. No sharing with Aurora or anyone else. "I don't think there's anything we can do. You made your choice. I wasn't it."

Dorian shakes his head and closes his eyes in frustration. "You were always my choice, Gabriella. You and only you. And you always will be. But I can't turn my back on my obligations, especially when they could potentially save your life."

"What are you talking about?" I take a step back, hoping to gain some clarity with the space.

Dorian leads me to my bed where we sit down at the foot. "It means that by me marrying Aurora, my father has agreed to step down. I will be king, Gabriella. He has ruled for over 4oo years and finally I have the opportunity to right some of his wrongs."

I blink, stunned at his confession. "Is that what you want? To be king?" I am all too aware that I am half naked and pull my comforter around me. That's about enough eye candy for him.

"It's necessary if I am to try to keep you alive."

I shift my body towards his to assess his expression. As always, he gives nothing away. "So what if I choose the Light. Will you still try to protect me?"

Dorian nods. "Yes. Because it's the right thing to do. Even if you never speak to me again. Even if the Light wages war against us with you on their side."

I let out an exasperated huff. "I never asked you to do that, Dorian. I never asked for any of this. The bond, the mark . . . hell, I never even asked you to pop into my life and turn it upside down! Do you know the mess you have created in all this?"

"You know I did it for you. I did it for-"

"Right, right! You did it for us!" I cut him off before he finishes the thought. "Dammit, Dorian! What happens if the rumor of your curse is true? What if you were only spelled to love me? Your father could break that spell and freakin' kill me. Then what? Huh? What happens then?"

Dorian stares at me blankly, giving nothing away. I can't even be sure he's breathing.

"Answer me, dammit! What happens if he breaks the curse?" I demand with a vicious glare.

Finally, he sighs and puts his face in his hands, rubbing the growing stubble. "You die, little girl," he whispers. "And I acquire your power."

His words resonate in my clouded head, roaring louder and louder until I have no other choice but to acknowledge them. "What?! Do you see what you have done?" I shout scrambling to my feet. "This was the plan all along, wasn't it? You knew about the curse and you knew bonding me would keep me under your thumb! You want my power just as much as your sadistic fuck of a father!"

"No!" he growls, on his feet in a flash. He towers over me, his seething sneer causing my anger to falter for just a second. "I am nothing like him! And you know good and damn well that I don't want that!"

"How do I know that? How can I ever trust you again? You are following right in his footsteps. You keep doing this shit, Dorian! Stop trying to dictate what's best for me! You do not own me!" I dig a finger into his hard chest to drive my point home.

The air around us hums with tension as we exchange threatening stares, neither one of us willing to back down. And I won't; I won't let him have his way with me. Whether or not his intentions were good, he can't own me. I'm not his to control. There may have been a time when I would have been complacent with solely being his, a time when his love was all I needed to survive. A time when I tried so hard to be good enough for him that I had become someone I didn't recognize. But that time has come and gone.

The sound of the front door opening breaks our heated trance and I am thankful for the disturbance. "You should go," I whisper.

Dorian looks down at the floor, his shoulders falling in defeat. "Is that what you want?"

"Yes. At least for now. I need time to think," I force myself to say. As much as I long for his touch, I know it will only make things harder for me in the future. I can't have all of him and I've never been the type to share.

Dorian steps forward and presses his lips to my forehead, pouring life into my numbed body. He lingers for just a moment longer than usual and I feel him inhale. Yes, he needs me just as much as I need him. Then just as Morgan steps into my room, he's gone.

"Oh shit, Gabs, sorry," she stammers, seeing my nearly naked frame. "I was just so worried about you! Girl, what the hell happened?"

I make my way to the dresser, pulling out a pair of pajamas. "I don't know. I was in the bathroom when I heard the screams. Niko gave me a ride home since it was nearly impossible to find you in that chaos."

Morgan nods, a frown creasing the space between her worried, brown eyes. "I heard a girl was murdered. Like at the mall that one time. We got out of there just as the cops and paramedics showed up. It's a massive clusterfuck over there."

"Yeah." I busy myself with pulling my shirt over my head, avoiding eye contact. I don't want her to see the guilt painted on my face.

"What are the odds of this happening again? It's like trouble is following us," she says quietly, her eyes unfocused.

Not us. *Me.*

I know I could never be totally honest with Morgan. I guess, in a way, I'm no better than Dorian. Maybe his omissions really were for my protection. And maybe, just maybe, I could find a way to get over the lies and the secrets and forgive him. Especially since I have a few secrets of my own.

I am only too anxious to take my lunch break the next day at work and speed down to the coffee shop on Union. I pull up five minutes early and settle into a table in the corner of the empty café with a large latte, too nervous and excited to eat anything. After checking my watch for the hundredth time and downing my hot brew, I realize that the Light Enchantress isn't going to show. She must have just said she would to appease me. Either that or last night's scare changed her mind. With a disappointed huff, I gather my things and rummage through my purse to retrieve my keys.

"You really should be more aware of your surroundings, Gabriella."

My head snaps up and my hands reflexively form hard fists. My surprised eyes narrow with question. "You came."

"Yes. I've been here the entire time," she smiles tightly.

I tear my eyes from the radiant woman and glance around the café. I could have sworn no one else was in here. In fact, other than the barista, it has been completely empty for the past hour.

"I served you coffee," she says, reading the confusion etched on my face.

"Come again?" That can't be right. The girl behind the counter was plain looking–drab even–with flat brown hair and lifeless eyes. I remember thinking how miserable she looked. I glance over at the counter but there's no one there.

The beautiful woman chuckles, her voice sounding like the tinkling of harmonious bells. "You need to realize how incredibly easy it is for us to change our appearance. You need to learn to *see* those around you. To *see* your own kind." She waves a hand in front of her face, transforming her soft, feminine features into the bored barista's.

"Holy shit!" I shriek, nearly flipping backwards in my chair.

"Focus, Gabriella. You need to learn to see with more than just your eyes. Let the magic within you guide your sight."

"Why?" I ask, trying to steel my rapid beating heart.

"Because you are living in a world of illusions. All this," she waves her hand, "is an illusion. This world full of pain, depravity, immorality and violence is all an illusion. As is your human life."

"But I have no power. Not until I ascend," I say casting my eyes down, as if I am ashamed of the notion of being remotely human.

"Can you truly believe that? Do you feel powerless?" she runs a hand through the flat, brown hair masking her golden locks.

My eyes quickly snap to hers. "No."

"Ever wonder why? Considering you haven't ascended yet?"

I look down at my empty disposable cup. "I thought it was because of my involvement. With *him*." I can't say anymore. Not without revealing who and what Dorian truly is, though I'm certain she knows exactly who I mean.

"Ah," she says nodding, leaning back in her seat. "The Dark One. Yes, that does contribute to it. But not all. Have you ever felt uneasy or paranoid when danger was near? Like maybe something within you was telling you to flee?"

I gaze at her knowing smile with shocked hazel eyes. "Yes. The mall . . . Breckenridge . . . the salon."

"All times when a threat was prevalent." She sits up straight and reaches her hand towards mine, tentatively inching it closer and closer before stopping it just centimeters from contact. "We never abandoned you, Gabriella. Our absence from your life was only so you could make your decision objectively without feeling any pressure. Though the Dark deem it necessary to play games with your heart to lure you."

"So it was you? The Light?" Suddenly my throat is bone dry, causing my weak voice to crack.

"Yes," she smiles, making even the dull mirage seem attractive. "So now, I want you to strip away the illusion before you and see me. You can do it; you've done it before. You just have to stop looking as a human and embrace *the sight* that is already strong within you."

The sight. What Donna has. What intensified when my mother,

Natalia, healed her when she was attacked by the Dark. The gift of knowing and accepting the supernatural.

I nod and look intently at the Enchantress, willing myself to see past the façade of muddy brown eyes and pale skin. My skin heats as I concentrate and tiny beads of sweat form on my forehead. Bit by bit, the vision before me dissipates. Brown hair turns into a blonde radiance; brown eyes morph into golden honey. Filtering rays of sunlight glint against her perfect complexion making her skin shimmer brilliantly. An impulsive gasp falls from my mouth as I take in the beauty before me.

"I . . . I *see* you," I say just above a whisper.

She smiles. "Yes. And I see you. The question is–do you see yourself?"

A small frown flashes across my features and I lean back in my chair. "What do you mean?"

"Do you see what you are meant to be? What your true destiny is? How imperative your existence is to this world and beyond?"

Her words slice through my stoic guise and I feel the threat of fresh tears at the rims of my eyes. Seeing that I have no answer to her questions, she continues. "Gabriella, you were not meant to be on the arm of a Dark One. Your destiny is not to be an accessory or a play thing. Don't let your human desires dissuade you from achieving your true purpose. We have been waiting for you for centuries. Your time has come."

I'm rendered speechless as the tears spill down my flush cheeks. This is it. *My destiny.* What I was created for. What my parents–the people who loved me so much yet never even got the chance to meet me–were sacrificed for. All this time, I had been trying to be good enough for Dorian, hoping that I could be worthy of his affections. I've never felt like I was truly *Somebody.* Yet this ethereal being before me is telling me–showing me–that I was made to be phenomenal. And something within me is dying to claw itself out, ready to prove to her and everyone else that I can do it. I can surpass all their expectations. I can be great.

"I must go, Gabriella," she smiles. "But we are never far. You are never alone."

"Will I see you again?"

She nods. "When you need to."

"How will I know?" I ask with a hint of desperation. I don't want her to leave. I need to know more. "I don't even know your name."

The Light Enchantress stands and looks down at me adoringly. "Solara."

Then she's gone. And I am no longer in my seat. I'm not even in the coffee shop. I am back in my car, facing an empty lot where the coffee shop was just seconds before. I can't even begin to understand what just occurred here. But I'm not afraid. I'm not worried in the least. I am filled with an inexplicable peace that carries me through the rest of my day, reviving the parts of me that were broken and battered.

When I arrive home that evening, to my surprise, Dorian is waiting for me, furiously pacing back and forth in my bedroom. I don't even have the chance to ask what he's doing here or demand he leave before he is in my face, grasping my shoulders.

"Gabriella, what were you thinking?" he asks though it sounds like a demand.

I shrug out of his hold and take in his slightly disheveled appearance. "What are you talking about, Dorian?"

"You went to see the Light? Are you insane? Did you forget that there is a fucking killer after you? You could have been slaughtered on the spot!"

I roll my eyes, kicking off my shoes and flinging them across the room. "Oh, like I could have been the moment I laid eyes on you?"

Dorian glares at me with vehemence yet my stance doesn't falter. "Where is this coming from? What did she say to you? I told you I wouldn't hurt you."

"You didn't know that then! You weren't even sure what you

were doing with me! This was all a ploy, remember? An *illusion*," I sneer, conjuring Solara's words. "Tell me, Dorian–the first time we kissed, was that real for you? Or were you just playing along to see how close you could get to me?"

He steps forward, boldly cradling my face in his palms. "Is that what you think?" His blue eyes sparkle as they earnestly search my face for understanding. "You think it was meaningless to me? That I wasn't forever altered the moment my lips touched yours? That I didn't obsess every second of every minute of every day until I could feel them again?"

His words strip away my tenacity and my body relaxes under his touch. "I don't know. I don't know what to think any more. But I do know that I've been a fool. I trusted you with everything in me. I trusted you with my life, my heart. And you've played with both."

Dorian brings his face closer to mine, close enough that I can smell the cool sweetness of his breath. "I never meant to. If you never believe a word I say again, you have to believe that. That I would rather die a thousand fucking times than hurt you. Believe me. Just please be patient, little girl. Just wait . . . for me."

"Wait?" I shriek jerking my head back. "You want me to wait? For what? Until you are done with your little sham of a marriage?"

Dorian's eyes dart around the room in suspicion. "My words are not safe. You told me you trusted me. That you loved me and wouldn't be afraid. I need that from you now. I need you to trust me wholeheartedly, no matter what. Just believe me, ok?"

"You seriously want me to wait for you? Why? You can't ask this of me and not explain. Shit, Dorian, you are immortal. Hell, *I'm* immortal! I could be waiting for centuries!"

"I've waited for you for centuries, Gabriella. When you have eternity, decades pass in a blink of an eye."

I shake my head turning away from his hypnotic gaze. "You can't ask that of me. You didn't even know me then. You had no idea who you were waiting for. I can't stand by and watch you marry another woman and potentially . . . have a family with her." I catch a glimpse of the little blue anchor on his hand that he and I share. "And how is it that you can even do that in the first place? We're both marked," I explain, holding up my own marked hand.

Dorian reflexively brings his hand up to his chest and rubs it with his other. "But it was me who did it."

"So what? You're exempt? The rules don't apply to you?"

He reaches a hand towards mine and intertwines our fingers so that our anchors are side by side. "Gabriella, if you were able to do it, I would gladly wear your mark. It would be my honor. But you can't until you ascend. And if you will have me, I want you to claim me as I have claimed you."

The fuck?

"*Claim* me? Did you just say you *claim* me?" I ask dropping my hand from his.

"That is what the mark means. You know that." I can see the exasperation in his weary eyes. He looks older, as if he hasn't slept or eaten in days. The sight causes me to abandon my previous question.

"Dorian, are you ok? You don't look so good." He looks like he could drop from exhaustion at any moment. I grab his hand and lead him to sit on the bed. "You've been using?"

He shakes his head and looks away, refusing to let me see him up close. "No more than usual."

"Then what's wrong?" I know I've seen better days but with last night's senseless murder still fresh in my mind and Dorian out of my life, it's hard to muster up the strength to care too much about trivial *girl* worries.

"It's just been . . . difficult," he mutters still looking away. I pull his face towards mine and though I know he doesn't want me to see him, he doesn't fight.

"What happened to you? Tell me. Please," I whisper, taken aback by the obvious wrinkles at his eyes.

Dorian sighs in defeat. "You, Gabriella. I lost you. I wasn't exaggerating when I said I was addicted to you. I need you to live.

You sustain me."

"You need to breathe me." It's not a question; it's a fact.

"Yes," he replies casting his eyes downward in shame.

"You're dying?"

Dorian nods. "Slowly but surely. Unless I breathe another source or acquire a life. I don't want to do either." His eyes finally meet mine, and they are filled with so much regret and pain that my chest aches for him. "I would never ask that of you. It's . . . personal. Intimate. And I know I don't deserve that of you."

"But you'll die, Dorian," I nearly beg. This world isn't meant for me and neither is a world without Dorian.

He shrugs and looks away again. "I deserve much worse for how I hurt you. You have no idea how much I hate myself for putting you through all of this. For being so selfish that I need you to live."

A long moment passes between us as we both fight the questions in our heads. "Do you want to?" I finally ask.

Dorian whirls his body to face mine faster than I can see. "Of course, I want to. I have never wanted anything or anyone so badly. But I wouldn't ask that of you. I can't guarantee my restraint."

"Restraint?" I ask with a raised brow.

His eyes are on my lips. "Sexually."

"Oh," is all I can reply with wide eyes. Just the reminder reignites the fire deep in my belly. It's been so long, and my body craves him just as much as my heart does.

We sit in silence, unsure of what to say next. "Do you want to try?" I ask after a beat.

Dorian's lips curl into a smirk, his eyes settling into his sexy smolder. I can almost feel my panties melting right off me. "Are you sure?" he asks already inching towards me, preparing to strike.

"The breathing, Dorian. That's it. Nothing more."

He fails at hiding his disappointment yet agrees, taking my hands in his and putting them to his lips. "Thank you," he sighs between tender kisses. Then he breathes the inside of my palm, his chest rising and falling with an audible *"Mmmm."* But he doesn't stop there. He moves up the length of my arm, leaving another kiss on the inside of my elbow. Then his hands are on my shirt, unbuttoning stealthily.

"Ummm, what are you doing?" I ask pulling back a bit, but not bothering to retract my arm. *Ugh, the flesh is weak!*

Dorian's intense gaze falls on me, his eyes already awakening with his arousal. "Gabriella, as much as I want to lie you down right here and make love to you until you pass out with immeasurable pleasure, I'm not going to try. It's just easier this way. More . . . potent." He carefully finishes unbuttoning my shirt before sliding it off my shoulders. Then he removes his own. Minutes tick by as we take in the sight of each other, both of our expressions tortured and hungry for more.

"Lay back," he whispers, easing me down. "I want you to be comfortable. I promise I won't do anything you don't want me to."

I nod and comply, not even bothering to cover up the cleavage sitting atop my black lace demi bra. Dorian settles beside me, propping himself up on an elbow as he admires my nearly trembling frame.

"Are you cold?" he asks frowning.

I shake my head and try to swallow, my mouth going dry. "No. Just a little . . . nervous."

Dorian gently splays a warm hand on the width of my stomach. "I told you I won't hurt you. And if you want me to stop, I will. Do you believe me?"

"Yes," I nod breathlessly. The rise and fall of my chest perks my nipples and they ache against the thin fabric. I am almost certain Dorian takes notice though he is trying to be a gentleman.

"I want you so bad, little girl. So bad it hurts me just to look at you, so unbelievably stunning. But if this is what I must endure just to be near you, than I gladly accept this torture. I happily burn for you." He places a soft kiss on my navel, then another right above it. Before I can react or object, he is kissing a trail up through the middle of my breasts and I fail to stifle my contented sighs. He really is trying to rein in his passion, and all I feel are his soft lips, not the rousing tingles that usually accompany his touch. He wants to make this moment as innocent and tender as possible.

By the time Dorian's lips are at my neck, I am a writhing, panting mess. I want him on top of me, all over me, and inside of me. And the fact that he is restraining himself, refusing to touch me in all the ways I know he wants to, is driving me insane.

He buries his face in my neck and inhales, groaning his relief. The visceral sound rumbling his chest stimulates my already damp sex and I squeeze my thighs together. He does it again, brushing his lips against my collarbone. The feel of his skin on mine, his intoxicating scent, the feather-soft tickles of his hair, pushes me to a place where all I know are my carnal instincts. I can't fight them. And a part of me, the impulsive part that shuts down all logic and reasoning, doesn't want to.

"Dorian," I breathe, my eyes tightly shut as sensation takes over me. He doesn't stop yet his actions don't go any further. *Dammit!* I just want him to touch me. "Please."

Dorian lifts his head from my neck, his now sparkling eyes meeting mine. "Please what, little girl?"

"Kiss me," I find myself saying before I can change my mind.

Without the slightest indication of movement, Dorian is on his back and my lace covered breasts are pressed against his hard, bare chest. "You have to do it, Gabriella. You have to take control. Because the moment I feel your lips, the second I taste your sweet tongue, I won't be able to stop. If you want this, you need to show me. I need you to take it."

The look of sheer need and passion on his face resembles my own and I know that I am a goner. I don't even bother to argue with myself about all the reasons this is not a good idea. I crush my lips to his and let his flavor nourish my body and soul after over a month of famine. His taste–all eroticism and freshness–scream of comfort and healing. As our tongues slide together, our hands roam the bare skin of our torsos. I feel like he could very well shatter me in this moment with just a kiss. And if it were to happen, I wouldn't object.

The gravity of our actions hit me like a ton of bricks and I pull away begrudgingly. "Wait!" I command, my palms pushing my body from his chest. "What are we doing? With everything that happened . . . with you and me. You are engaged. What about Aurora?"

Dorian's primitive growl vibrates my breasts, perking my nipples. "Fuck Aurora!" he grits before pulling my face back down to his.

Well . . . can't argue with that.

Our bodies remain fused together for what seems like hours. I hadn't had a make out session like this since . . . ever. Any and all things involving him completely surpass any experience I could ever imagine. And while I can feel the strain in his taut muscles, struggling to not take this too far, the bulge in his pants clearly wants to.

As I relish in our skin to skin contact, the doubt, the frustration, the sheer confusion seem to evaporate. I know this is wrong; I had never been the cheating type. But this is Dorian. And like he has always told me, we were not meant for this world. I need to stop trying to fit into my human mold. And when it comes down to it, knowing that I can share this with him and it is me whom he desires–not Aurora–gives me a sliver of triumph.

After kissing ourselves stupid, I lay in Dorian's arms, tracing little circles on his chest as he plays with my hair. This feels so right, so real. It's as if the last month or so was a terrible nightmare and this is my reality. And even with Solara's words still ringing in my head, telling me I was not meant for this, urging me to turn away, I let myself savor the stolen moments with the man I so desperately love. Lord knows if I could turn it off, I would. Because my true reality, the one that keeps trying to resurface from the depths of my denial, is that Dorian still isn't mine. He will return to his world–a world that I am not destined for. A world where he belongs to

Aurora. A world where the sad little boy inside him still wants his father's approval. I know I have to choose; I either have to let him go for good or choose to wait for him to return to me.

Twenty-One

I never understood how people got hooked on drugs. It just seemed pretty stupid to me. Like, why would you take something that you knew could fuck up your life and turn you into something that you don't even recognize? Like the shriveled carcass of yourself? Now I understand. I could relate. Because since Dorian came to my room where I let him breathe me, allowing the moment to turn into a searing, endless kiss, I knew I was addicted. Just as he, evidently, was addicted to me.

Dorian is my drug. I am a freakin' fiend.

That was over a week ago, and I still can't swallow the taste of him from my mouth. I told myself that I would be strong and not call for him. But every time my cell phone signaled a call or text, I wished like hell it was him. Every time I stepped into my room, I prayed he would be there waiting for me. I knew it was a dangerous game we were playing and I didn't care. My body craved him, just like it did the very first time I saw him. And every day that ticked by without him, it felt like I was crawling towards death.

"You got it bad, baby girl," Niko says shaking me from my depressing thoughts.

"Huh?" I ask with glassy eyes. I drop my hand from the diamond pendant around my neck that I had been absentmindedly fiddling with while lost in thought.

"You wanna tell me why you got me over here on a Friday night and we're not naked?" he chuckles.

I look back at the devastatingly handsome Warlock on my couch. "You're the one who showed up at my doorstep. And what makes you think I would get naked with you on *any* day of the week?"

He shrugs. "I'm just usually not fully clothed at a woman's house. Or a man's, for that matter."

My eyes nearly bulge right out of my head. "What? Are you trying to say that you're bisexual? That you play for both teams? That you like to double dip?"

Niko smirks, and I shudder at how much he resembles Dorian when he does that. "We don't put a label on sexuality, Gabriella. We aren't limited by human taboos. We do what we feel. We, the Dark, are free to express ourselves intimately with whomever we please." He runs his hand through his blonde highlighted perfectly messy hair and gives me a mischievous grin. "But no, I'm not bisexual. I was just seeing if you were paying attention. I've experimented but it was never my thing. I prefer the tight, warm feel of a woman."

"Oh," is all I can say in response. His words make my face flame and I look away to mask my discomfort.

"Geez, girl, you are easy to ruffle!" he laughs. "So what movie are we watching? Got any popcorn?" He stretches his arm across the back of the couch and kicks his feet up on the coffee table.

"Ummm, what are you talking about? Who said anything about a movie?"

With a wave of his hand, the TV flickers to life. "Well, I'm not leaving and you already turned down my offer of the best sex of your life," he snickers, "so I figured a movie would be appropriate for two platonic–although amazingly sexually attracted–friends to engage in. What kinda stuff are you into? Chick flicks, action, drama?"

I roll my eyes at his statement and shake my head. "Fine. Anything funny. And don't try to put on some porn to try to trick me!" I say heading to the kitchen to make some microwavable popcorn.

"Damn! You're no fun!" I hear him exclaim behind me.

As we are enjoying the insane comedic delights of Will Ferrell and munching on Jiffy Pop, I turn to Niko who seems overly comfortable reclining on the living room sofa. "Niko, what made you come tonight?"

"What do you mean?" he asks not even bothering to turn to look at me.

"I mean, why did you just show up? Last time I saw you it was Halloween and Dorian instructed you to watch me. Now you're here. What's up?"

Niko exhales and turns down the volume before turning towards me. "Father's here."

"He is?" I ask, my voice laced with shock and horror. "Why?"

He ponders his words carefully before answering. "Preparations. And your little meet and greet with the Light hasn't set well with him."

"Is he really gonna be a hypocrite like that? I mean, he sent his own son to seduce me then tried to do it himself. Your dad's hot and all but he's a real asshole," I let slip out, clamping a hand over my mouth.

"You think Father's hot?" he replies with disgust. "Yet, you turn *me* down? Really, Gabs? He's like 600 years older than me!"

"I didn't mean to say that. And it isn't the age thing, obviously. Just be glad that I actually like you, Niko. Your father is a fucktard though."

Niko breaks into guffaws over my assessment. "Yeah, I guess you're right about that. But he's the king. What can you do, ya know?"

"So you don't agree with the way he is?"

"No," he shakes his head. "I think what he did to your dad and to Dorian is unforgivable. He's done a lot of crazy shit but everything he's put D through is just heinous." He winces at the memory.

I nod. "Is that why you do it? Why you watch over me?"

"No. I watch over you because D asked me to. He's my brother and I owe him as much. He's saved my ass enough times to span a human lifetime. And I do it because I like you and I don't want to see you get hurt."

I can't stop myself from smiling at my new, albeit unlikely, friend, though I'm pretty sure he wouldn't hesitate if I agreed to sleep with him. But having him here actually does put me at ease. Just as much as the Dark, along with other paranormal beings, seem to be drawn to me, I feel as if I am just as attracted to them.

I nestle into the crook of his shoulder and shift my legs onto the couch. The tranquil feeling we experienced on Halloween returns and we both let out an audible sigh as we continue to laugh at Will and his antics.

By the time Niko leaves for the evening, it's after midnight and I am exhausted. His goal was to ensure that I stayed in for the evening and he certainly succeeded. I didn't even feel the need to drink in order to numb the pain and loneliness. And with Morgan having plans with Miguel for the night, that was exactly what I was planning to do before he showed up.

When I enter my bedroom, I jump with fright at the sight of Dorian sitting on my bed. He's dressed in a dark tailored suit though he has ditched the tie and unbuttoned the top few buttons. His hair is its usual dark, tousled and oh so sexy style. It's hard to believe that his effortless beauty even exists.

"Dorian," I gasp. "What are you doing here? And do you not know what a front door is? You're gonna give me a freakin' heart attack!"

The corner of his mouth curls into a smirk. "Sorry."

I busy myself with pulling out a tank top and some boxer shorts before shimmying out of my jeans, wholly aware of Dorian's heated gaze. "So why are you here?"

"I wanted to see you. And I felt it was best if one of us were here. There's no way I was going to let Niko spend the night. And don't think I don't know how touchy the two of you are."

I turn to assess his venomous expression. Is Dorian *jealous*? "So you're here to stay over? Won't your *fiancé* get worried and wonder where you are?" I gag at the thought.

"Gabriella, we don't live together. She stays at her condo and I still have my suite. Nothing has changed."

Now that's news. "Oh. So you two aren't . . ." I try to finish my thought but just can't bring myself to do it.

"Hell no. I love you. Do you think I could go through with something like that?" Dorian almost looks offended at the insinuation.

"I don't know. You are engaged. And you do plan to . . . procreate so you obviously have to sleep with her someday. Plus Niko told me that you all aren't as strict with things like sex. Like it's no big deal to the Dark."

"Well, it's a big deal to me," he replies standing and striding over to me. He grasps my bare hips and pulls my body into his. "The last woman I made love to is currently half-naked and pressed against me. And when she looks up at me with those big hazel eyes and bites her bottom lip in anticipation, all I can think about is how bad I want to feel her again. How I would do anything to bury myself in her for hours and hours until she is too exhausted to move. Until she tells me that she'll never leave me."

The desperation in his voice causes an audible gasp to escape me, rendering me absolutely speechless. God, how I want those things; there is nothing that I could imagine wanting more. But I've led with my desires before. I've pushed aside sense and logic to sate my body's craving. And look how far it got me. Now all I have is a broken heart, a killer (still) out to get me, the impending doom of my ascension, and a borderline drinking problem.

"I want you, Dorian," pushing out of his grip and contradicting my words. "But until I know we can actually be together, I can't go down that road with you. It will hurt too badly when we have to say goodbye again."

Dorian sighs and hangs his head before nodding. "I know, little girl. And I would never ask you for that. Can I just stay with you? To ensure you are safe tonight? I won't touch you if you don't want me to. I can just sit and watch you sleep like I usually do."

My face tenses into a frown. "Uh, that's kinda creepy. Do you really come here and watch me sleep?" A shiver runs up my spine. What else does he watch me do? My stomach roils at the possibilities.

"Only when you call me."

"Call you? What the hell? I don't call you, Dorian." I think back to my lowest points. Could I have drunk dialed Dorian?

Dorian smiles. "In your sleep you do. I don't go around stalking you if that's what you're afraid of. But I can feel you calling out to me at night sometimes and I come to you. You'll be thrashing around, tangled in the sheets. You dream about me." He runs a hand through my hair and a frown dimples his forehead. "And sometimes when you're asleep, you cry. It breaks my heart into pieces to see you so saddened knowing that I caused your anguish. I just want to kiss away every tear you've ever shed and make it better. You have no idea how bad I want that, Gabriella."

"I cry in my sleep?" I ask with a wavering voice. I suddenly feel sorry for myself. How much has losing Dorian really hurt me? I have hardly let myself cry over the loss and to know that those tears were so desperate to get out that they made their escape while I was unconscious kind of depresses me.

"I'm sorry," is all he says in response. He feels responsible and though he is partly to blame, I can't put this all on him.

I finish slipping into my sleeping clothes under his lustful gaze and retreat to the bathroom to brush my teeth. Then I slip under the covers of the bed that has felt so cold and empty since Dorian left it.

"Well, are you getting in?" I ask him still standing in the middle of the room dressed in his suit.

"You want me to sleep with you?" he asks with a raised brow.

"Well, I damn sure don't want you staring at me all night like some type of creeper while I drool," I chuckle. He still looks confused. "Yes, Dorian! I want you to sleep with me. Sleep though. Not sleep-sleep with me."

Dorian's face lights up with a beaming smile as he makes his way over to the bed. He takes off his suit jacket and steps out of his shoes before pulling back the covers.

"You're not getting in like that. Either lose the stuffy clothes or put on some pjs."

"But you know I don't have any. We never had a need for them when I was here." He waggles his eyebrows suggestively, causing me to giggle.

"Fine. Just take off your shirt and those pants. You do have on underwear, correct?"

"I'd be happy to lose those too," he grins.

"Uh . . . No! No! Um, yeah, not such a good idea," I stammer, unable to tear my eyes away from the pronounced bulge in his boxers as he lets his pants fall to the floor. "We should probably keep those. Yeah, uh, definitely . . . shit."

Dorian chuckles at my flustered tirade and I cover my face to hide my embarrassing blush. After he is stripped down to his undies, he climbs into the bed next to me, instantly rekindling the warmth and security it once exuded. He pulls me into his arms and without a second thought, I lay my head on his warm chest. His hand begins to stroke my hair and the tension that had strained every muscle begins to unravel.

"Do you think this could work? Do you think one day we could actually be together?" I murmur against his skin. I reflexively take a whiff and revel in his scent. *Ahhhh.*

"Yes. We just need to be careful. And you need to trust me when I tell you certain things. Things that may be difficult for you to understand at first but necessary."

I take a deep breath and muster up all my courage, putting the nagging voice in my head on mute. "Ok."

"Ok?" Dorian lifts me slightly and pulls my chin up to meet his gaze.

"Ok. I'll try. If you say that this is all a ploy and things will work out for the better, than I'll try to wait."

Dorian crushes my body to his, wrapping his arms tightly around me. "Thank you, Gabriella," he breathes, his voice cracking with emotion. “You have no idea how happy you have just made me.”

“I can tell,” I squeak under his bicep that’s about the size of my head. “Can’t . . . breathe . . .”

“Oops,” he mutters, loosening his hold but refusing to pull his arms away. “I know this doesn’t mean that we are together. But just the possibility that one day we will be is enough for me. I’ve waited so long for you. I can’t lose you now. This will work. Just trust me, little girl. It will work.”

“I just hope you’re right,” I reply, forcing a smile and trying to let Dorian’s radiant warmth and love blanket the doubts clouding my jumbled mind.

“So I wanted to talk to you about the job you’ve been doing here, Carmen,” I say, ushering her into the stuffy back office.

Carmen furrows her brow and horror washes over her. “Oh gosh, Gabs. What did I do? I know I was late last week, but I seriously had major cramps!”

I chuckle heartily and wave her off. “Relax, Carmen! You’ve been doing great here! Better than great. I just want to see how you would feel about taking on some extra responsibility.”

She sighs her relief before leaning against the closed door. “*Ay dios mio!* You had me worried! You’ve been so up and down lately; I didn’t know what to think!”

“No, it’s nothing to be worried about. But I do need some help. Now that I am technically the owner,” I say with air quotes, “I need to start delegating some responsibility around here. And there is no one I could think of to fill those shoes but you.”

Though acquiring Cashmere totally threw me for a loop, I decided to keep it rather than selling or letting it crumble to the ground. It had become home for more than just me and I knew that everyone here was dedicated to their job. Plus, there's no way I could put seven devoted employees out of a job just because I got dumped. Since then, I have been trying to make Cashmere my own and even toyed with changing the name.

Ever since I told Dorian I would try to wait for him almost two weeks ago, he's been helping me understand the ins and outs of the business. The bank account he kept for bills and expenses was still intact plus a few added zeros that Dorian insisted on. It was actually his idea that I delegate some of the responsibility.

"So what do you think, Carmen?" I ask with a raised brow and a smile. "Think you'd like to be my store manager?"

Carmen's eyes bug out of her head and her jaw drops. "Are you shitting me, Gabs?" she shrieks before clamping her hand over her mouth and muttering apologies.

I laugh heartily at her outburst. "Yes. I need some help around here and no one knows Cashmere or fashion like you. It pays well, and you will have the opportunity to put your stamp on this place and interact with some designers. How does that sound?"

"How does that sound?" she squeaks with wide eyes.

Before I can ask another question, Carmen wraps her tiny arms around me and is jumping up and down, squealing with glee. After she's accepted my offer and has calmed her jubilation, she gives me another warm hug before stepping back onto the sales floor with a giant grin. I smile to myself, genuinely happy that I could do something for her that will potentially advance her career. She deserves it; through all my bullshit over the last couple months, she has been a stellar employee and friend. I owe her this opportunity. Besides, after my ascension, there is a good chance I will have to fully leave the store in her qualified hands.

Right on cue, my cell phone dings to life and I am greeted with a text message from Dorian, causing my smile to broaden to mega-watt status.

From Dorian, 5:46 PM

– Dinner at my place tonight? Thought we could try something different.

My mind drifts to the painful memory of the last time I stepped foot in Dorian's suite. It was undeniably the worst day of my life, as I felt my heart being snatched from my chest and ripped into a thousand shreds when Dorian admitted that he would have to marry Aurora in order to protect me. Returning to the scene of the crime just seems unbearable. Yet, I know I have to eventually. If I am going to try to trust him again, if we are going to try to make this work somehow, I have to take baby steps.

I knew my decision to try to work things out with Dorian could somehow bite me in the ass. And I knew that after everything, it would make more sense for us to be apart. But when it came down to it, I just couldn't. Being with him, with all the supernatural politics and bullshit, is hard. Trying to see past his betrayal and deceit . . . hell, that's even harder. But living without him, not feeling his love and warmth blanket me every day? That is intolerable.

I accepted Solara's words that day in the coffee shop mirage. My sole destiny was not to be Dorian's lover. But something deep within me, something that penetrated straight to my bones halted my every advance to try to forget him. As if he was placed in my life for a purpose. Not to be my assassin. Not to persuade my choice of alignment. But something else that compelled me to stay anchored to him in an intangible way. Maybe Dorian isn't my destiny. Maybe I am his.

To Dorian, 5:58 PM

– Sure you can handle that? I wouldn't want to tease you ;)

I smile to myself, knowing exactly what his endgame is. Though

I had agreed to try, I felt it was best if we kept sex out of the equation, which was a painful feat for us both. We had dived in so quickly with it before, sometimes I'd feel like that's all we had. Like intimacy was our love language.

So we slowed things down and started doing things like normal couples do. We'd watch movies cuddled up on the couch, order takeout, and even play cards or board games. And at night, when he climbed into bed with me and slid his body next to mine, Dorian never crossed the line into sexual territory. And even though he could split bricks with what he was packing under his boxer briefs, he still tried to appease me and fit that normal 'boyfriend' mold. He tried to be human for me.

– For you, I can handle anything. Just having you here in my space and in my bed again is enough. I miss you so much. And I love you even more.

My smile multiplies into an ear-splitting beam at his words. *He loves me.* That's all I could really ask for, and every fiber of my being believes him completely. Suddenly the urge to be with him in every tangible way overwhelms me and I happily tap out a reply.

– I love you too. And I'll be there. I can't wait to be back where I belong.

I go back to finishing up the paperwork and bills sprawled out in front of me on my desk, eager to get out of here and rush to Dorian's waiting arms. I make a mental note to stop by my apartment to slip into something sexy, scrapping all thoughts of taking it slow. When death seems to be knocking at my door every five minute, why wait?

Just as I am packing up my things to go, my cell dings, indicating a text. I giddily pick it up, expecting another love-laced message from Dorian. However it's from a number I don't recognize, and contains no words, just a media attachment. I shrug and open it up, realizing it's some sort of video. *What the hell?* Who would send me this?

The first thing I notice is a bedroom I've never seen before. It's all deep purples and elegant décor, along with a massive canopy bed fit for a princess. The click-clack of high heels becomes louder as someone approaches the recording device. Shuffling ensues before a familiar face comes into focus. Aurora. She positions the camera then smiles menacingly into the lens, as if she is smiling right at me. Straight through me. My blood freezes in my veins.

Aurora turns away from the camera and makes her way to the entryway of the door. I hear her talking to someone, her high-pitched sing-song voice assaulting my eardrums. Then another set of footprints joins the clang of her expensive heels. And as he comes into focus in the frame, every inch of him looking downright edible in blue jeans and a dark V-neck sweater, the icy feeling in my veins begins to sizzle and burn in the most uncanny way, immobilizing me where I stand. Dorian. The love of my pathetic life, the object of every desire, my very own walking, talking fantasy is being led to the canopy bed by my arch-fucking-nemesis and his current fiancé.

What. The. *Fuck?*

Dorian settles onto the bed with a huff, clearly uncomfortable in the intimate space. Aurora nestles between his legs, placing her hands on his shoulders. He mumbles something but it is too low for me to make out. Aurora chuckles then begins to knead his shoulders. Dorian visibly tenses at the contact but then slumps into relaxation. Her hands shift from gentle kneads to a deep squeeze of his solid muscles and I am all too aware of the handfuls of fabric in her hands, pulling his sweater upwards. In what seems like hours yet happens faster than I can look away, Aurora pulls Dorian's top right over his head, revealing his tight, rippling torso.

My breath catches in my throat as my mind tries to absorb what I'm seeing. Aurora's hands fly to her own shirt where she works to undo each button, Dorian watching impassively, making no move to stop her actions. When she stands before him in her tight skirt, heels and lace black bra, she takes a step closer into him, aligning her breasts with his mouth. Then she grasps his chin to meet her line of vision, causing him to release a contented sigh.

I know what this is; I've been here before. Dorian is going to breathe Aurora. And though I've been a live spectator of the act before, the fact that I'm not there to stop it, not there to be a reminder of all the reasons why Dorian shouldn't go through with it, my heart clenches in my chest.

The shift in the air, the visible shimmer around them indicates the beginning of the ritual. Aurora's manicured hands clutch Dorian's bare shoulders as she submits to him. They both pant wildly, the faint sounds of ecstasy ringing through the receiver of my phone. I am only too aware of the hot tears trying to make their way over the threshold of my eye rims. I quickly blink them away and grit my teeth, knowing that any minute now Dorian will come to his senses and push Aurora away. He has to. He loves me. Right?

The next few seconds are beyond brutal as I watch Aurora push Dorian back onto the bed and straddle him, revealing her scanty thong. As she lowers her body on top of his, never breaking eye contact, the tears regenerate, and slide down my face. I swipe them away, refusing to show weakness, even in the isolation of my office.

With eagerness, Dorian buries his face in Aurora's cleavage and grips her bare backside, just as he did months before when I witnessed their exchange for myself. Then he is successfully ripping her bra off, the delicate fabric almost disintegrating in his enthusiastic hands. And as her pert mounds fall around his face, the puckered skin if her nipples grazing his perfect lips, the screen goes black. The torture ceases and the video ends. And I'm left alone in dejected silence, unable to fully accept what just went down. But I know what happened next. I know what I just saw. And even my affinity for denial can't blanket that truth.

I'm not sure how I made it out of the Cashmere, or how I even made it to the bar a few blocks away. But as I slide onto a barstool, I remember that I came here for a purpose. I came to forget that text message. I came to forget Dorian. And Aurora. And the Dark, the Light. And everything else fucked up in my life, making it impossible to just breathe easily for one second of the fucking day.

The full shot glass in front of me is almost too blurry to distinguish through my watery eyes, but I reach for it and gulp it back anyway, slamming it down on the bar. That's when I notice the number of empty shot glasses before me.

Five. I have sat here and taken five shots without even feeling it. Without even really knowing why I was here.

It's almost as if my heart and mind had gone into self-preservation mode after seeing that video. Like they wouldn't let me feel the immense pain it would undoubtedly cause. But now as I sit on my rickety bar stool, staring at the empty glasses yet not truly seeing anything at all, the feeling of dread and sorrow slowly flood my system. Like a creeping disease that eats away at every part of you bit by bit. And before you can look up and assess the irreparable damage, it's too late. You are already too mangled and rotted to even begin to heal. There's no way to come back from that. Death would have been much kinder.

"Whoa, honey. Another?" the bartender asks, suddenly in front of me. I nod my response and he goes about refilling a glass with light brown liquor. I signal for him to keep them coming despite his reluctance.

I throw back one. Then another, hoping the burning elixir would somehow disinfect and soothe my afflicted body. The warm effects from the liquor sweep through my veins and I let my eyes close, relishing the feel of bottled contentment. I want it. I want it all over me. I want to feel good. Not the incarnate hell that currently occupies my senses.

Time passes in a blur of empty shot glasses, blaring rock music and faceless bar patrons eager to hold my attention. I don't feel it. Any of it. I just fall into my own slice of oblivion and my carnal senses guide me. And as the room spins and blurs out of focus around me, I grin lazily in triumph knowing that I have once again achieved it.

Numbness. Nothingness. Emptiness.

"Baby girl, what the hell have you done to yourself?" a smooth as silk voice coos in my ear, brushing a lock of hair out of my face as I lean against the bar.

"Niko! You came!" I shriek, throwing myself into his arms with as much force as I can muster. My eyes are so low, I can't even see him. Yet his scent overwhelms and arouses me in a way that makes my mouth water. The feel of his hard frame against mine makes every sensitive area tingle with expectation.

"Yeah, Gabs. I came. But you shouldn't be here," he says pulling my body away from his to look at my face. "What are you doing here?"

I tug my arms away from the restraint of his hands and turn towards the bar, signaling the bartender for another round. "What does it look like? I am having a drink!"

"A drink? Or twenty?" He puts his palms on either side of the bar, imprisoning my body and making my heart sputter with the contact. His lips graze my earlobe. "You're supposed to be with Dorian right now. You know he's been crazed with worry."

"Fuck him!" I spew, drawing the attention of nearby barflies. "I don't want to be with him. I want to drink!" I pick up the first thing the bartender sets in front of me and down it without blinking, hopelessly trying to push away the pain that the mere mention of his name brings. "And I want you to drink with me!"

Niko's chest rumbles with a chuckle against my back, his warmth washing over me. The way his body surrounds mine makes me feel safe and cherished. But even in my jaded state of mind, I know it's not real affection for me. It's all an illusion. And at this point, I really don't give a damn.

"Baby girl, there's nothing I'd like more. But not here. And since you are way ahead of me, I suggest we take this little party back to your place."

I spin around on the stool and force my eyes open enough to look into his hooded gaze. "Mmmm, now you're talking. Ready to give me the best sex of my life?" I slur, biting my lip suggestively.

Niko makes a pained noise and looks away, running a hand through his styled coif. "Shit, you have no idea how bad I'd like to do just that. But you know the rules." He grabs my hand lightly and rubs his thumb against my little blue anchor. "I can't," he frowns.

I pull my hand away, stowing it behind my back. "I don't care about that and neither should you. You know just as well as I do that it will be amazing," I coo with a cocky, yet lazy, grin.

Niko chuckles and then leans into me, brushing my cheek with the back of his hand. I nestle into the touch and don't stop myself from inhaling his intoxicating scent. "Is that right? What makes you so sure? What makes you think you can even handle me?" he breathes seductively in my ear, sending shivers up and down my spine.

I turn my head, letting my cheek graze his. Feeling emboldened with liquid courage, I grasp his shirt and pull his body into mine, parting my legs to welcome him. "You know we all have superpowers, Niko. Mine just so happen to be fighting and fucking. And I'm exceptionally good at both," I rasp, my lips mere centimeters from his neck. "Now the choice is yours. Do you wanna fuck or fight?"

I hear Niko take in a sharp breath and he pulls away, taking a step back to put some distance between our warm bodies. He frowns, his blue eyes searching my face for any trace of humor. "You're serious." His hands grasp my shoulders firmly and not in an intimate way.

I shrug out of his hold and turn back towards the bar to down my poison. "Yes, I am serious, Niko," I murmur grabbing a shot glass. Before I can bring it to my lips, Niko snatches it away, gulping it down before I can stop him.

"What happened to you, Gabs? Talk to me. This isn't you."

I snort and roll my eyes. "What happened to me? Maybe you should ask your brother that."

Niko raises a brow. "Ask him what?" He shakes his head and puts a hand up to halt any further explanation. "Let's just get you home. We can talk once I sober you up." He fishes out a bill and slaps it on the bar before wrapping his arm around me to usher me out of the bar. Realizing that there are no more shots in front of me, I let him pull my alcohol-laden body from my chemical sanctuary.

Niko leads me into the backseat of a dark SUV and slides beside me. After breathing in the fresh, frigid air, I suddenly feel completely hammered and slump against the door frame. I can't even see who's in the driver's seat and am too far gone to care enough to ask. Niko mutters something under his breath and the car begins to move, making the swimming in my head turn into a full-on tsunami.

"Come here, baby girl," Niko says pulling me into his lap, realizing how drunk I really am. He cradles me lovingly and I rest my head on his shoulder, breathing in his freshness. I feel his lips on my forehead and his hands stroking my hair. It feels so good and so amazingly comforting, I fight the urge to let down my guard and release the emotion festering inside me.

We're at my apartment in what feels like seconds. Niko helps me inside though I insist I can somewhat walk on my own. However, what is waiting for me behind my bedroom door completely sobers me.

"What the fuck are you doing here?" I spew, glaring violently at a solemn-face Dorian. Niko steps from behind me and eases the door closed.

Dorian looks to his baby brother and frowns. "What happened to her?" He steps towards me but I recoil, trudging to the far end of my room, muttering an endless stream of curses and infuriated babble.

Niko shakes his head. "I don't know, bro. I found her at some bar, already sloshed out of her mind. What did you do?"

Dorian looks to me, his blue eyes painted with confusion. "Nothing. I don't know. I thought we . . . She said she was coming over. We had plans . . . I don't know," he grimaces.

Even in my inebriated haze, even with rage and pain eating me from the inside out, his beautiful face nearly brings me to my knees. I just want to run into his arms and let him kiss it all away. Even after how deeply he has wounded me time and time again, I can't turn it off. I can't make my heart stop loving him no matter how bad I want to.

"Gabriella," he breathes. "Tell me what happened. Tell me what's wrong. Please, little girl."

An audible growl escapes through my clenched teeth. "Do. Not. Call. Me. That," I grit. "You don't get to call me that ever again, you lying sack of shit."

Dorian looks to Niko and frowns before turning his softer gaze back to me. "Please, Gabriella. I don't know why you're angry with me. Tell me so I can make it right," he pleads.

"You can't. You can't make this right. You did this! You destroyed us! You destroyed *me*!" I shriek, moving towards him with balled fists. The room erupts into violent tremors, emitting a low roar.

Niko steps in front of me to try to calm me down. The moment he places his hands on me, he winces with pain and jerks away. "Aw, shit!"

Dorian keeps advancing but stops a good three feet away from me. He has experienced my wrath for himself and it would be stupid of him to come any further. "What did I do? I can't fix this if you don't tell me what I did."

"You can't fix this!" I scream.

Dorian takes a tiny step forward, putting his palms up in caution. "Now, Gabriella, tell me what I did. Tell me how to make this right. Whatever it is, I can fix it. Let me fix it for you. For us," he pleads.

"Us?" I sneer. "There is no us, Dorian. Not anymore. You broke us."

"How? I thought we were . . . I thought this was working," he says, gesturing between us.

Niko takes a step back, hoping to give us just a bit of privacy, yet keeps his eyes trained on me just in case he needs to intervene. They both seem . . . hesitant. Maybe even a bit nervous. What could these deadly forces be afraid of? How could they see a threat in *me*?

"You," I growl, jutting a finger towards him. "You want to know how? You want to know how you ripped me apart, limb from fucking limb?" I forcefully stuff my hand in my coat pocket to fish out my cell phone. Then I throw it at his head, hoping it will somehow clock him in his beautiful face. Of course, he catches it without blinking.

"Check the unknown text message, asshole," I add, taking a step back. I don't need to see it again. There's no way I could survive witnessing his betrayal once more.

Dorian presses a few buttons and looks at the phone with a stern expression. Then he makes a pained groan, causing Niko to instantly ghost to his side to see the cause of his agony. After a few seconds, Dorian's younger brother cringes then shakes his head at him. Then he looks up to me with sympathetic eyes. I almost want to slap the look from his perfect face. I don't need his pity.

After the torturous sounds of passion have ceased, my gaze locks on Dorian's staggered expression. "Little girl . . . Gabriella . . . it's not what you think," he stammers, eyes widened in horror.

"Not what I *think*?" I shout, angry tears stinging my eyes. "Do you think I'm stupid? I can see what the hell is going on with my own damn eyes, Dorian! Don't you dare try to twist this around to make me think otherwise! You are a liar, a cheater, and the scum of the fucking Earth! You are just like your father. No . . . you're worse. At least he is honest about what he is."

"But that's not-"

"Shut up!" I shriek. Hot, salty tears finally stream down my cheeks with the outburst. "Shut the hell up, Dorian! Everything you say or do is to benefit your fucked up agenda to control me! I don't want to hear it anymore! I don't want *you* anymore!"

Dorian flashes directly in front of me with no regard for his own safety during my tirade. In the same instant, Niko positions himself at my side. "But it meant nothing!" Dorian shouts. "Listen to me! She means nothing! I love you and only you! Nothing happened!"

The very words cause my ears to burn fiercely. As if my mind and body have somehow become disjointed, my hand is swinging in front of me and connecting with Dorian's cheek with more force than I have ever exuded, causing him to stagger to his side. Unable to detect how and where I conjured that type of strength, I gasp yet maintain my unrelenting anger.

Dorian composes himself instantly though I can see a small trickle of blood in the corner of his mouth. He sucks the inside of his lip, tasting the metallic substance, his nostrils flaring with unshed fury. Both of our chests heave rapidly as we glare daggers at the other with glassy eyes. The humming tension in the room evolves into a rumble, the air around our heated bodies shimmering with an iridescent current.

"Gabriella . . ." he whispers, his voice cracking with emotion.

I shake my head at the sound of my name on his tongue. It's wrong; it's all wrong now. It's all a lie. I knew that he could never truly care for me. I knew he could never understand the depth of my feelings for him. Even now, accepting his deception as truth, I can't help but love him, though every fucking part of me wants to hate him.

"I hate you," I whisper, hoping to breathe truth into my thoughts by saying them aloud. “I hate you and I never want to see you again. You are dead to me, Dorian.”

“But you can’t believe this. It’s not what-”

“Save it,” I say raising a hand in front of my face. I grasp the necklace around my neck and pull, causing the chain to scrape the bare skin of my neck before snapping. I gather the precious diamond pendant in my palm before launching it at his chest. “Get the fuck out. And don’t ever come back.”

Still clutching the necklace to his chest and looking at me with a myriad of tormented emotion, Dorian lets a lone tear slide down his flushed cheek. The sight causes the crumbled remains of my heart to stir yet it is not enough to break my resolve. It’s not enough to put me back together again. We are dead and gone. What Dorian and I had cannot be resuscitated.

He looks to Niko, another tear escaping yet he makes no move to swipe it away. “Stay with her . . . please,” he rasps.

Niko nods then claps a hand on Dorian’s shoulder, looking as if he is fighting his own tears at the sight of his brother’s pain. Everything inside me is shouting, urging me to go to him and wrap my arms around him. To give him the chance to explain and forgive him. To kiss away his anguished tears and hold him close to me until we both drift off to sleep. But I can’t. I can’t give him that because I honestly have nothing else to give.

Dorian looks back to me, tears trickling down his face. Seeing him so broken makes the compulsion to comfort him that much stronger but I fight against it, closing my eyes to erase his wounded beauty from my vision.

“I love you, little girl,” I hear him whisper with a cracking voice.

I reopen my eyes only to see dissipating clouds of grey before me. He’s gone; it’s over. And the finality of that thought tears me in two. With a loud, soul-shattering sob, I fall to my knees and grip my chest, my entire frame shaking violently as the giant tears gush from my eyes and drip into my mouth and all over my shirt. I cough and choke, my chest aching with every pained howl. I feel like I'm dying the slowest, cruelest death in history.

Niko drops to his knees, scooping me into his arms. He coos and whispers his sympathies, trying desperately to calm me. "Shhhhh, it's ok, baby girl. It's gonna be alright." He rocks me back in forth in his arms, allowing me to bury my tear-streaked face into his chest.

"I . . . can't . . . he . . . why," I sputter between gut-wrenching sobs.

"I know, I know," he whispers, kissing my hair. "I know it hurts."

After I have regained control of my breathing and can stop shaking enough to stand, Niko leads me to my bed. Gently, he helps me out of my clothing, not even fixing his lips to make a licentious remark. His gaze doesn't even rest on my body in a lustful way. Once I am stripped down to my underwear and bra, he sits me down and goes to rummage through my drawers in search of a t-shirt. He puts it over my head and even eases my arms through as if I am helpless. And in this moment, that is exactly how I feel. Helpless, hopeless, and absolutely lifeless.

Niko eases my head down onto a pillow and my endless stream of tears quickly drenches the pillow case. He scoots my body under the covers and tucks me in gently, pressing his lips chastely on my wet cheek.

"Don't," I croak, sniffling, looking up at him with bloodshot eyes. "Please don't go. Don't leave me. Please."

Niko gazes down at me, his face full of compassion and understanding. He nods then undresses, slipping under the comforter in his t-shirt and boxers. He pulls my body into his and wraps an arm around me, holding me close to his chest. His warmth and comfort squeezes out a fresh wave of tears, yet he doesn't let go or push me away. Niko holds me even tighter, randomly kissing my forehead and hair and murmuring calming words until I have cried every drop of moisture in my body and fall into a wistful slumber.

I awake pressed against a warm, hard chest, a thin white t-shirt the only thing deterring skin to skin contact. Strong arms are wrapped tightly around me and my leg is slung over a bare, muscular thigh. I peel my eyes open and the bright sunlight assaults my sore eyes, causing me to groan.

"Are you ok?" a hoarse, yet sexy, voice asks. I prop my body up to peer at Niko. He allows the movement yet doesn't remove his arms from around me. "How do you feel today?" He gives me a hopeful half-smile and runs a hand through my wild hair. He, on the other hand, looks absolutely perfect.

I shrug and lay my head back down on his chest, refusing to look him in the face with a lie. "I'm ok."

"Mmmm," he hums. "Well, I'm here. Whatever you need, I'm here for you."

I nod against him and let my eyes close. "Thank you, Niko. I mean it. Thank you." I inhale the scent of him and let out a small sigh. "Just keep holding me for now. Just don't let go. Because right now, you're the only thing holding me together." Then I drift back to sleep, not ready to face the world just yet.

When I finally wake up for the second time, I can see it is afternoon. I am still against Niko's body, our legs tangled together under the sheets. Though this could be misconstrued as inappropriate, feeling his body next to mine only feels comforting and innocent. Plus he isn't pitching a tent, thank God.

"Hey you, feeling rested?" he murmurs.

Though my body feels stiff and sore and my head is pounding from crying and drinking my weight in Jack Daniels, I sit up and nod. "Yeah. Thanks for everything." I try to muster up at least a small grin, but I just don't have the strength. It still hurts too much to pretend.

Niko cracks a smile and strokes my cheek adoringly. "Good. Are you hungry?"

I shake my head, unable to even stomach the thought of food. "Nah. I'm good. I just want to take a shower and try to figure out what to do next."

"What do you mean?" he asks, pushing himself upright.

"I need to get my stuff outta here and go back home." I look down at my hands and bite my trembling lip, desperately trying to push away the hurt.

"Gabs, you can't do that. It's not safe. You need to stay here until your birthday."

My eyes snap to his. "Why?"

Niko huffs out his resignation. "Because you are too close to your ascension and you could hurt your human parents. Plus, you are easier to detect. You could lead someone right to them. Especially now that you don't want Dor–"

"Don't say it! Just . . . don't say it!" I command, shaking my head. "Ok, I get it. But what makes you think I am safe here? That anyone is safe around me?"

"The apartment is spelled. Very few forces can penetrate the wards. And Morgan is probably the safest person you know. She's protected in a way that none of us can understand or alter." He reaches out to take my hands in his. "And right now, it just isn't a good idea. I know you are upset and hurt. Rightfully so. But you have to be smart. You only have a few more months. Stick it out. And if you feel like you still don't want to be here, then you can go where ever you want."

"Hurt?" I scoff. "Upset? Niko, do you understand what . . . he did? Do you realize how many times he has torn me apart? I was fine before. I didn't need him to come into my life. I was content. But he just wouldn't leave me alone. And even after the first betrayal, when I finally found out who and what he is, he still wouldn't leave me alone. He just keeps hurting me just so he can dust me off and make it all better." I blink furiously and try to swallow down the knot of emotion in my throat. “And like a fool, I keep letting him.”

Niko nods solemnly, unable to say anything in his brother’s defense. “I understand. I truly do. But think about who else may get hurt in all this. How much harder it will be for you if your family is hurt. Just please consider this.”

I look down at my hands, to the blue anchor burned into my skin. The constant reminder of the man I loved and lost. Still love. Maybe it was all in my head. Maybe I was the only one who felt that urge, who felt compelled to be with him at all costs. It was never real for him, I know that now.

“You ever been in love, Niko?” I ask, my eyes still fixed on my hand, cursed to forever wear that reminder.

He shifts on the bed uncomfortably and nods. “Yes.”

“Truly in love? In love enough that just the thought of losing them ripped you apart? That you felt like you wanted to die just to make the pain cease?”

Again, he nods. “Yes.”

I look up at him curiously. “What happened?”

Niko looks away and swallows, grimacing as if there is a painful knot in his throat. “She was human.”

“She died?” I ask, though I know the answer.

“Yes.”

Compassion falls over me and I grasp his hand. “Did she grow old and pass away?”

Niko brings his glassy eyes back to me, his face flush with sudden emotion. “No.”

I can see the memory is still fresh in Niko’s mind so I don’t press for more. He’s hurting, and judging by the strained look on his face, he may be hurting just as bad as I am. He lost his love, just like I did. Our heartbreak is just another element of our solidarity.

“You may never stop loving him,” Niko suddenly whispers, reading my anguish. “But slowly the pain of loving gets easier to handle. It eventually goes from a debilitating burn to a dull ache. Sometimes you’ll be reminded of that love, and it will pierce you in a way that makes you believe that you are dying again. But with time those reminders become few and far between. You'll be able to find joy in the things you did before your love came into your life. You'll be able to push down the rising panic whenever you hear their name. You'll be able to live again. And even though the memory of that love may never leave, it will remain just that: a memory. A memory that one day you'll be able to smile through when you recall it."

I let Niko's words sink in and tuck it away to carry with me. Dorian, my crazed love for him, my all-consuming need for his touch will eventually become a memory. A ghost of a time when I felt safe and adored. A time when I felt alive. I know I will survive this; I will live through it. But I'll never again feel alive. And just as Dorian will become a ghost of my past, I know I will find myself fading into a ghost of myself.

Twenty-Three

I walk down the hallway of manufactured memories, refusing to acknowledge the happy, carefree girl staring back at me. She was so naïve. So stupid. She thought that she'd grow up, fall in love, get married, have a family . . . be happy. She knew there were unanswered questions in her life, but she was content with her ignorance. She wanted to believe she had a purpose, that she would one day be *more*. She still believed in happy endings.

That girl was a fucking idiot.

I enter Chris's office, unsure of why he has requested to see me before our traditional Christmastime festivities. I know I've been ditching them lately, unable to stifle my pain and anger long enough to see them. But the state I've been in, what I have become . . . I couldn't let them see that. They wouldn't understand. No one does.

"Hey Kiddo, have a seat," Chris says once I enter. I do as he requests and flop down, meeting his concerned gaze blankly. He takes a deep breath before pinching the bridge of his nose and removing his reading glasses. "I need to know what's going on with you, Gabriella. Your mother and I are worried sick. Tell me what's wrong."

"What do you mean?" I ask in a flat voice.

"Well, for starters, look at you," he replies with a wave of his hand towards me. "The few times that we have seen you in the past few months, you look visibly thinner. You're pale, there are bags under your eyes. You look worn down. And you never smile. What happened to girl that was always cracking jokes and laughing? Where did she go?"

I cast my eyes downward, focusing on a scuff on my Converse. "She's gone," I whisper.

I hear Chris let out an exasperated sigh yet I don't lift my head. "Talk to me, Kiddo. I don't like what I'm seeing in front of me. You look . . . defeated. And don't even get me started on the tattoos. You know how your mother feels about them."

I smirk and roll my eyes, though I know he's right. In the span of a month, I've managed to acquire 5 more pieces of body art. But it was unintentional. Each time, I'd arrive at the shop to get the anchor covered, and each time something inside me wouldn't let me go through with it. I'd be so sure, so certain that I could get something to mask that reminder of my old life yet some invisible force kept the needle from touching it. So I'd leave each time with something totally different than what I initially intended.

I look up to finally meet Chris's brown eyes with the lifeless hazel orbs of mine. "There's nothing to say."

My dad shakes his head and purses his lips in irritation. Then he pulls something out of the top drawer of his desk and slides it across to me with a painful grimace. I pick up the adorned folded cardstock and run my fingers along the embossed lettering, my stoic expression giving nothing away. I swallow down the rising panic and will the tightness in my chest to unravel. Then I slide it back to Chris.

"Why didn't you tell us, Kiddo? We had to find out about you and Dorian splitting up with a wedding invitation? We would have been there for you. We could have helped you through it. Look what it's doing to you." His voice is soft and his eyes are full of pity. Exactly what I was hoping to avoid.

I open my mouth to speak, yet can't find the words to tell him that there's no need to worry, that I'm ok. Because it's a lie. I am far from ok. Nothing about the way I feel, what I have been doing to cope with the . . . loss . . . is ok.

"I don't need help," I finally settle on.

"Gabriella, everyone needs help sometimes. Stop trying to take on the weight of the world. You are only one girl with a lot of growing to do. You are not expected to be fearless."

I nod, indicating that I understand. “Is that it?” I ask, not even a sliver of emotion in my voice.

Chris huffs out his frustration at my tenacity yet his expression is sympathetic. “Sure, Kiddo. Just remember . . . your mom and me, we are here for you. We love you. No matter what the future holds for you, you’ll never stop being our little girl. We’ll never stop loving you.”

I nod again then rise, urging my face to crack into a smile. But I can’t do it. I can’t even pretend anymore. In order to repress my pain, to numb the constant agony, I have to turn it off. I have to stop feeling completely. The day I told Dorian to leave and never come back, I emptied myself of any and all emotion. And it evaporated in the wisps of grey smoke with him.

Deciding that holiday visiting hours are over, I leave the warmth and security of my parents’ home and head to the nearest bar. It is sparse except for the few depressed souls drowning their sorrows. I can relate to them. This is where the lonely come to escape the pain that this time of year represents.

I could have gone home but I didn’t feel like dealing with the rising awkwardness between Morgan and me. My indifference was infuriating her and she couldn’t understand why I couldn’t open up to her. But there was nothing left to open. I was already torn apart at the seams.

Every day had been the same for me. I’d wake up, go to work for a few hours, try to force down some food and end my night at a bar. I didn’t want to be at home anymore, and I especially didn’t want to be in my room for more than sleeping. It had been haunted with his ghost. And sometimes I’d see mine as well. So I’d get drunk enough to ignore the ghosts long enough to drift off to sleep. Sometimes I could make it a few hours without waking up covered in sweat and trembling. But most nights those ghosts haunted my subconscious as well.

This had become my existence. Not my life; that ended the day I felt my heart stop. It lost its reason to keep beating when I said goodbye to Dorian.

My night is a blur, like most nights. I sit at the bar, drinking until the urge to feel leaves me completely. And when the numbness overcomes me, pretending becomes easier. I can smile, I can laugh. I flirt with random men, I dance like I haven't a care in the world. I can act like I am just like everyone else. I can pretend I'm alive again.

"Hey baby, can I buy you a drink?" a faceless man asks. I don't even bother to look at him; I just nod.

The stranger slides onto a barstool next to me. I plaster on a carefree smile and thank him. It's the same song and dance, night after night: guys buy me drinks, I get smashed then I somehow make it home to pass out.

The stranger slides two shots in front of us. I down mine without tasting it. Then another appears. And another. It's not until I have lost count when a heavy feeling begins to creep over me. I feel . . . weird. Not just drunk, but different. It's like I am having an out of body experience and can actually see myself stumbling off the barstool onto shaky legs.

"Here, baby, let me help you," the stranger offers. He's told me his name yet I haven't bothered to remember it.

"Uhhh," I groan, my head swimming viciously. "I need some fresh air."

The man grasps my arm to steady me and helps me outside. I'm appreciative because I honestly feel like I could not have made it out on my own. The cold, winter air only intensifies the sinking feeling and I feel like my legs could not carry me one more step. He wraps his arms around me to hold me up and my head rolls back onto his shoulder. I can't even begin to explain what's happening to me. It's as if my entire body has been submerged in quick drying cement and though I fight to get free internally, I can't move. I'm aware–dreadfully so–but it seems like I am watching a movie of myself being dragged towards the dark alley on the side of the bar.

Cold, wet, bricks scrape my back as the man buries his face in my neck, groaning expletives as he gropes my body. His odor of booze and sweat assaults my nostrils, coaxing the fear-induced bile rising in my throat. I will my arms to push him away yet they flop at my sides. My jaw drops and I try to scream for him to get off me, yet only a whimper escapes. He's tugging at my clothes, his hands forcefully gripping my flesh. I feel his dirty fingernails breaking the skin on my hips. It's not until I feel hot tears sliding down my cheeks that I realize that I'm crying.

This isn't happening to me. This can't be. But as the disgusting predator fumbles at the fly of my jeans, I can't deny what is about to happen.

Someone please help me. God . . . please. Doesn't anybody hear me? Isn't anyone there? This can't happen to me. I don't want this. Please . . . anybody. Help me . . . Dorian? Please?

My eyes, the only thing with mobility, dart around wildly, almost certain that he's heard my cry yet there is no movement in the dingy, dark alley. He should be here by now. He wouldn't let this happen to me, right?

A million reasons for his delay run through my head, followed by a million more scenarios of the impending minutes. I want to shut my eyes and block out the ugliness looming ahead. I don't want to feel it; I don't even want to be conscious. But I can't turn it off. No matter how bad I've wanted to be completely numb these past few months, there is no denying the sheer dread I feel. I try to summon my inner strength, try to will the auburn flames to enrapture my hands but nothing happens. Not even the icy prickles jab my eyes whenever my wrath takes over. I've been completely abandoned by both the Light and the Dark.

A tingling, creeping feeling sweeps over me suddenly. Tiny prickles like the sensations that Dorian delivers with every kiss. They sting my desensitized nerves, rousing them from their chemical paralysis. In the next second, feeling returns to my fingers and I wiggle out the stiffness in my joints. Sensation crawls up my arms and legs, stirring them awake and flooding my body with a renewed tenacity. I feel empowered, emboldened, and with a grunt, I use my newfound strength to push the vile bastard away.

"Get off me! Get your fucking hands off me!" I scream, my fists clenched at my sides.

My would-be rapist stumbles backwards, clearly stunned at my sudden coherency. "You filthy bitch," he sneers, gaining his footing and lurching towards me.

This time, I'm prepared for his attack. My fist collides with his face so hard that I hear an audible *crack!* from his jaw and teeth. I know I should run like hell. I know this is the perfect opportunity to seek safety. But I can't; I don't want to run. I don't want to feel weak or helpless for another second. I don't want to be a victim.

I approach him as he staggers while holding his ugly face and pummel him again. And again and again. With hard fists and feet, I beat the asshole until he is nothing but a lifeless pile of blood and flesh on the pavement. And I can't stop. I don't want to stop. I want him dead for what he was about to do to me. And for what he has more than likely done to countless other young women.

As I stand crouched over him, bawling, still kicking and punching his unresponsive body, strong arms wrap around me, whirling me around and depositing me several feet away from the scene.

"Let me go! Get off me!" I scream and fight though I don't move an inch.

"Shhhh, Gabriella," a familiar voice coos. His lips brush my earlobe as he murmurs soothing words. "I'm here, baby. Calm down."

Finally, he lets me go and I spin around to face him. "Niko?"

"Are you ok? Are you hurt?" he asks, assessing my torn clothing. I hadn't even noticed. He reaches over tentatively to button my coat to hide my exposed stomach then grabs my fists to look them over. They're covered in blood.

I shake my head. I am anything but ok. "I'm fine," I say panting wildly. My entire body trembles violently. "Where . . . were you?

And Dorian? What happened to me?" My voice cracks with emotion at the end of my question.

"I'll explain everything once I get you out of here." Just then, a tall, impossibly broad man approaches, causing me to tense once more. Niko wraps his arm around me, feeling my anxiety. "Just clean up when you're done, Cyrus," he says to him.

The man that Niko referred to as Cyrus nods then turns to me momentarily. He looks as if he could be very handsome, however, his irises are blood red and horribly frightening. My eyes widen with fear. Cyrus gives me a swift nod then makes his way to my offender's battered body still crumpled on the cold ground.

"Who is that?" I whisper.

Niko looks down at me, a mischievous smirk on his lips. "Cleaning crew."

Before Niko can turn me towards the parking lot, I get a glimpse of exactly why he referred to Cyrus as the cleaning crew. Cyrus grabs the still unconscious pervert by the collar of his bloodied shirt and swiftly raises him up to meet his face. What happens next is something I couldn't imagine in my wildest dreams or my darkest nightmares. Cyrus opens his mouth wide, unnaturally wide, bearing a pair of razor sharp distended fangs and sinks them into the man's neck viciously. The wet, guttural sounds of teeth tearing into flesh causes my stomach to roil. My attacker's body flinches and twitches before resting into a deadened slump as Cyrus drains every drop of his blood. Then he drops him to the ground like the disgusting garbage that he is and drags him away into the shadows.

"What the hell was that?" I ask Niko with horrified eyes. "He was a . . . ?"

"Vampire. Yes," Niko simply states, ushering me to his car.

"But . . . no. That's impossible. There's no such thing!" Inside, I want to scream but the words pass my lips in a hoarse whisper.

Niko shrugs. "Months ago you probably thought we didn't exist either. But here I am. And here you are."

I try to wrap my muffled thoughts around everything that has just transpired in the span of 10 minutes. I am sure I was drugged and was about to be raped. Just when I thought that I had been completely defenseless, a powerful force swept over me, filling me with the strength to fight him off and beat that asshole to a bloody pulp. Then Niko swept in with a vampire? This shit just keeps blowing the lid off my sanity.

Niko ushers me into a dark SUV then climbs into the driver's seat, hurriedly starting it up just as a clap of thunder rocks the sky. Rain pours down in a sheet of water and it seems impossible for him to be able to see far enough to drive though he makes it to my apartment complex effortlessly. Neither of us are eager to exit.

"Is he . . . dead?" I already know the answer but I have to ask anyway. I'm not quite sure how I feel about it yet.

"Yes."

"Really, Niko? Vampires?"

"Just imagine that everything you thought was myth is actually true. And everything you thought was real is an illusion."

An illusion. My human life, everything I've known, has been an illusion.

"Gabriella, do you have a death wish?" Niko asks, breaking me from my musings. "Because if you do, just tell me now so I can stop caring so much. I don't like that feeling. And it's selfish of you to put us all through hell just because you feel slighted."

"Niko, that's not what I'm doing."

"Really?" he asks, whipping his head towards me, suddenly furious. Lightning flashes across the sky followed by a horrifying clap of thunder, making him appear ghostly ominous. "Because you could have fooled me. You've been drinking yourself to death for weeks, not giving a damn about being cognizant about your surroundings. I've had to follow you every night just to ensure you made it home in one piece. But tonight takes the cake. You fucked up, baby girl."

I let my head fall, knowing that he is right. "I know. I know I did. I just felt so . . . I don't know. Alone. Dead inside."

"You feel alone? You are probably the person least alone on Earth. And you have no idea what it means to be dead inside. No fucking clue. You don't know what feeling deadened is until you have to suck the life out of an innocent just to survive."

I lift my head to meet his gaze, his eyes glassy and bright in the darkness. "I'm sorry, Niko. I really am."

He shakes his head. "I'm not the one you need to be apologizing to. Dorian almost killed himself tonight. He nearly killed himself to save you. I almost lost my brother, the only person that gives a damn about me, so he could save you from being raped. I know you have your issues with him but just think about that the next time you try to throw your life away. Think about how many people will hurt."

"What do you mean?" Dorian almost *killed* himself? *How?*

"Whatever drugs were in your system made it impossible for you to defend yourself. And now that you have chosen not to wear the pendant he gave you, it's harder to track you. But whatever you took tonight . . . it made you impossible to find. He felt your fear and he was also weakened. And since we knew we couldn't get to you fast enough, he used through you. He willed power to you so you could fight your attacker."

He shakes his head then turns to me with a softer yet stern expression. "I'm not saying you have to forgive him for what he's done. But if you still doubt his affections for you, than you are a fool. And being who and what you are, you can't afford to be foolish. Get it together, Gabs."

I look at Niko in disbelief, part of me wanting to be annoyed at his candor but the better part of me knowing that his tough love is necessary. I've been more than careless with my life. I felt that because my heart was broken that somehow my life was as well. Even with knowing everything I was meant for and all the people that are counting on me, I didn't care. Only Dorian mattered to me. I had become everything I had always despised. I had let my pathetic, irrational 'girl' instincts override my sanity.

"You are absolutely right, Niko." I reach over and grasp his hand, my knuckles covered in drying blood. He doesn't seem to mind and relaxes under my touch. "Thank you. I needed to hear this. I'll do better, I promise."

Niko nods and flashes me a sheepish half-smile. "I know you did. I care about you, baby girl. We all do. Don't make it for nothing." And with that, he opens the car door and we brave the elements on the way to my front door.

Luckily, Morgan is fast asleep and we are able to sneak in without any questions about my blood-stained clothing. Niko heads straight to my bathroom and begins to run me a bath. He urges me to undress so he can dispose of my bloodied clothing and doesn't even bat an eyelash at my naked, battered frame. Then with a kiss on my cheek, he retreats hastily to give me some privacy.

Soft music wafts from the stereo system in my room as I soak in the tub, eager to scrub the blood from my skin. I wash my body until it is pink and raw, not even aware of the tears streaming down my face. Tonight could have ended totally different for me if it hadn't been for Dorian. I could have been killed at the hands of that monster. And I have no one to blame but myself. Niko was right; I've been careless with my life for weeks. I wasn't being fair to my family and friends and they deserve so much better. They deserve for *me* to be better.

Muffled voices come from the other side of the door and I sit up to hear more clearly. I can't make out what they're saying but I can tell that they are two distinct male voices. As quietly as I can, I lift myself out of the water and wrap myself in a towel. I hold my breath as I press my ear against the door.

"How is she? Is she hurt? Did she go into shock?"

"She's fine. She's stronger than you think she is. And you gave her a lot. Too much."

"I know."

"Father isn't going to be happy with you."

"Fuck Father. I wasn't going to keep her defenseless. And if he had been holding up his end of the deal, she would not have even

been in danger."

"I know." A long beat passes. *"So now what? What are you going to do?"*

"I don't know. Not much I can do."

"I won't let you die. I'll bring someone to you. A willing soul-"

"No, Brother. I will not allow you to do that. I'll be ok."

A painful groan rings out. *"No. You won't be. You're all I have left. Please let me help you."*

Dorian is here. And judging by the conversation, he's in trouble. Before common sense has the opportunity to kick in, I swing the door open, startling them both. He's really here. And though he looks weary and weakened, his beauty causes the knot in my throat to break with a sob.

"Dorian," I gasp. I drink in the sight of his tall frame, dressed in dark clothing and drenched in rainwater as if he walked all the way here.

He nods solemnly. "I'm sorry. I know I shouldn't have come here. I just had to know you were safe." His voice is hoarse and almost ancient-sounding. Visible lines around his eyes and mouth mar his face and he is ghostly pale.

I suck in a breath and try to regain my resolve. With tentative steps, I make my way to him and extend my hand. "This doesn't change anything between us, but let me help you. I owe you that much."

Dorian furrows his brow slightly then looks to his brother, who is nodding enthusiastically. I can't fully understand why he is being so unsure of himself. He's never hesitated to breathe me in the past.

"I'll be right here if you . . . lose control," Niko says reassuringly, reading his apprehension.

Dorian looks back to me, shame and sorrow painting his haggard face. "I can't let you do this, Gabriella. I don't deserve it, not after what I did to you." His eyes sweep my frame and I know he is blaming himself for the negative changes in my appearance.

I shake my head, dropping my hand. "Dorian, you may have

broken my heart, but I broke me. I did this. What I've been doing, what happened to me tonight, that wasn't your fault." Take another step forward, close enough to smell his intoxicating scent mixed with rainwater. "Let me do this for you. It would make me feel better. I don't want to feel like I owe you anything." Again I extend my hand to him.

After a long beat, he takes my hand, and we both gasp at the contact. It's been so long since he's touched me and with his hand grasping mine, I feel whole again. I know it isn't healthy to be so reliant on him for comfort, but I can't help what my body feels or what my heart wants. I instantly forget that Niko is standing merely feet away from us or that anyone else even exists.

"Gabriella," he whispers, bringing my hand to his face. He kisses my palm gently before resting it against his cheek. I feel his skin heat under my touch.

I nod. "It's ok. You need to heal. I owe you this much," I reply in a breathy voice. Feeling his lips on my skin again revitalizes every weakened, dejected part of me.

Again he kisses my palm then inhales. He continues this ritual until his lips travel from my hand to the inside of my elbow, successfully making me weak in the knees. At feeling my legs buckle, he leads me the chaise lounge only a few feet away without even looking up or stopping. I'm a panting, sighing mess by the time he looks up at me with bright, glowing blue eyes.

"I missed you so much, little girl," he murmurs against my skin, the breath of his mouth warming my insides and heating my core. "I haven't breathed since the day you left me. I ache all over for you."

I close my eyes and turn my head, not quite sure how to respond. What does this mean? Have I totally just confused things even more? How could I possibly turn away from him now when my body begs for his touch?

"Nothing has changed, Dorian. You hurt me beyond repair. But that doesn't mean you deserve to die." It takes every ounce of willpower for me to pull my hand away but I do, my head still turned away from his perfect face. Somehow I feel it will be easier to say goodbye if I don't have to look at him but it still hurts like hell nonetheless.

"Of course," he replies quietly. "I love you, Gabriella. More than my next breath. More than anyone could ever love another."

The air shifts and emptiness fills me once more. I know he's gone but I still don't bother to open my eyes. Facing that immense loneliness is more than I can bear at this point.

"You want me to stay?" Niko asks after a few silent moments. I had forgotten he was here.

I shake my head just as the first tears escape. "No. I need to be alone," I sniffle. Finally I bring my watery eyes to him, his face filled with sympathy. "Don't worry. I heard you tonight. I won't go down that road again." Niko nods and begins to turn towards the door. "Hey, Niko, wait. Can I ask you something?"

He stops in his tracks and turns to face me. "Anything."

I swipe away my tears and take a few calming breaths. "Tonight . . . Cyrus . . . how?" I can't even bring myself to say the word *vampire.*

Niko walks over and sits beside me on the chaise. "You know how legend states that vampires were first created by a curse? That witches made them?" I nod my reply and he continues. "Well, that wasn't entirely false. We, the Dark, created vampires. When a Dark One dies, the magic leaves its vessel, which is the human body. It becomes completely lifeless. A spell was cast centuries ago that made it so that we could resurrect our fallen brothers and sisters, though they would still be technically dead. In order for them to continue to walk the Earth, they would have to consume human blood. Now they serve us, so to speak. We don't turn all of the fallen Dark, only the most elite."

My eyes broaden with shock and my jaw drops. Holy hell! How do I even begin to digest this revelation? *Un-fucking-believable!*

"Don't worry," Niko continues, smirking at my expression. "They won't hurt you. We control them. They are completely under the Dark's rule. And if you should ever find yourself in need, they are completely at your disposal."

I swallow laboriously. "But I . . . I thought that vampires were like the most powerful, feared creatures in history?"

Niko guffaws as if I have stated something outlandish. "Far from the truth, baby girl. But we don't correct the rumors as a way to keep the secret of our existence concealed."

I nod, letting it all sink in. There is still so much to learn. I feel like I have even penetrated the surface. I try to give Niko a reassuring grin. "Thanks for telling me. It was a good distraction."

He returns with a genuine, warm smile of his own. "I thought it would be." He leans forward and presses his lips against my forehead. The gesture is sweet and chaste, causing my eyes to flutter closed. He's gone before they even reopen.

No ghosts came to me that night as I lay down to sleep. No haunted dreams plagued my subconscious. Just the precious memory of Dorian's lips against my skin and my newfound tenacity to begin to live a full life without him.

Twenty-Four

New Year's Eve

I told myself I wouldn't take my dreary disposition into the New Year. It just wouldn't feel right to be down and mopey when everyone would be so buoyant and happy. I used to be the same way and honestly, I want to be way again. As much as I hate to admit it, I craved the mediocrity of the old Gabs. The Gabs that got excited about a night out with friends. The Gabs that relished an evening of carnival games and rides. The human Gabs. I want to be that girl again.

"You look . . . good," Morgan remarks behind me as we assess my outfit choice in the full-length mirror. We'd been working at healing our friendship in the past week or so. I really owed her an apology for my behavior and as always, she forgave me without question. She really is a better friend to me than I am to her.

"But?" I ask with a grimace.

"Well . . . let's be honest. Your ass has always been one of your best assets. And right now, it's pretty non-existent," she snickers. "If you don't start eating, I will pin you down and force feed you. I am not above bodily force."

"I do eat," I say quietly, though even I can't deny the negative effect my weight loss has caused.

"But I gotta admit, the tats are hot! I love them. They really fit your whole 'I'm-a-bad-girl-and-I-just-don't-give-a-fuck' persona."

My mouth works into a small smile as I adjust the strapless shimmery top I've chosen for our night on the town. Morgan wanted me in a dress, of course, but she didn't press the issue once I had agreed to go out. It was a big step for me, officially showing that I had returned to the living. Yes, I was alive. Not a ghost, not an empty shell. I had chosen to live again for my family and friends. And for me.

If I am being honest with myself, I had become pretty damn pathetic. Some girls cry and scream for days after a breakup. Some eat their feelings, trying to fill the void with pints of Ben & Jerry's. Others even take bats and bricks to their estranged lover's car. Well me . . . I drank myself into numbness and became withdrawn. In many ways, my coping mechanism was worst. It not only hurt me, it hurt everyone that I cared for. I became exactly what Jared said I was–a liability.

So I am on a mission, Operation: Happy Back. Sure, my love life had turned to shit and there was pretty much a supernatural bounty hunter after me. But somehow, some way, I am alive and for that reason alone, I have something to live for.

After another twenty minutes of the Morgan once-over, we hop in her Mustang and head towards Mansion, a super trendy club known for its once a year blowouts. We check our coats and thrust ourselves into the rambunctious crowd, the sounds of noise-makers, cheers and music vibrating the vast space.

"What? No VIP, Morgan?" I ask, as we flag down one of many bartenders.

"Girl, please! On New Year's Eve? Not even baby Jesus himself has that kinda clout!"

We make our rounds, stopping to chat with former classmates and friends. I plaster on my most carefree smile, hoping like hell that I even slightly resemble my former self. It's a feat, and between the sideways glances and sympathetic smiles, I know that word has gotten around. It would be so easy to just fall back into my old habits. With all the alcohol circulating, I could simply grab a few shots and numb the ache slowly making its way back into my chest. I'd be able to ignore the uncomfortable looks and half-hearted greetings.

But I can't return to that, not only for my sake but for Morgan's as well. That night in the dark alley really opened my eyes. The thought of feeling so violated and helpless is one that I hope to never revisit. I still haven't told any of my friends or family about the incident in fear that they'd try to force me to report it. And there's no way I could explain why there is absolutely no trace of my attacker anywhere.

"Hey, look who's here." Morgan points to three faces I hadn't seen in weeks. Maybe closer to months. It's hard to really tell how long I had been buried underneath my own grief.

"Hey, ladies," Miguel smiles, moving in to kiss Morgan on the cheek. He gives me an awkward one armed hug and I instantly feel like shit. When did things get so weird?

"Gabs!" James exclaims, pulling me into his arms. He squeezes me tight before pulling back to assess my frame with a raised brow, yet he doesn't comment. "See you got some new ink. Nice."

I smile at James warmly before turning my attention to his younger brother. Jared's guarded green eyes scan the length of my body before resting on my face. The uneasiness that presented itself upon his approach is quickly replaced with warmth and familiarity.

"Hey, Gabs," he says, his mouth working into my favorite boyish grin. Any iciness I felt moments before instantly melts.

"Hey, Jared."

We stand just taking in the sight of each other, not quite sure if we should make any move to embrace. Jared finally makes the first move, wrapping his arms around me and pulling me close to his chest. He feels just like I remember–full of goodness, comfort and security. And the smell of Irish Spring is still prevalent though he is wearing cologne. He smells of Jared. *My* Jared. The man I once loved since he was a boy.

"Oh shit! I love this song! Remember this, Gabs?" Morgan squeals, causing Jared and I to pull away, though our eyes are still joined. I force myself to focus on the blaring beats vibrating the room. Great, it's Danity Kane's "Damaged." How fitting.

Before I can protest, we are pulled onto the dance floor and thrust into the raucous crowd. Somehow Jared and I are crammed together, dancing closer than either one of us are really comfortable with. But instead of making it awkward, he takes each of my hands and dances with me as if it is the most natural thing in the world. As if I was made to be in his arms.

"You look really good, Gabs," he whispers in my ear, his warm breath washing over me.

I pull away a bit to give him a skeptical look. "You don't have to say that. I am well aware that my ass has run for the hills," I chuckle.

Jared gives me a sheepish smile and shakes his head. "But you look better. Happy."

I nod though I can't admit to being truly happy. Not yet, at least. I know I'll learn to let go and live and accept everything this life has to offer me. But it will take time to heal. My heart is slowly mending. I know I'll get there eventually and that sliver of hope brings a smile to my face. I can learn to be happy again.

We dance through song after song, slipping back into our once seamless companionship. Having him here with me makes me realize just how much I've missed him and I am quickly flooded with fond memories. My mind drifts to St. Patrick's Day when Jared confessed his true feelings for me. It seems like years ago though it has only been about 9 months. Have things really changed so much in that short span of time?

"I owe you an apology," Jared murmurs in my ear. He has led me off the dance floor and we are stationed at the bar in search of beverages.

I shake my head, not wanting to spoil the mood. "It's fine."

"No, no it's not fine. I was a total dick to you, Gabs," he

explains. “And I hate to admit it, but part of me blamed you for everything that happened.”

I give Jared a pointed glare. He blames me?

Reading the confusion on my face, Jared quickly continues. “I blamed you because I thought if you had chosen me, if you had just tried to see yourself happy with me, you would have never been with Dorian. You would have never fallen for him. And I would have never met Aurora. It could have just been me and you. Like it was supposed to be.”

I give him a small smile though I’m not quite sure what to say. “Everything happens for a reason,” I finally offer though it sounds generic. Part of me really does wish I had chosen Jared. I could have saved us both the heartache of finding out just how cruel love can be. We could have been happy together.

“Maybe so,” he shrugs. “But you have to know that I never meant to hurt you. Everything I said was out of hurt and anger. I didn’t mean a word of it.”

Before I can respond, the rest of the gang comes bounding through the crowd, laughing jovially. I grin inwardly as the conversation was becoming too intense for the lively atmosphere. Miguel pulls Morgan’s svelte frame into his and I cock a brow at the public display of affection. Morgan plants a kiss on his full lips and wraps her arms around him, causing a nearly audible gasp of surprise to leave my lips. Have I been so caught up in my own drama that I have totally failed to see what has been going on right in front of me? I silently scold myself; I’ve been a horrible friend.

Realizing how much all of us have been through in the past year yet somehow we are still intact makes me smile. Our friendships have changed, we’ve grown, we’ve matured, but we are still together. These four people before me have seen me through the toughest times of my life. And though things have been shaky between us, I know we’ll survive anything that life may throw at us. We have to. Because if there is anyone who is worth surviving for–is worth fighting for–it’s them.

"Hey Gabs, get a picture of us!" Morgan shrieks, laughing into Miguel's neck as he hoists her leg up around his waist provocatively.

I fish out my little rinky-dink digital camera and capture the moment. "Ok, now all of you get in it!" I exclaim, gesturing for Jared and James to join the frame. They all strike equally silly poses while I snap a few more.

"Oh, crap," I frown down at my camera. "Says my memory is full. Let me clear out some pics." I hit the button to review my photos and scroll through. Then it tumbles from my fingertips, crashing to the floor with a clatter.

Jared rushes to my side, picking up the camera before assessing my stunned, watery gaze. "What's wrong, Gabs?" he asks, his brow furrowed with worry.

I can't answer him. I can't say a thing in fear that every squelched emotion will come flooding back to me. Jared looks down at my camera and begins to scroll through the photos that caused me to freeze in horror. Photos of Dorian and me that day at the park music festival back in the Spring. Photos when I thought I was truly happy. Pictures of us smiling, kissing, hugging, making funny faces. Candid shots of him looking away thoughtfully. A few of him looking at me with my favorite crooked, mischievous grin as if he adored me.

I look over at my friends who are none the wiser at my impending meltdown then my eyes lock with Jared's emerald green pools. He's worried and maybe a little sad for me. I open my mouth to say something but no sound escapes.

"Hey guys, I'm not feeling well all of a sudden," he shouts over to our group of cackling friends. "You guys party on. Gabs, think you could give me a ride?" he asks looking down at me sympathetically. I nod and Jared gingerly intertwines his finger with mine.

We bid our friends goodbye and make our way back to Paralia per Jared's request. I don't question him; I am just thankful for the distraction. Now more than ever I am thankful at how well he knows me. Maybe he is just as hell-bent on protecting me from myself as everybody else is.

I retreat to my room to strip out of my tight clothing and slip on some sweats while Jared rummages through the kitchen. I need comfort right now. I need to feel somewhat whole again.

"So let's see . . . we've got grapes, cheese and some frou-frou girly pink champagne," Jared smiles entering my room just as I am removing my makeup.

"Sounds good," I grin genuinely before joining him on the floor where he's laid out my comforter and some throw pillows for a makeshift picnic. I take a hefty gulp of the champagne, urgently trying to wash away the memory of the picnic Dorian prepared for us months ago. No matter how hard I try to ignore it, he consumes every thought and I hate it.

"So . . . ," Jared begins, fingering a grape nervously. "Have you seen him? Since then?"

Great. He wants to talk about the very thing I need to forget. I shrug. "Yeah. We've talked. I've tried to forgive him but there are just some things that are unforgivable."

"Yeah, I know," he replies, not meeting my gaze. He frowns into the champagne flute in his hand. "She called me and tried to explain. But I couldn't believe it, you know. I couldn't let her keep lying to me."

A sympathetic hand grasps his, causing him to look up. I plaster on my best reassuring smile. "You really did care about her, huh?"

"I thought I did," he shrugs. "But honestly, I was more upset about losing you than losing her. I was just mad and I didn't know why. I knew you were hurting and I couldn't even comfort you because I was too caught up in my own selfish anger."

I nod, not quite sure what to say but don't move my hand away. Jared squeezes it gently. "Ok, enough of the heavy stuff. We need music," he announces, jumping to his feet to tinker with my sound system. He settles on Justin Timberlake before flopping back down and kicking off his shoes. "Ok, truth or dare?"

My eyes grow wide with playful shock. “Oh, hell no! I haven’t played that game since high school!”

“All the more reason to play it with me now. Come on, Gabs, it’s only us!” he smiles brightly.

I roll my eyes and let out a puff of air. “Fine, fine! But I get to go first!” Jared gestures for me to proceed and I perk up into a wicked grin. “Truth or dare?”

“Hmmm, I’ll go with dare.”

I look up to the ceiling, thinking of what I could dare him to do without crossing any unseen lines. “I dare you to down the rest of your champagne.”

“Too easy,” he snorts before tipping the glass up and downing its contents in one gulp. “Ok, my turn. Truth or dare?”

“Truth,” I say with an exasperated sigh. This could go very wrong in about 2.5 seconds.

“Is it true that . . . you hooked up with Trevor Mason in the 11th grade?”

“What?” I exclaim, more than happy that he didn’t ask me anything about Dorian or the past 9 months. “No way! He told you that?”

Jared shrugs refilling our champagne glasses. “Hey, according to him, you guys got it on in the coat closet at Becca Franklin’s house.”

“Well, that is so untrue. I should totally kick his ass the next time I see him.” I take a sip of my champagne then pop a grape into my mouth. “Ok, your turn. Truth or dare?”

“What the hell, I’ll take truth,” he smiles before taking a sip.

“Ok. I’ve always wondered but never thought it was my place to ask. But . . . why slum it at community college? Why didn’t you just enroll at UCCS to begin with? Your grades were surely good enough. Mine, not so much. But you could’ve definitely gotten in.”

Jared runs a hand through his wild auburn locks and makes a face at the ceiling. His green eyes fall back to me as he sighs, releasing his reluctance. “Honestly? You, Gabs. I went for you. I wanted to be wherever you were."

Shock paints my face. "Really?" I ask with a wavering voice. "Why?"

He smiles and grasps my hand in his, studying our conjoined fingers. "Because I knew a long time ago that you were the one for me. There may have been other girls but they were just temporary placeholders for you."

He lifts his head, his dazzling greens finding my eyes and holding them captive with his intensity. "Gabs, I know you. I know you like to play tough to keep people from getting close to you. I know you crack jokes to mask your insecurities. And I know you think that being alone will keep you from getting hurt. And knowing all that, plus everything else that makes you the crazy as hell, shit-talkin' chick that you are, I still wanted you. And I still do."

I have no idea how to respond to that yet a million thoughts rush to the forefront of my mind. I've loved this man for longer than I can remember. There was a time that I would have done anything–been anything–for him. I can't deny the love I have for him, and I know that those feelings will always be there. Whether or not that type of love could grow into a romantic relationship is the question.

Maybe I am meant to be with Jared. Maybe he is exactly what I need: stability, compassion, goodness. Maybe he is the one anchoring me to my human life, a life that I so desperately need to hang on to. Everything that has happened to me has proven that I have no place elsewhere. I'm right back to where I started. I still don't fit in.

Jared assesses the mix of emotions flashing across my face. "Gabs?" he squeezes my hand a bit, trying to bring me back to the here and now. "Gabs, truth or dare?"

Here it is–that pivotal moment when you're standing at a proverbial crossroads. Jared has just bared his soul to me and in turn, he deserves that I do the same. With just a few simple words, I could give him what he wants. I could make him happy. But in the same token, I could completely crush him. And that's the last thing I want to do to him, no matter which way this goes.

"Dare," I whisper.

Jared tugs my hand a bit, pulling me forward and closing the distance between us. Then he utters the words that have been on the tip of his tongue since he divulged his true feeling for me. "Kiss me."

Instinctively, I moisten my lips with a sweep of my tongue and sit up on my knees. It's just a kiss, a simple show of emotion towards someone I care about deeply. And who's to say that I could not love him like I used to? Dorian may consume a large part of my heart, and maybe he always will. But there's room for Jared. There's always been room for Jared.

The moment our lips touch, I melt into him. Jared holds me gently at the small of my back, pulling me close to his body. It feels safe and inviting here. It feels like home.

We pull away after a few moments, not able to do much more than stare into each other's eyes. So much has gone unsaid yet there are really no words to sum up what has just transpired.

Jared breaks into a sultry grin and grips my hips. "I think we can do better than that."

His lips collide with mine, searing me with years of unspoken love and passion. I gasp at the sudden contact and he easily slides his warm tongue against mine, tasting of sweet grapes and champagne. This is different from any other we've shared. This is what our first kiss should have been like. Because if it was, I would've picked Jared. I would've felt just how deeply he adores and desires me in that kiss. I would have moaned my gratitude into his mouth and tried to convey the same. I would have given him, and him alone, my whole heart.

Jared pulls his mouth away with a groan, resting his forehead against mine. "I'm not asking to be a replacement. I know that's something I could never be." His fingers rake through my hair and he presses his lips to mine for just a moment before pulling them away again. "But if you could just . . . try. Try to let me love the hurt away, Gabs. Try to let me in so I can heal the parts of you that are broken. Because I swear . . . I will never hurt you. I will never do what he's done. I'll make it my mission to bring you back to life."

I close my eyes and absorb his earnest declaration. Every part of me believes him; there is no one I trust more. And in that moment, I want the same. I want Jared to bring me back to life. If anyone could do just that, it's him.

"Ok," I whisper just centimeters from his lips. "I can try."

With our foreheads still joined and my eyes still closed, I feel him smile. His mouth unites with mine as he slowly eases our bodies down onto the comforter. "Oh God, Gabs, you don't know how happy you've made me," he mumbles against my lips. "I just want to show you how much you mean to me."

I return his smile and wrap my arms around his neck, running my fingers through his hair. "Happy New Year, Jared."

"Happy New Year, Gabs," he murmurs, stroking my cheek. His green eyes shine as he looks down at me with so much adoration, I can literally feel his warmth embrace me. "I love you."

The shrill dinging of my cell phone rouses me from the most contented sleep I've had in months. I stretch my arms above my head and slowly peel my eyes open before quickly shielding them from the bright sun streaming through my curtains. Then it hits me.

Last night . . . Jared . . . Us. The memories flood my mind in a rush, causing me to sit up abruptly. Then I smile, letting my eyes close to savor each remembrance of the previous hours. It was . . . absolutely perfect. Everything I imagined about Jared could not live up to how remarkably sweet and tender he was. My eyes scan the empty space next to me and my smile falters. He's gone. Before panic sets in, my cell phone–conveniently resting on the pillow next to mine–perks again signaling another text message. I quickly grab it.

From Jared, 9:34 AM

– Good morning, beautiful. I can't tell you how amazing it was to wake up next to you. Sorry I had to cut out but I have to work & I didn't want to wake you. I want nothing more than to lay with you all day and night.

– I want you to know that I have no regrets. And I meant every word of what I said. I love you, Gabs. Call me later?

I hug my phone to my chest and grin, falling back into the mound of pillows and giggling to myself.

"Are you trying to kill me?"

I gasp in surprise, clutching the comforter and drawing it up to my chin before sitting back up.

"What the hell are you doing here, Dorian?" I all but scream.

Dorian slowly makes his way to the side of my bed, his expression stoic as he sits down beside me. He looks as beautiful as I remember him and while my heart aches at the memory, it doesn't kill me. Not anymore. Jared's love has cushioned the blow.

"Have you no feelings for me at all? No concern for how that would feel to me?"

I swallow my trepidation, taking in the sight of his anguished face though he refuses to look at me. "I'll ask you again. What the hell are you doing here?"

Finally his blue eyes sink into mine, so full of pain and anger that I take in a sharp breath at the sight. "How could you?" he grits though a tense jaw. "You are mine, Gabriella. You belong to me. Do you know what you have done?"

"Belong to you?" I spit back with a frown. "Dorian, I'm not yours. Not anymore. And furthermore, I am completely justified in moving on. You obviously have."

Quicker than I can see, Dorian grasps my hand, his touch nearly burning me with vicious tingles. He brings it up, exposing his mark. "This says otherwise, Gabriella. You are mine, whether you like it or not. Mine." His murderous glare penetrates my own annoyance and I pull my hand free, tucking it back under the covers.

"Only in the supernatural sense," I reply, more meekly than I intend. "Isn't this what you wanted? For me to find someone safe? Someone human? To lead a happy life with someone that could love me the way I deserve?"

Dorian takes my words like a blow to the gut and he closes his eyes to compose himself. "But *I* love you," he shouts fervently. "And I don't want any of this! You know that! I don't want you with him or anyone else."

I shake my head. "That's not your call to make. Not anymore. You made your choice. You chose Aurora. She's the one you're marrying, Dorian. Not me. Concern yourself with her."

He takes a deep breath before facing me again. "What is it going to take? You want me to give it all up? Fight against my father and my people? Commit mutiny. Shit! Fine, I'll do it! Will that make you happy?"

I reel back with a disgusted look, confused by his anger. "I don't want anything from you! I didn't ask for this! I didn't tell you to invade my life. You did this!"

"Little girl, you are my world," he says, clutching my hand firmly. "But you are crushing me. You're killing me. Knowing you want someone other than me physically makes me sick."

I shake my head and pull away from his touch. "Welcome to the club. I've been in my own personal hell for months. I can't deal with your pain and my own, Dorian." I swallow against the knot in my throat and let my eyes close, conjuring strength. "You have to stop this. You have to stop coming in and out of my life. You have to leave me alone for good if I'm ever going to get over you."

He cringes as if my words have sliced right through him. My first instinct is to comfort him but I resist. No. He's no longer mine to console.

"You want me to let you go?" he asks, pain etched on his face.

"I want you to let me be happy. I can't do that if I keep hoping you'll turn up. I know you're not good for me, but that doesn't make me stop feeling what I feel for you."

He nods though I can tell it's a nearly impossible feat for him to accept. "I'll never stop loving you, you know that."

I smile through my pain, knowing that I'm doing the right thing. It has to be. Even as the newly mended pieces of my broken heart quiver and crack, I know this has to be done. We both need to let go so we can live again.

"I know," I whisper hoarsely around the lump in my throat.

I watch through watery eyes as Dorian flashes me his wickedly sexy crooked smile one last time. Then he's gone, leaving me to hold on to that precious memory of him.

I cry one last time for the man that I love and will probably always love. I may learn to live again, and I may even learn to love again but it will never be the way that I love him. It will never be the all-consuming way that penetrates every bone in my body. I'll always love Dorian Skotos, the Dark One who captured my soul and ruined me for anyone else.

Twenty-Five

Routine had become my friend over the passing months. It was the only way I could get through each day without anxiety completely overwhelming me. I wasn't miserable; I wasn't even unhappy. I had become . . . resigned. This was my life now. Well, for the next few weeks or so it was.

With my ascension quickly approaching, I could no longer sweep it under the rug. I couldn't ignore the changes taking over my body. My eyesight was clearer, sharper. My hearing was magnified. My reflexes were quicker than any ordinary human. And I felt *good.* Better than good. I felt incredibly empowered in a way I never knew possible. And I loved it.

That's why I needed to see Solara. I had so many questions for her and I needed to know I was making the right decision. I had been visiting the abandoned parking lot for weeks, hoping to see the illusion of the coffee shop. But it never returned. She never came to me, no matter how hard I tried to conjure her memory.

Resolving to head home, I click on my seatbelt just as my cell phone buzzes. Seeing the name on the screen, I smile and open the attached message from Jared. It was hard not to smile these days when he had made it his mission to brighten each one with his presence.

From Jared, 8:07 PM

– Thinking of you. But that's nothing new. It seems like I can't stop these days. Can I see you tonight when I get off? xx

– Absolutely. Only if you promise to behave ;)

I chuckle to myself and click over the ignition. Things between Jared and I had been . . . interesting, to say the least, since New Year's when we shared a searing kiss that would forever alter our friendship. We spent the night holding each other, our tongues tangled, before falling asleep in each other's arms. It was perfect and tender. Jared reopened a part of me that I wanted to keep sealed away. A part that had been previously crushed by Dorian. But somehow, some way, Jared's love had begun to heal that broken part of me.

However, I'm still not ready to commit fully to him; it wouldn't be fair to him considering my heart is still completely captivated by Dorian. And Jared has been adamant about not crossing any physical lines until I can give myself to him emotionally. I don't have the heart to tell him that that day may never come. How do you get over someone who has loved you in a way that transcends all rationality and logic? Dorian has loved me from the inside out, and knowing that he is still out there yet we can't be together kills me every day.

The last thing I want to do is make Jared feel like he is second best but in reality, there is no competition. But unless I want to be alone for the rest of my life, I have to close that chapter of my life. I have to move on. Dorian and I will never be. We can't. He's Dark and that will never change, no matter how much goodness and love is in him. He'll always choose his own kind. He'll always play by his father's rules. And I can't sacrifice my soul and my sanity just to be with him.

"Hey chick, how was dinner with the 'rents?" Morgan asks as I settle at our breakfast bar. It appears she is cooking though she can barely boil water. I mentally calculate how long it would take to get to the fire extinguisher under the sink.

"Good. I brought you back some leftovers. Donna got a puppy. You can take Dolce over there for a play date," I reply, stowing the plastic container of food and grabbing a cold soda from the fridge. I pop the top and it suddenly explodes in my hand, soaking the sleeves of my shirt. "Shit!" I squeal, grabbing paper towels to sop up the mess.

"No! Don't open that!" Morgan shouts just as I flip open the lid of the trashcan.

I give her a confused glare before peering into the trashcan. It's littered with magazines and newspapers. I grab one on the top and instantly see the source of her trepidation.

"I didn't want you to see them," she says quietly. "You've been doing so well and I didn't want you to get depressed again."

I study the cover for just a moment before flipping to the featured story in the local gossip magazine. A full article on Dorian and Aurora, deeming them the *It Couple of the Rockies*, explains their future wedding plans, along with a full color photography spread of the happy couple. Pictures of them together at formal black tie functions and even Denver Nuggets basketball games sitting courtside stare back at me, and I suddenly feel like I can't breathe. I take a few calming breaths, hopelessly reminding myself that I'm ok. That it's normal for couples like them to be in the public eye. That no matter what, I'm alive so he must at least have an ounce of love left for me.

"I'm fine," I say through a strained grin. I pop open the trash, seeing more editorials with similar themes and drop the magazine among them. "Really, you don't have to shield me from all that. I know that they're together. I accept it."

"I hope you know this is all Aurora's doing. I swear, ever since she sank her acrylics in Dorian, she has been on a damn rampage. She even had some camera crew at the salon the other day. And had the nerve to tell us that we should just start calling her Mrs. Skotos. I've wanted to slap the bitch for weeks."

"Well, that'll be her name soon enough," I shrug. "This is what she's always wanted. The spotlight, the wealth, the status. I guess that comes with being part of Dorian's life. She can have it."

Morgan places a hand on my shoulder and gives it a little squeeze. "You're really ok with this, huh? You're really over him?"

I look up at her big brown eyes, full of genuine concern and love and try to come up with a semi-truthful response when the doorbell rings. I sigh with relief and go to answer it, thankful for the lifeline.

"Hey babe," Jared smiles, his green eyes glittering against the darkened backdrop. He looks gorgeous as always, and his enthusiasm to see me quickly pushes my mood back to the positive side of the spectrum.

"Hey yourself," I grin back, lifting my face so that he can kiss me as he enters. His lips feel so warm and comforting, dispelling the chill of rejection I felt just moments ago.

"Jared! Geez, back again? We may need to start charging you rent," Morgan winks.

Jared laughs off her mock insult and flops on the couch, dropping his overnight bag. "So what'll it be tonight, ladies?" he asks, nodding towards the television.

We all quickly settle in on the living room couch to watch a movie. I get about two-thirds into it before falling asleep in Jared's lap as he runs his fingers though my hair with one hand and traces little circles on my arm with the other.

"Let's go to bed, baby," he whispers in my ear, leaving a kiss below my earlobe. I give him a sleepy smile and nod. He's making it entirely too easy to fall in love with him.

We change into pajamas and cuddle under the comforter of my bed. I curl into his chest, his large bicep capturing me and pulling me closer still. I sigh with contentment and relish my slice of peace and happiness.

"You know I would never hurt you, right?" he whispers in my hair.

I nod against his chest. "I know."

"And you know that I want to give you as much time as you need to heal. That I would never rush you to make any decisions."

Again, I nod. "Yes."

He pulls my face up to meet his eyes, his lips just inches from mine. "I just want you to know that I want you. So bad, Gabs. I've imagined making love to you for longer than I can remember. And whenever you're ready, I promise that I'll make you happy. I'll help you forget."

His words seep right into my skin and attack my heart, the warmth of his affection melting the last layer of ice protecting it. I don't even think. I simply lean forward into his lips and let his love enrapture me. The kiss quickly ignites from a spark to a flame and before long we are grasping each other's clothes and hair. Jared eases me onto my back, pulling my tank over my head simultaneously before removing his own. He rests his naked chest on mine, the skin to skin contact creating a new depth of sensation. I give myself over to my body's wants and just allow myself to feel.

Jared's lips and tongue move from my mouth, down to my jaw and neck. He sucks and nibbles, groaning his pleasure in the base of my throat. My hands pull handfuls of his soft, auburn hair.

"Gabs," he murmurs against my skin. "I want to feel you so bad."

Words fail me again and I just tug at his hair even harder as he makes his way down to my breasts. His tongue finds a hardened nipple and I moan loudly. His body on top of mine feels so good, so right. Every nerve ending stirs awake after months of slumber.

Jared's mouth explores my torso, tasting and teasing enthusiastically. He covers every inch with wet kisses as I continue to sigh and fondle his hair and shoulders. My body wants this. It damn near needs this.

I force my mind to focus on solely pleasure and try to push the emerging guilt from the forefront. I don't want to think about all the reasons why this is a bad idea. I don't want to stop Jared's hands from pulling down my pajama bottoms. And I damn sure don't want to stop him from hooking his fingers into the waist of my panties.

"Stop," I sigh before my body ignores my mind any further. Jared's mouth is on my stomach, his fingers beginning the slowly, torturous descent of my undergarments.

"What's wrong?" he asks still swirling his tongue in my navel. I groan my displeasure at halting his efforts.

"I can't do this, Jared. Not yet." I pull him up by his shoulders so we are eye-level and sweep his ruffled almost-sex hair out of his face. "When I give myself to you, I want it to be completely. I don't want to be focused on anything other than feeling you. I'm sorry, but I can't right now."

Jared rests his forehead against mine, his breath coming out in short, excited pants. His lips brush against mine and I feel him smile. "I understand, and I'm cool with it. I swear. You don't need to apologize." He gives me one last deep kiss before grabbing my tank top and maneuvering it over my head and sliding it over my breasts. I nearly whimper when they lose the warmth of his skin.

He settles next to me and pulls me into his still bare chest and I eagerly nuzzle into the contact, breathing in his familiar scent of Irish Spring. I leave a chaste kiss just below his nipple, smiling to myself as I let myself drift to sleep. It won't be long now. I'm falling for Jared hard and fast. Maybe even enough to give him my whole heart. But what will that mean for Dorian? Will giving my love to Jared, in turn, snatch it away from him? Will allowing myself to fall in love with Jared kill Dorian?

And the most obvious question . . . What will that mean for us in a few weeks when I ascend? Having a conventional human relationship could potentially put Jared in danger. And will he even want me then? Will I want him?

Cool fingertips stroke my cheek, trailing down to my jaw before landing at the base of my throat. I jerk awake and sit up straight, my quick fists balled in front of me.

"Easy there, killer," Niko laughs, holding up his palms in mock defense.

I slump against the pillows and roll over with a grunt. It's my day off and I was hoping to sleep in, not be disturbed by overly playful Warlocks with boy band hair.

"Come on, Gabs! I want to take you shopping!"

I roll back over and narrow my eyes at him. "Shopping? Why?"

Niko runs a hand through his perfect coif. "It's the least I can do considering what I am about to ask you." When I continue to glare at him, he continues. "I have to make sure you come to the party this weekend."

Ok, that didn't make me any less confused. "What party?"

He chews his lip and looks away, visibly stalling before letting out a resigned sigh. "For Dorian and Aurora. Father is throwing them some kinda grand affair to celebrate the wedding in a few weeks. And he requests your presence."

My tired eyes pop open instantly. "Oh hell no! *Hell-fuckin'-no!* I am not going to a party for my ex and his ho-bag bitch fiancé! Hell no!"

Niko pokes out his lip. "I thought you'd say that. And I get it. But it's important that you come. Father insists. And denying him will not be good for anyone. I'm trying to keep him from coming near your friends again, Gabs, but you have to help me out."

"No!"

He lets out an exasperated groan, desperation marring his angelic face. "Ok, I didn't want to say this, but Gabs, you have no choice. Either you go to him, or he will come to you. And if your friends or family are around, it won't matter. He gets what he wants. Don't you get that yet? You either play by his rules or you don't play at all!"

I sit up with an irritated huff. "So are you telling me that if I refuse to go, your father will come to me? And that my loved ones may get hurt in the process?"

"Yes."

I purse my lips and shake my head, beyond pissed and unable to successfully unleash my contempt. I know it's not his fault and I shouldn't blame Niko, but all I want to do right now is slap the Dark out of him. "You know this is complete bullshit, right?"

He nods, his shoulders slumping with relief. He's knows I'm considering it. "I know. And I wouldn't ask you if it wasn't necessary. He only wants to talk. He wouldn't try anything around so many witnesses. And even if he did, I'll be there. And so will Dorian. Do you think any one of us would sit back and watch him hurt you?"

I shrug, unsure of what to think at this point. It's true that Niko has been undoubtedly loyal to me. But he's still Dark. And deception and betrayal seem to come second nature to his kind.

"Look, I'll come. But you don't need to take me shopping. I do happen to own a clothing store. And I'll stay long enough to hear him out then I'm gone. I don't need to see them flaunting their fucked up love for one another."

"Thanks, Gabs," he says leaning forward and kissing my cheek. "I promise it isn't what you think. And for the record, I just have to say . . . I don't believe he did anything with her in that video. I would bet my life that he didn't have sex with her."

"Doesn't matter," I shake my head, trying to erase the conjured memory of the video from my mind. "He's with her now. What they do is none of my business."

After he says goodbye, I begrudgingly roll out of bed. Jared had an early class so I know he was out of here hours ago. Waking up to the Dark King's demands was not how I pictured starting off my day.

"Morning!" Morgan chimes, sipping her coffee at the breakfast bar. I give her a half-grunt and head for the pot. I'm still too annoyed to be cordial. She taps her acrylic nails against the marble top impatiently, indicating that something is on her mind.

"What?" I ask after taking the first sip of caffeinated heaven.

"So this Friday, I have to go to this function for work. I'm dreading it but I absolutely have to go, Gabs. All the Luxe employees do. And I wanted to tell you but I didn't know how you'd react. But now that you see how the tabloids are blowing up with information, I'd rather you hear it from me," she rambles nervously.

"The party for Dorian and Aurora. I know," I say, putting her out of her misery.

She sighs with relief. "How did you know?"

"Because I'm going too," I reply stoically. "I guess with Cashmere formerly being owned by Dorian or something, I'm required to make an appearance. I'm just popping in for five minutes then leaving."

"Are you sure you can handle that, Gabs?" The space between her big brown eyes puckers with doubt.

"Yeah, what's not to handle? He and I have been broken up for like six months now." Before I am forced to convince her any further, the doorbell rings. Fortunately, I am greeted by Jared's smiling face, bearing a paper sack full of bagels.

"Now that's what I'm talking about! Did you remember to get smoked salmon cream cheese?" Morgan asks, snatching the bag.

Jared makes a disgusted face and fishes the individual servings of cream cheese out of his pocket. "Yeah. Gross." He drops a kiss on my smiling lips, cradling my face in his large hands. "Good morning, beautiful. Sorry I left so early."

"It's ok," I grin, folding my body into his arms. "You're here now. And you brought bagels." We both look over at Morgan who is muttering her thanks between large bites of bread and sesame seeds.

"So Gabs, I'll stop by the store later and look for a dress. You wanna meet me there so we can shop together?" she asks after washing down her bite with a gulp of coffee.

I shrug, not sure what I plan to do for the day. The last thing I planned to do was shop for formal dresses for an event that I don't want to attend. I'd rather cut off my left foot than go to a party to celebrate Dorian and Aurora's upcoming nuptials.

"A dress for what?" Jared asks, grabbing himself a mug. Morgan and I lock gazes. Shit.

"Oh nothing. Just some bullshit party Morgan and I are being forced to attend on Friday. But I was planning to OD on Thursday so my RSVP is still tentative."

"A party? What kind of party?" he asks eyeing me curiously. He knows I'm dancing around the truth, trying to throw him off the scent of my anxiety. I look to Morgan and plead for help with my eyes.

"A party for Dorian and Aurora," she answers. "You know how ruthless these socialites are. We are practically being dragged there against our will."

I mouth my thanks to her behind Jared's back before he turns back to search my blank expression. "And you're ok with that? You'll be fine to be in the same room with them again?"

I don't have the heart to tell him that Dorian and I tried to work things out and that I had seen him on New Years. But I hadn't even really considered Aurora. Can I really stand to be anywhere near her without wanting to snatch every single hair from her corrupt little head? Doubtful.

"I guess we'll find out," I shrug.

"Ok," he nods. "What time should I pick you up?"

Huh? "Pick me up for what?"

"For the party. You really think I am going to send you to deal with those soulless assholes by yourself? If you have to suffer through it, so do I."

I cock my head to one side and look up at him questioningly. "You'd really subject yourself to that for me?"

Jared sets down his coffee mug and takes mine from me as well, placing it on the breakfast bar. Then he wraps his arms around my waist, pulling me into his body. "When are you going to realize that I would do anything for you? Of course, I'm going."

I snuggle into his embrace and forget for one moment what I've committed myself to do. In a matter of days, I will be face to face with the Dark King and God knows what else. I could be walking into my own assassination. But I can't tell Morgan or Jared that without raising suspicion. I just have to see this through and hope like hell that Niko is right about my safety.

Twenty-Six

I stand in front of the full length mirror, adjusting the delicate straps of my dress. My hair falls in soft ringlets from an intricate knot atop my head and my eyes are perfectly smoky with a touch of golden shimmer. It all seems oddly formal for just a party but of course I know nothing about black tie formal affairs. Most of the parties I attend are BYOB or include beer funnels.

"Oh . . . Em . . . Geee, Gabs, you look stunning!" Morgan says from behind me after putting the final touches on my hair.

I run my hands down the front of the cream beaded gown. "You really think so?"

She beams at me through the mirror and places her hands on my shoulders. "I know so. Do I look like the type of chick that dishes out compliments just to blow your head up? Now tell me how fabulous I look so we can go."

I turn around to face my best friend decked out in head to toe emerald green satin. "You look absolutely beautiful, Morg," I smile. She truly does, and for a moment I feel the threat of tears forming at my perfectly lined eyes. I quickly blink them away. Morgan would kill me if I ruined her hard work. But being here, her arsenal of beauty products splayed all over my room while she treats me like a life-sized Barbie, feels like old times. I almost feel normal.

A tap at my bedroom door interrupts the sentimental thoughts going through my head. "We better get out there," I remark. "The guys are getting impatient."

"Oh, screw them," Morgan replies, adding another coat of mascara to her dangerously long false lashes. "Perfection takes time!"

When we emerge from the bedroom, appreciation is written all over Miguel and Jared's faces. Miguel quickly wraps his burly arms around Morgan's tiny waist and kisses her senseless, eliciting quite a few squeals. Jared takes a smoother approach, grasping my hands and pulling me into his body. He rests his forehead against mine and lets out a breath.

"You look incredible, Gabs. I'm tempted to skip the party and keep you here all to myself."

I smile genuinely at him, looking downright scrumptious with a dark suit and tie draped over his sculpted build. "I'm tempted to let you."

Coincidentally, the event is at in the grand ballroom of the Broadmoor hotel. As we approach valet, I can't help but feel a shudder of apprehension. We're walking into the lion's den. And even though it will be filled to the brim with high society types, anything could happen. The Dark will certainly be prevalent.

We enter the extravagant hall cautiously, yet no amount of preparation could prime us for the sight before us. The massive space screams opulence .from the soft gold and ivory color scheme to the twinkling crystal chandeliers. The affluent crowd is decked out in tailored suits, lush ball gowns and diamonds. I'm nearly blinded by the flare and even with my beautiful dress, I feel out of place.

You know that feeling where you think everyone is looking at you? Like you can almost literally hear the screeching of the record and all conversations cease? Well, that's how I feel at this very moment. I know most of it is in my head, but it's evident that some people recognize me. Or sense me.

"You ok, babe?" Jared whispers in my ear, feeling me stiffen next to him. I smile and nod, feeling anything but ok. My eyes scan the room for Dorian and Aurora though I don't want to see them. I know I can't avoid running into them. Even if seeing them cuddling and canoodling completely demolishes me from the inside out, I can't hide from the inevitable.

A waiter stops at our group, offering glasses of champagne and we gladly accept. I gulp mine down easily and place it back on the tray before he even leaves us. It will most likely be the first of many.

"Ready for this?" Jared whispers in my ear. He nods his head to the side and I reluctantly follow his line of vision. Dorian and Aurora enter the room with grand flourish, her petite hand secured in the crook of his arm. Her mega-watt smile blinds me as they meet the growing applause of their reception. Dorian's face is passable. Not quite a scowl yet not a smile either. He almost looks bored. He nods politely and shakes a few hands yet his impassive expression never falters. Something inside me smiles.

The more they move into the room, the more I see of them, and my face heats with unleashed fury while my chest tightens in agony. Aurora looks spectacular, in a catty, diabolical bitch kind of way in her red floor length gown and sparkling diamond accessories. Dorian is just as flawless in a tailored black suit and tie, his black hair meticulously styled and glossy. They look like the perfect couple. Evenly matched and supremely beautiful.

"Shame that someone so attractive can be so extremely ugly," a smooth voice says behind me, drawing my attention from the fanfare. I turn to smile at Niko who looks just as mouth-watering though he's scrapped his tie, exposing the top of his tan chest. Always the rebel. Jared follows my movement and gazes at the devilishly handsome Warlock with a slight frown.

Niko extends his hand to him with a friendly smile. "You must be Jared. I've heard a lot about you. I'm Nikolai Skotos."

Jared accepts it tentatively, confusion in his eyes. "Skotos?"

Without missing a beat, Niko nods, his smile never faltering. I turn to Jared and lay a hand on his shoulder, feeling the tension in his muscles. "Niko is Dorian's younger brother. He's been a good friend to me," I state with a comforting grin.

"Has he," Jared mutters. I can tell he's annoyed with all things Skotos and I really can't blame him. Just the name alone works as an instant cock-block. "Good to meet you, Nikolai."

"Please, call me Niko." Dorian's younger, more playful sibling greets my friends warmly, completely ignoring Jared's awkward stance. I've totally caught him off guard. He wasn't even aware that Dorian had a brother, let alone one that I consider a good friend.

Niko makes a small gesture with his finger and right on cue, servers approach us with fresh flutes of champagne and hors d'oeurves. He engages the guys in conversation after complimenting Morgan and I on our ensembles, slipping into the polished aristocrat he was bred to be. This is a side I've never seen of him and while I appreciate his hospitable demeanor, I miss his crass sense of humor. And I have to admit, I have missed him.

Once Jared is engrossed in conversation with Miguel and Morgan about an attending heiress's latest scandal, Niko comes to stand next me. "If he doesn't stop staring, Aurora may sink her claws right through his Armani," he murmurs with a sly smile.

I turn to my head fractionally to him and smirk before following his gaze. As if we are trapped inside our very own slow motion sequence, my eyes lock with Dorian's from across the room. He's surrounded by dignitaries and politicians yet his ocean blue stare doesn't falter. A momentary flash of painful regret plays on his exotic features before settling back into impassivity. It takes everything in me, every ounce of strength and determination, to close my eyes and turn away from him. The ache in my chest returns.

"He's being a rude host," I whisper to Niko before taking a sip of champagne.

"He doesn't care," he replies as if it's obvious. "He doesn't care about any of this. When are you going to see that, Gabs? He only does this to . . ."

I whip my head towards him to gauge his expression. "To what? Why is he doing this?"

Niko shakes his head. "I've said too much. It isn't . . . wise to speak here. But you have to know . . . carrying on with another guy is really killing him. It's crippling him, baby girl."

I look down, focusing my glossy eyes on a sparkling bead on the hem of my dress. "Like him marrying her isn't crippling me?" I say only for his ears.

"You know he has to do this, right? That he is sacrificing himself to save you. He would never do this if there wasn't a good reason."

I look back up and gaze into his endless blue eyes. Eyes so similar to Dorian's that it nearly hurts to look at him. "Do I? Can I really trust that?"

"What are you two whispering about?" Jared interjects with mock easiness. Hopefully I'm the only one who can detect the aggravation in his voice.

I smile warmly at him, brushing his cheek with the back of my hand to soothe him. "Just catching up. Want to check out the terrace?"

The four of us excuse ourselves from Niko and head out to the magnificent terrace overlooking the lake on the resort grounds. It's pretty chilly, even with the outdoor heaters, so we don't stay long. However, the frigid air seems to have cooled Jared's suspicions.

"Have I told you how beautiful you look tonight?" he whispers in my ear, holding me close to his body. He plants a soft kiss along my jaw and I gladly nuzzle into his touch.

"Hmmm, I can't remember. So obviously one more time wouldn't hurt."

Jared cups my face between his large hands and pulls my face up to meet his heated gaze. "Gabriella Winters you are the most beautiful girl I have ever seen. That was my first thought when I met you seven years ago. And it's still true today."

I decide right then and there that tonight will be the night that I give myself to Jared mind, body, and soul. I want to make love to him. I want to let him love the last bits of hurt away. And I want to give him my whole heart, even if that is never possible. I truly want all those things. I want to be able to love Jared the way he deserves to be loved. I want a life with him. One that isn't filled with corruption, secrets, and deception. One where I am just regular, old Gabs and he is Jared, the boy I've always loved.

Just as I am about to relay my desires, something out the corner of my eye catches my attention and draws my gaze. Over Jared's shoulder, several feet away, I see Niko, a stern expression on his face. It's a total contrast from his normally easygoing guise and instantly puts me on guard. He nods his head to the side, and I know that it's time. Time for me to do what I came here to do.

I smile up at Jared, sliding my hands up his chest. "I have to go talk some business for a minute. But when I return, I want you to take me home so we can . . . properly . . . finish this discussion." I bite my lip suggestively, letting my words sink in before giving him a kiss. I just hope it's not a kiss goodbye.

I make my way to Niko, my legs shaking with every step in my four inch heels. I need to channel every bit of confidence in me when I face Stavros. Showing any signs of weakness will undoubtedly give him the leeway he needs to sift through my head.

Niko and I approach a large built man dressed in all black and wearing dark shades. His presence is ominous, yet Niko greets him with familiarity. It's not until I let myself look at him that I realize who it is. Cyrus. The vampire that cleaned up my . . . mess. My skin goes clammy at the remembrance.

"Where are we going?" I ask, unable to mask my uneasiness once we are all concealed behind the elevator doors.

Niko punches in a code into the keypad under the illuminated numbers. "Penthouse."

Of course. I wouldn't expect anything less. I nod then force my eyes to Cyrus, standing a few feet away to my left. "Thank you, Cyrus. For what you did . . . that night."

His head whips to me faster than natural, his expression unreadable. He gives me a stiff nod, also unnaturally fast. "My pleasure, ma'am."

My heartbeat stutters and I hear Niko chuckle next to me, causing me to narrow my eyes at him. When the elevator slows to the top floor, he clutches my hand, intertwining our fingers, and leads me out of the car and into the penthouse.

If concentrated panic didn't already ooze through my veins, I may have been able to take in the magnificent splendor of the top floor. But knowing that I would be surrounded with Warlocks and vampires, not to mention the most diabolical of them all, the Dark King, I can't focus on more than putting one foot in front of the other. I work to steady my breathing and let Niko's soothing touch wash over me. Having my hand locked in his is the only thing keeping me from bolting back to the elevator and getting the hell out of there.

Niko gives my hand a little squeeze as we step into the vast living area and I stop before crossing the threshold. Sitting in an elaborate high back chair, reminiscent of a modern day throne, sits Stavros, the king of the Dark. To his right stands the man that I couldn't stop loving even if I tried. His eyes instantly find mine as if he's been anxiously awaiting my arrival. He makes a slightly pained grimace before his lips curl into a smooth half-smile. That, along with another squeeze from Niko, is enough to make me continue into the room. Niko gives me a swift kiss on the cheek before going to take his spot on his father's left side. I stifle the whimper at the loss of contact and knot my fingers in front of me.

"Gabriella," Stavros coos silkily, his intense blue gaze molesting my body. Of course, he is impeccably dressed and downright edible. I hate my physical attraction to him. It is the most maddening, sickening feeling in the world and I'm tempted to claw my eyes out just to escape his beauty. "I'm so glad you could join us this evening," he adds with a devilish smile.

I take in the sight of the three most gorgeous, deadly men alive. It's hard to accept that such beauty could harness such evil. Between the three of them, they could probably demolish Colorado Springs in the blink of an eye. I swallow back the rising anxiety.

"Did I have much of a choice?" I ask quietly. Shit. He needs to know I mean business. I clear my throat and flick my cold eyes back to him. There's no way I'm letting him think I'm intimidated.

Of course, Stavros isn't ruffled in the slightest at my icy

demeanor. He smiles, his grin sickly sweet and devastatingly handsome, before licking his lips. “Can I get you a drink?” He raises a finger and another dark suited wall of muscle with dark shades appears before I can even answer. Another vampire. I begin to wonder where Cyrus is but the thought leaves me as quickly as it manifests when I catch Dorian’s gaze. His eyes haven’t left me since I arrived.

I shake my head, my hazel orbs still fixed on Dorian’s stoic expression. *God, he’s magnificent.* How could anyone get over someone that extraordinary? How could you ever settle for anything less?

“Very well then,” I hear Stavros say. “I don’t suppose introductions are in order, considering you and Dorian are well acquainted. And you’ve met Nikolai.”

I tear my eyes away from Dorian and look to Niko at the mention of his name. He gives me the famous Skotos crooked grin and winks, causing me to smile genuinely for the first time since arriving. I look back at Stavros, squaring my shoulders and ready for the onslaught to ensue.

“Gabriella, first I want to sincerely apologize for any inconvenience you have suffered at the hands of my sons.”

I narrow my eyes viciously. “Bullshit.”

Stavros looks as if I’ve just slapped him across the face. Niko fails to stifle a chuckle and earns a sharp look from his father. “Excuse me?”

He wants the truth; I’ll give him every ugly truth he’s conspired to show me for the past year.

“That’s bullshit and you know it. This is exactly what you wanted. You sent your son after me, remember? And you’ve done everything in your power to ensure that I can’t forget him.” I give each of them, even Niko, a stern glare. Each wears the same blank face, not even allowing a crack of emotion to give way to their solidarity. I realize now that I’m an outsider. No matter what type of relationship I have with Dorian and Niko, they will stand with

Stavros. They won't defy their king.

Stavros breaks into a menacing leer before chuckling darkly. I'm certain he isn't used to being addressed like this, especially in a room full of his supernatural subordinates. "Don't be ridiculous, Gabriella."

"Ridiculous?" I spit out venomously. "As ridiculous as sending a wedding invitation to my parents' home? Or sending me a sex tape?" My eyes snap to Dorian whose icy façade cracks at the mention of his betrayal.

"I can assure you," Stavros says, his gaze darting between Dorian and me, "that I had nothing to do with either of those infractions."

"But it was you who orchestrated this little marriage, correct? You couldn't have me so you ensured that Dorian couldn't either."

Stavros gapes at me for just a second, caught off guard at my accusation. I can see he's growing angry at my challenging behavior. I can nearly taste the shift in the atmosphere. I let my eyes close for just a moment and suck in a breath, an almost metallic flavor resting on my tongue and simmering. The thin hairs on the back of my arms stand at attention and a sensation sweeps over me, causing my skin to slightly tingle.

The three men send each other questioning looks, no doubt silently communicating the sudden change in the air. Stavros appears to be on the brink of fury, Niko seems amused, and Dorian looks almost hopeful. I'm not exactly sure what has penetrated their impassivity but whatever it is, I know it has them on guard.

Stavros clears his throat before addressing my claims. "You do realize that the arrangement between Dorian and Aurora is necessary. That it is imprudent to assume that it was done for any other reason than to assure your safety."

I take a small step forward, suddenly feeling bold. I can almost feel Dorian's growing tension at my advance. "My safety from whom? People keep claiming that this is all to keep me safe but no one has told me who has threatened me. Other than you, Stavros, I'm starting to believe that there is no one out there that wants to hurt me."

He steeples his fingers in front of his face, resting his chin on the very tips. His eyes grow colder with every tense second that ticks by. "I don't want to hurt you, Gabriella. If I wanted to, I could. Very easily," he spits back, causing both Dorian and Niko to flinch at his tone. "But there is still someone out there who does. It would be wise of you to remember that. We don't want any more of your . . . loved ones . . . to be hurt."

His words sound like a threat, and I shift uneasily on my high heels, fingering a bead on my dress. "What are you saying?"

The corner of Stavros's mouth pulls up on one side, his icy gaze fixed on my fidgeting. I hear Dorian take in a sharp breath and my eyes fly to his. A frown puckers his forehead and his jaw is tight with anger. I look at Niko who mirrors his brother's expression before turning back to Stavros, who seems oddly amused at my discomfort.

"How far would you go to protect your family, Gabriella? Your friends?" He leans forward, resting his elbows on his knees. "That human boy you seem to be so fond of? What's his name . . . Jared?" He turns to his oldest son and smiles menacingly. "Hmmmm."

The subtle shift in the air evolves into a low hum and my skin prickles. A hiss escapes through my teeth involuntarily. "Is that a threat?"

Stavros shakes his head, waving off the thick tension between our bodies. "Of course not. But accidents do happen. It would be most unfortunate if one were to happen to any one that you care about."

"Cut the shit. What do you want? Why did you call me here, Stavros?" I snap, growing tired of his games.

He sucks his teeth at my crassness and sits back on his mock throne. "You know what I want. Give me your allegiance. I can make you great, Gabriella. I can ensure that you are the most feared force this world has ever seen."

"What if I don't want that? What if I don't want to be feared?"

Again, Stavros's eyes flick to Dorian, then back to me. "Then what is it that you want?"

Reflexively, I also look to Dorian, whose eyes have been locked on me since the moment I stepped in the grand room. His face is a tortured mix of anguish and hope, so painfully beautiful that my heart aches for him. "I want you to undo the link," I say quietly, not even bothering to look at Stavros. Dorian's eyes widen with horror but I continue. "And then I want you to break his curse. His curse to love me."

Physical pain rocks my entire frame as the words leave my mouth and I blink back scorching hot tears. However, a stubborn one escapes, sliding down my cheek as I take in the look of sheer agony on Dorian's face. Yet, I can't look away. Neither one of us can turn away though it hurts us both. It seems like putting each other through hell is what we do best.

Niko gasps. "Gabriella, you shouldn't-"

"Silence, Nikolai," Stavros demands, raising a palm to halt any further influence. "What curse do you speak of?"

I finally pull my gaze away from Dorian and bring it to Stavros. "You cursed him to love me for the sole purpose of making him suffer when he had to kill me."

"Hearsay," he says dismissively. "But if you would like me to break the link, I'd be happy to. Is that what you really want?"

"Yes," I whisper breathlessly.

"No," Dorian growls.

Stavros ignores his threatening tone. "Upon your ascension into the Dark, I will break the link. And whatever . . . curse . . . you speak of. Do we have a deal?" He extends his palm for me to shake.

"No!" Dorian spits more forcefully, his clenched fists shaking at his sides.

My shaky legs carry me the few feet to Stavros, my eyes trained on Dorian's murderous expression. His jaw ticks violently. Time seems to cease as I approach, holding my hand out to receive

Stavros's deal. I know I shouldn't do this but I'm tired of people making decisions for me. I'm sick of feeling helpless.

As soon as my skin grazes his, a sizzling current rips through me, emitting its charge through my fingertips. Stavros inhales sharply and recoils from my touch as if it's on fire. I take his unease as my chance to drive my point home. I lean forward, close enough to feel the warmth of his body and the sweetness of his alluring scent, placing my palms on the armrests of his chair.

"Isn't this what you wanted?" I sneer, my searing gaze penetrating his once composed face. "For me to embrace what I am? To be the goddess I was intended to be?" I move in a fraction more. I want him to feel the heat of my vengeful words. "I am nobody's pet, Stavros. You are not my king and I will never take orders from you. It would be wise for *you* to remember *that*."

I stand up straight and smooth my dress over my hips. "I'll do what you ask of me and after you fulfill your end of the bargain, we are done. You won't ever threaten my loved ones again and you will stay the hell out of my life."

I look to Dorian and try to give him a smile that he struggles to return. Soon I won't be more than a passing memory to him. He'll be able to move on, find happiness in his new life with Aurora. And maybe one day, when the ache of loving and losing finally ceases, I'll be able to do the same.

After one last satisfied glare at Stavros, I turn on my heel and exit the vast living area and don't stop until I am pressing the elevator call button. Niko is next to me in the next instant, pressing his lips to my cheek without caution. I look up to him and beam, trembling yet proud of myself for standing up to his father. If only he and Dorian could do the same.

"You amaze me, baby girl," he murmurs, giving me a wink.

I let out the breath I had been holding and lean against his shoulder, suddenly feeling drained. Luckily the elevator makes it to the top floor with a ding and the doors slide open. Niko ushers me in with a hand at the small of my back then drapes an arm around my shoulders, pulling me close to his chest protectively. His hand strokes my shoulder gently and I feel the binds of fear and anxiety leave my body. Just as the doors slide closed, Dorian's panic-stricken face comes into view yards away. But it's too late. I'm already gone.

You wouldn't know there had been a nearly hostile showdown just upstairs by the looks of the vibrant gathering in the ballroom. The band is remarkably good and plays everything from big band swing music to Top 40s favorites. I spot Miguel at the bar across the room, contently watching Jared and Morgan cut a rug. They look so happy and carefree, there's no way I could bring myself to disrupt their good time. I gaze at them admiringly. I'm not sure how many more times I can see them like this.

"Dance with me?" Niko asks, offering his hand. I roll my eyes playfully and take it, letting him lead me to the crowded dance floor, out of my friends' line of vision. Dozens of ice blue eyes focus on us the moment he wraps his arms around me.

"Looks like we have an audience," I note as Niko sways me from side to side. Of course, he's an excellent dancer.

He smirks and nuzzles closer to me, yet keeps his hands above my hips. "They're just curious. Screw 'em. I'm sure they are more interested in me and all my fuck ups than you."

I give him a question-laced frown. "What makes you say that?"

"Black sheep, baby girl," he shrugs. "Surprisingly, Dorian's transgressions pale in comparison to mine. But when you've been alive for centuries, you get bored. And you get desperate."

"Desperate for what?"

Again he shrugs, pulling me a bit closer. I know he's doing it solely for the comfort. "Death. Life. Love. We're all looking for something."

I give into his intense, saddened blue eyes, my affections for this absurdly handsome Warlock causing me to press for more. What hidden pain lies behind his playful façade? "What are you looking for, Niko?"

He smiles coyly and just shakes his head. We continue to dance for the remainder of the song in companionable silence. I can't even begin to deny the magnetic charge between us. I feel safe in his arms, though I know I can only have that sense of security for just a moment longer.

A slower ballad begins and I lay my head on Niko's shoulder, forgetting where I am and letting his intoxicating scent surround me.

"I always wondered," he whispers into my hair, "what it would have been like if it had been me who came for you, and not my brother."

I lift my head and gauge his torn expression. "What do you mean?"

"Would I have been able to go through with it?" He looks away, taking a moment to formulate his thoughts. When his blue eyes meet mine, they look a bit glazed. "Could you have loved me like you love Dorian? If you had met me first?"

My cheeks heat at the question, and my own undefined fondness for him. "Of course," I smile. "What's there not to love?"

He gives me his famous dazzling white smile. "That's what I keep saying!"

I laugh and settle my head back on his shoulder, closing my eyes and letting the music combined with his contact soothe me. It feels so nice, so familiar. Like a small remembrance of something I once had.

"Are you angry at me for asking Stavros to break the link and the curse?" I ask quietly.

Niko takes a beat to think and I feel him shake his head. "No. I'm not angry."

"I don't want to be loved out of obligation. I don't want him to be cursed with me forever."

"I understand. But that's not a curse. That's a privilege," he says giving me a little squeeze before letting out a huff of air. "I hate having to say goodbye to you."

I quickly pull my head up and frown. "Goodbye?"

Niko nods and tries to smile but it doesn't meet his eyes. "We're all going back. For the wedding. Your birthday is soon and you'll no longer need us."

"You're leaving me?" I ask with a cracking voice, sounding needier than I intended.

Niko places his warm lips on my forehead. "We'll see each other again, baby girl. I won't forget about you. It's impossible to." He brushes my cheek with the back of his hand and I lean into his touch, all thoughts of Dorian and Jared forgotten. My heart is now breaking for someone else. For the Warlock I had grown to care for deeply.

"Promise me you'll visit." Tears sting my eyes. For some reason, I feel like this will be our last encounter.

Niko smiles and gives me a wink. "I promise. But you have to promise me something." He takes in my narrowed, suspicious eyes. "It's nothing bad! Or naughty. Just promise me you'll have an open mind. Promise me you'll listen."

"What are you talking about?"

Niko answers my question by unraveling his arms from my waist and turning me to the side. Dorian is mere feet away, weaving his way through the crowd. My breath catches at the sight of him. I could never get used to seeing his face. He stops before us with a contented grin on his face, as if he had been looking for me all night. As if I am the very air he needs to breathe.

"May I cut in?" he asks in his seductively smooth voice. I scowl at Niko who raises his hands and shrugs with mock innocence. Of course, he planned this.

With a deep breath, I gently place my hand in Dorian's, my breath instantly hitching at the contact. With his eyes trained on mine, as always, he pulls my body into his, holding me close as if he's afraid I'll run. I can't be entirely sure that I won't.

I feel Niko and the rest of the world slip away from us the moment I wrap my hands around his neck. Just the feel of the small patch of exposed skin between his collar and his hairline under my fingertips brings back a flood of memories. Dorian kissing me . . . holding me . . . telling me he loves me . . . gazing down at me as he eases himself inside me, both of us gasping with the pleasurable intrusion. I've tried to stifle these memories for months yet I know they will never die. Just like my insane love for him.

"What are you doing, Dorian?" I sigh into his shoulder. His scent instantly fills my senses and I feel almost intoxicated. I close my eyes and take it all in, wishing his exotic freshness could wash over me permanently.

I feel his lips in my hair. "Dancing with the most beautiful woman here."

"Won't your fiancé mind?" I don't even try to mask the snarky tone in my voice.

"I don't know and I don't care. She won't bother you. She knows if she even comes near you, she'll be out on her ass. Besides, she'd rather keep up the charade than admit to the world that I'm not in love with her."

"You seem to want the same," I whisper.

Dorian pulls away to look me in the eye. He looks . . . sad. Defeated. "You know what I want. But you told me I couldn't have it. That I couldn't have you. I'm trying, Gabriella. I'm trying to let you go so you can live."

My heart clenches at the sight of his pain. "I'm trying too. That's why we have to break the link, Dorian. Once your father reverses the curse, you won't have to-"

"Gabriella, I love you unconditionally. No curse, no link, nothing else could influence or take that away. One day you will see that. I'll prove it to you."

I shake my head. "And how is that letting go? How is that closure?"

Dorian looks away, pondering my questions with a slight frown. "Maybe I don't want closure."

"Than what do you want?"

He brings his gaze back to me, passion burning brightly in his impossibly blue orbs. His hands tighten around waist, grasping the skin of the small of my back through the thin fabric of my dress. “You. Forever. Just you.”

I’m left gaping at him, eyes filled with tears and seconds away from telling him that I want the same–*need* the same–when I hear a familiar, albeit irritated, voice. “What the hell is this?”

We both spin around to face a furious Jared, staring daggers at Dorian. I drop my hands from his neck, yet Dorian’s are still clutching my lower back. He doesn’t look ruffled in the least. Maybe he’s even a bit amused.

“Jared, um, I,” I stammer weakly. “I was just coming to find you when . . .”

“I asked her to dance,” Dorian replies coolly. “I insisted. I wanted to say . . . goodbye.”

My eyes snap to Dorian’s and he gives me a weak half-smile. I nearly choke on the knot in my throat.

Jared clears his throat and grasps my hand, tugging me towards him possessively. “Ok, you’ve seen her,” he mutters angrily.

“Jared, stop.” I pull my hand away from his grasp and place it on his chest to halt his temper then look back at Dorian.

“Dorian . . .” Words fail me. I know this is goodbye. I know this is the closure we both need yet I can’t get it out.

“Gabriella . . .” He sucks in a breath, his sad eyes glossy. Then in his native language, the Dark tongue that I can somehow understand, he mutters his final declaration to me.

“We’ll be together. I’ll make this right for us. For you. I love you, little girl. In life and in death.”

He slowly withdraws his hands and backs away, his beautifully pained face the only thing I can see. Our eyes don’t leave each other until he has melted into the crowd yet I still gaze after him, willing him to fill my sight and come back to me.

I force myself to look back at Jared, his face displaying a mix of hurt and confusion. His shoulders slump with resignation and his head falls to his chest. I know that I’ve lost him. I know that he and I cannot move forward. Not like this.

My hand cups his cheek as guilt and remorse tear me in two. "Go home. I'll get a ride with Morgan and Miguel."

Jared lifts his head and I nearly break at the sight of his tear-rimmed eyes. I've hurt him, the one thing that I've tried so hard to avoid. I thought if I withheld, if I just kept him at a distance, than it would be easier to let go. Because I knew it would come to this. I knew I'd eventually break his heart.

"I'm so sorry, Jared. I'm so, so sorry."

Though he couldn't understand the words Dorian uttered just moments ago, the intense longing in our eyes was undeniable. He saw it . . . felt it. He knows he could never compete with that magnitude of need. He knows that I could never look at him the way I look at Dorian. I can't lie to him; I won't. He deserves so much better than that. He deserves better than me.

Without another word, Jared turns and stalks out of the ballroom, leaving me standing alone on the dance floor, a few remorseful tears dripping onto my dress. While the surge of emotion is rare for me, I can't contain my pain. Silently and unapologetically, I cry those tears for Jared, the man I loved since he was a boy. The man I wish I could love again.

Twenty-Seven

I stare at the half empty bottle of Jack sitting on my desk. It's the last of my post-breakup stash that I kept here at Cashmere. And while I hadn't needed the numbness it brought in months, I am thankful for it today. Today was a different beast. It would be my last day as a twenty year old, semi-regular girl. It would be the last day I could even consider myself remotely human. And it would be the day that my heart would stop beating. The day that I would forever remember with loathing.

Dorian's wedding day.

I know it's no coincidence that he and Aurora would be getting married the day before my ascension. It's just another way for Aurora to take a jab at me. My fists clench reflexively. It would take more than just a jab if she even dared to come near me. Apparently she knew that because physically she had kept her distance.

I unscrew the bottle and set it on my desk, still unsure if I want to go back down this road. It's only late morning after all. I had planned to just come in to finish up some paperwork in the event that my ascension goes terribly wrong then spend the rest of the day with my parents. It could be my last day with them. Neither of us knew what the future held in the next twenty four hours. They had done all they could do up to this point. Now it was time for me to make a choice.

I take a deep breath and pick up the bottle, the scent of the strong liquor burning my nose. I know it would help ease the rising anxiety of the unknown. It would help me forget the last year, not to mention the next hours. I just can't decide if that's what I truly want. I had made peace with the fact that I would probably be alone forever. Not in the pathetic 'whoa-is-me' kinda way. But in the 'it-is-what-it-is' kinda way. Normal, healthy relationships were reserved for normal, healthy girls. That no longer applied to me. Not after today.

Before I can bring the bottle to my lips, my computer chimes, indicating a new email message. I put it down and open the application, more out of distraction than anything else. I can't help but smile when I see the name of the sender.

Subject: Happy Birthday, Beautiful

Baby girl,

Since I can't be there to celebrate your birthday with you, I thought this may be a close second to gracing you with my actual presence. I pulled a few strings and recovered some info that I'm sure you will find interesting. I know you don't like to talk about it, but I was able to find the original of the video that was sent to you. Of course, Aurora was the one who sent it . . . heartless bitch. But more importantly, the original had a time and date stamp.

Gabs, that video was recorded in March of 2012. Exactly a year ago. And I swear to you, it didn't go any further than what you saw. I told you . . . Dorian would never do that. You have no idea what he has already been through with that woman. He wouldn't let himself get hurt again. I actually think she created that file for a different purpose, maybe to gain leverage for another one of her convoluted plans. I don't know. But whatever the reason, Dorian didn't betray you. He loves you.

I have attached the original video in case you wanted to see for yourself, though I doubt you do. But just know, he was telling the truth. He never did anything with her other than what you saw. As hard as that was to stomach, it wasn't how it seemed.

I have half a mind to send you a plane ticket to come stop this bullshit wedding. But we both know how that would end. Father still has a stick up his ass about the last encounter. Did I ever tell you I fucking love you for that?

Well, I better let you go and enjoy your last day as ordinary. Get fucked up, stir up some trouble, make some bad decisions, and oh yeah . . . think of me the entire time.

See you on the other side of forever,

Niko

I let out the breath I didn't realize I was holding and slump back in my chair, letting myself process what I've just learned. My heart told me that Dorian was being honest, that he had not betrayed me. But after playing the fool for so long, after being beaten down and broken, I felt like I could no longer trust my own instincts. I had turned a blind eye for so long. I let denial blanket my rationale. I have never been so happy to be wrong.

But it doesn't matter. None of it does. Sure this information gives me peace of mind but that's as far as it goes. Dorian is getting married today. It's too late to change the inevitable.

I screw the top back on the bottle and shove it back into the bottom drawer of my desk. I don't need to be numb. Not when this may be the last time I feel human. And it's ok. I'm . . . ok.

But there is something I do need to do. I need to make things right with Jared. I need him to know that I never meant to hurt him. I don't know how much time I actually have left. What if something goes . . . wrong . . . and I'm never able to see my friends and family again? What if the consumption of power completely alters who I am?

I finish up what I came for, writing down important contact info, securing legal documents, and recording account numbers, before placing everything in the safe for Carmen. The task is almost morbid, as if I am getting my affairs in order, waiting for death. Maybe on some level I am. My human life must end so my destiny can begin.

I decide to walk down to Luxe before trying to find Jared. I need Morgan's opinion. For weeks, since he stormed out of the

Broadmoor ballroom, he's avoided me. I tried to give him space and time to heal but even after a few days, he still refused to take my calls. I had really destroyed him. But no matter what I did, Jared would have ended up hurt. If I went along with it, if I just tried to make it work with him, I still would have eventually crushed him. Either my love for Dorian would have floated back to the surface, tainting the relationship we were trying to build, or my ascension would have made things too difficult to try to carry on normally. Even if I would have been honest from the start, I still would have hurt him. There was no painless way to do this.

"Hey chick," I say, greeting Morgan with a smile. I wave over at Carlos and the rest of the stylists who look like they've seen a ghost. I don't fault their surprise; I haven't stepped in the salon since Dorian and Aurora got engaged. It doesn't even feel like it's been over six months, but at the time, it felt like an eternity of loneliness and grief.

Morgan narrows her brown eyes. "Everything ok?"

I give her a warm smile and nod. "Yeah, everything is fine. I just wanted to stop by and see you before I went over to see the parents. And I was thinking I would go by the campus and see Jared."

Morgan turns from her station where she is sanitizing a collection of combs and brushes. "Really?"

"Yeah. I gotta make this right before it's too late. Before I lose him for good."

Morgan claps a hand on my shoulder giving it a little squeeze. "I think that's a great idea. Tell him how you feel. Fight for your friendship. I know he has to miss you."

I perk into a half-hearted smile. *God, I hope he does.*

"Thanks, Morg." I wrap my arms around her and pull her in for a tight hug. "You're my best friend, you know that? And I owe you so much. Thank you for always looking out for me. I hope I can do the same for you . . . one day."

Morgan slowly wraps her arms around me, taken aback by my

bizarre display of affection. I'm not exactly the warm-and-fuzzy type.

"Sure, of course, Gabs." She pulls my body away from hers to gauge my expression. "Are you sure everything is ok?"

I blink my glazed eyes rapidly, dispelling the rush of vulnerable emotion. "Of course. I just want you to know . . . just in case I never told you."

I smile away the awkwardness and make my way to the other stylists, embracing them as if I'll never see them again and earning quite a few questioning glances. Just minutes ago, I had done the same with my own employees, even getting a bit choked up while hugging Carmen. I couldn't help it. It felt like goodbye and I couldn't let the moment pass without acknowledging it.

I pull out my phone as I exit Luxe, eager to dial Jared and tell him that I want to see him. Need to see him. Something inside me can't let his avoidance go another second.

"Oh shit!" I shriek, running right smack into a hard chest and dropping my phone. I had been so intent on scrolling through my contacts that I hadn't been paying well enough attention to what was right front of me.

"Gabs?" a surprised voice says from above me.

Embarrassed, I flick my gaze up to twin chocolate brown eyes and perfectly styled brown hair. "Xavier?"

"Hey, long time no see!" he says, smiling brightly, causing his eyes to sparkle in the sunlight.

I give him a quick, friendly grin before bending down to scoop up my phone. I cringe after seeing the cracked screen. Shit.

"Are you walking back to Cashmere?"

"Yeah," I reply, still frowning at my destroyed cell phone. I take a deep breath and give him a weak smile.

"Ok, cool, I'll walk with you."

We walk the couple blocks to Cashmere, Xavier catching me up on all the guys' wild trysts. "So Carlos goes home with the man and . . . OMG, his wife jumps out of the closet with a baseball bat!"

"You're kidding!" I laugh.

"No. I shit you not. What makes it worse, is that I knew him from somewhere. I couldn't put my finger on it until I ran into him again at the mayor's office. He's the chief of police!"

"Oh my God!"

We laugh the entire way to Cashmere, my foul mood at my broken cell phone screen completely forgotten. I'm thankful for the distraction. Xavier's goodhearted nature and easy humor have somewhat restored my faith in humanity. He's probably faced adversity every day of his life because of his sexuality. Yet he is able to laugh and smile through it all. If he can overcome hatred and pain, maybe so can I.

"Well, this is me," I say waving towards the parking lot. I move in to give Xavier a hug when a buzz from my cell phone startles me. *Whew!* At least it works. After an awkward wave as I try to answer the call without slicing off my finger, I fumble for my keys, making my way to my little Honda. Unfortunately, the caller hangs up before I can answer and I curse under my breath.

"Oh, Gabriella?"

I whip my head around to see that Xavier has followed me to my car and stands only a foot away.

"Yes?" I ask with narrowed eyes.

Xavier gives me another bright, beaming smile that lights his eyes with flecks of gold. "Happy Birthday."

And before I can process the words, let alone respond, staggering, unimaginable pain grips my entire frame before plunging me into the dark, frigid depths of unconsciousness.

Twenty-Eight

I hurt.

God, I hurt. *All over.* But the pain in my head is by far the worst. Just the tiniest flutter of my eyelids causes excruciating pain to rip through my skull. It feels like a hatchet has been embedded in my brain, the pressure pushing on the vital bundle of cells that controls all movement. *I can't move.* I'm not sure if it is out of immense pain or if there really is a hatchet crippling me.

Oh God, am I paralyzed?

No. I can feel pain. Shit, it's all I feel. But my leaden body won't move. Maybe it's out of complete and utter fear. Or maybe I'm being bound by restraints. I urge myself to crack open an eyelid, fighting through the agony with a clenched jaw. I stifle the whimper building in my throat, resorting to biting the inside of my cheek. Great. *More* pain.

I try to peer through the tiny slit of my lid for any clue of my location. The room is unlit yet a small stream of dim light floods from a high window. From that, I can see that the dank, stuffy room is barren. Cement floors, bare cinderblock walls, all grey and desolate. It's depressingly silent except for the annoying sound of a leaky faucet somewhere. Every drop feels like a stab to the temple. I inwardly groan. If I could cry, tears would be streaming down my face. But it hurts too much. It's all . . . too much.

I try to swallow but the saliva in my mouth feels too thick. Even my tongue seems swollen. The metallic taste on it makes my stomach roil. If my aching body could withstand the heaving, I would vomit.

"Oh good," a haunting voice says from somewhere out of my line of vision. "You're awake."

I feel my already sluggish blood freeze in my veins, my dry lips parting fractionally in my attempt at a gasp. I know this voice. It's one that I considered friendly and warm. A voice that was always attached with a smile.

Xavier steps into my line of vision, moving silently in the shadows. He grins adoringly, scanning the length of my body with rapt fascination. When his eyes flick to mine, I nearly choke on a labored breath and my sore eyelids pop open widely.

He's Light.

Golden irises twinkle brightly in the dim, drab room as he continues to gaze at me with wonder. He doesn't seem hostile at all. He still looks like the warm, sweet man I always thought he was. And he's Light. He's the embodiment of goodness and healing. I just don't understand.

"Oh, don't look so surprised, sweetheart," he says taking a step towards me. "You are one hard little thing to find. I had to kill all those poor, helpless girls yet you were right under my nose the entire time. Ha! Could you really not sense me?"

Again I try to swallow, my eyes darting around frantically. Even the horrific ache dulls in comparison to the concentrated panic binding my body.

"You can speak, darling. I have many questions for you and I need you to be cooperative. Your compliance will be the determining factor in what happens next."

"What's that?" I choke out in a raspy, broken voice. The vibrations of my voice rip through my throbbing head, causing tears to spring to my eyes.

Xavier smiles again, tilting his head to one side. "Whether or not I kill you quickly or torture you until your human body eventually gives into an agonizing death." He takes another step towards me and looks down at the ground. "But judging by the amount of blood you are losing, your death may be quicker than I originally planned. But I think we are still on schedule."

Blood? I take a deep breath through my nose and let it out through my mouth, tasting the metallic ting in the air. I try to give myself over to my senses and focus on my hearing. The dripping nose magnifies as I concentrate and I inhale again, this time through my mouth. It's not a leaky faucet. It's blood. *My blood.* And judging by the mere second between drops splattering to the ground, I'm losing a lot of it.

"What do you want from me?" I whisper. I can't even think about the pain it brings. Soon I may not be able to feel pain, or anything else, ever again.

Xavier slowly extends a hand towards me, causing my already weak heartbeat to sputter frantically. "Shhhhh, love," he coos. He strokes my cheek lovingly then cradles my head, raising it up a few inches. I can't even fight against it. I still can't move.

After gazing at me adoringly and causing my tears to spill, he gently eases my head back down on what feels like a concrete slab. When he removes his hand from underneath my head, it's covered in bright, red blood. He rubs his fingers together, working it into his hand like a balm, before wiping it clean with my shirt. Bile rises in my tight throat.

"Isn't it obvious what I want? Isn't it obvious what everybody wants from you?"

Of course I know the answer, but I want to keep him talking until I can figure out what to do. What *can* I do? I am brutally injured and I am pretty sure he is manipulating my body so I can't move. But I have to do something. I can't–I won't–lay here and die without a fight. I've come this far. I've fought through heartache, confusion, denial, and fear just to get here. The finish line is in sight. I have to make it. I have to survive.

"What is it?" I croak.

"Dear Gabriella . . . Did you know I knew your mother?" he asks, halting all thoughts of escape with his change of subject.

I take in a sharp breath, choking on the thick saliva that I am sure is mixed with more blood. "My . . . mother?" I sputter between raspy coughs.

"Yes," he smiles, tilting his head up to the ceiling in remembrance. "She was very strong. Very efficient and talented. Fierce. And beautiful. What a beautiful woman she was," he remarks breathlessly. His expression suddenly turns dark and contemplative. "I envied her. She was better than the rest of us and she knew it. She felt invincible. I hated her arrogance."

Xavier swallows laboriously and runs a hand through his neatly styled brown hair. He takes a deep breath before letting his shoulders slump. "But I loved her. I loved her so much," he says in a broken voice.

I almost feel sympathetic at the sight of his pain when a tangible shift in the atmosphere steals my breath. The shell containing his immense power, his human form, falls away piece by piece, unleashing a ghostly form. This is different from anything I've ever seen from Dorian or even Aurora. It's bright, blindingly so, and nearly translucent, more like a premonition. A whisper of a body.

He convulses as he shifts, fighting against his rage, trying to put himself back together again. He wants to remain in control. Once he's got his emotions in check, and the pieces of his humanity have fallen neatly back into place, he scowls at me, as if I am to blame for his momentary lapse.

"She couldn't love *me*, though! She couldn't give me her heart. Because of him!" he screams pointing at me. Wind whips through the desolate space causing my blood-matted hair to fall into my face. The cement slab under me rumbles with his sudden outburst.

"I could have given her everything! But she wouldn't love me. She would rather commit treason than be with me. To be with him!"

He's at my side quicker than my eyes can see, crouching down, his face just inches from mine. I can see the reflection of my terror in his wide, crazed eyes. "We could have been so happy together," he whispers, though his soothing voice doesn't match his insanity. "And look at you . . . just like my dear Natalia. Drawn to the Dark treachery. Did he fool you, love? Did he make you fall for him with his mind games? Make you believe that he loves you too?"

I'm too afraid to answer him, too frozen in overwhelming fear to even whimper a semblance of a response. If I could move, I'd be trembling violently. If I could sob, I'd be drowning in my own tears.

"Answer me, dammit!" he screams, spewing spittle in my face. He grasps my shoulders and shakes my limp body, causing the pain to spread even more.

"No!" I cry. "He didn't do any of that. He really does . . . he does love me."

"Impossible," Xavier sneers, dropping my body back onto the slab. My head throbs viciously and I'm sure the wound has opened even more. My vision goes blotchy and I feel cold. So unbearably cold. It won't be much longer now.

Seeing me slip away, he grasps my cheeks in his shaky hands. "No, no, dear love. I need you to stay with me." Then he leans forward and presses his open mouth on mine. Comforting warmth spreads through me, and I feel some of the debilitating ache subside in my head. However, I still don't have usage of my limbs.

Xavier pulls away after only a few seconds. "That's enough," he says with a satisfied grin. He looks over me, lost in his thoughts and rubbing an index finger over his lips. "Maybe it was you all along. Maybe you knew consorting with the Dark would help conceal you. Would throw me off your scent. Maybe you knew I would have to deflect, and in turn, would not be able to detect you. Is that it? Is that why you want him?"

I try to shake my head but it's no use. "No. I didn't know what he was. Not at first."

"And once you uncovered the truth? Surely you knew what kind of sheer, unrelenting evil he harbored. Didn't you try to escape him?"

"No," I answer confidently. "I . . . I love him."

Xavier snorts. "And where is your prince? Where is your dead father's best friend and brother in arms? Ah . . . that's right. Marrying his own kind. You see, Gabriella. They can bed our women and create . . . monstrosities . . . with them. But they always go back to their kind. They would not dare taint their precious bloodline."

"My father didn't leave my mother," I reply, rage taking over my trepidation. "He was killed for loving her. He died for love."

"They. Can't. Love!" he shrieks, increasing the rumble of the concrete slab beneath me. "They are monsters. Demons. All of them! They are the reason your world is riddled with hate and violence! The reason why your mother was slain!"

My tears flow freely, the hot saltwater diluting the thick blood caked in my hair. I know arguing with this maniac is pointless. His rage will only intensify and he may end up killing me out of sheer anger. I need more time. I need to try to make him see why this is wrong.

"But you can love, X," I say in a small voice. "You can right these wrongs. You can show everyone that the Light stand for good. You don't have to do this."

He reaches a hand towards me and cups my cheek. "Oh, but I do, Gabriella. I really do. You shouldn't be allowed to exist. You don't deserve the gifts of the Divine." He brushes away a few trickling tears, and moves my soiled hair out of my face. "And it is just my luck that I've found you right before your ascension. As long as I keep you immobilized and breathing, I can kill you right as you ascend and acquire all your power. And with that, I will make everything right. I will erase the ugliness that the Dark has created. Starting with your precious prince."

I resist the urge to crack a weak smile and tell him that his plan is botched. That, even though I may die, he will never have my power. I am still linked to Dorian. And when I die, he will acquire the magic that has lain dormant in my human body.

"But I thought . . . I thought the Light didn't kill innocents. That they wanted to help and protect humans. I haven't done anything to you. How are you any better than the Dark?" Even as I say the words, I am going over a thousand different escape scenarios in my head. There's no way I am going to lay here and die.

Xavier's hand travels down from my cheek to my neck before resting on my chest where my heart pounds fiercely, despite my injuries. His small token of healing has ensured that.

"You may have not done anything *yet*, but you are far from innocent. You have Dark blood running through your veins. You consort with the Dark freely." His hand travels down to my hand where the tiny blue anchor sits. He grasps it gently, running his thumb over my inked flesh. "And you have been marked."

I open my mouth to protest but before a sound escapes, he squeezes my hand, causing me to scream out. I hear the crunch of my splintering bones breaking like glass under his grip. I feel the jagged pieces slicing through my skin, the wet sounds of tearing flesh causing the acid in my stomach to churn. I cry and shriek in agony until I am hoarse, my dry lips splitting and bleeding. He lets my hand fall with a torturous thud, as if it's nothing. As if *I'm* nothing.

Xavier wipes his bloodied hand on my clothing and backs away casually, watching me whimper and cry from the excruciating pain. I want to die in this moment. I can't take it anymore. And from the way his demented gaze sweeps over my body, only God knows what else he has in store for me.

Exhausted from the overwhelming pain and sobbing, I let my eyes close, praying for unconsciousness to take me again. Let him do what he wants with me. I don't want to be awake for it.

"Wake up!" he shouts, slapping me across the face swiftly. My mouth fills with blood and it dribbles past my split lips and down my chin. My cheek is on fire and I suspect that the skin has been broken there as well judging by the way my salty tears sting the area.

"Fuck you!" I spit, thick bloodied saliva flying into his face. "You are worse than the Dark, you piece of shit!"

Xavier's eyes grow wide and frantic, as if he's gone mad. He smiles menacingly as he brings a hand up to wipe my spit from his face. Then faster than I can see, his hand is around my neck, squeezing dangerously tight. "You stupid girl. Do you realize how easy it would be for me to snap your little precious neck? To rip off every limb like paper? Have you no regard for your life? No sense of worth?"

I struggle to get free from his grasp but of course it is futile. "I'd rather die than let you have an ounce of my power," I rasp through the tight strain.

He retreats at my words, looking down at me with contempt. "Funny. That's what Solara said as I drained every drop of her essence from her body."

I flick my gaze to him, a disgusting smile creeping onto his face. "What did you do to her?"

"Isn't it obvious? I killed her. I knew she had been in contact with the Dark Light, yet she refused to disclose your identity. She fought hard and well. Just not hard or well enough. Being a hunter has its advantages."

So he was a hunter. No wonder he was able to elude Dorian and Aurora. My cloudy mind drifts to all the times Xavier was right under Dorian's nose. He probably didn't even expect the Light to be that bold. But Dorian was an assassin as well. How could he have missed this? Was he driven to distraction to the point of oblivion? Was he just as blinded by his affections as I was?

Too bad I'll never get the chance to ask him.

I focus my thoughts on my surroundings, again letting my senses take the reins. There's only one high window from what I can see. Beyond that there's grass and dirt. I have to be in a basement. I don't hear any cars or foot traffic. The only thing I smell is blood and maybe . . . paint? The light seems dimmer. How long have I been down here?

Noticing my roaming eyes, Xavier closes the distance between us in one swift step, clutching my jaw in one of his large, blood-tinged hands. "Don't even think about escaping. There's no way you can get away. No one can save you. Just accept this death as your destiny, child."

"No," I grit through my sore, smashed cheeks between his

fingers. "It's not. And you don't have to do this, Xavier. You're a good guy. Don't do this."

He rips his hand away and doubles over into a theatrical guffaw. "What? You think by telling me I'm a good guy, I will miraculously change my mind?"

The sound of his hearty laughter infuriates me but I resist the urge to spew insults. "But you are good, X. Me and you could've been good friends. What would Carlos and Jackson and Morgan do once they learn what you've done? You can't tell me you don't care for them."

"Care for them?" he sneers. "I don't even like them. I despise them. What they are, what they represent . . . it's every corrupt thing in this world. The reason why you should not be able to live. It will be just one more example of depravity & immorality."

I muster the last bit of awareness in me, the tiny bit of sanity I am hanging onto for dear life, and try to give him a sympathetic smile. "But you can change that. Right here and now. You can show that goodness and Light always prevails. You can walk out of here knowing that you did the right thing. Please, Xavier," I plead. "Don't let your pain push you into something you're not. Don't let your Light die and become a ghost of what you were because you were hurt. You're better than that. Stronger than that."

He looks at me for a thoughtful moment, contemplating the alternative. Somewhere deep inside him, goodness stirs, beckoning him to return to what he truly his. To his true purpose. To the Light. I hold my breath, hoping–praying–that part of him isn't gone forever.

Xavier's mouth turns up into a menacing leer, shattering my last shred of hope. All remnants of sympathy for him seep out of me with my trickling blood. "You think I'm stupid, girl? You think you can trick me into letting you go? Do. You. Know. Who. The. Fuck. I. Am!?" he screams in my face, suddenly hovering over me. Then his fist slams down onto my chest, stealing all the air from my lungs with a crack. I try to take a breath through the immense pain, but I can't. I can't breathe. Something is terribly wrong. My eyes grow horrified and panicked, as I silently plead for relief. *Oh my God, I'm dying.* I am really dying. I wheeze and pant, only swallowing tiny wisps of air. It's not enough. Not enough to keep me alive.

Xavier looks down at me with a satisfied grin, amused at the labored sounds of my injured lung. He could easily heal me yet he enjoys seeing me struggle for just the tiniest bit of oxygen. After a minute or so, he slowly brings his face to mine. He sees the life slipping away from me and wants to keep me alive just so he can kill me later. Sick, sadistic, twisted fuck.

Just before his lips touch mine, his head snaps up, his golden irises blazing with fiery rage. "Impossible!" he seethes.

Instantaneously, the entire room erupts into a quake, the slab underneath me shaking violently. I can feel the shift in the air turn dense with cracking energy. I can almost see tiny particles of electricity swirling around me, cocooning our bodies.

"No!" Xavier grits. His hand is now on my neck, squeezing harder than I thought was possible, cutting off the sliver of oxygen I had just seconds ago. He hisses at something out of my line of sight. "No! If I can't have you than neither can he!"

The strain is too much, and I've been without air for longer than my battered body can take. I can't fight anymore. There is no more fight left in me. It's bled out of the gaping wounds that riddle my entire frame, staining the grey cement a deep crimson. Unconsciousness is so close, its warm blanket of comfort and oblivion outstretched to greet me. I want it. I need it in these final moments. Then with the wet, sickening crunch of my windpipe, my horrified eyes fall to small slits. And just as I let them close completely, before diving into my painless oasis, I see a flash of brilliant blue light and hear a low, terrifying growl.

It's all black now. Still. Cold.

Numb.

Twenty-Nine

White sands caress my bare toes, feeling as soft and warm as tiny silken diamonds. I lift my head to the sky, my eyes closing tightly against the intensity of the sun, and take a deep, cleansing breath. The air is so fresh, so clear. My lungs expand gratefully and take in as much as possible. It feels good . . . so good to breathe.

My lips curl into the most genuine smile I've worn in months. My cheeks almost ache with the nearly foreign movement. But I smile through it. It's a welcomed ache. Just as the bright, intense sun delivers a delightful burn, I relish in the sensation. It makes me feel vital. And happy. Finally happy.

Crystal blue waves crash against large boulders in the distance. A breeze strokes my face and hair, ruffling my white sundress. My skin is flawless and clear, no remains of brutality anywhere to be found. I smile again. Maybe I can be beautiful here. Maybe scars don't exist in this place. Maybe there are no broken spirits or crushed hearts. Just peace and bliss. Two things I never thought I'd ever truly achieve again. Two things that were ripped from me at only twenty years old.

"Beautiful, isn't it?" an incredibly smooth voice coos from beside me.

I turn my head towards the voice, a voice I know as well as my own. A voice that has whispered anecdotes of love and adoration while warm, strong arms held me tight. A voice that could melt away all the fear and anxiety I've ever felt with just a simple 'I love you.' The only voice I have ever wanted to hear.

"It is," I smile at him. "So beautiful."

Dorian's eyes sparkle against the backdrop of seawater and cloudless blue sky. His full lips curl up on one side as he gazes at me adoringly. "Only because you're here." He moves a curl from my face, tucking it behind my ear. I turn into his warm touch.

"Mmmm," I hum. "Where am I?"

He brushes my cheek, his other hand finding mine. "Home."

I smile at the word and turn back into the gorgeous view of stone mountains, endless aquamarine, and distant clay houses. "Home."

We sit in perfectly comfortable silence for a long moment, enjoying the smell of saltwater and the feel of cool wind whipping through our loose clothing. I dig my toes deeper into the soft sand. I nearly giggle as the tiny granules tickle my sensitive digits.

"Will you stay with me?" I ask in a small voice, still gazing out at the water.

I feel Dorian shift beside me. "If you want me to."

"For how long?" I turn to face him, my expression free from worry and doubt.

"However long it takes."

Satisfied with his response, I scoot next to him and rest my head on his shoulder. Dorian wraps his arm around me in response, holding me close to him. I turn into the bare skin of his neck and breathe in his sweet, alluring scent. It feels me with euphoria, and my body relaxes even more.

"I'm not afraid," I whisper, letting my eyes close for a moment and enjoying his closeness.

His lips are in my hair. "I'm glad. You shouldn't be afraid ever again."

I sigh with contentment. "I've missed you."

"Little girl, I've missed you more than you could ever imagine."

"So stay," I murmur against the fabric of his white shirt. "Stay with me."

Dorian's lips brush my forehead. "I'll never leave you again."

We sit for several minutes, maybe hours, watching the waves collide with the giant jagged rocks until the sky begins to darken. Before night falls upon us completely, I turn to him. "I have to go, don't I?"

"Yes."

I nod, understanding washing through me. "Will you come with me?"

I see Dorian smile in the dimming light, his eyes shimmering and luminescent. "I can't. But I'll be waiting for you." His hands come up to cup my face and he brushes away tears I didn't even know were there. He leans forward and presses his soft lips on my forehead. Then they caress each cheek. When his warm lips finally meet mine, I instantly melt into his touch. Sensation rips through me, spiking my heart rate and stirring the butterflies in my stomach from hibernation. When he pulls away, I see a single, glistening tear roll down his cheek.

"Close your eyes," he whispers.

I take in his beauty once more before steeling myself to do as he says. I'm not afraid. I'm not nervous. I just don't want to end this. I don't want to lose him again. But I know what I must do. I know that this is the only way. So with a deep, calming breath, I press my lips against his once more, close my eyes, and cross over to the other side.

Air fills my lungs in a rush, so much so that I almost feel high with oxygen. My wide open eyes dart around frantically, looking for any sign of familiarity as my rigid hands grip the slick fabric underneath me. I know this place. The satin comforter, the black and gold motif, the smell of rainwater and fresh linen. I've been here before.

Dorian's suite.

As if he could hear my realization, he's at my side, cradling my head. "How do you feel?" he asks, concern etched on his troubled face. His blue eyes twinkle in the dim light flooding from the en suite bathroom.

Immediately, my concern goes to my debilitating injuries. I stretch my hand in front of me, expecting to see mangled flesh and bone. It's perfectly fine, and I wiggle each digit, ensuring full mobility. My hand touches the back of my head. I can feel knots of dried, caked blood yet there is no gash. Not even a touch of soreness where the wound would have been. My lungs and neck feel fine, no trace of labored, shallow breathing. And the pain . . . it's gone. I look to Dorian with a puzzled, borderline panicked, look.

"What happened? I was . . . he had me . . . I thought," I stammer, clutching my chest. I realize it's draped in feather-light silk, not tattered, bloodied rags. "Was it a dream?"

Dorian shakes his head solemnly, grasping my hands in his. His thumb traces small circles around my anchor mark. "No. It wasn't."

Fear and confusion grip me, causing Dorian to pull me closer. "What happened to me?" I whisper.

Tension rolls off him in waves and his jaw begins to tick wildly. Though his body has stiffened, his hands are still gentle and calming as they stroke mine. "The Enchanter captured and tortured you. You lost a lot of blood. You suffered several broken bones, including a punctured lung and crushed cervical vertebrae."

I frown. So it wasn't a dream. I remember all of those things happening. I felt every broken bone and gaping wound. I could taste and smell the iron of mass amounts of blood loss in the air. I remember my fear and desperation. "But . . . I'm fine. What happened? How could all of that have happened, yet I'm here with you, unharmed?" I think back to just minutes before, to my vision on the beach of Skiathos. The wind whipping through my white dress. The smell of seawater. The feel of the sun's golden warmth . . .

"Oh my God, Dorian," I say in a horrified whisper. "Am I dead?"

He looks away, avoiding my tear-filled gaze as he battles his own emotions. "You were."

"And . . . now?" It suddenly dawns on me that it's completely dark outside. I try to pull away to stand but Dorian has a firm hold on my hands. "Oh no, what time is it?"

"10 PM. The fourteenth."

So I haven't ascended. I sigh with relief, but only for a split second. I still don't know what I am. I don't even know if I'm still dreaming. Or if I'm . . . "So I'm not dead?" I choke out, my throat suddenly as dry as chalk. "Is this an illusion?"

Dorian looks back to me, a slight frown puckering his forehead. "No, little girl."

I open my mouth to speak, the questions bombarding me all at once. I decide to go with the most obvious question. "How?"

He swallows slowly, the movement of his throat captivating my gaze. Then he cups my cheeks with his warm, soft hands. Hands I haven't felt on my body in way too long. "I felt you. I felt your pain, your fear. It crippled me. That feeling of pure dread filled me, stole my breath, and brought me to my knees. I had to come to you. I had to save you."

His thumbs brush tiny circles on the apples of my cheeks as he takes a calming breath. His beautiful endless blue eyes freeze over, becoming distant and cold. "I found you just as that bastard crushed your neck in his hands. I heard it, and it was the most terrifying sound I have ever heard. I felt the life slip away from your body. I saw you lying there ghostly white and limp."

His bottom lip trembles ever so lightly before he sucks it into his mouth, digging his teeth in it and taking a deep breath. "And I did to him what he wanted to do to you. I slaughtered him until he was nothing more than a pathetic speck of dust. I wanted to do more. I wanted everyone he has ever known to suffer. He took away the only thing I cared about. The only person I have ever loved. He took my reason to live."

A hand brushes away a few tangles that have fallen in my face. "I kneeled over your lifeless body and I sobbed. I felt myself break into a million pieces. Losing you completely shattered me and I wanted to die, Gabriella. I wanted to die with you because living without you isn't an option for me."

His eyes begin to well up with tears, matching my own. I don't even breathe as his pained grimace turns into a hopeful half-smile. "So I did something I hadn't done for centuries. I prayed. I wailed out to the Divine, begging him to help me. Asking the he take me instead and leave you to live a happy life. I screamed and cried until I had no voice left, until the sobs tearing through me made my body ache. All the while, I kept trying to save you. Kept trying to heal you. I couldn't accept that you were gone. I couldn't."

He pauses, his eyes searching my face for reaction. All I can do is look at him in disbelief. Dorian leans forward and rests his forehead against mine. We sit there for several long moments, soaking in the closeness, before he speaks again. "I don't know how, but I healed you," he whispers, his cool breath washing over my skin. "Don't you see? My love for you is so deep and so strong that the Divine heard my cries. Felt my excruciating pain. And something within, something that had been dead inside me awakened. And I healed you."

He pulls back just a fraction to press his lips against mine. "I love you," he says between feather-light kisses. "So much, Gabriella. I love you so much."

He kisses every inch of my face, yet I am too shell-shocked by his account to reciprocate. I *died*? Dorian *saved* me? Then I was on a beach in Skiathos? It all doesn't seem real to me. Like a fuzzy, bootleg version of *Inception* . . . a dream within a dream. Yet while the view may be hazy, the memory of the pain–the excruciating ache throughout my entire body–is crystal clear. I remember the agony, the desperation. The unrelenting fear that consumed the fight in me. The sudden need to survive it all though I knew I couldn't.

"I was in Skiathos. On a beach. With you," I say, trying to make sense of it all.

"Yes," he replies, a ghost of a smile on his lips. "I gave you that illusion while your body healed. I didn't want you to feel any more pain. And I didn't want you to be alone."

"Thank you."

My eyes search Dorian's hopeful face, taking in the sight of his relief. Then I spy his attire, all thoughts of hope leaving me. I push against his chest a bit to put some distance between our bodies. "Are you wearing . . . a tuxedo?" My eyes grow wide at his stoic silence. "Oh my God, Dorian, you did it, didn't you? You married her." His tailored black dress slacks, crimson-stained white dress shirt, and unraveled bow tie say it all. He was at his wedding.

Dorian shakes his head, releasing a breath. "No. I didn't. I couldn't. I felt how badly you needed me. I knew I had to come to you. I left her . . . at the alter."

Relief creeps in but I quickly push it away in exchange for skepticism. "But if I hadn't been in trouble, if you hadn't felt those things from me, you would have done it, right? You would have married her."

Aggravation flashes across his face, colliding with the visible regret spilling from his eyes. He can't lie. And his silence tells me everything I need to know.

"That's what I thought," I mumble, pulling away from him altogether.

Dorian tries to recapture my hands but doesn't fight against my refusal to let him. "Gabriella, I need you to understand what this marriage would have meant to me. It would have given me the influence–the power–to end my father. Once the throne was mine, I had planned to kill him. I couldn't tell you that because, as you know, my thoughts and words were not safe. There's no reason to hide this from you now. I'm as good as dead. I've committed my final act of treason by walking out on that mockery of a wedding." He smiles weakly but it translates as a grimace.

I nod, soaking it all in. "So all of this . . . was just a trick? To get to Stavros?" Part of me knew. But after all the lies and deceit and half-truths, I just couldn't follow my instincts. I want to believe that Dorian has always been completely honest with me but the truth is he hasn't. He's fed me too many betrayals. Betrayals that were eclipsed by my love for him.

"It was. And to be rid of Aurora. I had planned to imprison her. Strip her of all her power and leave her with just enough to exist . . ."

"Petrify her," I whisper, speaking of the same punishment that still haunts him.

"Yes," he nods. "But none of that matters now. I had to come to you. There's no way I could go through with all that while you were suffering." He runs his hands up and down my bare, unmarred arms, igniting pleasurable goosebumps on my skin.

I let myself relax under his touch, my body fighting fatigue from the day's events. The thought brings me up short and my eyes snap to Dorian's. Without thinking, my hands are on his face, pulling it within inches of mine. His eyes close reflexively as if expecting me to kiss him, and as much as I want to–*need to*–I know there is so much more that we have to discuss.

"Why do you look . . . fine? You still look like yourself. Not tired or weak." I stretch the taut skin on his high cheek bones, looking for any sign of wrinkles or dark circles.

He shakes his head in my grip. "The Enchanter was easy enough to defeat. He was too distracted by you to put up much of a fight. I acquired his power then destroyed him. Light energy has its . . . perks. I didn't want to take it, but I knew I needed it if I were to try to save you."

I release his face from my hands and let them slide to his sculpted shoulders, resting my forehead against his. "I have to go," I say just above a whisper. "I don't know what I am gonna do, but I have to go."

"I know," he replies matching my tone. "I won't tell you how to choose. I can't. But know that whatever side you align to, whichever way you ascend, I love you." My bottom lip quivers before Dorian soothes it with the sweetest, softest kiss. "I know you'll do what is right. I know you'll make Alex and Natalia proud. They loved you so much. Maybe even as much as I do," he says with a chuckle.

Through my confusion and fear, a smile curls my trembling lips. "Thank you."

After one last chaste kiss, he pulls away. "I'll give you some privacy to clean up. All your clothes and toiletries are still here. I never got rid of them. I expected . . . both of us to be back soon."

I smile as he exits the room then make my way to the bathroom to shower and wash out the matted blood in my hair. I feel an overwhelming gratitude to Dorian for changing me out of my ripped, bloodied clothing. He must've known the sight alone would have raised even more turmoil in my head.

I wash and dress on autopilot, my thoughts completely consumed with my last moments on Earth as a somewhat normal, human girl. I've lived a good life. I've been blessed with good friends and great parents. By aligning with the Dark, I would be going against all they have taught me. I would be playing right into Stavros's hands. And now that Dorian has gone against his wishes, I am almost certain that our deal is off. He would have no reason to uphold his end of the bargain.

Then again, the Light have proven to be just as cunning and deceitful. I can't blame their entire race for the acts of one but Xavier has clearly shown me just what they are capable of. They can be evil, menacing and murderous. They are no better than the Dark in that respect.

I make my way out of the bedroom and spot Dorian at the French doors, looking out into the night, a glass of scotch clutched in his palm. The sight tugs at my heartstrings and I fight the impulse to wrap my arms around him from behind like I had done so many times before. He would tell me all the wonders that the darkness revealed as I trailed kisses on his back before resting my cheek against it, taking in his exotic freshness. It would be so easy to slip back into that habit. Being with him, showing him that affection that he craves so much, would be as effortless as breathing.

"I called Chris and Donna," Dorian says before turning to face me. His expression is cautious, and a little bit sad. "I went there before I found you and told them what I felt. I promised I would do any and everything to save you. I nearly had to restrain Chris from coming with me but I couldn't risk him getting hurt. I told them you would call once you had a chance."

"Thank you." I stop just a few feet from him, unsure of where we stand. But I can't think about that right now. My thoughts are reserved solely for what is to come in the next hour.

Dorian fishes something out of his pocket and extends his palm, revealing a set of keys. "Here, take my car. Yours is still in front of your store."

I take the keys from him with a shaky hand, now even more nervous about driving his ridiculously expensive sports car. "Thanks. I didn't realize you still had it here."

"I told you that I had intended to come back. All of my things are here. But most importantly, you're here. I wasn't lying when I said I couldn't be without you."

I nod, clutching the keys to my chest. I don't know how I should respond. I have a major decision to make and I don't want to give him false hope in case it doesn't go the way he wants. Hell, I don't even know how it's going to go. But it will be midnight soon and I can't run from that. I can't escape my destiny, no matter what it entails.

On slightly wobbly legs, I make my way to the door, leaving Dorian at the French doors watching me intently. I turn towards him just before he is out of my eyesight.

"Dorian," I say in a quiet voice, though I know he can hear me. "I'll be back. I don't know for what. I can't be sure if it will be as your friend or your foe, but I'll be back. Thank you . . . for everything. For saving me. And for loving me."

One corner of his mouth curls into a smirk. "Why does this feel like goodbye?"

I shrug, feeling the distance between us growing wider and wider with every passing second towards my ascension. "Because maybe it is goodbye. Or maybe it's something else entirely. Maybe it's forever. I don't know."

And with that, I turn on my heel and exit the suite, wondering if I've seen the last of the man I love. The Warlock who opened me in a way that no one else could, and showed me all the wonders of the world through hauntingly ice blue eyes.

I pull into the abandoned, dark parking lot of Garden of the Gods and kill the engine. I have twenty minutes to spare so I take the few quiet moments to contemplate my next move. I know I've had a year to prepare for this moment, and honestly, I thought my mind was made up. Even with the knowledge of what the Light and Dark were originally created for, my interpretation of them was pretty black and white. But the last twelve hours have completely shattered that decision. It's not only created grey areas, it has made me doubt any and everything I've ever learned about them. How can I choose one when I am still so tied to the other?

My tortured thoughts are interrupted by a sensation crawling up my arms and legs. It's not the prickles of pleasure that Dorian gives me. It's not even the creeping, tingling feeling that indicates that danger is near, causing the fine hairs on my arms to stand at attention. It's something else entirely. Like a burning coldness that singes the surface of my skin, stripping off the very top layer. It doesn't hurt but it isn't exactly pleasant either.

I take a moment to absorb it all, holding my arms in front of me to look for any visible change. Even in almost complete darkness, I can see every line and pore in my skin. I can hear the tiny pelts of rainwater falling silently on the windshield, even smell them in the light breeze. And I can feel the shift in the Earth's atmosphere, indicating that an extreme surge of power is on the horizon. It's time. It's time for me to cross over into the unknown and embrace eternity.

I step out into the chilly dampness of the night and take a deep breath before beginning my trek. Ascending here at Garden of the Gods just made sense when I planned it weeks ago. I had always marveled at the fascinating rock formations and thought of them as somewhat supernatural even long before I even knew the Light and Dark existed. And now that I have an idea of all that is out there, coupled with its name, I am almost certain that paranormal activity played a part in its creation.

Then there's the most obvious reason for its significance: Garden of the Gods is the place where Dorian and I shared our first kiss. Though our future together is murkier than ever–hell, *my* future is murkier than ever–I will hold that memory close to me. It was a happy time. I don't want to lose sight of those moments in fear that I may never feel happiness like that again.

I stop at a tall, sandstone structure with a flat surface and with one last calming breath, I begin my climb. It's pitch black out but I can see perfectly. Even the climb is almost too easy, which brings a tiny smile to my tense face. I've never been really athletic but right now I feel like I could climb Pike's Peak.

The rain begins to pick up just as I reach the top, shifting from a light mist to a moderate downpour. My hair has already begun to curl and stick to my face and back yet I make no move to seek refuge. I know what is coming and if what Dorian has told me is correct, it could very well get much worse. I close my eyes and tilt my head to the sky. Maybe it's him who is actually making it rain right now. Maybe this is his way of being with me through all of this.

Lightning slices through the sky so bright that I yelp in surprise. Deafening thunder immediately follows it, indicating the storm's close proximity. The heavens open completely, rain pouring down in a sheet so thick that I feel as if I'm submerged in water. The static in the air meets the cold burning sensation still attacking my skin with millions of tiny shocks. I hold my hands in front of me, looking at the miniscule volts glowing on my skin with rapt fascination. This is happening. This is really happening. And instead of being afraid or confused, I feel absolutely enlightened and secure. Like this is totally natural. This ethereal feeling just seems *right*.

Bolts of white hot lightning dart from the sky, scorching the earth around me. Sparks fall over me like electric rain, illuminating the haunting shadows created by the huge sandstone boulders. The earsplitting boom caused by the constant thunder sounds more like a roar mixed with the howling winds. Everything around me rumbles and shakes, yet I stand tall, fierce and completely unmovable.

There is no little girl here. She no longer exists. That girl has grown, has lived, has loved and has lost. She has been broken and beaten. She has been hurt and mended. And now she is free. Free to be everything that she was destined to be.

The numerous bolts of ominous lightning inch closer and closer, only a few feet standing between them and my stock-still form. I don't even recoil. I simply stand and wait, welcoming the surge of power I know they will deliver. Rain still falls around me, drenching me to my bones yet I don't even feel the slightest chill.

In ceremonious fashion, I lift my head back up to the sky and give myself over to my supernatural senses as I make my internal declaration. As I pledge my allegiance to the side that I wish to be tied to for eternity. The side that I will live, fight, and eventually, die for. I want that magic to fill me to the brim. I want to be engulfed in that overwhelming power. I want to *be* the magic, just as my mother, Natalia, intended for me to be. I hope I make her proud. I hope she is somewhere looking down at me with joyful tears in her beautiful golden eyes as she clutches my father's hand. I hope he, too, is smiling at me with pride etched in his magnificent face.

I am not sure if time stops, or slows tremendously, but as the first bolt of lightning pierces me, everything suddenly pauses. Every raindrop freezes to a halt, looking like a million congealed jewels suspended in the air. The strong gusts of wind die, not even whisper of a howl to be heard. Everything around me is completely silent and still. Another strikes me, lighting every cell in my body on fire with its intense current. I gasp at the feeling yet no cries escape my lips. It's . . . jolting, just like Donna said it would be. I smile through the odd sensation, my thoughts now on my adopted parents as the third bolt zaps me. They will never again have to be afraid. They'll never have to worry about me again. It's my turn to protect them. My turn to show them that twenty-one years of sacrifice was worth it.

The lightning flies down in a seamless blur, shocking my body from every angle and causing me to writhe and convulse with the intensity. It continues for several minutes, or maybe hours, I can't be completely sure. There is no sense of time in this realm where all other life is frozen. But as the last strike rocks my entire frame and brings me to my knees, I know no time has passed at all. Life returns yet the tumultuous rain and wind cease. The lightning and thunder have also dissipated. All is still in the night. And I can see all of it. I embrace it. I thrive in the looming darkness as if this is my natural element.

A scared, bemused girl came here, not knowing who and what she was. Unsure of the path she should choose. Uncertain of what her place was amongst the violence, rage and turmoil between two ancient enemy forces.

Now a goddess emerges, leaving behind the confusion that kept her bound with anxiety. She was made for this. She was chosen to undo the wrongs that have plagued this world and beyond. To bridge the gap between the Light Enchanters and Dark Ones and a tainted history of conflict. Her parents died so she could live and achieve her destiny. A destiny to be great, to be fearless. A destiny to be utterly extraordinary.

THIRTY

Seeing the world through brand new eyes is almost jarring. *Hell, have I been blind for twenty-one years?* Even the way I walk, the way I move, is different. It's not so much that I'm afraid that I'll move unnaturally fast, it's keeping myself planted on the ground that seems to be the real feat. It seems easier to somewhat ghost to where I want to be. To think of a spot and somehow manifest there. Now I realize how much restraint Dorian had been using just to appear normal.

I walk down the cobblestone path, my head snapping at every creak and rustle of the leaves. It's not so much hearing as it is *knowing*. Like an instinctual force within me that knows what is there without truly hearing or seeing it. It's as if all my senses have combined and I've become somewhat omnipresent. Yet I still feel normal. I still feel like *me*. Yeah, the superhuman senses and the way my eyes and fingertips seem to constantly tingle is a bit weird, but for the most part, I am still Gabs. New & improved Gabs. Gabs 2.0. But still Gabs.

I step off the familiar elevator without hesitance and face the double doors. I know what I've come here for. My once clouded, jaded mind is now crystal clear. No amount of influence from him or anyone else can dissuade me from this. The truth is screaming at me and I can't ignore it any longer. I can't continue to live a lie.

I face the doors, contemplating my next move. Do I just bust in, guns blazing? Should I knock? Would he even answer, especially if he knew what I am? Can't he already sense the power rolling off of me in iridescent waves? *Damn, I really am* me. I still can't make up my mind.

The door swings open, disrupting me from my thoughts, though

I expect it. I heard the footprints lightly padding across the carpet. I smelled the cool freshness of his skin. I heard his heart hammering with nervous expectation as I approached. I could even taste his flavor on my tongue. He knew I'd be coming for him. He knew this moment was inevitable.

"Gabriella," Dorian breathes, a hint of desperation in his usually smooth voice. I watch as his brilliant blue eyes take me in, a myriad of vibrant emotions displayed clearly on his face. From relief to confusion to shock to horror to fear, every one of his reactions do not go unnoticed by my skillful eyes. I know what he sees, and I know what that must mean for him. *For us.* But this is what I have chosen. And honestly, there was no other choice.

"Dorian," I reply confidently with a slight nod of my head.

He swallows, my eyes studying the movements of his throat and the rapid pulsing of his jugular. He's nervous. Even a bit afraid of me. I know because I can *feel* it. I can feel every one of his emotions just as he can feel mine. My ascension has brought our link full circle.

"What have you done?" he rasps, his eyes growing wide. "How? How did you . . . Why?"

I lick my lips, though they feel as smooth as silk under my tongue. "Let me in so I can tell you."

Uncertainty furrows his brow and he looks away, contemplating his next move. After a beat, he steps aside, realizing that I would make my way inside no matter what he decided. His eyes stay trained on me, taking on the icy glaze reserved for hostile threats. Once I cross the threshold, I spin around, faster than even he can probably detect.

"You can relax, Dorian. I won't attack you from behind," I smirk, giving back the same words he spoke to me the day I found out who and what he is. "It's not my style."

The look of sheer disbelief mars his gorgeous face, his jaw dropping in surprise. He quickly closes it and composes himself, ushering me through to the living room with a wave of his hand. I take the liberty to make myself comfortable on the couch, totally at ease with what I am about to do. I don't even have to think about it. I know there's only one solution and I don't want to waste time dancing around it.

"Sit with me," I say, patting the cushion beside me.

With masked hesitance, Dorian complies, yet stays a good two feet away from me, his cold, calculating eyes still focused on mine, no doubt predetermining my next move. We spend long moments sizing up the other with rapt awareness. I had always known Dorian was absolutely beautiful. Yet seeing him now, being able to unveil the mask he wears for the world is really a sight to behold. He is powerful, terrifying and magnificent. It still hurts to look at him, but in a different way entirely. He's trying to keep me out. Trying to keep up the façade to protect himself, yet he can't deny me access. His anxiety is my anxiety. I am more powerful than he is, and effortlessly tear down the barriers that he struggles to put up to hide his true form.

"Why?" he finally whispers, giving up on trying to delay his fate.

I smile. "There was no other option. I knew what I had to do. I know what I was made for. It's *this*. This is why I was created," I say.

Dorian shakes his head and looks away, unable to stand the sight of me. "But it's impossible. It's not supposed to be like this."

Before he can turn his head back, I am beside him, clutching his face between my hands. He gasps and nearly recoils at the contact.

"But don't you see? It *is* supposed to be like this. This is what was meant for me all along. I am half Dark and half Light equally. Both good and evil. I was meant to rule the night and the day. And that's what I am going to do." I give him a reassuring smile. "It's ok. I'm ok, Dorian. I was meant to be both. I was never supposed to choose."

His eyes never leave mine, searching for some semblance of rationality. "But your . . . *eyes*."

I shrug, dropping my hands from his face and grasping his hands instead. He jerks a bit at first, still growing accustomed to the prickles *I* give *him*. "Yeah, that will take some getting used to. One blue and one gold eye isn't exactly normal, is it? It kinda scared the shit out of me."

Dorian finally cracks the faintest of smiles. "So you're . . . ok? You're not hurt? You're not . . . different?"

"Well, other than the eyes, do I look different?"

His eyes begin their study at the crown of my head, my semi-wet hair in a tangled, curly mess that oddly seems perfectly styled and intentional. He takes in the luminescent skin stretched over my high cheekbones, and my full pouty lips that part reflexively with his notice. Then his eyes are on collarbone, traveling down to where my wet shirt clings to my round, heavy breasts.

"Yes," he breathes, a smile curling his succulent lips. "You are absolutely breathtaking. Even more so than before because you finally know it. You finally see what I've seen in you all along."

I beam at him, relief flooding my chest. I lift his hands and brush them with my lips. This time, he barely flinches. "I have never been more certain of what I was created for, Dorian. I'm not supposed to be solely Light or Dark. I was made to be the Dark Light. Once I accepted that, everything just clicked into place. I didn't question it anymore."

I brush his cheek with my hand, trying to be as gentle as possible. He instinctively lets his eyes close and nuzzles into the touch. "And I didn't question you anymore. You have sacrificed so much for me. You gave up everything you knew–your family, your life . . . for me. For love."

"Yes," he rasps, his voice thick with emotion.

"I know that now, and I thank you." I inch forward, closing the small distance between our bodies. "Let me do that for you. Let me protect you and sacrifice for you. Let me show you what it is like for someone to care for you and want to keep you safe against all odds. Let me love you like you love me."

Doubt puckers the space between his brows. "You would do that for me?"

I stifle the giggle in my throat and shake my head before resting it against his forehead. "When are you going to realize that I am stupid, crazy in love with you? That I never stopped loving you? That I simply cannot live another day without you? Didn't you know? The Dark die for love. I think I inherited that trait from my dad's side."

"I think I did hear that somewhere," he chuckles. "So this is it? This is what you really want?"

I lift my face to study his features. I didn't realize it before but Dorian has been scared this entire time that we've been together. Since the day we met, he has had to fight against his nature, to try to go against what has been engrained in him from birth. Stepping out on faith–on love–has been as terrifying for him as it has been for me. Yet he did it anyway. He loved me in spite of it all.

"Dorian, I've tried to be as human as I could possibly be. I've tried to embrace the ways of the Light like my mother wanted me to. I even tried to accept that I may very well be Dark. I have done everything that people wanted me to. I've rejected what I have wanted because I thought that was what I was supposed to do." I take a deep breath and beam at the exotic Warlock in front of me, letting conviction shine through every pore. "Hell yes, this is what I want. You are what I want. I know what it meant for you to come to my rescue. I know what that fate entails for you. And now it's my turn. Now I want to show you what it means to be loved unconditionally."

I turn over his hand displaying the tiny blue anchor that matches my own. "We're anchored, Dorian. Not by an impulse. Not by a curse. But by love. And I'm ready to fight for that love. I'm ready to fight for you."

I only have a split second to take in his awe-filled expression, his eyes glazed and full of ardor before I am on my back, his weight crushing me into the couch cushion. Our mouths waste no time reuniting, our tongues and breaths conjoining simultaneously. His kiss is nothing like I had remembered. It's better. So much so that I moan against his lips. I can actually taste the depth of his affection for me. I feel how much I mean to him with just the slide of his fingertips against my skin. I can see how much I affect him even with tightly closed eyes.

Dorian pulls away, yet stays situated on top of me. His fingers rake through my wild curls as he smiles down at me adoringly. "I am going to love you for eternity. I know we have adversity stacked against us but I promise to always fight and protect you. I'll never give up on you. *On us.* It's just me and you. This is our destiny. I love you, little girl."

I bite my bottom lip and smile, gazing up at him with sultry, hooded eyes. Then without even thinking about, I instinctively let the words fall from my lips in the language that we now both share. The ancient language of the Dark that now comes as natural to me as breathing.

"I love you too, Dorian. Forever."

EPILOGUE

DORIAN

I can't tear my eyes away from the sleeping, naked woman in my bed. I don't even want to blink, for fear that she will disappear. I've had to tell myself time and time again that this isn't an illusion. This isn't a dream. She's real. She's here. And she's mine. *All mine.*

I still can't believe that less than 24 hours ago, she was snatched away from me. I lost her. I lost the only thing still anchoring me to this life. I was ready to end it all. It wasn't even a question. But I held on, I kept trying. *For her.* Her life was worth saving.

I trace the lotus blossom tattoo at the nape of her neck with my fingertips, brushing it gently down her spine. My hand lingers at the dip of her lower back where it merges into her round, delicious ass. *Fuck, she has an amazing ass.* One that should be worshipped by the gods. I grab a luscious handful and squeeze, her taut flesh sizzling hot underneath my grip. The things I want to do to it are downright sinful. I know she'll let me . . . eventually. And she'll like it. She'll love it when I ruin every little perfect part of her.

My hand slips farther south, slipping between her slightly parted legs. I can already feel the humid heat emitting from her beautiful sex. That's right . . . *beautiful.* Her soft, pink folds are truly a work of art. And the things I do to it, the way she arches her back and mewls softly when I work her over with my tongue . . . shit. It's the most magnificent thing I have ever seen. She comes in Technicolor, her reaction to me so vibrant and colorful whenever I bring her to the brink. I am fascinated by every quiver and moan.

"Mmmm," she sighs sleepily, her eyes still closed. "What are you doing?"

"Shhhh, go back to sleep, baby. I'm just exploring."

I slip a single finger between her already slick folds, eliciting a small whimper. "I don't want to sleep anymore. I've been sleeping for twenty-one years."

Her eyes pop open and I nearly gasp at their brilliance. *Shit,* she is still the most gorgeous creature on Earth. And now that she can see me just as I see her, I can't help but be even more taken by her. I've got it bad. Really fuckin' bad.

She's straddling me in the next second, pinning my arms above my head much like I have done with her in the past. Shit, I love how she is able to take control. I love it when she has that fiery look in those big, dazzling eyes. And the energy they emit when she lets them pool into mine . . . I can't even describe it. I've honestly never come that hard in my life. But even more than that, I have never felt so much love and passion fill my once empty heart. We were both surprised at the intensity, yet I couldn't help feeling embarrassed at my almost tearful reaction. Yeah . . . I had a near-bitch experience.

My awe-filled gaze takes in her round, bare breasts mere inches from my face. I flick a hardened nipple with my tongue instinctively. *Fuck, she tastes good.* I suck the rigid nub into my mouth eagerly, nibbling and licking until she reflexively writhes her bottom half against my hard dick.

"Oh God, Dorian," she pants, loosening her grip on my hands. It's all I need to break free from her hold and grasp that amazing ass of hers, grinding her wetness onto my rock hard erection even more and sucking harder on her breast. She likes it like that. I know what makes her go mad with lust for me. I know what she craves. Me and only me.

I flip her onto her back, my cock still pressed against the sliver of her entrance. I press it into the hypersensitive bundle of nerves of her mound, teasing her relentlessly. I can't help but smile in wonder. We made love for hours after she came back to me. Both of us could hardly wait to taste and feel each other again. Yet she still wants me. She still yearns for me. Her body still needs mine just as I need hers.

How the fuck did I get so lucky?

"Careful, little girl," I murmur against her still hardened nipple before pulling the other into my mouth. "You may be stronger, but remember who owns this." I rotate my hips, pressing my cock against her wetness with delicious friction. She moans my name again, making it pulse furiously against her. Shit, I need to be inside her now. I won't be able to hold off much longer.

"Yes, oh God, yes," she coos as I slide into her. I don't stifle my own moan at the sensation. She's so warm. So tight. So fucking perfect in every way.

I begin a slow, drawn out pace, careful to reach every tingling area within her walls. She moves with me, meeting me stroke for stroke, grabbing handfuls of my hair and tugging at the root. I love it when she does that. Just like she loves it when I nuzzle my face into her neck and graze her collarbone with my teeth. Or how she goes wild when my fingers dig into the skin of her ass. And of course, I know that she likes it when I wrap my hand around her throat just as she begins to climb higher into euphoria. And when she takes that dive, her walls pulsing around my cock, milking every last drop of come from me, she likes me to slowly release my grip, letting her tumble down from her orgasm-induced high.

After giving her everything she craves and more, we recline on the couch, flipping through the room service menu. She's wearing one of my dress shirts, only a few buttons securing her stunning, naked skin. I run my hands up and down her bare legs, gazing at her lovingly as she flips through the menu.

"What?" she asks, not even bothering to look at me with those startling blue and gold irises.

I shake my head and chuckle. "Nothing. Just . . . watching you. Touching you. It still seems unreal."

Her gaze flicks up to mine and she smiles. "But it is real. What we have is real, Dorian."

"I know that." I laugh and let my head fall back on the cushion. *Shit.* Her emitting her incredible power to me last night has me all types of fucked up in the head. I feel vulnerable, juvenile, yet *free.* All the things I admire so much about her.

I shake my head against the back of the couch. "I sound like a bitch, don't I? Like a stupid fool taken by infatuation."

My beautiful Gabriella tosses the menu aside and straddles me in a blur before my eyes. "No, you don't. You sound like a man in love. And lucky for you, I am perfectly fine with sounding like a bitch when it comes to you. We can be bitches together," she smiles.

I attack her mouth with mine before she can say another word. *Damn, I love this woman.* More than two and a half centuries of a half-hearted existence yet I didn't start living until the day I met her. Gabriella breathed life into me.

"Ok, ok," she giggles pulling away. "At this rate, we'll never eat and I'm starving." She grabs the phone off the nearby end table and thrusts it against my chest. "Here. Order whatever. And get as many desserts as you want. We'll need them," she says with a sly smile.

"Yes, ma'am," I reply, tickling her ribs, the alluring sound of her laughter filling every vacant part of me.

I do as she wishes, ordering all her favorite dishes plus every dessert on the menu. I never want her to go without. I want to give her everything she desires before she even realizes she desires it. I want to do any and every thing to make sure her smile never falters.

We're kissing and cuddling on the couch, working ourselves into a frenzy when a knock at the door disrupts us. We're both on our feet before the sound of the first rapt dissolves.

"That was quick," she remarks, turning for the door. I grab her arm before she even takes a full step.

"Where do you think you're going?"

She scrunches her cute little nose and rolls her eyes. "To open the door for the concierge. Duh. You have on your boxers which, quite frankly, boy scouts could camp under with the tent you're pitching. I'll be 2 seconds. Relax."

I shake my head. "Your eyes, baby. You need to change them if you are going to fit in."

My gorgeous little goddess smiles and shrugs out of my grip. "Who said I wanted to fit in? Besides, what's the use in being a freak show if you can't have a little fun?" Then before I can stop her, she is at the front door, turning the knob, with only my half-buttoned shirt obscuring her naked frame.

I see her freeze and hear a tiny gasp, putting me on alert. "Who is it, baby?" I call out, shrugging on my forgotten pants from last night.

Without turning around, she answers in a small, shaky voice, "My dad."

Shit. Chris did not need the evidence of me fucking his adopted daughter slapping him in the face. No dad wants to see that. He'll never forgive me now. I take a deep breath and make my way to the door, not looking forward to the awkward conversation ahead.

Gabriella widens the door just as I approach, giving me full view of a pair of cold, venomous eyes and a threatening snarl. I freeze in my tracks, unable to articulate a semblance of a response to what stands before us. The only thing that breaks me out of my trance is Gabriella's tear-filled eyes gazing up at me full of confusion and fear. I open my mouth to soothe her anxiety, knowing that she needs an explanation for what greets us just two feet away. Shit, I need one too. But what do I say? How do I even begin to rationalize this?

Fuck.

So I start with the obvious, knowing that I have to say *something*. Whether or not it's enough to diffuse the situation is the real question. But I doubt it. He's always been a stubborn son of a bitch. Yet, I plaster on my most rigid grin and extend my hand anyway.

"Hello, Alexander."

Gabriella and Dorian's story

continues . . .

Book 3 of The Dark Light Series

Light Shadows

Coming Soon

SHOUT OUTs, THANK YOUs & IOUs

Without question, I could not have done this without the love and support of all the fans and readers. It was your encouragement and enthusiasm that kept me going when I wanted to scrap The Dark Prince (which happened more than a few times). Thank you Thank you Thank you from the bottom of my heart for believing in this crazy dream of mine.

Throughout my journey creating TDP and trying to spread the DLS love, I have met some amazing authors that have inspired the hell out of me. Thank you Madeline Sheehan, Claire Contreras, T.K. Tuitt, Karina Halle, Gail McHugh, L.B. Simmons, C.C. Brown, MJ Abraham, Nicole Deatherage, Emma Grayson and the rest of my lovely ANGTFD book bitches (geez, there's a lot of you). I have learned so much from you all and love each of you dearly. I couldn't have picked a better bunch of crazies to laugh, cry, rant, curse and be inappropriate with. And special thanks to the PB to my J, my sista from anotha mista, E.L. Montes, whose friendship and support have encouraged me beyond measure.

I had kick ass beta readers who ensured that TDP wasn't crap. And if you thought TDP was crap and you are still reading this, well . . . sucks for you. Anyway, extra special shout out to Ashley Hartigan Tkachyk (Love you, Ash!) , Karinna Baez (my eye candy pusher), Kari Acebo (I owe you SO much for all you have done!), Ena Burnette (my smut peddler/pimp), Gina Tobin (thank you for everything!), Andrea Kelleher, Nikki Sebben Narvaez, Aimee Bentley, Gina Stough, Judy Ruiz and Jennifer Baumgart Heim.We did it ladies! Now how about that shot & ugly cry?

There were a few awesome book blogs that took a chance on me and consistently showed love for me & DLS. Thank you to The Sub

Club Books, First Class Books, Books, Babes & Cheap Cabernet, SMI Book Club, Mommy's Reads & Treats, Sugar & Spice Book Reviews, Erotica Book Club, Swoon Worthy Books, Jennifer's Book Addiction, Alphas, Authors & Books Oh My, Red Hawt Romance, and everyone else that posted, shared, tweeted and recommended. Much love.

Ah yes, my DLS girls, DLROs :) . . . IOU all so much for all you have done to promote and spread the Dorian love! Thank you for everything you have done & I hope I can still create stories that inspire you to post man candy pics ;) Thank you for having some of the strongest pimping hands this world has ever seen!

To my fabulous friends that didn't gripe (too much) when I was stuck in the writing cave for weeks on end. Thank you for not making fun of my unarched eyebrows and lack of makeup when I was too sleep deprived to give a damn. IOU a girls night. With mustaches.

Shout out to the amazing Stephanie White of Steph's Cover Design to creating such gorgeous covers for The Dark Light Series. You rock, woman!

Most importantly, thank you to my beautiful family, who traded home-cooked meals for frozen pizza, family nights for writing nights, a clean house for a not so clean house, and a nice, perfectly sane mom/wife for a bloodshot-eyed, tangled haired, neurotic, crazy lady who talks to the voices in her head. IOU the world. And one day I'll give it to you. I love you.

And if you're reading this, thinking "Why the hell didn't she thank me?" well, guess what? I was saving the best for last :)

Thank you insert name here . I couldn't have done this without you.

xoxo,
Syreeta

About the Author

S.L. Jennings is a wife and mother of three. Her husband is a member of the United States Air Force and they currently live overseas in Germany. While *Dark Light* is her very first full-length novel, she has always had an unshakeable love for writing short stories, poetry and music since childhood. She hopes to continue to share her passion for writing and entertaining with *The Dark Light series* and her contemporary romance novel, *Fear of Falling*.

For more info, visit:

www.facebook.com/darklightseries

www.facebook.com/authorsljennings

Twitter: @MrsSLJ

www.goodreads.com/SLJennings

BOOKS BY S.L. JENNINGS

THE DARK LIGHT SERIES:

Dark Light
The Dark Prince
Light Shadows – COMING SOON

TO BE RELEASED SUMMER 2013:

Fear of Falling

The Soul Mate

The Holy Trinity Trilogy: Book One

by

Madeline Sheehan

The world won't end with a bang.
The world won't end with a whimper.
In fact, the world won't end at all.
But it will change and if we refuse to change with it . . .
It will be us that ends.

PROLOGUE

Bulgaria, 1056 A.C.E.

"The screaming has stopped, Emilian. Time to go." Ferka gestured toward camp where Zora Petulengro's birthing screams had previously seemed unending. Emilian had never been so thankful before that he'd been born a boy.

He had no desire to go back to camp, even though a few minutes ago he'd felt the sudden urge to run straight there, straight to . . . that baby.

That baby, a little girl that was to become his. No, she was already his. She had been given to him, as a gift of sorts. They would be bound together as soon as he could muster up enough courage to make his feet move. She would become his bride when they were of age and eventually bear his children.

He closed his eyes.

His soul mate.

He'd scoffed at his tată and mami when they'd spoken to him of this foretold prophecy. How could a seven year old have a soul mate? How could he have a soul mate?

But he wasn't just any seven year old. He was the first born son of Baró Gavril Drágon, the leader of their Romani Clan, who already had more magic inside him than his full grown tată. Magic that would grow too powerful for any one man to contain without going mad. He would need to have an outlet, a vessel with whom to share his gifts with. This was where this baby came in.

"You look green my friend, but methinks you better go before the Baró comes looking for you himself."

Ferka was right. Green or not, the wrath of Baró Drágon was indeed something to be feared; especially if you were his son. Dragging his heals in the dirt, Emilian began to walk slowly back to camp.

"Where have you been, you cowardly little fleabag?!"

He winced as his mami grabbed him by the ear and yanked him in the other direction toward the Petulengro's wagon.

"You were supposed to be close!"

He didn't answer her; he knew no answer was good enough for Violca Drágon when she was angry.

As his mami dragged him across camp, much to the amusement of the entire clan, he could only stare longingly toward where the horses were tied. He wished he could yank free of his mami's hold, grab a horse, and be gone from here forever.

Boldo Petulengro thrust open the small wooden door of the wagon as they reached the steps, his large overbearing frame dwarfing the entire structure. The look of disfavor on the man's face belied any happiness he thought the man might have had for the birth of his new daughter.

Cowering beneath Boldo's simmering glare he slipped into the wagon and approached his tată. Lying on a pallet of rushes in the corner, Zora was holding a tiny bundle in her arms. The new mother looked exhausted, covered in sweat with small bruises under her eyes. A pile of bloodied rags lay near a bucket of equally bloodied water.

"Come here Emilian," Zora said hoarsely, a strained smile on her face. "You must touch her; make her yours so there will never be another."

Ignoring the dark penetrating gaze of his tată, the anxious stare of his mami and Boldo's disapproving glare, he instead focused only on Zora, the only person who was treating him with any sort of kindness.

On skinny, shaking legs he knelt down beside her, waiting with bated breath as she unwrapped the small bundle. A tiny head covered in black fuzz appeared.

The babe was sound asleep.

"Wake up, love."

Zora stroked her daughter's cheek. The baby blinked sleepily a few times and opened her mouth in a toothless yawn. He fought the urge to smile. Just because she was adorable didn't mean he had to like her. Then she opened her eyes wide and the entire group gasped.

"Green?" Violca squawked.

"What does that mean?" Boldo demanded of the Baró. No Roma had green eyes. They had varying shades of brown, some almost black, other's had hazel or even caramel colors, but not a blue or a green among them; it was simply unheard of. Gavril stared at the tiny girl as a smile began to spread across his face.

"She is perfect, my friends. do not fret, for green represents balance, harmony and stability, everything that Emilian will need. She is everything we could have hoped for."

This answer seemed to delight the parents. Violca, however, continued to study the baby with narrowed eyes.

"It is time."

Gavril lowered himself down on one knee with Violca and Boldo following suit. Together they said the proper Romani blessing over the two children, binding them together in love, family and clan. Their union had been foretold by nature and would be upheld by the very people who had sworn their lives to protecting nature's blessings and gifts.

"Touch her, child," Zora urged, smiling at him.

Deciding to touch only the top of the babe's head, he leaned forward. As he crept closer his body responded to the nearness of her and, without thinking, he kissed her cheek instead, breathing in her scent. Shocked, he stumbled backwards and landed awkwardly on his backside.

"Son?" Gavril asked. "Did it work? Did you feel something?"

Struck dumb by the sweetest perfume he'd ever smelled, he couldn't yet speak. He could only stare at the most beautiful pair of sparkling green eyes he would ever see.

CHAPTER ONE

Catskills Mountains, NY
Present Day

Too afraid to move, I continued watching with trepidation the daddy longlegs spider that was poised directly above where I lay. It was a creepy looking little devil, with its tiny little body and obscenely long, spindly legs.

Bugs, I am convinced, have been placed on this earth to make my life miserable. Then again, there wasn't much that didn't make me jumpy these days. The end of the world will do that to a person.

I blew out the breath I'd been holding as the spider took off running. It skittered across the stained brown canvas ceiling of my 1980's pop-out tent trailer and disappeared.

"Ugh," I told no one in particular. "I am having a bad day."

"The day hasn't even started yet, woman. It isn't possible yet for it to be bad."

I huffed at Becki, my trailer mate. "You don't consider waking up to giant arachnids hovering over your head, waiting to eat you, a bad day?"

I ducked the pillow that came flying from the other end of the trailer. It hit the canvas wall directly above me where possibly hundreds, maybe thousands, of hungry daddy longlegs spiders could be living.

"You could have scared the spider back out!"

"Trinity, it's a spider."

"Do you know how vengeful spiders are?" I asked in my haughtiest voice, "Especially to the Greeks?"

I couldn't quite tell, since her head was still buried in her mattress, but she mumbled something that sounded suspiciously like, "Here we go again."

"Well," I continued, "The Greek Goddess Athena . . ." I paused. "You know who she is right?"

"How could I not? You talk about her all the time."

I chose to ignore that comment.

"Anyway, Athena and a mortal princess, named Arachne, had a competition to see who the better weaver of the two was. Arachne won and Athena was furious, so she destroyed Arachne's tapestry and cursed the princess to live a life full of disgrace. Arachne, unable to bear the weight of her curse, hung herself. Then, Athena took pity on her and brought her back to life . . . but as a spider!"

"Trinity, if I had known living with you was going to be a constant lesson in Greek mythology, I really would have reconsidered."

"How would you like to be brought back to life as a spider? Wouldn't you be angry? Or vengeful even?"

Becki scowled at me as I sat up. Her long, brown curly hair was hanging in front of her dark brown eyes, but I could see enough of them to know that if looks could kill, I would have been dead two or three times by now. Becki Bălan was most certainly not a morning person.

"Good morning sunshine." I grinned at her.

"I wish I could turn you into a spider," she grumbled, cocooning herself inside of her blankets until all I could see was the tips of her toes.

I was about to respond with another little tidbit of Greek myth when I smelled it: Christmas in the middle of July. The sticky sweetness of fresh pine trees and the thick, pungent odor of cinnamon flew in through the open window alongside the warm morning breeze.

"Gerik's coming," I told her, jerking my head toward the doorway. The scent of the man preceded him wherever he went.

The screen door swung wide open and a 6 feet 4 inch shirtless Viking came bounding through the small doorway, dominating the entire trailer, bringing with him his unique scent. He always smelled so amazing, so intoxicating . . . but only to me. The one and only time I'd asked another person if they smelled what I did . . . Well,

I'm pretty sure Alana still thinks I'm insane.

Gerik paused just inside the doorway and shook out his long, soaking wet hair, spraying water everywhere.

"Oh. My. God," Becki moaned. "Why is everyone against me today?"

He turned to grin at her while stretching his long muscular body. The magical runes tattooed on his chest rippled with the sinuous movements.

Gerik Hjemsäter looked like none of the other Gypsies in this Romani camp that I'd been calling home for the past few months. Most of the men and women in camp were of Romanian origins and had darker shades of skin combined with dark, alluring features; others had olive complexions, also with dark hair and eye colors.

Gerik was different. He was strong and tall like most of the Roma men; his forehead wide, his cheekbones high and predominant, but that was where the resemblance ended. Like many of his Scandinavian ancestors, his hair was the color of ripe wheat and his eyes were a deep ocean blue that misted and swirled like a stormy sea. Gerik's nose was proud and strong, unlike the majority of low rooted muzzles here, and his jaw was strong and square, standing out around the many rounded chins in camp.

Needless to say, Gerik was like nothing I'd ever seen before.

I watched him wipe his wet face and chest with his t-shirt before slipping it on; easily picturing him covered in heavy animal furs and a horned helmet. Before I knew it, I was giggling.

Becki was watching me. She rolled her eyes. "Yes, Trinity, we all know how sexy Gerik is."

Her correct assessment of my thoughts embarrassed me, but Gerik hadn't been paying her any attention. As usual, his focus was solely on me.

"Do my braids, yeah?" He held out his pony holders.

My giggles turned into full on hysterics. Gerik always wore his hair in two long braids that hung down his chest, making him look even more the part of the Viking warrior. I patted my bed, "Come

Viking, I'll plait yer hair before ye go off to battle."

Still grinning, Gerik grabbed the corner of my old red quilt and with one quick tug yanked it off me. I shrieked and lunged for my covers, managing to keep the sheet over my legs.

"Ugh!" Still in her pajama's, Becki jumped out of bed and shot us a disgusted look. "It's a little early for the mushy stuff. I'm out."

The screen door slammed hard behind her as she stormed out.

Gerik and I exchanged confused glances. Since I'd come to camp, Becki hadn't been a gracious morning person, but she'd never been outright mean.

I scooted closer to him when he sat down, taking the beaded pony holders out of his hand. The sheet that was still covering me slipped down my legs. I followed his gaze to my underwear and exposed thighs.

The air in the trailer grew hotter, heavy and thick with anticipation. I knew without having to look that Gerik's eyes had turned gray.

Gerik made me tremble with want; he could make me forget everything around me except for him. Even without the knowledge that Gypsies still roamed the earth and that magic truly did exist in our world, I would have felt the power in this man.

He was a force of nature and muddled my brain with energy the likes of which I'd never felt before. He zapped my body of will and strength just by being near me. Gerik was the stuff gods and goddesses were made of. Only . . . a Viking God. Well, actually a Gypsy god, but tomato, tomáto.

His hands slid up my sheet covered calves; the material of the sheets thin enough for me to still feel the rough and calloused skin on his fingers, caused by years of physical labor. The kind of labor you didn't see in the world I had been accustomed to.

I couldn't stop the shiver that tore through me in appreciation of his masculinity.

Gerik was strength incarnate; it showed in how he carried himself, how he spoke, and now in how he was deliberately, oh so slowly and very neatly, sending me down a path he knew I wasn't ready to travel.

I pushed at his chest.

"Stop," I whispered hoarsely.

Gods, he was just too much, too intense, for someone as inexperienced as I was.

His voice was a deep rumble in his chest when he answered, "Is that what you really want?"

I was breathing heavily, our lips nearly touching, his hands now gripping my sheet covered knees. It was a sliver of sanity he had allowed me to keep; one I was thankful for. If Gerik touched me, skin on skin, I would be los—"

"Gerik!" I gasped, as he gripped my naked thighs. Roughly pulling me underneath him, he was suddenly situated over top of me.

Heat flooded me as his hand slid up under my t-shirt to wrap around my waist. Everywhere he wasn't touching began to quiver with need.

Gerik and I had this crazy chemical reaction to each other, something I'm sure scientists would have loved to have gotten their hands on and studied until there was nothing left of us but blood and guts, if that.

We were like that ridiculous song, "Just one look, that's all it took." Except in my case it was, "Just one touch and Trinity turns to mush."

"Tell me to stop Trinity. Tell me to stop right now . . . and I will."

He ran his lips across my cheek, then down my neck where he sucked softly and my body involuntarily clenched. Gods, he was such a liar.

My skin tingled, my limbs trembled, and my body's sensitivity heightened to unbearable amounts as the fever of his touch raced through me. I couldn't tell him to stop because I couldn't speak. I was so desperate for him, so focused on the completion of our joining and how magnificent it would be.

He wasn't playing fair at all; once he touched me, he knew I was lost to a world of only sensation, where only feelings ruled. Awareness of the outside world was sucked away to a teeny tiny part in the back of my brain that I could barely reach.

Stop! Stop! I thought over and over again. This wasn't right; this wasn't the way I had imagined losing my virginity. Not in a haze of magic and desperation.

As if he'd heard my silent plea, he released me. I scooted backward until my butt hit the canvas.

"Trinity . . ." His voice was so ragged, so full of hunger, full of . . . everything a girl would want to hear in a man. "I didn't mean . . ."

"Save it," I snapped, trying to shake the haze of lust that, to my embarrassment, so easily consumes me in his presence. He stared at me for a moment, then in a quick singular movement reminding me of an acrobat, jumped off my bed.

"You touched me," I accused, trying to right my clothing. "Skin on skin. We made a deal, Gerik. We would only do that if we prepared each other. Which," I gave him a deliberate look, "you definitely did not."

He didn't even have the decency to look apologetic. He stood there, in all his Viking glory, looking as proud and as indifferent as ever. If it weren't for his refusal to meet my eyes, I wouldn't have even known he was feeling anything at all.

"It wasn't a conscious thing, yeah? I got . . . caught up. Don't freak out." He ran his hand through his wet hair and headed for the door.

"Gerik?" I called. "Do you think that maybe someone could fix us?"

I braced myself for his anger. It always surfaced when I brought this up.

He took a deep breath before answering. "There's nothing wrong with us."

"But . . . it's magic; it has to be."

"Trinity," he said, turning to face me. "I don't know how many times I have to tell you that no one cast a spell on us. There are no witches casting love spells, like in your Greek stories. And before you even suggest it again, there are no fairies either. The magic the Romani possess is ancient and was gifted to our people by nature. It isn't something that is thrown around for silly little things like love or lust spells, but that's all I can tell you about it, my little Gaje princess. You know the rules."

Yes, I knew them. Being a Gaje, a non-Gypsy, I wasn't privy to the Roma secrets, the origins of their magic, or their true history; unless I was allowed to marry into the clan, something that could only happen if I cut my ties with the Gaje world completely and a council of elders deemed me worthy. Then, a ceremony that consisted of purging my Gaje blood would be performed, all before the marriage could even occur . . .

According to their laws, it was forbidden for me to even live here. An apocalypse changes everything.

I crossed my arms over my chest. "Stupid rules."

He shrugged. "They have protected my people for centuries."

"Fine, whatever. You go on protecting your Viking sex hoodoo and keep me in the dark."

"I'm not purposely keeping you in the . . ." He paused and his eyebrows rose. "Did you say Viking sex hoodoo?"

I narrowed my eyes and snarled. "Don't make fun of me!"

"So, what you're saying is, no one is actually attracted to me, hmm?" He grinned "They only want me for my long ship and battle axe skills, yeah?"

I couldn't look at him when he started flirting with me; it was nearly as bad as him touching me. I cleared my throat, embarrassed. "You are such a guy."

"You want me too, Trinity." He spoke softly. "And don't pretend it's magic."

I couldn't share the sentiment. "Shoo." I waved him away. "I need to get dressed."

CHAPTER TWO

The Romani camp was set up in a clearing, roughly the size of a football field, in the Catskills Mountain Region of New York State. The Gypsies had strategically parked their trucks, vans and motorcycle trailers in a circle surrounding camp. Outside of the clearing a thick forest kept us hidden.

Camp consisted of three main areas, the biggest being the very center where a hodgepodge of RV's, trailers and two and three room canvas tents were parked in neat rows, called the living lot. The trailers ranged in age and style from a typical 70's aluminum Winnebago to top of the line Recreational Vehicle's that could comfortably house families of five. Every home had its own small fire pit for cooking or heating water, and individual light, since propane was hard to come by these days.

A small stream ran through the front lot that deepened into a water hole that the clan utilized for bathing. The front lot was used mainly for chopping wood, cleaning dishes, doing laundry, and gutting and cleaning the animals hunted in the area. It was also home to a family of chickens and one mean-as-Hades rooster that I'd nicknamed Frank, after my old next door neighbor who refused to give out Halloween candy.

The back lot was strictly for fire meetings. A large fire pit had been dug out for entire clan gatherings. The area was roomy enough for nearly eighty clan members to fit comfortably together.

Everyone was already hard at work when I left my trailer, working in sync together like a well oiled machine. That was the way of the Gypsies. Not even an end-of-the-world like assault could stop them from living their lives the way they always had.

At first it had seemed impossible for me to fit in among this close-knit group of people, half of whom related in some way.

I was an outsider, a Gaje, someone that they'd learned through generations of persecution, incarceration and genocide not to trust. After hearing portions of their history, mainly of the relatives lost in the WWII concentration camps, I really didn't blame them.

Yet, when Gerik had brought me here, no one had questioned his judgment. Jericho Popa, the Baró, leader of the entire clan, and his wife Maisera, had welcomed me with open arms.

When Jericho made a decision it was final. He had final say and was the enforcer of the Roma Laws. Their legal structure had totalitarianism written all over it, but from what I had witnessed in my time here, both he and Maisera were kind and fair and loved every one of the clan members as if they were their own children.

As always, when I left my trailer, part of my personal morning routine, I checked to make sure the wards that surrounded camp still held. The wards were a magical wall of protection, invisible to the naked eye. It protected what was held inside and kept what lie outside from entering. It didn't, however, keep us from seeing the horrors it held at bay.

Today, the number of creatures our camp had attracted seemed to have grown. I counted six of them staring around confusedly, wondering why they could smell us yet couldn't see us. That was Romani magic for you. Unless you were Roma, you couldn't see the wards. Those standing on the outside see nothing but an empty clearing . . . just like I would see if I were out there with those . . . things. I shuddered at the thought.

They looked human enough. I suppose that was because not all that long ago they had been human. Then everything changed. I lost everything, my family and the world as I'd always known it.

Two of the creatures closest to the wards suddenly bolted across the clearing toward the edge of the forest line where a lone deer had wandered. Simultaneously, fangs bared, they ripped into the squealing animal and within minutes tore the poor creature apart. Then, eyes glowing red, they turned on each other.

They were a deadly combination of both animal and human. They not only possessed great speed and agility with heightened senses and the incredible ability to heal almost instantly, they also had the power of reason, making them the ultimate predator.

The one and only way to kill them was destroying their brain.

"Trinity?" I jumped as a large hand came down on my shoulder. Stefan Sava Sr., a man around the age my father would be if he was alive, was smiling down at me.

"You're shaking, child. Come away from here."

With his big arm around my shoulders, Stefan pulled me from the gruesome sight beyond the wards and began walking me back to the innards of the living lot.

I saw Gerik sitting by a small fire near the tent where food was prepared. Made first thing in the morning and kept heated all day, it was available for the clan to eat at their leisure. I would have gone over to him if not for the prostitute sitting next to him. Onyx, not really a prostitute, had a long standing thing with Gerik. Whereas typically I find the Gypsy women in camp gorgeous, Onyx just reminds me of a cheap impersonation. Maybe it's the emptiness I sense inside of her.

I watched her press her tiny, devoid-of-curves body up against his in an obvious sexual invitation. For a moment I fantasized that he would tell her exactly where she could shove it, even though I knew he wouldn't. He never did.

As I continued to stare, I was growing more and more jealous by the second. According to Becki, Gerik and Onyx had been an on and off item since Gerik was seventeen. Now, at twenty-nine and thirty, their twelve year relationship made our couple of months look like chump change.

I knew I didn't have any right to feel as I did, I didn't have any sort of real claim on Gerik. I had made that perfectly clear to him time and time again, refusing to make any real commitment to him. It wasn't for his lack of trying. I just couldn't seem to wrap my head around what was really between us.

But watching him with her, seeing the hunger in his eyes heighten as her actions grew bolder, stirred something ugly inside of me. I had never been outwardly jealous of my two sisters, but being an averagely pretty girl in a family of supermodels will give you a complex whether you want one or not.

Both of my sisters had taken after our father; Greek-born with black hair, dark brown eyes and flawless olive skin. With their slender sleek frames and legs that went on for miles, both men and boys alike had gone out of their way to stare at them.

I suppose I was an odd mix between both my father and my mother. At five feet two inches tall, my mother was a second-generation Irish spitfire with blue eyes, flaming red hair, pale freckled skin, and a body with curves that rivaled Betty Boop's.

Then there were my eyes. Not one person in either side of my family had bright green eyes.

"Ah, Trin. Looking most miserable this morning."

Xan Deleanu.

The guy loved getting under everyone's skin. I was starting to think it was his mission in life. He was frustrating, annoying and downright arrogant.

Shirtless and wearing only a pair of weathered green cargos and work boots, he was covered head to toe in chunks of mud and bits of wood. A pair of goggles sat atop his mound of waist-length dreads, currently tied up in a thick knot.

Xan wasn't classically good looking, or quite as muscular as Gerik. His body was built more like a boxer; more meat, less definition, but raw strength all the same. He had beautiful, dark bronze skin and sharp exotic features that gave his face a hardness he used to his advantage; his bad boy image.

"When did you get back?" I asked him. Last I'd known he and a few others had gone on a supply raid a few weeks ago.

"This morning."

Xan's dark gaze looked back to where Gerik and Onyx were huddled close and he smirked at me. I shifted uncomfortably, wanting to avoid his merciless teasing.

"How was it out there?" I asked, curious about the state of the world.

“Worse. A god damn ghost town full of Skin Eaters."

“Skin Eaters?”

He shrugged. “Gotta call ‘em something, right? But, you don’t wanna hear the gory details.”

He was wrong; I did want to hear them. I wanted to hear everything about the outside world. I’d been in camp since the very beginning of the disaster with my ear glued to a radio until the batteries had run out. After that, I’d begun bombarding the raiding teams for as much information as possible. But Xan interrupted me before I could push.

“Next time we go for a raid, can I get you something? Maybe some Midol? Or I could just offer my own services. It’s so obvious what you’re needing, Trin.”

It was my turn to smirk.

“Xan the fact that you even know what Midol is makes me happy enough. I’m feeling better already.”

His grin turned upside down and he scowled at me. “I have a mamă you know.”

I nodded knowingly. “Uh huh, I’m sure that’s why.”

Xan pulled a black t-shirt from his back pocket and wiped the sweat off his face. Next, he pulled a cigarette out from behind his ear and a lighter from another pocket. He took a long drag, blew the smoke out slowly and then pointed the cigarette at my chest.

“You’d be a worthy sparring opponent, Trin . . . if only you didn’t have those pesky boobs distracting me all the time.”

I didn’t answer him. I was momentarily fascinated by a bead of sweat running down his chest; I watched it hit his rippled abdomen and dissipate into his skin.

Xan snapped his fingers in front of my face as the corners of his lips began to curve. “You with me, fată?”

I looked away, embarrassed. This morning’s encounter with Gerik had left me feeling quite unsatisfied.

“You know he’s only using her to take the edge off. They’ve

been doing that dance since we were kids. I don't really understand what the hell is up with you and Gerik and I don't really care. But if you want me to take that lush little body of yours for a ride . . ."

My head snapped up. Xan was grinning at me.

"It's not like it would be a chore, Trin. Not with those sweet curves of yours and that long black hair . . . damn fată, how many times could I wrap that ponytail of yours around my hand? Five, six maybe?"

He snapped his teeth at me and I felt my entire body flush. Bastard.

Xan caught my fist long before it connected with his stomach. Not that my punches would have done him much damage anyway.

"You know where to find me . . ."

He released my fist with a wink and headed towards his motorcycles, his movements hard and predatory. Whereas Gerik reminded me of a large cat, his movement's fluid and graceful despite his size; Xan was more like a bear. He would never waste time stalking his prey, he'd barrel right into it without thinking twice and his jaws wide open.

He was reckless in a way no one else in camp was. Not only was Xan an adrenaline junkie but there was a chip on his shoulder that was dug in deep. It made him cocky, hot-headed and downright mean at times. I believe it had a lot to do with the fact that he'd been born without magic in a clan of Gypsies that held magic in such high regard. He had a Gaje father, some biker that his mother Drina had some whirlwind love affair with. His father hadn't been allowed to join the clan and Drina hadn't wanted to leave.

Like the rest of the clan, he also had followed the carnival circuit. Xan had performed dangerous show stunts riding his bikes, but unlike the rest of the clan, he'd developed outside relationships with the Gaje world. He'd grown extremely good at refurbishing old motorcycles and selling them, amassing in quite a lot of connections outside of his Roma life. Some thought he might have even preferred life outside the clan, according to Becki.

The smell of cooking meat and steaming vegetables finally tempted my empty stomach enough to bring me meandering over to the food tent. Becki and her mother, Jaelle, were dishing out stew. I helped myself to a large bowl.

"Saw Gerik." Becki pursed her full red lips and winked at me. Becki and I weren't just roommates; she was the closest thing I'd ever had to a best friend. She was only two years older than me and had befriended me instantly upon my arrival. We shared a common interest in a lot of things, especially our hatred of all things Onyx. In my opinion, that made us soul mates.

"Yeah," I muttered. "I screwed up but—"

"Bah!" Jaelle jumped backwards causing her enormous breasts to bounce as she spattered stew all over herself. "Too hot!"

Taking a helping of stew herself, Becki threw an arm around me. "Taking a break, mami."

Outside, we leaned against the back of a truck. She didn't say a word. That was what I loved about Becki, she wasn't chatty and annoying. She didn't push. She was just there when I needed her and let me come to her in my own time.

"It happened again this morning," I sighed.

"Woman, you need to just let nature take its course. You'll feel a lot better once you get it out of the way."

"He's going to want more than that and I can't give it to him. I can't even bring myself to give him that. I'm not ready."

"You might change your mind once you take that ride." She cut her dark brown eyes at me, a knowing smile on her face.

"Ugh." I rolled my eyes. "Clan living . . ." I shook my head.

"Hey! It was a long time ago. But it was . . ." She grinned. "Memorable."

"Speak of the devil." She nodded back toward the food tent. Gerik was rounding the corner, coming directly from the living lot.

I crossed my arms over my chest. "His hair is braided."

"Let it go. It's just hair," Becki muttered.

"I doubt it was just hair."

His long, blonde hair was braided with a few new beads woven throughout. I always braided his hair in the morning and took them out in the evening; he'd had me doing it for the past two months and it had become part of our routine. I liked it, it felt . . . good; not just because being near Gerik felt abnormally good. I had always brushed my little sister Tahyra's hair and styled it.

Three guesses at who braided it today. I wondered about what else they had done. My stomach knotted at the thought of them together intimately.

"Nice hair," I said, without thinking about it first. That was me, always doing without thinking. My mouth had a brain of its own. My daddy always said one day it was going to get me in a world of trouble.

He froze mid-step at the sound of my voice and turned to look at me. "Don't start this with me, yeah?"

Start this with him? What a joke. He'd completely crossed the line this morning and he knew it.

I crossed the distance between us, my body instantly reacting to the nearness of him. I ignored it, as much as anyone could ignore an onslaught of emotional and physical perfection. But he didn't, he never could or would; his eyes grayed and his face tightened.

Willing my frustration and lust to turn to anger, I shoved hard against his massive chest. He didn't move. I was sick of all these men and their bodies made out of solid rock. Give me a pudgy stomach to sink my fist into. I'd at least like to hear a nice grunt or something. Any sort of acknowledgment of pain. Even a little grimace would've been nice.

I pushed him again. In return, he heaved forward with his chest. It was just a small movement, but it was enough and I stumbled backwards.

"Is something wrong, Trinity?" His nostrils flared. "Something you want to talk about?"

I laughed. It wasn't a nice laugh and I shouldn't have done it, but there was no middle ground when it came to Gerik. In order to ignore this anomalous attraction, I had to try and shut down completely. I had to become cold and distant and repress my brain's normal responses to him to be flirtatious and sensual. It was the only way: black or white. There was never any gray area with Gerik and me, unless it was the color of his eyes and that color was for me and me alone.

I turned to leave but he snatched my wrist, causing heat to flare where he touched me. It shot up my arm, arrowed through my chest making my breasts swell and ache, then spiraled down toward my stomach before settling in between my legs.

I faltered.

It took every ounce of sanity left inside of me to glare at him, but I managed it and he glared right back, unwilling to release me.

Both our bodies were tense and strung as tight as wires as we silently fought. He wanted everything from me and I wanted . . . Well, that was the problem, wasn't it? I didn't know what I wanted. The emotions pouring out of us were already past excessive and well on their way to redundancy.

"You feel that, yeah?" He leaned down and pressed his lips to mine. His kiss was like a shock to my already overloaded system. My heart was thumping hard and fast against my chest feeling like, at any moment, it might explode.

"That's me inside you, Trinity. I've always been there and always will be."

I gasped against his mouth as my body betrayed me and swayed forward, collapsing against him. The electric sensations he was somehow creating within my womb spread like wildfire across my nerve endings. My insides writhed and stilled, thrashed and throbbed until the final explosion left me grasping to stay standing, fighting for breath, as it threatened to end me completely.

Gerik held me steady against him until the quivering inside of me had subsided, and I was again able to hold my own body weight. Never mind the fact that I was still breathing quite heavily.

"Feel better?" He whispered, his breath against my cheek

beginning to stoke a fire inside me that had yet to die. A fire I feared, that with Gerik, would never die.

I swallowed hard and tried to nod.

"It's only you, Trinity. I keep telling you that, yeah?" He tilted my chin up until I was drowning in his two deep blue pools of blue. I never wanted to leave his arms, never wanted to let go, never –

"Gerik?" Becki said softly, appearing next to us. "Trinity and I have clothes to wash and, if you don't let her go, we're not going to get them done before daylight runs out."

I'd never been so grateful for dirty underwear before.

******

I followed Becki to a large metal basin where three piles of clothes waited for us. She threw me a large clump of soap and I dutifully started scrubbing clothing against a washboard.

I had never before been a big fan of manual labor. It had also never crossed my mind that someday I would find myself burdened with such a large amount of it. Here my days are longer than ever before, eaten up by washing clothes and dishes, cooking and serving food and playing with children who are not mine. I fall into bed at the end of the day bone tired with aching muscles and sore feet and yet . . . I feel a fulfillment that I can honestly say I'd never experienced before.

Technology, even the simplest forms of it, had made people's lives so much more accommodating but it had also disconnected us. But here, in this Romani camp, we are forced to interact just to survive. It was a forgotten way of life, yet, to the Romani it was all they'd ever known and they worked hard to keep it that way.

Staying in tune with the earth, keeping their families close and passing knowledge along to the next generations was what the Gypsies considered the right way to live. They never wasted a thing. They didn't litter or purposely pollute. Everything had a use or a purpose. The land we lived on was sacred; it gave us life and in return they gave back to it. That, to me, felt right and I respected them for it.

"So . . ." Becki said.

I paused in my scrubbing to rub the itch on my nose with the inside of my elbow, careful not to get soap on my face. "What's up?"

"How would you feel about cooking duty tonight?"

I narrowed my eyes. "No one cooks at night, what are you talking about?"

"I'm supposed to make jerky tonight, but I promised Hockey I'd meet him in the back lot later." She scrunched her face up at me like a cute little puppy dog. "Pretty please, Trinity? I'll be your best friend!"

I rolled my eyes. "You already are."

She jumped up, clapping her hands. "Great! I so owe you one! I'll be right back, I'm going to go tell him we are on for tonight." She ran off, her hands still covered in soap.

Hockey (Stefan Sava Jr.) and Becki had been together for a few months. They were polar opposites. Whereas Becki was loud, Hockey was quiet. Becki liked to drink and Hockey didn't. Becki wouldn't read a book to save her life and Hockey constantly had his nose buried in them. Becki had dated half the guys in camp and I'm pretty sure Hockey hadn't dated anybody until Becki. Still, they were pretty adorable together; she did all the talking while she dragged him around behind her.

"Trin, do you ever smile?" Xan appeared out of nowhere and threw a large green duffle bag at my feet.

"Didn't you already fill your harassment quota for the day?" I asked.

"I'm just dropping off dirty laundry, not here to fight." He nodded at the canvas bag he'd left at my feet. "Mostly Pitti's underwear and socks. Knock yourself out."

I groaned. Pitti Moldoveanu had the smelliest feet in the world.

"Xan?" I called out as he turned to leave, wanting to ask him something that maybe only he might have a familiarity with.

He turned, one eyebrow raised, his eyes dark and hard. I thought about his explosive temper and changed my mind.

“Never mind," I said quickly.

“Fată, what’s bothering you?” He leaned up against the basin a few inches from me, his dark eyes assessing. It was too close for comfort. I often felt uncomfortable around him, exposed in a way I wasn’t used to feeling.

“Your father couldn’t stay with the clan because he wasn’t a Roma, right?”

Surprise lit his features and for a moment I didn’t think he would answer me. Then, “Yeah.”

“So, what makes me any different? Is it just because it isn’t safe out there? If it was, would I have to go?”

Xan just stared at me, his body ridged. I knew his father was a sore subject.

“I don’t know,” he finally said. “Now, my laundry?” He nodded toward the bag and walked away.

I huffed. “Jerk.”

3402490R00238

Made in the USA
San Bernardino, CA
29 July 2013